ATTORNEY-CLIENT PRIVILEGE

Books by Pamela Samuels Young

Vernetta Henderson Series

Every Reasonable Doubt (1st in series)

In Firm Pursuit (2nd in series)

Murder on the Down Low (3rd in series)

Attorney-Client Privilege (4th in series)

Lawful Deception (5th in series)

Dre Thomas Series

Buying Time (1st in series)

Anybody's Daughter (2nd in series)

Short Stories

The Setup

Easy Money

Unlawful Greed

Non-Fiction

Kinky Coily: A Natural Hair Resource Guide

PAMELA SAMUELS YOUNG

ATTORNEY-CLIENT PRIVILEGE

GoldmanHOUSE PUBLISHING

Attorney-Client Privilege

Goldman House Publishing

ISBN 978-0-9864361-3-0

Copyright © 2012 by Pamela Samuels Young

For information about special discounts for bulk purchases, please contact the author or Goldman House Publishing.

Pamela Samuels Young
www.pamelasamuelsyoung.com

Goldman House Publishing
goldmanhousepublishing@gmail.com

Cover design by Marion Designs

Printed in U.S.A.

For Eric and Daisy Barnum,

I am truly blessed to have
amazing friends like you.
Thanks for all your support.

CHAPTER 1

"Girlfriend, you need to relax." Olivia Jackson gave her co-worker's shoulder a gentle squeeze. "We won't be able to get through this if you don't. You want me to pray for you?"

Judi Irving inhaled and pretended to busy herself inside her battered locker. Prayer was her co-worker's answer to everything.

"Uh, that's okay," Judi mumbled, mostly to herself. "I'm fine."

She stripped off her purple Big Buy blazer and stuffed it inside the locker. The second she'd entered the room, the pain swelling her feet went from uncomfortable to unbearable. Her body's way of rebelling against another twelve-hour shift.

Olivia took a step closer to Judi, as her eyes crisscrossed the empty locker room. "Did you bring the documents?" she asked.

"Not here," Judi snapped, her voice tinged with panic. She had told Olivia a thousand times. It wasn't safe to talk about their lawsuit at work.

Judi was a fit, strawberry blonde, who usually masked her worries with a pleasant smile. Today she felt anxious and frayed. She stared up at the ceiling. She wouldn't put it past Big Buy to have listening devices or even video cameras hidden in the locker room.

"You worry too much," Olivia said, raising her right hand as if preparing to take an oath. "Not a soul can be against us because Jesus is for us."

At only 33, Olivia spoke with the confidence and zeal of a Baptist minister. She had skin the color of slightly burnt straw and a body stacked with curves. Her tell-it-like-it-is personality significantly heightened her five-two frame.

"Ida can't meet us tonight," Judi said. "So you'll have to wait until tomorrow to see them."

It baffled Judi how Olivia could be so fearless in the face of what they'd just done. Two weeks ago, the three sales associates had filed a sex discrimination lawsuit against Big Buy, the largest discount chain in the state of California. Fed up with seeing women repeatedly passed over for promotions and subjected to crude, sexist jokes, Judi and her two co-workers decided to do something about it. The only way to make change, they'd agreed, was to shove it down the company's throat.

The Big Buy documents Judi now possessed—documents Olivia was dying to see—should have emboldened her. Instead, they only heightened her fears.

Olivia's face flushed with exasperation. "You're way too paranoid, girlfriend. I'm praying for you whether you want me to or not." She took both of Judi's hands in hers, closed her eyes and bowed her head. "Father God, please protect and strengthen Judi for the battle we—"

"That's okay." Judi eased her hands from Olivia's grasp and stepped past her, never meeting her eyes. "I have to go."

It was close to ten by the time Judi pulled her black Camry into the driveway of her modest rental house in Mar Vista. Unfortunately, being home did nothing to lift her spirits.

A year-long divorce battle that was still in full swing had left her emotionally drained. And now, her starving-actor boyfriend was exhibiting the same evasiveness her husband had displayed right before he'd dumped her for a big-breasted beautician. At 42, Judi was still picking losers.

She made her way inside and headed straight for the bedroom, longing for a hot shower and some deep sleep.

Phillip walked out of the attached bathroom, bare-chested and beautiful, his coal-black hair slicked back with a shiny gel. His grayish-green eyes matched the tint of his silk boxers.

Phillip barely looked at her. "Hey."

"Hey," Judi said back.

That had been the extent of their communications lately.

In the beginning, her affair with a 28-year-old she'd picked up in a bar had been nothing short of a thrill ride. At the time, a young lover was the boost her self-esteem needed. Now, it was simply a whopping mistake in judgment.

Judi undressed, while Phillip returned to the bathroom. It was close to five minutes before another word passed between them.

"You still going through with the lawsuit?" Phillip called out.

Judi snorted. "Why wouldn't I?"

"Because it's a stupid thing to do."

Judi smiled. She relished this newfound power over her live-in lover. As the TV pitchman for Big Buy stores, Phillip feared her lawsuit might ruin his career—if you could call a few commercials, three plays and a B movie a career. He'd been constantly badgering her to drop it.

"Whoever sent me those documents doesn't think my lawsuit's stupid," Judi shot back.

The thick package had arrived in the mail only three days earlier. With Phillip peering over her shoulder, Judi opened it to find several dozen documents and a typed note: "Good luck with your lawsuit against Big Buy. These documents should help."

"You don't even know what they are," Phillip pressed.

True. They had both skimmed several pages and could see that they were financial records. Beyond that, they might as well have been written in Russian.

Judi had immediately left an excited voicemail message for her attorney. At the moment, Vernetta Henderson was defending a football player in a civil sexual assault case. As soon as that trial ended, their lawsuit against Big Buy would receive Vernetta's full attention. For now, the documents were in a safe place. Not even Phillip knew where she had stashed them.

"They're probably stolen," Phillip said, refusing to drop the subject. "What happens if you get fired?"

If I get fired, then you'll have to get a real job.

Judi should have kicked him out weeks ago, but she had a long history of letting men trounce all over her. Maybe that was why the Big Buy lawsuit meant so much to her. She was finally standing up for herself.

Having been out of the job market for most of her eight-year marriage, returning to retail had been her easiest option. She had expected a quick promotion, but soon realized the fast track at Big Buy was reserved for men.

"Can I borrow a few bucks?" Phillip asked from the bathroom.

"What's a few bucks?"

"A hundred?"

"I don't have it."

Phillip strode out of the bathroom. He had changed into jeans and a body-hugging sweater that showcased his muscular arms. "Stop being a bitch."

Judi charged up to him. "I told you not to talk to me like that. And where the hell do you think you're going?"

"I have a meeting with Harold."

"It's almost ten o'clock. Since when do you schedule meetings with your agent this late at night?"

"I have no reason to lie."

Those were certainly words she'd heard before. "Who're you screwing, Phillip?"

He threw up his hands. "I don't have time for this nonsense. Get out of my face." Phillip shoved her so hard, she stumbled to the floor.

Judi laid there totally stunned. Their arguments had intensified in recent weeks, but Phillip had never put his hands on her. The rage began to build as she slowly got to her feet.

"We're done. Pack your stuff and get out!" Judi shouted.

Phillip turned back around to face her. An ugly smirk marred his face. "I'll leave when I'm ready to leave."

Judi charged at him and gouged her fingernails deep into the left side of his face.

For several long seconds they both seemed stricken with paralysis.

Phillip finally pressed three fingers to his cheek. His eyes expanded as he stared at the specks of blood on his fingertips. Phillip's precious face was his bread and butter.

"You bitch!" he sputtered. "You scarred my face!"

He snatched Judi by the upper arms, lifting her high enough for her feet to dangle in the air.

Judi tried to wrestle free, but Phillip only squeezed harder. Sharp stabs of pain rocketed down her arms. "Let me go! You're hurting me!"

Phillip hurled her onto the bed, then bolted over to the dresser to inspect his face in the mirror. Three short, red gashes lined the left side of his face. He turned back to Judi, who lay coiled in the middle of the bed, sobbing.

"If you ever touch my face again," he seethed, "I'll kill you."

Snatching his keys from the dresser, Phillip stormed out of the room.

The sound of movement coming from the kitchen woke Judi from her sleep. She was still curled up in the same spot where Phillip had discarded her. She checked the clock on the nightstand and was shocked to see that it read 3:27 a.m.

"A meeting with your agent my ass!"

She scrambled out of bed. Enough was enough. Phillip had to go. Now. Right now.

Striding into the hallway, she flicked on the light switch. No illumination appeared, but that did not interfere with her mission.

"Phillip! We need to talk!"

She stepped into the kitchen and pounded her fist against the light switch just inside the doorway. This time, when the light that should have flooded the room didn't, her body constricted with fear.

"Phillip, is that you?" Her voice was smaller now and had lost most of its bravado.

Judi sensed the presence of someone nearby and whirled around.

"Who's in here?" She could hear a loud, steady thud, but wasn't sure if it was her heartbeat or someone else's. "Phillip, is that you?"

She darted into the living room, each step compelled by an innate instinct to flee. Terror, however, had distorted her sense of direction. She was uncertain now whether the front door was to her left or right, north or south. She plowed clumsily through the room, arms extended like a mummy.

"Ow!" Judi yelped as her knee collided into the corner of a coffee table. She ignored the fierce pain and continued to hobble across the room.

When she finally made contact with a wall, she slapped the surface like a mime palming an imaginary window. Her hand found the doorknob and she fumbled with the lock before finally tugging it open.

Judi whimpered in relief as the cold morning air stroked her face.

Just as she was about to cross the threshold to safety, a hand gripped her shoulder and snatched her back into the living room. The door slammed shut as something hard and heavy careened into the back of her head. She crashed face-first into the wall. Blood gushed from her nose with the force of a geyser.

"Help! Somebody help me!" Judi screamed.

The intruder pinned her right shoulder against the wall and pounded her in the back of the head a second time. A heavy fog enveloped her senses, but Judi fought hard against her body's desire to give in. She flailed at her attacker, raising her left hand up and over her shoulder. When she felt skin, she grabbed and pinched and scratched. But her efforts did nothing to free her from her attacker's grasp.

Another hard blow to Judi's head sapped any remaining strength. She began to drift toward unconsciousness as her co-worker's earlier request flickered in her mind.

If only Olivia could pray for her now.

CHAPTER 2

Show no fear.

That was my mantra whenever I walked into a courtroom.

For the past eight days, I'd been sitting at the defense table in Department 26 of the L.A. Superior Court, wearing my game face like a coat of armor. When my nerves threatened to flare up, I straightened my back, gritted my teeth and mentally squashed them like ants.

Show no fear.

Every eye in this media-infested tinderbox was now riveted on my opponent, Girlie Cortez, who was winding down her closing argument.

A salacious mix of Filipino and Caucasian, Girlie was a junior partner at the litigation firm, Donaldson, Watson and Barkley. Petite and slender with dark, ominous eyes, her shiny black hair spilled down her back like a curtain of silk. Born Lourdes Amelia Cortez, Girlie had legally adopted her childhood nickname and wore it like her personal marquee.

Any opponent who judged Girlie based on her feminine appearance would live to regret it. A tigress of a lawyer, she had a reputation for doing whatever it took to win—no matter how unscrupulous, unethical or just plain scandalous. I learned *that* from personal experience.

The Honorable Rafael Pedrano nodded in my direction as Girlie returned to her seat at the plaintiff's table. "Ms. Henderson, you may address the jury."

I slowly stood up, my facial expression confident, my stance relaxed.

Show no fear.

"Good morning, ladies and gentlemen," I began with a respectful smile. "As you know, I'm Vernetta Henderson and I represent Lamarr 'The Hero' Harrison, the Los Angeles Legends' star wide receiver."

At five-eight, my height was ideal for commanding attention in a courtroom. My shoulder-length hair was parted on the side and conservatively swept back behind my right ear. My navy blue, pin-striped suit conveyed both self-assurance and power.

"I'd like to commend Ms. Cortez for that spectacular story she just told you. But this is a court of law. Stories are of no value here. To carry her burden of proof, Ms. Cortez must present you with credible evidence. She hasn't done that because she doesn't have any."

I took a moment to make eye contact with a few of the faces in the jury box. Juror number six, a dental assistant with perfect teeth, gave me an encouraging nod. I was already counting on her vote, having caught her giving Lamarr a seductive smile that bordered on flirting.

"There were only two people in that hotel suite on the morning of June twenty-fifth when the plaintiff alleges that my client sexually assaulted her. So only two people—Lamarr and the plaintiff—know what *really* happened."

Using her name would make her human. Human was not what I wanted her to be.

"When you head back to the jury room to begin your deliberations, I'd like to ask yourself one question: Who's the *real* player here?"

Out of the corner of my eye, I could see that Lamarr was sitting up straight, just as I had instructed, his hands clasped on the table in front of him. He was 26 years old, ten years my junior, with a boyish face and deep-set dimples. A tall, sturdy 230 pounds, Lamarr traversed the football field with the speed and grace of a prized race horse.

"My client plays games for a living," I told the jury. "That's his job. The plaintiff plays games too. The one game she plays best is manipulation. She manipulated my client and she's been trying to manipulate all of you by walking into this courtroom day after day with her conservative suits, her mousy demeanor and her crocodile tears. But let me remind you who she really is."

I took four short steps over to the defense table and pressed a button on my laptop. A life-size picture of Tonisha filled the screen to the right of the witness box. She was wearing purple eye shadow, ruby red lipstick, and a thick auburn wig that fanned out across her shoulders. Her long legs were shamelessly snaked around a shiny brass pole. She was also butt naked.

Extending my arm, I pointed up at the screen like it was my smoking gun. "That's the *real* player in this courtroom."

Although the jurors had seen this photograph when I cross-examined Tonisha, they still seemed jarred by it. Juror number nine, the computer geek, leaned forward and blushed. Juror number two, the Lutheran minister, averted his eyes.

"The plaintiff," I continued, "is an admitted sports groupie who was on a mission to *hook up* with a professional football player—any football player. But Girlie Cortez wants you to believe that the plaintiff only accompanied Lamarr to his suite at the W Hotel so they could *talk and get to know each other.*"

I dramatically rolled my eyes.

"She wanted to *talk*? At two-fifteen in the morning? We all know the real reason we're in this courtroom."

I raised my left hand and slowly rubbed my thumb back and forth across my fingertips. "So that the plaintiff can collect."

Point by point, I meticulously reviewed the evidence, then reminded the jury that the plaintiff changed her story so many times, that the L.A. District Attorney's Office elected not to file criminal charges against Lamarr. By the time I finished recounting *my* version of the facts, I hadn't exactly come out and called Tonisha a dishonest, opportunistic skank who didn't deserve a dime, but the jury got my drift.

"Ladies and gentlemen, I'm not here to convince you that Lamarr Harris is a choir boy. He's not. But he's also not a rapist. His only mistake on June twenty-fifth was failing to recognize that he was being played by the plaintiff."

I pressed my lips together and paused for three long beats. "Please don't let her play you too."

Even before I was settled in my seat, Lamarr leaned over to whisper words of praise. "That was tight, counselor!"

It felt great to have such a satisfied client. I just hoped he still felt that way *after* the jury's verdict.

Girlie Cortez took to the floor again and was about to begin her rebuttal. She abruptly stopped and turned to the judge. "Your Honor, could you ask Ms. Henderson to please remove her exhibit?"

I tried not to smirk as I took my time fiddling with my computer. I'd watched other opponents complete their entire rebuttal with a damaging photograph or document looming in the background. I didn't think Girlie would be that sloppy, but it was worth a try.

Recognizing that the jury was antsy, Girlie didn't speak long. "Ladies and gentlemen, I won't waste your time rehashing facts you already know. I just want you to remember that the defendant is a handsome, wealthy young man who's used to getting what he wants, whenever he wants it, no matter what the consequences. And Lamarr 'The Hero' Harrison wanted Tonisha."

She made a show of gazing over her shoulder at Lamarr, which drew the jury's attention his way.

"My client is a naive young woman who was infatuated with a celebrity football player she'd just met. Please—"

Girlie's voice cracked and her eyes started to water. It was an act I'd witnessed before.

"Please don't punish her. Punish the man who raped her and make him pay for his brutal crime."

When I saw Lamarr's hands curl into tight fists, I firmly tapped my foot against his and his thick fingers instantly sprang loose. I'd repeatedly warned him not to show any sign of aggression in front of the jury.

In just over an hour, the judge finished the instructions to the jury and dismissed them to begin deliberating. Lamarr walked toward his friends huddled in the back of the courtroom while I stuffed papers into my satchel.

"Nice closing," Girlie said, breezing past me. "Maybe the third time'll be the charm for you."

I didn't bother to respond. I'd lost my last two cases against Girlie and it still smarted. The fact that we were both minority women in a profession dominated by white males should have created some level of camaraderie between us. But Girlie wasn't the collegial type.

As I closed my satchel, I felt a hollowness that had nothing to do with my disdain for my conniving adversary. I'd done a good job, but the verdict, I knew, could go either way. And even though I'd love a win against Girlie, I wasn't sure my client deserved one.

When you spend close to a year prepping a case for trial, you see sides of your client that no one else ever will. Not their wives or girlfriends, not their parents, not even their life-long homies. And the man I'd come to know wasn't the stand-up guy I'd just presented to the jury.

Despite his celebrated nickname, as far as I was concerned, Lamarr Harris was nobody's hero.

CHAPTER 3

Detective Dean Mankowski stepped across the threshold of the two-bedroom home where Judi Irving had been viciously attacked. He grimaced as his eyes took in the chaos. Overturned chairs, ripped cushions, a cracked coffee table, and a bucket of blood spatter on the door and wall.

"I think my gut's already got a line on this one," he announced to his partner.

Mankowski was tall and solidly built. A committed bachelor in his mid-40's, his wavy, dirty-blonde hair and TV cop's swagger enhanced his raw good looks.

Detective Mitchell Thomas scratched his head, then exhaled. "Okay, let's hear it. What's your gut saying this time?"

Mankowski smiled. "It's the boyfriend."

Upon their arrival almost thirty minutes earlier, the two detectives received a quick recap from the first officer on the scene, then briefly spoke to Phillip Peterman. Mankowski's dislike for Peterman was instantaneous. One, the guy didn't have a real job. Two, he was an actor. And three, he waxed his eyebrows.

"Man, you go with your gut way too much," Thomas complained. "We haven't even interrogated him yet."

A few inches shorter than his partner, Thomas had skin the color of almonds, an angular nose and pencil-thin lips. He was a married father of three with a salesman's demeanor.

Mankowski took a step back to allow an officer carrying two large plastic bags to walk by. A female crime scene tech hovered near the front door, snapping pictures of the blood spatter. A man on his knees dusted the coffee table for prints.

An hour earlier, paramedics had rushed Judi Irving to St. John's Medical Center in Santa Monica. Their hysterical housekeeper had discovered Judi bleeding and unconscious on the living room floor.

"I just hope the woman makes it," Mankowski said. "Then *she* can tell you how right I am."

His gut wasn't always on the money, but it had racked up enough hits for him to still confidently rely on it.

Thomas let out half of a chuckle. "Here we go again. We'll probably spend the next three months going after the boyfriend only to find out it was a burglary gone bad. Look at this place."

Mankowski shook his head in disagreement. "This is a staged scene. Somebody just wanted us to *think* this was a burglary. And that somebody is Phillip Peterman."

"Maybe," Thomas said, rubbing his dimpled chin, "maybe not. A back window was jimmied open. Somebody also went to the breaker box out back and shut off the electricity. Sounds like a burglary to me."

Mankowski grinned like a proud papa. Thomas had only a fraction of his partner's two decades of chasing down criminals, but he was on his way to becoming a solid detective.

When they'd first been paired up, everyone expected friction because Mankowski was a cowboy and proud of it. But Thomas had learned how and when to rein him in, so it worked out well. Mankowski also liked having an easy-going black guy for a partner. Most of the youngsters coming out of the Academy were too headstrong to appreciate the importance of listening to their elders.

"Nice analysis," Mankowski said, "but this is overkill." He stopped and surveyed the room. "Every piece of furniture in here was turned over, even the coffee table. Every cabinet opened, every drawer pulled out. What burglar takes the time to search the linen closet? This is a sloppy setup by somebody who wanted us to think his intent was to rob the place."

"Maybe the burglar was searching for something," Thomas said, resisting his partner's theory. "Let's wait to hear what Peterman has to say when we take him downtown."

Mankowski exhaled. Interrogations at the station had to be videotaped. "I'd rather talk to Actor Boy here first."

Thomas grunted, then followed his partner outside.

They found Peterman standing near a patrol car. He jumped to attention when he saw them approaching.

"Can I go now?" The words rushed out of him. "I need to get to the hospital to find out how Judi's doing."

Mankowski gave Phillip a quick once-over. His hair was uncombed, his sweater wrinkled, his eyes were swollen and bloodshot. *Definitely booze*, Mankowski thought. *Not grief.*

"We need you to tell us what happened," Mankowski said.

"I already told you that." Phillip's voice was a smidgen short of surly. "I don't know what happened. I have to get to the hospital. I don't even know if Judi's still alive."

Mankowski zeroed in on what appeared to be scratches on the side of Phillip's face. He'd done a piss-poor job of trying to cover them up with makeup.

"We won't keep you long," Mankowski said. "We'd appreciate your cooperation."

Mankowski hated having to be polite. He missed the good old days when you could slug a suspect and get away with it. Rodney King and camera phones screwed up everything. People actually thought they had rights.

Phillip perched himself on the hood of the patrol car.

"So how did you learn about the attack on your girlfriend?" Mankowski asked.

"I got a call from Imelda, our housekeeper." Phillip rubbed his forehead. "We can only afford to have her clean once a month. I'm just glad this was her day to come."

"When did she call you?"

"Just after eight this morning."

Mankowski and Thomas had already questioned the distraught housekeeper, who was of little help.

"So what kept you out all night?"

Phillip stared down at his laced fingers. "I...uh...I had a meeting with my agent in the Valley. I left home around ten. We didn't finish talking business until after midnight, so I stayed at his place instead of driving home."

Mankowski nodded. The guy didn't look gay, but you could never tell these days. "Do you spend the night at your agent's house very often?"

"Every now and then," Phillip sniffed.

"How'd you get those scratches on your face?"

Phillip's hand absently flew to his cheek. "I...uh...I was doing some yard work a couple of days ago and got swiped by a tree branch."

"Which tree?" Thomas asked.

"The one out back."

"I only saw one tree in your backyard," Thomas pressed. "It didn't have any branches?"

"The gardener trimmed it."

"I thought you just said you did the yard work," Mankowski said.

"I do. Sometimes." Phillip's eyes darted left, then right. "But we have a gardener too. What's this got to do with anything?"

"Those scratches on your face look pretty fresh to me," Mankowski continued. "You sure it wasn't your girlfriend who scratched you?"

Phillip jumped to his feet, his nose inches from Mankowski's. "This is ridiculous. Why are you treating me like a suspect? I don't have to take this."

"Yes, you do." Mankowski pressed his palm flat against Phillip's chest and pushed him back against the car.

"You can't treat me like this," Phillip protested. "I know my rights."

"Rights? You don't have any rights."

Detective Thomas stepped between them. Thomas rarely thought it was a good idea to piss off a person of interest. It made it harder to get what you wanted. But Mankowski preferred to lay it on with a heavy hand.

"Mr. Peterman, let me apologize for my partner." Thomas emitted a friendly smile. "He's a little worked up this morning because he really wants to find out who attacked your girlfriend."

"I don't care how worked up he is. He can't talk to me like this."

"You're absolutely right," Thomas agreed.

"I'm leaving." Phillip tried to brush past Detective Thomas, who took a step sideways, blocking his path.

A smile eased across Mankowski's lips when he saw his mild-mannered partner's jawline go taut. Thomas was always Mr. Congeniality. Until a perp pissed him off.

"Yep, you are leaving," Thomas said. "And you're coming to the station with us for further questioning."

CHAPTER 4

It took me a few minutes to round up Lamarr and his homies and hustle them out of the courtroom.

The judge had ordered both sides to stay within fifteen minutes of the courthouse in case the jury had a question or reached a quick verdict. We walked across the street to Kendall's Brasserie, a high-end restaurant in the Los Angeles Music Center. We'd eaten lunch there nearly every day.

A horde of reporters trailed after us like a pack of wild dogs, shouting questions they knew we wouldn't answer. Lamarr and his entourage—Keyshawn, Baby Duke, and Mo—followed my instructions and kept their mouths shut.

It was almost three o'clock, so I was hoping the restaurant would be empty. It wasn't. The fuss our entrance created no longer fazed us. People whispered and pointed as the maître d' escorted us to a large, semi-secluded table. I'd been too nervous to eat breakfast or lunch, so I was famished. I ordered a bunch of appetizers for the table as soon as we were seated.

"I know we won," Keyshawn declared.

Keyshawn's left eye was noticeably smaller than the right. The result of a BB gun injury over a decade ago. He and Lamarr went all the way back to second grade. "Don't nobody believe that skank."

"It's all good," Lamarr said with a half-smile.

He was putting up a brave front for his boys. In my office two nights ago, he'd broken down in tears, fearful of the impact a loss would have on his career. Lamarr earned ten-million dollars a year on the football field and almost as much in endorsements. A week after Tonisha went public with her rape allegations, Red Bull cancelled his commercials. Two weeks later, Nintendo followed. Four more companies were in a wait-and-see mode. Under the NFL's conduct clause, Lamarr had been barred from playing, pending the verdict.

A waiter arrived with four trays of appetizers colorful enough to be Christmas tree ornaments. I was the first to dig in.

"I can't wait to see that bitch's face when the verdict comes in," said Mo, who resembled an overdressed sumo wrestler. Gargantuan diamonds sparkled from his meaty earlobes. He and Lamarr played Pop Warner football together.

I let my fork fall noisily to my plate and glowered across the table at Mo as if he'd used the B-word to describe me. I'd repeatedly asked them not to use that word or any other vulgar language in my presence.

Mo raised both hands in surrender before I could say a word. "No disrespect, counselor. That girl know she gave it up. She just tryin' to jack my boy."

His statement set off a murmur of approval from Lamarr's other two buddies.

"Oh snap!" Baby Duke pressed his fist to his lips as if it was a microphone. "Check out the babe at ten o'clock."

He was attempting to whisper but there was way too much baritone in his voice. All four of the guys gawked as an attractive Latina sauntered by in a tight spandex dress.

"Jennifer Lopez ain't got nothin' on that." Lamarr smiled and rubbed his chin.

"I told you guys to cut it out," I whispered. I felt more like Lamarr's mother than his lawyer. "You never know who's watching."

Lamarr rubbed his boxy jaw. "It's all good."

"It won't be *all good* when TMZ runs a clip of you guys acting like a bunch of sexual predators. Somebody could have a cell phone camera pointed at you right now."

Lamarr stopped chewing as his eyes zipped around the restaurant.

"We was just admiring the scenery," Baby Duke said with a gap-toothed smile. "You need to lighten up, counselor."

What I needed to do was flee from the restaurant and find some civilized lunch mates. But I had two good reasons to stay put. The food was fabulous and my client and his knucklehead cronies needed a chaperone. If I left, they'd probably get even rowdier.

"Let's just finish eating and get out of here," I snapped.

When I received the call from Lamarr's agent asking me to represent him, I was more than flattered. This was my first high-profile criminal case since defending a local socialite accused of murder. Though the pressure was intense at times, it was exciting to be at the center of such a scandalous case.

I'd recently opened my own law practice, renting space in the law office of a friend. I left my old firm, O'Reilly and Finney, after my partnership chances nosedived, due in part to the antics of a female attorney who was almost as ruthless as Girlie. But that's another story.

As soon as the verdict was in, I could finally dive into my next big case, a sex discrimination lawsuit on behalf of three female sales associates at Big Buy department stores. One of the plaintiffs had recently left me an excited voicemail message about some mysterious documents she'd received. I'd been too busy putting the finishing touches on my closing argument to call her back.

The mood at the table had lightened considerably by the time we'd finished our meal. Lamarr and his homies were laughing at some off-color joke and getting way too loud. Before I could quiet them down, I spotted Girlie Cortez, minus her client, at the maître d's stand.

Lamarr's eyes followed mine. "I hate that bit"—he caught himself—"I mean female. She knows I didn't force that girl to give it up. Still, I'd love to hit *that* one day."

The iced tea I'd just sipped spewed all over the table. "Are you nuts?" I said through clenched teeth. "Didn't I just warn you guys to knock it off?"

"Chill out, counselor. It ain't that serious. We just blowin' off some steam." Lamarr slouched down in his chair and pouted like the spoiled, overpaid celebrity that he was.

The hostess was leading my nemesis to a table a good distance away when Girlie did an about face and marched in our direction.

"Hey, everybody," Girlie said, sidling up to our table. Her eyes landed on me, but lingered on Lamarr. "Hope you guys aren't celebrating too early."

"Might as well," Keyshawn said, raising his wineglass in a makeshift toast. "'Cuz we gonna win."

Girlie put a hand on her hip and protruded her ample bosom. "Is that right?"

"Yep, that's right." Keyshawn's hooded eyes moved up and down her body as if he liked what he saw.

I wanted Girlie to disappear. Her close proximity to these goons could easily lead to another sexual assault allegation. "Is there something I can help you with?" I asked.

"Not really. See you back in court."

The guys ogled her ass as she pranced away.

I picked up my fork and stabbed my plate so hard they all flinched. "Turn around. Now!" I had to fight off the urge to slap each one of them in the back of the head.

I never told Lamarr how much I despised Girlie Cortez nor had I mentioned my prior losses against her. Our first match-up was a race discrimination case a few years back. I lost at trial after she withheld an investigation report crucial to my client's defense. During our second case just last year, I couldn't understand why my star witness told a completely different story on the witness stand. I figured it out a couple of months later when I saw him holding Girlie's hand across a dinner table.

My iPhone vibrated. I recognized the court clerk's number on the display as soon as I pulled it from my purse. I swallowed hard and held my breath. The jury hadn't even been out two hours. There was no way they could be done deliberating already. Maybe they had a question.

My hand trembled slightly as I raised the phone to my ear.

"The judge wants everybody back in court," the clerk told me. "The jury has reached a verdict."

CHAPTER 5

Mankowski snagged a patrolman to drive Phillip Peterman to the station in the back of his squad car. Phillip wasn't officially a suspect yet. Mankowski just wanted him to feel like one.

"Where'd they put Actor Boy?" Mankowski asked, returning to his desk after making a pit stop.

Thomas didn't answer. His thumbs were busy tapping the screen of his iPhone.

"Please tell me you stopped day trading long enough to get going on those subpoenas?" Mankowski asked with a scowl.

"Hey, man, my latest stock pick just reached an all-time high. My investment savvy is going to put my kids through college. And yes, I'm almost finished with the paperwork to get Judi Irving and Phillip Peterman's bank, home and cell phone records."

Another detective walked up. "Your perp's in interrogation room seven. Want me to sit in?"

Detective Charlie Hopper was a balding, overweight grump who should've been put out to pasture decades ago. The last time he'd cracked a case, the first George Bush was president.

"Thanks, Pops," Mankowski said, walking past him. "But I think we have this one under control."

"I guarantee you a confession in thirty minutes or less," Hopper bragged.

"Yeah, right," Mankowski said.

Thomas slipped his iPhone into his pocket and followed Mankowski into the interrogation room. Phillip sat wedged behind a short metal table, his cell phone jammed against his ear.

"They won't tell me how Judi's doing because I'm not a family member," he griped, hanging up the phone. "I need to get to the hospital. Exactly how long is this going to take?"

Mankowski spread his hands. "Depends on what you have to say."

"It shouldn't take long." Thomas pulled up a chair and offered one to Mankowski. He set two cans of Pepsi on the table. "I thought you might like something to drink."

Phillip reached for one of the cans, popped it open and took a healthy gulp. "I'm doing you guys a favor. I really don't have to talk to you without a lawyer."

"You're not a suspect," Mankowski said. "Why would you need a lawyer?"

Phillip shrugged. "Let's just get this over with."

"Can you think of anyone who would want to hurt your girl-friend?" Mankowski asked.

Phillip's face flushed with surprise. "I thought it was a burglary? You think somebody was out to hurt her?"

"What made you think it was a burglary?"

"The place was a wreck. The small flat screen we had in the kitchen was missing. That cop wouldn't let me look around to see what else they took."

Mankowski's brows arched. "They?"

"That was just a manner of speech. I have no idea how many people it was."

"Let's get back to my initial question," Mankowski said. "Is there anyone you can think of who might've wanted to hurt Judi?"

The Pepsi can made a crinkle sound as Phillip's hand tightened around it. "Maybe her husband. Their divorce isn't final yet. He's been paying her a grip in alimony based on the court's temporary order and he's not happy about it."

"So Judi's married?"

"Yeah. He dumped her for some bimbo. His name is Robby Irving. He's a pharmaceutical sales rep. You should definitely check him out."

"Does he own that house where you guys were living?"

"Nope. Judi and I rented it a few weeks ago. We were staying in a condo in Westchester at first, but the rent was too high."

"What about you? Did you have any reason to hurt her?"

Phillip set down his Pepsi and cracked his right knuckles against the palm of his left hand. "Of course not."

"Those are some nasty scratches on your face."

"And I already told you how I got them. You need to get Robby Irving down here. He should be your number one suspect."

"Anybody else?" Mankowski asked.

"Nobody I can think of." Phillip paused as if he was torn about how forthcoming he should be. "I don't know if this is important or not, but Judi had a lawsuit going."

"What kind of lawsuit?" Mankowski asked.

"Discrimination."

"Against who?"

"Her employer."

Mankowski drummed his fingers on the table. The way Phillip was parceling out information was beginning to irritate him.

"Mr. Peterman, we can stay here for the next three hours as you dole out your little tidbits, or you can tell us what we need to know and you can go check on your girlfriend. How do you want to play it?"

Thomas tilted his head and gave Mankowski a glare that told him he didn't approve of his bullying tactics. They had no legal right to keep Phillip there since he wasn't under arrest. It was inappropriate for Mankowski to act as if they could.

"Okay, okay," Phillip huffed.

He spent the next few minutes telling them what little he knew about Judi's sex discrimination lawsuit against Big Buy.

"Sounds like you had a problem with her suing the company," Mankowski said.

"I thought it was a stupid thing to do. She was going to end up getting fired."

"Hey, wait a minute." Thomas grinned and wagged a finger at Phillip. "I recognize you. You're the Big Buy Guy!"

A modest grin lit up Phillip's face. "Yeah, that would be me."

Mankowski eyed his partner. "Big what guy?"

"Big Buy Guy. He does this commercial where he's running through the store slashing prices." Thomas started singing the Big Buy jingle.

"Oh, I get it." Mankowski leaned back in his chair. "You didn't like your girlfriend messing up your Big Buy gig by suing the company?"

Phillip took a long gulp from the Pepsi can. "I just didn't think the lawsuit was a good idea."

They continued to grill Phillip about Judi's lawsuit, his whereabouts while she was being assaulted and Judi's impending divorce. For the most part, his story stayed consistent.

"Would you be willing to provide a sample of your DNA?" Mankowski asked.

"DNA?" Phillip cracked his knuckles again and reached for the Pepsi, but didn't take a sip. "Why would you need my DNA?"

"Just routine," Thomas said. "We'd like to rule you out."

"Judi scratched her assailant," Mankowski added. "We want to know if your DNA matches the skin and blood we found underneath her fingernails."

Thomas shot Mankowski a chiding glare. His partner was sharing a little too much information. But Mankowski wanted Actor Boy to know that they had him. A worried perp was much more likely to make the kind of mistake that would leave him cornered.

Phillip visibly shuddered. "I...uh...I'm not comfortable providing my DNA."

Mankowski smirked. "Why not?"

"I'd just rather not, okay?" Phillip cracked his knuckles for the third time. "You need to get her husband down here and get *his* DNA."

"Alright, Mr. Peterman," Mankowski said, sliding a pen and notepad across the table. "Give us the name and number of your agent so we can confirm your whereabouts last night. Then you can go. But we'll definitely need to speak to you again. If you plan on taking any out-of-town trips, we'd appreciate it if you give us a call first."

Mankowski winked.

"I'll give you my agent's cell phone number," he grumbled. "But just so you know, he's out of the country. He left for Paris this morning. He won't be back for six weeks."

"How convenient," Mankowski said. "But I'm pretty sure cell phones work in Paris too."

Phillip scrawled down a number, ripped the paper from the pad and sailed it across the table. "Are we done?"

"Nope," Mankowski said. "We need a photograph."

"Of what?"

"Those scratches on your cheek." Mankowski pulled a tissue from his shirt pocket and slapped it on the table. "Wipe off your makeup."

"I don't have on makeup," Phillip said testily. "It's a medicated cream."

"Whatever. Just wipe it off."

"I'm not sure I want to—"

"You know what?" Mankowski said. "You're really beginning to make me think you have something to hide."

Thomas stepped outside and returned with a camera that he handed to Mankowski, who took pictures of Phillip's face from three different angles.

Afterward, Thomas found a patrolman to drive Phillip home, then met Mankowski back at his desk.

"Did you see how nervous he got when I asked for his DNA?" Mankowski said. "I think Judi scratched his face while he was bashing her in the head."

"He was sure trying hard to steer us in the direction of her husband," Thomas replied with a nod. "If he did do it, he must be sweating bullets not knowing whether she's going to survive and identify him."

Thomas called the hospital to find out Judi's condition.

"Good news," Thomas said, hanging up. "She's critical, but stable. We might be able to talk to her tomorrow."

They had already placed a guard outside her room and given the hospital strict instructions that no one, especially Phillip Peterman, should be allowed in to see her. Mankowski, meantime, tried to reach Harold Gold, Phillip's agent.

Mankowski slammed down the phone. "Asshole gave us a wrong number."

"That," Thomas said, "speaks volumes."

Mankowski turned to his computer to look up the agent's office number on Google.

"Well," Thomas said with glee, "at least we have this." He held up a plastic bag containing Phillip's empty Pepsi can.

"Criminals are so stupid," Mankowski said with a satisfied smiled. "That arrogant prick is going to piss in his pants when he finds out we have his DNA. Let's drop that off at the lab, then go have a little talk with Judi Irving's almost ex-husband."

CHAPTER 6

By the time we made it back to the courtroom, Girlie and Tonisha were already seated at the plaintiff's table.

Lamarr hadn't uttered one word during our short walk back and I could see the fear in his eyes. For him, this was the fourth quarter with a minute left on the clock. If the jury's verdict came back in favor of Tonisha, his future on the field was anyone's guess. As for his endorsement deals, he could kiss them good-bye. At least for the immediate future. Memories would eventually fade, but it would take time. Just ask Kobe, Ben Roethlisberger or Michael Vick.

Across the room, Tonisha rocked back and forth in her chair, while Girlie held her hand. Win or lose, the two of them would be hitting the talk show circuit so hard, they'd make Gloria Allred look camera shy.

A side door opened and the bailiff led the jurors to their seats.

Judge Pedrano wasted no time. "Madam Foreperson, have you reached a verdict?"

A middle-aged white woman with short, curly hair rose from her seat. "Yes, we have."

I was shocked that Juror No. 1, a bashful-looking fifth-grade teacher, had been selected as the jury forewoman. None of the jurors made eye contact with me or Lamarr. Even the dental assistant no longer smiled Lamarr's way.

Juror No. 1 cleared her throat. "In the matter of Tonisha Cosby versus Lamarr Harris, Los Angeles Superior Court Case Number LC-

983388, we find Lamarr Harris liable for sexual assault and award Tonisha Cosby two-million dollars."

"Two-million dollars! Hell naw!" Lamarr pounded the table with both fists. "This is some bullshit!"

One of his homeboys yelled some indecipherable expletive from the gallery. The entire room buzzed with chatter.

The unarmed bailiff was at our table in an instant, peering down at Lamarr like an angry school principal.

Judge Pedrano banged his gavel in quick, successive raps. "Order! I want order in this court!"

He aimed his gavel directly at Lamarr. "Young man, that kind of outburst is unacceptable in my courtroom. If it happens again, you and anybody else who's out of line will end up in a holding cell."

Tonisha apparently didn't believe the judge's admonition applied to her. "Thank you for believing me," she cried out in hiccupping sobs. "Thank you so much!"

Lamarr's chest heaved up and down and I thought he might be hyperventilating. I had explained the risks of going to trial and had even tried to convince him to settle shortly after Tonisha went public with her allegations. Back then, Tonisha probably would've agreed to drop her case for a tenth of the jury award. But Lamarr refused to pay *the lyin' 'ho a dime*. Days later, Girlie Cortez entered the picture and settlement was out of the question.

It took a few more minutes before the judge regained control of the courtroom.

I rose from my seat. "Your Honor, I would like to poll the jury."

The poll revealed that nine jurors voted in favor of Tonisha, with three for us. To my surprise, the dental assistant went against us. The Lutheran minister, a security guard and a grocery store clerk voted for us. Tonisha needed nine of the twelve votes to prevail. If we'd had just one more juror on our side, Lamarr would be the one celebrating.

"Let's go," I said, when the judge had finished thanking the jurors for performing their civic duty.

Lamarr gripped the edge of the table. "You gotta get me a new trial. She just fucked up my career."

No, you fucked up your own career.

The chances of the California Court of Appeal overturning the verdict was about as likely as Lamarr appearing on a Wheaties box tomorrow morning.

"I know an excellent attorney who specializes in appeals."

"I don't want another attorney. I want you."

It was nice that Lamarr still had confidence in me, but I was ready to punt. I had my Big Buy clients to think about. Not to mention the rest of my caseload.

I instructed Lamarr and his buddies to wait in the courtroom while I dashed off to the ladies' room. I wanted to freshen up before facing the throng of bloodthirsty reporters waiting outside.

Girlie exited the ladies' room as I approached. "I'll be giving you a call to discuss our next case," she said sweetly.

Her words stopped me cold. "What next case?"

"Your sex discrimination lawsuit against Big Buy. I'm representing the company."

Once her words registered, a slow grin radiated across my face. No case is a slam-dunk, but if half of what I knew about Big Buy was true, this case was pretty darn close. And those documents Judi Irving had called me about could only be icing on the cake.

"That's great news." I could almost kiss her for adding some sunshine to my downer of a day.

The bluster fell from Girlie's face. She had obviously anticipated a different reaction from me.

"Your client has a real problem with the way it treats women," I said, feeling chatty all of a sudden. "And I have the evidence to prove it."

"Is that right?"

"Yep, that's right."

I continued into the ladies' room with a renewed pep in my step. I was thrilled to have another opportunity to square off against Girlie Cortez. And this time, I was definitely going to kick her butt.

CHAPTER 7

Detectives Mankowski and Thomas kept a close eye on the BMW two car lengths ahead of them on Sepulveda Boulevard.

They'd been trailing Robby Irving since he left home twenty minutes earlier. They presumed he was starting his rounds to doctors' offices on the Westside.

"Judi Irving has lousy taste in men," Mankowski said, browsing the information they'd dug up on Irving. He earned a nice six-figure salary as a pharmaceutical sales rep. He also had three Facebook accounts, where he spent way too much time trying to meet women. "Both of these guys are pricks."

"You're just jealous because they're better looking than you," Thomas joked.

"You think so?" Mankowski grabbed the rearview mirror, turned it in his direction and examined his face. "Naw, I'm way prettier."

Irving turned left on a side street and drove his car into the parking lot of a large medical complex. Thomas pulled into a stall three cars away.

Irving was standing behind his trunk, opening boxes when the two detectives approached.

Mankowski held up his badge. "Mr. Irving, we're detectives with the LAPD."

Irving was just shy of six feet with dark hair and a too-thick mustache. His blue suit was expensive, his shirt monogrammed.

"You must be here about Judi."

Mankowski nodded. "Can you talk for a moment?"

Irving glanced at his watch. "Yeah, sure. How's she doing?"

"Still critical. So you know about the attack?"

"Yeah, her sister called me."

"We'll need to confirm your whereabouts between ten o'clock last night and eight a.m. this morning."

Robby tugged at his nose with his thumb and index finger. "I was at home."

"Can anyone verify that?" Mankowski asked.

"Yeah. My girlfriend, Camille. But I thought it was a burglary? I'm not a suspect, am I?"

"So you have a girlfriend?"

"Yeah, but it's not that serious."

Thomas asked for her number and address as he pulled a notepad from his shirt pocket.

"We heard you had a beef with Judi over alimony," Mankowski said.

"And who told you that?" A hot splash of red inched up Irving's neck. "That gigolo who's sponging off of her?"

"As a matter of fact, he was the source."

"You need to be interrogating that sleazebag, not me. He didn't care about Judi. She was just a meal ticket to him."

"If she was his meal ticket, why would he want to hurt her?" Detective Thomas asked.

Irving smirked. "I guess he forgot to tell you about Judi's insurance policy."

"What insurance policy?"

"The one Judi took my name off of and replaced with his. I couldn't believe it. She barely knew the guy. She only made him the beneficiary to piss me off. If Judi dies, that punk gets three-hundred grand."

That, Mankowski thought, was exactly the kind of motive he was looking for. He smiled over at his partner, then turned back to Irving. "We'll need you to come down to the station for questioning. We'll also need a sample of your DNA."

"DNA? Why? I didn't hurt Judi."

"We know that," Mankowski lied. "We just need your DNA to rule you out."

"I...I...uh, I hate needles."

"What about Q-tips. You scared of those too?"

"What?"

"We can get your DNA from your saliva," Thomas explained. "All they need to do is swipe the inside of your mouth with a Q-tip."

That seemed to make Irving breathe easier. "Fine. No problem."

"By the way," Mankowski asked, "how did you find out that Judi had replaced you as her beneficiary?"

Irving hesitated, "Uh...I, uh...I called our insurance broker."

"When?"

Irving shifted his weight from one foot to the other. "I know how this looks. But Judi put me through a lot. Her sister didn't think she was going to make it. I just wanted to make sure the policy hadn't lapsed. That's when I found out that punk was the beneficiary."

"So when did you call your insurance broker?" Mankowski asked again.

"A couple hours ago," he finally admitted. "But I didn't hurt Judi."

Thomas tossed his partner a triumphant smile, then flipped a page on his notepad. "So how much alimony were you paying her?"

"Thirty-one hundred dollars a month. Can you believe that? That's crazy."

Robby realized the implication of this revelation five seconds too late.

"I was upset about it, but I didn't hurt her." He turned away and started stuffing drug samples into a leather duffle bag.

Mankowski peered into the bag. "What kind of drugs you got in there? Got any Tylenol?"

Irving reached into one of the boxes, snatched a handful of Tylenol packets and handed them to Mankowski.

"If anybody had a motive for wanting to hurt Judi, it was Phillip Peterman," Robby insisted. "In fact, he had three-hundred-thousand dollars' worth of motive."

CHAPTER 8

For a lawyer, standing on the courthouse steps following a big victory, fielding questions from reporters is akin to having your moment on the red carpet. You smile humbly and talk eloquently about justice and the importance of the jury system.

But when you lose, it's like showing up for a public stoning.

Lamarr stood off to my right, his eyes steel-like, his lower lip tucked in. He had agreed to keep his mouth shut and let me do the talking.

"Ms. Henderson, how do you feel about the jury's verdict?"

My own doubts about my client's version of events were threatening to bubble to the surface. But like a highly paid mouthpiece, I did the job I was being paid to do.

"I'm extremely disappointed in the verdict. The man I've come to know did not commit the acts he's been accused of." I glanced back at Lamarr for effect.

The reporters all started shouting their questions at once. Too bad I couldn't respond honestly.

"So you think the jury got it wrong?"

How would I know? I wasn't in that hotel room with 'em.

"Are you going to advise your client to appeal?"

Why should I? He probably did it.

Well over an hour later, I pulled into the driveway of my home in the Los Angeles suburb of Baldwin Hills, my physical and emotional batteries completely drained. All I wanted to do was climb into bed and pull the covers over my head.

I stuck my key in the door just as someone yanked it open.

"Hey, girlfriend." Special swallowed me up in a bear hug. "Me and Clayton came over to cheer you up. We've been watching you on TV. Y'all got robbed."

Special Sharlene Moore, my best buddy, was a tall, curvaceous spitfire, who had an ultra-feminine air about her. She had recently abandoned her weave for long micro-braids. She took my purse and satchel and escorted me inside.

"I picked up some grub from Grand Lux." She looped her arm through mine and led me to the kitchen.

"Got everything you like. The duck pot stickers, the crispy Thai sushi rolls, the chicken jambalaya, and best of all, the red velvet cake."

Looking at the spread made my stomach churn. I'd been running on adrenalin for the last two weeks and was on the verge of a full-fledge crash. I had no appetite for food or company.

"Hey, babe, get in here," my husband Jefferson yelled out to me. "You're on channel seven."

Special and I dashed into the den where we caught the tail end of my sound bite. The video then switched to Girlie and Tonisha. They were both cheesing like they'd just won the lottery. And basically they had.

"Don't worry about it, babe," Jefferson said. "You'll kick her ass next time."

My husband was my staunchest supporter. Thick and compact like a tank, he sported a shaved head and a man's man demeanor. He ran his own electrical contracting company.

"Both of those heffas know they're wrong." Special turned up her nose. "According to the word on the street, Ms. Tonisha's been with half the NFL and a third of the NBA. And I hear her attorney gets around too. Can you believe she drives a Jag with a license plate that says *HotGirl*? How skanky is that?"

"Nobody knows what happened in that hotel room except La-marr and Tonisha," I said, rubbing my eyes. "And just because she slept around doesn't mean Lamarr didn't force himself on her."

Six pairs of eyes lasered in my direction. By the stunned expressions on their faces, you would've thought I'd just confessed to attacking Tonisha myself.

"So you believe her?" Clayton asked. Special's beau had the lean, athletic appearance of a baseball player. The two of them had recently reunited after a tumultuous breakup.

"I didn't say I believe her. But we weren't there, so we'll never know for sure what happened. Just like we'll never know for sure if O.J. really killed Nicole."

Special scrunched up her face. "Girl, please. You know damn—" she stole a sheepish glance at Clayton. Her foul language caused his face to instantly harden in disapproval.

"Excuse my language, everybody. You know darn well O.J. is guilty. If I had my investigator's license, I'd look into Lamarr's case myself and find out the real deal."

Clayton's face clouded. He didn't like the idea of his woman pursuing such a dangerous profession any more than her occasional use of expletives.

"My point is," I continued, "we'll never know with one-hundred-percent certainty because we weren't there."

"Well, I ain't buying Tonisha's story," Special insisted. "That girl was looking for her fifteen minutes of fame. She lucked up and got that plus two mil."

"I'm just glad you're home," Jefferson said, standing up. "'Cuz I'm starving and Special wouldn't let us eat until you got here."

He led Clayton and Special into the kitchen while I stretched out on the couch and instantly nodded off.

"Hey, girl, wake up."

I refused to open my eyes, even though Special was bent over me, shaking me by the shoulder.

"Leave me alone," I moaned. "I'm exhausted."

"This is important. I've been dying to show you something."

When I finally opened my eyes, Special's hand was so close to my face, it made me cross-eyed.

"I'm finally getting married!" she said, waving her sizable diamond ring back and forth like a QVC model. "Can you believe it?"

I bounced off the couch and gave her a big hug. "Congratulations!"

Jefferson embraced her too, then gave Clayton a bump of the fist. "It's about time, bruh."

It thrilled me to see Special so happy. After being charged in a highly publicized criminal case a year earlier, she'd lost her job and split up with Clayton. But my buddy was a survivor. With my help, the charges were dismissed. She later landed a new job in collections at Verizon and got her man back.

"So when's the big date?" I gave Clayton's shoulder a brotherly squeeze before sitting back down.

"Well," Special said, perching herself on the arm of the chair where Clayton was sitting, "we're keeping our engagement a secret for a little while. We're not even telling our parents yet."

"A secret? Why?"

Special looked everywhere except at me. "There's something we need to do first."

"Let me tell 'em, baby." Clayton took her hand. "We're joining the Community of Islam. We aren't announcing our engagement until we complete our orientation and get the blessing from our minister."

Perhaps I was still groggy from my short nap and hadn't heard him correctly. "Are you saying you're converting to Islam?"

My question was directed at Special, but she just sat there, biting the nail of her baby finger.

Clayton, on the other hand, beamed like a new headlight. "That's exactly what we're saying."

My mouth opened, but no words followed.

Jefferson bravely broke the awkward silence. "That's cool. If that works for y'all, more power to you."

Special smiled hopefully at me, no doubt waiting to hear me echo my husband's blessings. I'd seen my friend do a lot of crazy things in the name of love, but abandoning her Christian faith was something I couldn't cosign. Right now, I wanted to grill her like a hostile witness. The ringing of my iPhone put that on hold.

When I placed the phone to my ear, a frantic voice intermittently rambled and sobbed.

"Who is this?" I asked, trying hard to recognize the caller. "What's the matter? Slow down. I can't understand you."

All eyes in the den were on me as I listened for close to a minute without speaking. When I finally understood what the caller was telling me, I sank even deeper into the couch, then pressed the phone to my chest.

Jefferson threw an arm around my shoulders and pulled me close. "Babe, what happened? What's the matter?"

My voice cracked as I tried to speak. "My client is dead."

"Lamarr?" All three of them asked in starry-eyed unison.

I shook my head. "No, not Lamarr. It's Judi. Judi Irving from my Big Buy case. She's been murdered."

CHAPTER 9

Phillip plodded back and forth across the grungy motel room, cell phone in hand.

"Answer the damn phone!" he shouted, growing more annoyed with every ring.

Bleary-eyed and unshaven, the underarms of Phillip's white T-shirt were soaked with sweat. He could smell his own tart body odor.

When he heard his agent's recorded voice yet again, he hurled the phone to the bed.

It was imperative that Phillip reached Harold before those two cops did. He'd already left four messages. At least he'd been smart enough to buy himself a little time. When he'd written down his agent's number for Mankowski, Phillip had intentionally made both fives look like sloppy sixes.

A roach crawled across his shoe and he kicked it away. The cops still had the house cordoned off as a crime scene and Phillip had no place else to go. His newest sugar mama was usually good for some quick cash. But now that Judi was dead, they both agreed that it was best to lay low for a while.

Phillip couldn't believe how fast everything had spun so far out of his control. Sure, he'd wanted out of his relationship with Judi, but it wasn't supposed to go down like this. He just hoped he could collect on her insurance sooner rather than later.

He snatched the phone from the bed and hit redial. Still pacing across the room in a trance-like state, Phillip hadn't heard the voice on the other end of the phone. He stumbled to a stop. "Harold, is that you?"

"Do you realize there's a friggin' nine-hour time difference between L.A. and Paris?" Harold Gold barked, his usual arrogant self even when half asleep. "You better have a good reason for blowing up my phone."

Phillip fell into a cushionless chair in the corner of the room. "I need a favor, man. A really big one."

"I'm not giving you another dime."

"I don't need a loan. Did you get a call from a detective?"

"A detective? Why would a detective call me?"

"Judi was murdered," he said, his voice quivering. "They think I did it."

A bolt of silence shot through the line.

"Are you still there?"

"Yeah, I'm here," Harold said tentatively. "Well…did you?"

"How could you even ask me that? Of course not."

"Okay, okay," Harold said, annoyed. "I'm sorry for your loss. So what can I do for you?"

Phillip wished he could reach into the phone and grab the little shit by the throat. As soon as he was out of this fix, he was firing this pompous asshole. Harold hadn't gotten him a decent gig in months.

"I need you to cover for me. I told the cops I spent the night at your place last night."

"What? Why in the hell did you do that?"

"Just cover for me, okay?"

"Are you nuts? No way I'm lying to the police," Harold sputtered. "And why would you need me to lie for you if you didn't do it?"

"I swear I didn't kill Judi. You have to do this for me, man. I really need you to help me out."

"Since we both know you weren't at my place, where were you?"

Phillip paused. He couldn't tell anyone where he'd really been. That would open up a can of worms that would further complicate his predicament.

"I can't say, right now. Anyway, the less you know the better. But please, man, can you cover for me?"

"No way."

Phillip lowered his head and massaged his temples. If Harold didn't back him up, he was screwed.

"Okay, okay," Phillip said. "You don't have to lie. But how about this? Can you just screen your calls? If the cops leave you a message, don't return it. Maybe by the time you get back, they'll have Judi's killer."

"I don't like that idea either. What if they—"

"Man, please," Phillip begged. "Just don't answer your phone. You won't be committing a crime by not calling the cops back. If they do reach you, they'll probably want you to come back home and give a statement."

"That's bull. I'm not cutting my vacation short because of you."

"Then don't answer your phone," Phillip pleaded.

It took another five minutes of begging before Harold agreed to go along. Phillip just prayed he didn't change his mind. That would buy him a few weeks.

Phillip was up and pacing again. Now he had to figure out what he was going to do about his second, much bigger problem. If the police got a sample of his DNA, there was a good possibility it would match what they'd found underneath Judi's fingernails. He stared into the dresser mirror, still pissed at what Judi had done to his face. As soon as he got some money he was going to get a chemical peel to make sure there was no permanent scarring.

It was stupid of him to have claimed that the scratches came from a tree branch, but he hadn't been able to think up a better cover story on the spur of the moment. If he had admitted that he and Judi had fought that night, he'd probably be in jail right now.

Phillip collapsed onto the bed. All this worrying wasn't doing him any good. What he needed to do was relax. Shutting his eyes, he started doing the deep-breathing exercises he'd learned in acting class. He could actually feel his pulse slow to a trot.

A hot shower was what he really needed. He entered the bathroom, pulling his T-shirt over his head as he walked. Just as he reached for the nozzle to turn on the shower, he caught a glimpse of his torso in the mirror on the opposite wall. A brilliant idea began to slowly percolate.

Closing the toilet lid, he sat down as his mind began to whirl as fast as the blades of a fan. Yes, he thought, exhaling with relief. It would definitely work. He'd just come up with the perfect explanation for why his DNA would be underneath Judi's fingernails.

He laughed a loud, hearty laugh. He couldn't wait to screw with those obnoxious cops.

Glancing around the bathroom, he spotted exactly what he needed to carry out his plan. Picking up the metal soap dish, he ran his fingers along the sides, delighting at its jagged edges.

Yes, Phillip thought. Problem solved.

CHAPTER 10

Girlie pulled her silver blue Jag to a stop in front of the Anaheim Crest Country Club. She clipped her Ray-Bans to the sun visor as a parking attendant dashed over to open her car door.

"Good afternoon, Ms. Cortez."

"Hello, Jeffrey."

Girlie always remembered the names of the insignificant people who serviced her. It made them feel better about their menial jobs. Jeffrey's over-anxious grin confirmed that.

She swung her legs out of the car in a careful, dainty move. As she glided into the lobby of the club, she enjoyed the appreciative stares. The breast implants she'd purchased two years out of law school had been one of her wisest investments. On top of that God had blessed her with stunning physical attributes. Her fabulous legs topped the list.

Girlie was not looking forward to this meeting with the CEO and general counsel of Big Buy. The milquetoast GC was tolerable enough, but the CEO was a high-caliber bitch.

A hostess showed Girlie into a small, private dining room that overlooked the city's skyline. The CEO and general counsel were sitting in club chairs, sipping wine. Their meal was laid out on a table set with china and sterling silver.

"I have some good news," CEO Rita Kimble-Richards announced, once the hostess had left. "One of the plaintiffs, Judi Irving, is no longer with us."

Girlie froze. "You fired her?"

The CEO smiled and took a sip of wine. "Nope. She's dead."

That news was a shock, but Girlie was more taken aback by Rita's apparent pleasure in it.

"Please forgive my sister-in-law's lack of tact." Evelyn Kimble, the general counsel, was always quick to correct the CEO's foibles.

"Oh, I didn't mean it like that," Rita said dismissively.

The CEO was well past fifty, but her botoxed lips, tightened eyes and over-tanned skin, made her look like an aging freak. Girlie couldn't understand why someone with her money couldn't find a better plastic surgeon.

"What happened to her?"

"She was attacked during a break-in at her home on Monday," the general counsel volunteered.

Though close in age to the CEO, the prim and professional Evelyn was hot enough to pass for forty. Even Girlie admired her taut body, creamy skin and thick blonde hair.

Vernetta obviously hadn't known about the break-in when she was acting so giddy outside the courtroom.

"I'd like to get this case resolved as soon as possible," Rita said, taking another sip of wine. "Only the black and the Mexican are left. Offer them peanuts and get it over with."

The CEO's crass comment caused Evelyn's cheeks to color with embarrassment. "From what I saw of Vernetta Henderson during that trial you just had, she's not going to take peanuts to drop the case."

This was only Girlie's second case for Big Buy and she was still learning the quirks of her new clients—an important element in maintaining a successful lawyer-client relationship. She had quickly picked up on the unspoken hostility between the two women.

Decades earlier, Rita had been a secretary with the company. Once Big Buy founder Harlan Kimble laid eyes on her, Rita had become his lover and soon thereafter, his wife. She'd gained control of the company five years ago, after he died unexpectedly from a heart attack.

"I'm sure I can get it resolved," Girlie promised.

"Just make it happen sooner rather than later," Rita ordered.

"You seem unusually concerned about this case," Girlie said. "Is there anything I need to know?"

Rita reached for the wine bottle and refilled her glass.

"I've been chosen Woman of the Year by the Anaheim Rotary Club. My general counsel is a woman. In light of our positions of power in the company, an allegation that we're discriminating against women would be extremely embarrassing. For both of us."

What should have been embarrassing was the company's deplorable record when it came to promoting women. Despite a sprinkling of female floor supervisors, Big Buy's management was overwhelmingly white and male. Rita wasn't smart enough to recognize the existence of a glass ceiling at her stores. Nor did she even care. The sexist culture at Big Buy had been firmly entrenched by Harlan Kimble, a crusty Neanderthal who didn't think women had the hutzpah to manage a retail operation. When Harlan had passed on the company to his wife, he had assumed she would tap one of his vice presidents to step in as CEO.

During her first two years at the helm, Rita had nearly run the company into the ground. But by year three, Big Buy's profits had started to rise and had been on an upward track ever since.

"We also can't risk this case turning into a class action," Rita said. "Plaintiffs' attorneys are out there trolling for companies like us to sue."

Girlie glanced at Evelyn who did not meet her eyes. The CEO was not telling the whole truth about why this case was so high on her radar. But Girlie always did her homework. She knew exactly why Rita wanted the case to disappear as soon as possible and it had nothing to do with her precious reputation.

"If you're that concerned about getting rid of it," Girlie said, "I suggest we throw some real money at the plaintiffs."

"I'm not sure we should offer significant money this early on," Evelyn said, finally sounding like a real general counsel. "If we do, every woman in the company will be lining up with their hands out."

The general counsel had little legal experience outside of Big Buy. Harlan Kimble had hired his sister as general counsel just three years out of law school. Nepotism at its finest. They'd been very close, up until the time he'd married Rita.

"We can open with a nuisance-value settlement offer," Girlie said. "If they reject it, I'll take their depositions for several days and hit them with boatloads of discovery. I'll make it so tough that they'll want out of the case just to get me off their backs."

Girlie smiled at the thought of all the hoops she planned to have Vernetta and her clients jump through.

"I like it," Rita said. "But I want this case resolved in weeks, not months. And do everything you can to keep it out of the media."

"That shouldn't be a problem." Girlie repositioned herself on the couch. "I doubt that a two-plaintiff discrimination case would be of much interest to the media."

"Oh, I forgot to mention something else." There was a phony casualness in Rita's tone. "One of our regional managers says there's a rumor that Judi Irving had some documents with damaging information about the company."

"What kind of information?" Girlie asked.

"No one knows for sure, but according to the gossip making its way around the store, they may have been financial records."

"Who has the documents now?"

"Who knows?" Rita said. "Ironically, Judi Irving's live-in boyfriend appears in one of our TV spots. I would think he has them. If they even exist."

"I'll dig around and see what I can find out," Girlie said. "But I don't want anyone from the company contacting the boyfriend about those documents. If they exist, I'll find them. And make sure the management at the store is aware of the lawsuit."

The CEO ran her finger along the rim of her glass. "If either one of those women even blinks the wrong way, they're out."

"That's not a good idea," Girlie cautioned. "You'd just be handing them a retaliation claim. No one should take any kind of action against them without clearing it with me first."

Evelyn silently nodded her agreement.

"I'll work on getting the case resolved as soon as possible," Girlie promised.

And she would use whatever ammunition she could find to get the job done.

CHAPTER 11

My iPhone rang just as I pulled into a metered parking space in front of the Center for Justice on Crenshaw Boulevard. I glanced at the caller ID display and cringed.

I let it ring two more times before finally picking up. "Hey, Lamarr."

His calls to me had practically reached stalker level.

"'Bout time you answer! I been callin' you for two days."

"I had a lot of catch-up work to do on my other cases. What's up?"

"*What's up?* You know what's up. I need to know what's going on with my appeal. I ain't payin' that trick no two-million dollars."

"Lamarr, I've already told you. I'll put in a request for the trial transcripts. We have sixty days from the date of the court's entry of judgment to—"

"I don't know what all that legal mumbo jumbo means and I don't give a shit." His deep voice was elevated. "I just wanna know how long it's going to take before I get a new trial."

Finding some basis to appeal the verdict would not be difficult—an incorrect jury instruction, evidence that should have been excluded. But finding something significant enough to entitle Lamarr to a new trial was a longshot.

"Even if we're successful in getting a new trial," I said, "it's not going to happen overnight."

"*If?* I ain't tryin' to hear 'bout no ifs. I'm getting a new trial. You can bet on that. That lyin' bitch and her attorney are on TV every damn day calling me a rapist. If I can't stop her legally, then I'll do it *my* way."

I recognized the rage in Lamarr's voice because I'd witnessed it before. We were in my office late one night going over his testimony. The longer we worked at it, the more frustrated he became at having to repeat the sequence of events over and over again. In a snap, he went from frustrated to nearly deranged, picking up my files and hurling them across the room.

"You can't go around saying stuff like that, Lamarr. I understand that you—"

"You don't understand shit!" he said, his voice breaking. "She's trying to destroy everything I worked for. I didn't rape that girl. She's lyin' on me!"

I gave Lamarr a few seconds to compose himself before I spoke.

"I do understand what you're going through," I said softly. "I'm not living it, but I understand it. I'll be consulting with an appellate attorney to get your appeal filed. But it's going to take some time. Until then, I need you to promise me that you're not going to do anything stupid."

Lamarr did not say a word.

"Did you hear me, Lamarr?"

"Yeah," he mumbled.

"Maybe you should get out of L.A. for a while." Without your homies, I wanted to add. "Go visit your grandmother in Cleveland."

Lamarr's mother died in a car accident his senior year of high school. He'd chosen Ohio State over UCLA just to be closer to his grandmother.

"Yeah, okay," he said after a long beat. "That's probably what I need to do. I'm trying to keep my cool. But if one of those punks from TMZ sticks another microphone in my face, I'ma have to hurt somebody."

"Just do what I told you to do. Keep walking and don't say a word."

I gave him a few more words of advice that I expected him to ignore, then hung up and rushed inside the Center for Justice.

My excitement about suing Big Buy had waned after Olivia's call telling me about Judi Irving's death. Of the three plaintiffs, I'd spent the most time with Judi. I admired her passion to change things at Big Buy. It was hard to think of her dying in such a brutal way.

Benjamin Cohen, the Executive Director of the Center, and my law school classmate, greeted me in a cramped waiting area. The Center provided free legal services to people who couldn't otherwise afford it by relying on state grants and attorneys like me, who took on cases without a retainer.

"Olivia and Ida are pretty freaked out," Benjamin said, leading me back to the Center's only conference room. "Ida, in particular. Crazy as it sounds, she thinks Big Buy was behind Judi's death."

A skinny Jewish guy, Benjamin wore a multi-colored yarmulke atop of his Afro-like mass of curly hair. He favored blue jeans and owned an impressive T-shirt collection. Today, a picture of the Black Eyed Peas graced his chest.

Benjamin graduated at the top of our class at UC Berkeley's School of Law, far ahead of me. His decision to forego a big law firm salary and dedicate his time and talent to the poor said a lot about him.

When we entered the conference room, Olivia Jackson and Ida Lopez were standing near the window. We all sat down at a long table. I took one side, Benjamin the other, sandwiched between the two women.

"Good to see you again," I said. "I still can't believe Judi's gone. Our fight against Big Buy won't be the same without her."

I pulled a legal pad from my satchel.

"Did Judi ever show you those documents she called me about?"

They both shook their heads.

"Do you have any idea where they might be?"

"Her boyfriend probably has them," Olivia said, "which means we'll never see 'em."

"Why do you say that?"

"That man tried everything he could to get Judi to drop out of the case," Olivia explained. "I was proud of her for not bowing to his pressure. Some women will do anything to please a man."

That statement made me think of Special. I was certain that she was only joining the Community of Islam because it was what Clayton wanted her to do. We still hadn't found time to have a heart-to-heart talk about her decision.

"Why would he want her to drop the case?" I asked.

"He's an actor and he made a few commercials for Big Buy," Ida said. There was a tiny hint of a Spanish accent in her voice. "He was worried that they wouldn't give him any more work if Judi sued the company."

"That man is a heathen who needs Jesus," Olivia said.

Benjamin smiled and winked at me. We both thought Olivia's strong faith would play well to a jury.

I could hear the quiet patter of Ida's foot underneath the table. Dressed modestly in a loose-fitting dress, her long hair was pulled back into a bun. I'd never seen her in makeup, not even lipstick.

"Whoever Big Buy hired to kill Judi has those documents," Ida said. "Whatever they were, Big Buy couldn't risk letting them go public."

"You really believe that?" I asked.

She nodded.

"Do you have any evidence of that?" Benjamin asked.

"Not a shred," Olivia replied.

"Do you still want to proceed with the lawsuit?" My question was intended for Ida.

"Definitely," Olivia said with no hesitation. "We have to stop this mess."

A tear slid down Ida's cheek. "I have two girls I'm raising by myself. I can't afford to lose my job. And if something happens to me..." Her voice trailed off.

"Nothing's going to happen to you," I assured her.

"Were you guys able to gather any more demographic information?" It was time to steer the meeting in another direction.

Olivia pulled a piece of paper from her purse and handed it to me.

Her handwritten notations showed that eighty-three percent of the non-management workforce was female, while women held only seven percent of the supervisor positions. The numbers were even worse at the upper-management level. Women held only two percent of those jobs.

I would need to confirm these stats during discovery, but the information gave me a good starting point.

"I just discovered that there's a guy in our region who makes three dollars an hour more than I do," Olivia said. "And he does the exact same job and started a month after me."

"You think that's something?" Ida said, suddenly re-engaged. "One of the guys I supervise makes more than I do. When I confronted the store manager about it, he tried to make a joke. Said I was getting child support payments from my ex so that made us even."

I frowned in disgust. "What's the manager's name? I'm going to have a lot of fun with him in deposition."

"Anything else happen in the workplace since our last meeting?" Benjamin asked.

"Two weeks ago, they had the nerve to hold our regional convention at a casino in Temecula." Olivia waved her hand in the air. "That place is filled with sin. At the kickoff reception, the hostesses were wearing hot pants and push-up bras for tops. A couple of the regional managers got drunk and started telling sexist jokes."

"Can you remember any of the jokes?" I asked.

Ida jumped in on that one. "What do you tell a woman with two black eyes?" She paused for effect. "Nothing. Somebody already told her twice."

Benjamin and I gasped simultaneously.

"That's just the mild stuff," Olivia said. "When they got to cussin', I had to leave. I sat in my car and prayed for everybody in that place."

We spent another thirty minutes listening to more outrageous stories about what it was like to be a female employee at Big Buy.

"I want to be completely honest with you," I said, putting down my pen. "Since you're still working there, suing the company is going to be twice as hard as it normally would be. I need to make sure you're emotionally up to this."

"I'm all prayed up and ready for battle," Olivia said. "Besides, I want to do this for Judi."

I turned to Ida. "Are you still in?"

I knew her answer before she opened her mouth. I could see the renewed fire in her eyes.

"You're right," Ida said, turning to face Olivia. "We can't let Big Buy get away with treating us the way they do. We need to fight this fight for ourselves and for Judi."

CHAPTER 12

Girlie had never been a wait-and-see kind of person. She was a successful trial attorney because she anticipated problems—and, more importantly, their solutions—long before they ever materialized.

She welcomed Eli Jenkins into her office and showed him over to her custom-made hot pink leather couch. When the movers had first wheeled it in, the couch had caused a big stir among her stuffier partners. But they eventually saw the wisdom of letting Girlie be Girlie.

Big, bald and burly, Eli was the only investigator Girlie kept on retainer. He never breached confidentiality, and like Girlie, he was smart enough to never get caught.

Girlie took a seat at the opposite end of the couch.

"I was glad to get your call," Eli said, ignoring the cleavage she was putting on display just for him.

Eli claimed that he never mixed business and pleasure. That did not, however, stop Girlie from trying.

"I was a little disappointed that you were able to pull off a win against Lamarr Harris without my help," he joked.

Girlie laughed. "Sometimes raw legal talent alone is enough to get the job done."

Girlie reached for a folder from the coffee table and handed it to him. "I'm representing Big Buy department stores in a sex discrimination case. If the need arises," she said with a wink, "I'd like to have something I can use against the two sales associates who're suing the company. Their names, addresses and dates of birth are in that file."

"What kind of dirt you looking for?"

"Any kind you can find. Preferably something criminal or at least embarrassing enough to force them to drop their lawsuit or take a settlement they might not otherwise accept."

Eli had once found out that a principal who was suing a Catholic school for wrongful termination was screwing one of the nuns. Eli planted a video camera inside the rectory. When Girlie produced a picture at the principal's deposition showing his head buried under the nun's habit, he quickly dropped his case.

"Another plaintiff in the case was recently murdered during a break-in at her home," Girlie said. She supposedly had some financial records with damaging information about the company. I'd love to get my hands on those documents."

"Any connection between the break-in and the documents?"

"Not sure, but I doubt it."

"Any idea who might have them?"

"My best guess is her live-in boyfriend or her attorney, but I don't know that for sure either. The boyfriend's name is Phillip Peterman. There's a little information about him in the file too."

"I'll nose around and see what I can find out. Is it okay if I speak directly with Peterman?"

Girlie shook her head. "Hold off on that for now. I'm working on him from another angle. I don't want anyone to know the company is looking for the documents. But use any other means you find appropriate to locate them. There's a ten-thousand-dollar bonus if you can find them."

"Thanks for the additional motivation." Eli perused the folder Girlie had given him. "What else can you tell me about the plaintiffs?"

"Ida Lopez is a single mother with two daughters. Olivia Jackson is married, no children and a bit of a holy roller. I haven't taken their depositions yet, so I don't know much more than that. But I'm sure you'll find something."

Eli laughed. "Tru dat."

"The only problem is," Girlie continued, "I need the information fast. As in yesterday."

"I'm already on it."

He placed the folder inside his briefcase.

"So when are you going to let me buy you dinner so I can reward you for all your great investigative work?" Girlie asked. She'd never met a man she couldn't entice and it irked her that Eli repeatedly blew her off.

"You're my best client," he said with a smile. "There's no way I'm going to *screw* that up."

Girlie stretched her arm along the back of the couch. "You have no idea what you're missing."

Eli finally gave in and took a long, admiring look at her cleavage. "Actually, I do."

Girlie was about to end the meeting when another idea came to her. She stared over Eli's shoulder out of the window.

"There are two other people connected with the case that I'd like you to look into."

He readied his pen. "Fire away."

"The first one is Benjamin Cohen. He runs the Center for Justice in South Los Angeles. He helped the plaintiffs retain their counsel and is serving in an advisory role on the case."

"Got it. Who's the other person?"

"Vernetta Henderson. She's the plaintiffs' attorney."

Eli stopped writing and looked up. "I'm familiar with Henderson. She's squeaky clean."

"A lot of people are squeaky clean," Girlie said. "Until something mysteriously pops up."

"You know I don't go there." Eli scowled, then broke into a playful grin. "But I have people who do."

"If you do happen to find something interesting on Vernetta, I'll be very, very pleased," Girlie said.

"Pleased enough to double that bonus?"

Girlie's lips stretched into a devilish smile. "Pleased enough to triple it."

CHAPTER 13

"This is absolutely ridiculous. Robby wouldn't hurt a fly."
Mankowski scrutinized the shapely, gum-snapping blonde standing in front of him and marveled at her resemblance to Judi Irving.

When they'd first entered The Salon Haven in Westwood where Camille Watson worked as a hair stylist, Mankowski had picked her out right away. The curly auburn hair, pert nose and toned body mirrored the photographs of Judi that he'd seen in her living room—that is, if you take off ten years and add three cup sizes.

"Is there someplace we can talk in private?" Detective Thomas asked, after flashing his badge.

"Nope. I'm busy."

Camille's tattooed shampoo boy gasped in shock at her insolence. All eyes and ears in the salon waited for the detectives' next move.

Camille started spraying her client's hair with a tangy-smelling aerosol that made Mankowski's eyes water. He waved his hand in front of his face and took a step back.

"We only need a few minutes of your time," Thomas pressed.

"I watch the Investigation Discovery channel twenty-four/seven," Camille said boldly. "I'm not under arrest so I don't have to talk to you if I don't want to."

"You're right," Thomas replied. "If you don't want to help your boyfriend, that's fine with us."

She picked up another bottle and continued spraying.

Mankowski glanced around the shop and spotted a back door that he presumed led into an alley. "Maybe we can talk out back."

"Okay, fine," she said, finally relenting. "I'll be back in a sec," she told her client.

She followed the detectives past a row of hair dryers and through a pink door. The alley out back was neater than Mankowski's house.

"We're just here to confirm Mr. Irving's whereabouts during the timeframe we believe Judi Irving was murdered. So can you tell us—"

Mankowski stopped and glanced behind him. The door was open just a crack. "Can I help you?"

Camille's shampoo boy quickly shut the door.

"What we'd like to know," Mankowski continued, "is where you were between the hours of ten p.m. Sunday night and eight a.m. Monday morning?"

"I was with Robby." The fact that she didn't take a second to try to recall the date meant that Robby had prepped her.

"How can you be so certain?"

"I'm off on Mondays." She was still holding the spray bottle, punching the air with it as she spoke. "I always cook dinner for Robby on Sunday nights."

"Where?"

"At his place."

"How long were you there?"

"I got there around six and left at nine the next morning."

"Was Robby there with you the whole time?"

"Yep."

"You're certain of that."

"Absolutely."

"Did Robby ever talk to you about Judi?"

Camille rolled her eyes. "A little. They were trying to work things out without attorneys, but Judi was being unreasonable. He had to pay her way too much alimony. Look, I'll just slice to the chase. Robby's a wonderful man, but he wasn't happy in his marriage so he left."

Slice to the chase? Mankowski started to correct her, but let it go. "So Robby was pissed off about having to pay Judi alimony?"

"Well, not *that* pissed. Robby's not a murderer."

"How do you know that?"

"I've been dating the man for over a year, okay? I know him like the back of my palm."

Thomas looked away to keep from laughing. The woman's misuse of clichés was comical.

"When you're in a business like mine, you have to be very good with people. I'm excellent with people."

"Okay," Mankowski said. "So what did you two do that night?"

"We watched TV."

"What did you watch?"

That question stumped her. They had obviously neglected to rehearse the details of Robby's alibi.

"I don't remember." Camille scratched her upper arm and looked down at the ground. "I don't even remember what I watched this morning."

The woman was a lousy liar.

"Sounds like you might be lying to cover up for your boyfriend," Mankowski charged.

Camille laughed cynically. "I already told you, I watch a lot of cop shows. Your scare tactics aren't going to work on me." She pointed the bottle at Mankowski. "I know how you guys try to trap people. I need to get back to my client."

"Robby thought he was getting three-hundred-thousand dollars in insurance money," Thomas said. "That's quite a motive for murder."

"Sure is. And what's good for the duck is good for the duckling. So go talk to Judi's boyfriend. She barely knew the guy. I couldn't believe she made him her beneficiary. She obviously doesn't watch *Snapped.*"

Mankowski had no idea what she was talking about and decided not to ask.

"We'd like you to come down to the station so we can get a statement," Thomas said.

"You just got my statement."

"You know," Mankowski said, "if you watch as much TV as you claim you do, then you know we don't have to be so nice."

Camille's face puffed into a pout. "Okay, fine. But I can't do it until my off day. Can I get back to my client now?"

Mankowski didn't speak until they had climbed back into their sedan. "I don't believe she was with Irving that night. She's covering for him."

"I agree," Thomas said. "Which makes Robby Irving just as much of a suspect as Phillip Peterman."

CHAPTER 14

Special flitted around the kitchen as if she was organizing a dinner party for twenty. Clayton would be arriving any minute and she wanted to make sure everything was perfect.

It surprised her how much she enjoyed cooking for Clayton. She was used to men wining and dining her at the city's best restaurants. Now, she was turning out to be quite the chef since her conversion to Islam.

Her physical appearance had also changed. Her makeup was much more understated, just the way Clayton liked it. Just mascara, blush and a light-bronze lip gloss. The decision to give up her fake eyelashes had been tough, but the whole natural look was growing on her. Who would've thought she could look sexy without showing any cleavage? Tonight she was wearing a form-fitting black turtleneck and her black skinny jeans.

The doorbell rang and Special skipped to the door.

She reached out to give Clayton a hug even before he had stepped across the threshold. He barely hugged her back.

"Hey, babe," he said, wearily.

Clayton worked as an engineer for a small defense contractor, a job he seemed to be growing more and more disenchanted with. He was constantly talking about quitting and starting his own business.

Clayton took a seat in the living room and Special brought him a glass of apple juice.

"It's fresh squeezed," she said proudly. "From my new juicer."

"Thanks, babe."

"And I made—"

"Sit down." Clayton patted the couch. "We need to talk."

Special's entire body tensed. "Talk about what?"

"About us."

She didn't move for another three seconds. "Let me go turn off the oven."

In the kitchen, she opened the oven door and set the casserole dish on the stovetop. Her mind raced as she tried to recall the past few days. Had she done something wrong? A cuss word had slipped out every now and then, but other than that, she'd been a model Muslim woman. She walked tentatively back into the living room.

"Okay," she said, sitting down on the couch, a respectable distance between them. "What's up?"

"You know how much I enjoy being with you and how much I like having you in my life, right?"

Special stopped breathing. He was prepping her for some really bad news.

"And you know I've decided to dedicate my life to the Community. That means there are rules and principles that I'm—well, both of us—are required to follow."

Now she was completely confused. "What are you talking about? We've been doing everything we're supposed to do. Going to meetings three or four times a week, praying five times a day. I've changed my diet and I don't even cuss anymore." *Well, almost.*

"I'm talking about the big thing we've been doing that's straight-up wrong."

Special's face clouded. "What big thing?"

Clayton gave her a skeptical look that told her to stop playing dumb. "Special, we can't have sex anymore. Not until we're married."

Fear eased out of her body and astonishment skidded into its place.

Special laughed. "Boy, stop playing."

Clayton frowned. "I'm not playing. I'm serious."

She waited a beat, expecting him to explain this joke, but he didn't.

"Oh...uh, okay," was the only response Special could muster.

"I don't expect it to be easy," Clayton continued. "For either of us. But I want to follow Allah's will in every way."

"Okay," she said again, still shell-shocked.

"Let's pray." Clayton took both of her hands, lowered his head and closed his eyes. "Oh great Allah, we come before you as mere servants, humbled by your power. Strengthen us, Allah, so that we may be the worthy servants you deserve. . ."

Special opened one eye and pinned it on Clayton. *This has to be a joke?* Maybe this was some kind of test to see if she was really serious about Islam.

Once he'd finished praying, Clayton instantly seemed like his old self. "Whatever you're cooking smells good. I'm going to wash my hands."

As Clayton disappeared down the hallway, Special stayed put, still a bit dazed. This was crazy. She did not wait three decades to find the man of her dreams just to become a friggin' nun. Christians fornicated all the time. They just went to church Sunday morning and asked Jesus for forgiveness. It was no big deal.

A naughty smile suddenly graced her lips. They weren't planning to get married for another year. There was no way Clayton could go without sex that long. He was the most sexual man she'd ever dated. Her smile grew increasingly wider. Since Clayton was putting her to the test, she'd turn the tables and come up with one for him.

And she'd make sure there would be no way he could pass it.

CHAPTER 15

Girlie lowered her head and let out a quiet breath of air.

"Tonisha," she said into the speakerphone, "I need you to calm down and listen to me, okay?"

For the past ten minutes, Girlie had been trying to explain to her obstinate client why it was unrealistic to expect to have a two-million-dollar check in her hands three days after the jury's verdict.

"Were you even listening to me the last two times we discussed this? I already told you there's a good chance that Lamarr will appeal the verdict and if he does, it could be a long time before he has to pay you."

"I need my money now!" Tonisha yelled in a shrill voice. "Can't you file a motion or something? I can't even get a job strippin' no more 'cuz everybody's hatin' on me. How am I supposed to live?"

"*Star* magazine paid you twenty grand for that story they ran last month. Where's that money?"

"It's gone. I had a lot of bills."

"I don't know what to tell you. Maybe a family member can give you a loan."

"My family ain't got no money. You gotta make Lamarr pay me!"

Girlie bit her lip. "Tonisha, I want you to listen to me. There's nothing I can do to make that happen right away."

"Okay then, how about loaning me some money until we get paid?"

Girlie had advanced money to clients on a couple of occasions. She was fairly certain Tonisha would eventually receive the jury's award. Even if Lamarr appealed, it was unlikely that the court would overturn the verdict. But Girlie didn't want to be tied up with Tonisha anymore than she already was.

"My law firm doesn't allow us to advance money to clients," Girlie lied. "But maybe I could approach Lamarr's attorney and offer to accept a reduced award in exchange for their agreement not to file an appeal. I've done that in other cases."

"A reduced award?" Tonisha hissed. "That jury gave me two-million dollars and I want every penny of it."

Explaining to Tonisha that she wouldn't actually receive the whole two million was a battle Girlie would fight another day. After attorneys' fees, costs and taxes, Tonisha would be lucky to clear five hundred thousand.

Girlie looked at the clock. Time for a Tonisha break.

"I'm late for a meeting," she said. "I'll figure something out and call you later."

She ended the call with Tonisha still yapping about her money.

"Hey, how's the sexiest attorney in L.A.?" Christopher Biltmore stepped into Girlie's office and closed the door behind him.

Girlie grimaced. From an annoying client to an even more annoying colleague. Not a good omen for the remainder of her day.

"Hello, Christopher," Girlie droned.

He plopped into a chair in front of Girlie's desk. There was nothing attractive about her colleague. He was shaped like a potato with toothpicks for arms and legs. But everyone envied his brilliant legal mind.

"You know," Christopher began, "I thought it was really strange that you lobbied so hard to take on Big Buy as a client after Harrison retired. Everybody knows the CEO is a control freak and a first-class witch. So I've been scratching my head trying to figure out what you knew that I didn't."

The competitiveness between law firm associates paled next to the backstabbing rivalries that could erupt between partners battling over a new client. Like Girlie, Christopher was a junior partner at Donaldson, Watson and Barkley.

"You really have to stop it with all the conspiracy stuff, Christopher. I just saw an opportunity for a great new client."

Christopher leaned back in the chair. "No way. There's more to the story, so spill it."

There was indeed more to the story, but Girlie wasn't about to share the real deal with a loudmouth like Christopher.

"I was looking for a change of pace," she said. "Something a little more low profile."

Christopher laughed like he was being tickled.

"That's bull. I still can't turn on the TV without hearing a sound bite from you about that Legends player. How many talk shows did you do? Fifty? And by the way, if you ask me, your client was just as shady as that football player. How in the hell did you pull that off?"

"They call it legal talent, sweetie pie."

He chuckled. "So, are you going to tell me why you went after Big Buy? Or am I going to have to tell you what I know?"

That was more like it. Christopher was here because he had information he wanted to confirm. "I'm listening," she said. "Tell me what you know."

"I just heard that the Welson Corporation is planning a buyout of Big Buy. Nice move. You handle Big Buy's employment work now and once the buyout is complete, Welson is likely to consider you for their legal work as well. And voilà, you've got a new mega client."

"Welson is buying Big Buy?" Girlie widened her eyes in exaggerated shock.

Despite the strict secrecy surrounding the merger, Girlie had learned about it months ago from an investment banker she was screwing. The kind of blow jobs she gave could make a man give up his mother. The forthcoming buyout was indeed one of the reasons Girlie had lobbied so hard to win Big Buy as a client. But she would have to come up with a better cover story to appease Christopher.

"I knew nothing about it. I swear. You know how I like to win, right? Well, don't tell anybody, but I really thought I was going to lose my case against Lamarr Harris."

"No way. You walked around here acting like you'd already won even before you picked a jury."

That was part of Girlie's allure. She acted like a diva, thus she was a diva.

"Anyway, what does that have to do with Big Buy?"

"I found out that Vernetta Henderson was planning to sue Big Buy for gender discrimination."

Of course, Girlie only found out about Vernetta's case *after* she'd snagged Big Buy as a client.

Christopher spread his hands. "And?"

"Since I thought I might lose Tonisha's case, I saw another opportunity to go up against Vernetta and redeem myself."

Christopher took a few seconds to mull that over.

"Now, *that's* the Girlie I know. I could easily see you lowering yourself to work with a demanding client like Big Buy if it offered a chance for revenge."

Girlie smiled. "You know me too well, Christopher."

He stood up. "Not as well as I'd like to." His fuzzy eyebrows twitched.

Girlie had never had a conversation with Christopher that hadn't included some form of sexual innuendo. But Christopher didn't have enough juice in the firm to make a fling worth her while.

She batted her eyelashes. "Are you flirting with me again?"

"Yep, I think I am." His breathing was low and gruff now. "You sure you don't want me to stay? I give great back massages."

"Now what in the world would your wife have to say about that?"

"Mildred would have absolutely nothing to say because Mildred would never find out."

Girlie laughed. "How many times do I have to tell you? If I slept with you, it might jeopardize our wonderful working relationship. And there's no way I'd want to do that. Now get out of here. I have work to do."

She was relieved when Christopher finally left. The guy was nothing but talk. According to his legal assistant, he spent over a grand a month on calls to 1-900-ALL-PORN. If she had whipped out one of her perfect tits, Christopher probably would have fainted.

Girlie picked up the Big Buy complaint from the corner of her desk and flipped through it. She fully understood why Rita Richards-Kimble was so worried about the case attracting media attention or turning into a class action. That would jeopardize the company's merger with the Welson Corporation. The CEO was probably in line to pocket millions from the deal.

Girlie had been looking forward to another long, contentious match-up against Vernetta Henderson. Too bad this battle would be such a short one.

CHAPTER 16

Mankowski darted in and out of traffic on Sunset Boulevard, his eyes pinned on Phillip Peterman's white Ford Explorer.

"So just how long are we going to follow this guy?" Thomas asked, as he checked the latest stock quotes on his iPhone.

"Until we find out who he's screwing. I know he has a chick on the side. I can feel it."

The detectives spent most of the morning parked on Phillip's street, several houses away. They followed him to 24 Hour Fitness and back and were now tracking his second trip of the day. A review of Judi and Phillip's home and cell phone records revealed nothing helpful. The bank records showed that Judi saved every dime she earned, while Phillip didn't know how to spell *save*.

"Once we find out who he's screwing," Mankowski said excitedly, "we're going to scare the hell out of her until she spills the beans. The guy's so stupid he probably told her everything."

Thomas fiddled with his iPhone. "My new tech stock is up six points today."

"Put that thing away."

"I'm telling you, man, you have to get into the stock market. It's the only way to make a buck these days."

"The stock market is just legalized gambling."

"Okay, just wait until I'm rich." Thomas slid the phone into the pocket of his jacket.

Phillip pulled into the parking lot of a large strip mall off Fairfax. Mankowski hung back to give Phillip time to park. "Guess he's not headed for his broad's house, huh?" Thomas teased.

"You don't know that. Maybe she works someplace in here. She's probably some kid half his age. The guy looks like a pervert."

Phillip hopped out of his SUV, opened the back door and grabbed a knapsack from the seat. The detectives watched as he climbed a flight of stairs and entered Stars Acting Academy.

"He's probably banging some girl in the class," Mankowski complained.

He insisted on staying put until Phillip's acting class ended. Over an hour later, Thomas nudged Mankowski's arm, waking him from a deep sleep. He opened his eyes to see Phillip walking out of the acting school with a cute red-head in shorts and flip flops.

"Bingo!" Mankowski said, grabbing the steering wheel to pull himself up.

The pair talked and laughed as Phillip led the woman to his Explorer.

Starting up the car, Mankowski followed Phillip and the woman out of the parking lot and south on Fairfax. They stayed with him until Phillip pulled into the driveway of the house he had shared with Judi, which was no longer cordoned off as a crime scene. The detectives waited until the couple had entered the house before parking.

Mankowski grinned ominously. "I say we give 'em about fifteen minutes to get hot and heavy, then do a little coitus interruptus."

Thomas laughed. "You're having way too much fun at this guy's expense."

Mankowski constantly checked his watch. He could only manage to stay put for ten minutes before bolting from the car. He pounded on the door, expecting that it would take Phillip several minutes to answer.

Seconds later, he opened the door, but not wide enough to welcome them inside.

Phillip sneered at the detectives. "What can I do for you?"

"Just checking in to see how things are going."

"I'm fine."

Mankowski placed his foot across the threshold. "Mind if we come in?"

"Yep, I would mind."

"Why? You got company?"

"Actually, I do."

"Didn't take you long to get a new broad?"

"I don't have a new broad."

"Oh, so you admit you already had a woman on the side?"

"What's going on, Phillip?" The woman from the acting class walked up behind him.

"Just two cops who dropped by to harass me."

"Hello, ma'am," Mankowski said. "We know Mr. Peterman's been grieving since the loss of his girlfriend. We were just checking on him. I guess you're helping him through his grief."

"It's not what you think." Her wide eyes shined earnestly. "We were just rehearsing. Phillip needs to stay busy to keep his mind off of his loss."

"We don't have to explain anything to them," Phillip groused.

The woman softly touched his shoulder. "Yes, we do. Then maybe they'll leave you alone."

She stepped in front of Phillip. "I'm Traci. C'mon in."

Traci led them into the living room, where two Coke cans and several pages from a script were spread across the coffee table. "I have an audition tomorrow and Phillip was nice enough to help me rehearse my lines."

Mankowski wasn't buying it. His eyes bounced around the room. Acting in haste often resulted in people overlooking something. He was bound to spot a condom or a discarded bra.

"You satisfied?" Phillip grunted.

"How about if we check the bedroom?"

"How about if you get the hell out of my house?"

Mankowski wanted to punch him in the gut. Hard. Damn, he missed the good old days.

"You gave us the wrong cell number for your agent."

Phillip hunched a shoulder. "Did I? I've been told I have pretty sloppy handwriting."

"No problem," Mankowski said. "We got the correct number from his assistant."

Phillip stiffened. "Really? So…uh…did you…did you get a chance to speak with him?"

"Not yet. He hasn't returned our calls and we're actually a little concerned about that. You might want to urge him to do so."

Phillip smirked. "I'll do that."

"How come you didn't tell us about Judi's insurance policy?" Thomas asked. "Three- hundred grand is a nice payout for a few months as a boyfriend."

"That policy had nothing to do with my being with Judi. It wasn't important to me."

"Glad you feel that way," Mankowski told him. "We let the insurance company know that you're a person of interest in Judi's death. They won't be paying a dime on the policy until we give them the word."

Phillip's body puffed up like he was going to explode. "You had no right to do that. I didn't kill Judi."

"Yeah, sure you didn't." Mankowski took a step toward the door. "We'll drop by later to check on you. Call us if you need anything."

Mankowski groused to himself all the way back to the car. "They probably spotted us following them."

"I say we spend a little more time checking out Judi's ex-husband," Thomas suggested.

Both men had strong motives for killing Judi, but Mankowski's money was still on Phillip Peterman.

Actor Boy was the killer. He could feel it deep in the pit of his gut.

CHAPTER 17

Benjamin hopped off the Santa Monica Freeway and drove south on Crenshaw Boulevard, blasting Tupac's *Only God Can Judge Me* at eardrum-busting level.

He tapped the steering wheel and mouthed the lyrics in rhythm with Tupac. "That which does not kill me can only make me stronger," he rapped, completely off key.

Tupac was a friggin' poet laureate as far as Benjamin was concerned.

Although it was close to midnight, it was not unusual for Benjamin to be headed in the direction of his office. When he couldn't sleep, working was the perfect remedy. Lately, he'd spent more nights camped out on the lumpy couch in his office than in his rent-controlled apartment within walking distance of Venice Beach.

He eased his orange Volkswagen Beetle into a narrow alley and pulled into a stall near the back entrance of the building. He shut off the lights and finished listening to the rest of the song, his head bouncing in rhythm to the beat.

Turning off the ignition, Benjamin hopped out of the car. He planned to spend the next few hours reviewing a brief he was drafting in a mortgage scam case. Benjamin enjoyed the intellectual part of practicing law far more than arguing before a judge or jury.

As he approached the Center's back entrance, he frowned at the heavy steel bars. The place looked like a prison. But after two break-ins and the loss of three laptop computers, he had to face the reality of their South Los Angeles location.

He removed the two locks on the steel door, then unlocked the thick wooden door. Though the police had advised him to install an alarm system, it wasn't in the budget. As it turned out, they didn't need it. After the Center helped the mother of a local gang leader save her home from foreclosure, the gang had issued a protection order for the Center. That kind of security was better than any alarm system on the market.

Benjamin flicked on the lights and walked down a bright, yellow hallway dotted with motivational quotes.

You can if you think you can.

It's hard to fail, but it's worse never to have tried to succeed.

Be just and fear not.

Benjamin didn't just want to help his clients solve their legal problems, he wanted to change their lives.

He was about to stick his key into the door of his office when something stopped him. The door was already open just a crack. He tried to recall whether he'd forgotten to lock it. No way. Benjamin *always* locked his office.

He took an uneasy step inside and felt along the wall for the light switch. The breeze from the cracked window hit his face seconds before he noticed the open file cabinets and papers scattered about the floor. He stepped further inside, surveying the debris.

The office suddenly went dark.

"What the—"

A gloved hand rammed Benjamin's forehead into the adjacent wall. "Don't move and keep your mouth shut."

Brightly colored stars blinked on and off and Benjamin's head felt like it was on fire.

The gloved hand was clamped so tight around his neck that he could barely breathe, let alone speak, but he tried anyway. "Take my wallet," he managed to eke out. "It's in my back pocket."

"I said keep your mouth shut."

Benjamin sensed that his assailant was not some crack head. He was a head taller than Benjamin and heavyset. He also wasn't some neighborhood thug. He had the deep voice of an older man, an older white man.

"I want those documents you got from Judi Irving," the man spat. "Hand 'em over and I'm out of here."

"I don't have them."

The man pulled Benjamin's head back toward him, then slammed his face into the wall again. His yarmulke tumbled to the floor and he could feel his entire face puff up like a beach ball.

"I…swear…I…don't…have…them," Benjamin stuttered. "I don't even know what they are."

"Don't make this hard on yourself. Either give me the documents or tell me where they are."

Benjamin's panic level shot straight skyward. The guy was not going to take no for an answer. Right now, Ida's fears no longer seemed farfetched. Maybe Judi *was* dead because of those documents. And now Benjamin might be next.

He tried to swallow, but the hand around his throat made that next to impossible. "Okay, okay," he said. "They're in the trunk of my car. Out back."

"That's more like it," the man said.

Still holding him by the neck, the man twisted Benjamin's right arm behind his back. He ushered Benjamin out of the office and down the hallway toward the back door.

Benjamin's right eye was swollen shut now and everything around him was a blur.

"Open the door," the man ordered.

He kept a grip on Benjamin's neck, but let go of his arm. When Benjamin extended his right arm to reach for the door, pain vibrated through his whole body. He doubled over in pain.

"Open it!" the man shouted.

Benjamin used his left hand to ease the door open.

The man pushed him across the threshold, then immediately jerked him back inside. Their feet became entangled and they both tumbled into the wall to the right of the door. Benjamin landed shoulder-first with a painful thud.

"Turn off that spotlight!" the man ordered.

"The switch is up front, in the lobby. It's on a timer."

"Goddamn it!"

The man didn't speak for a long time and seemed to be weighing his options. He maneuvered Benjamin aside, leaned his head out of the door and peered from left to right.

"That your Volkswagen over there?" the man asked.

"Yeah," Benjamin mumbled.

The man marched him outside, stopping when they reached the back of Benjamin's Volkswagen. "Open it."

"The trunk is in the front," Benjamin blubbered.

The man cursed and trotted him to the front of the car just as Benjamin realized that he didn't have his keys.

"Uh…my keys are inside. I dropped them on the floor."

"You must think this is a game." The man pounded Benjamin's head against the car.

Benjamin cried out in pain.

"I don't have time for games."

"I…I just realized that I didn't have them."

Benjamin didn't know what he was going to do when the man opened the trunk and discovered that the documents weren't there.

"You little—"

"Yo, Ben, is that you?"

Benjamin couldn't see who was calling out to him, but he recognized the voice. It was Sonny, the security guard who patrolled the nightclub two doors down. Benjamin had saved him from eviction last year.

The man glanced behind him. "Damn!"

He shoved Benjamin aside and took off running. Benjamin tried to brace his fall, but couldn't prevent his head from careening into the pavement.

"You okay, man?" Sonny ran over and peered down at him.

"Yo, Ben, you okay?" He patted Benjamin lightly on both cheeks. "C'mon, man. You gotta wake up!"

CHAPTER 18

Olivia Jackson's wary eyes bounced around the sterile home of Judi Irving's sister. The place had all the warmth of a hospital operating room. Nothing but chrome and glass and colorless walls. Olivia doubted there was a single Bible in the whole place.

Along with Ida, she'd come to pay her respects. But there was also another, more pressing reason for their visit.

Olivia realized how little she knew about her friend. She wasn't even sure Judi was a Christian. Her nose wrinkled as she stared across the living room at Phillip Peterman. If Judi *had* been a Christian, she certainly didn't behave like one, shacking up with that sad piece of work. That boy was barely old enough to wipe his own behind.

For the past half hour, Olivia had been waiting for the right moment to approach Phillip. Ida sat next to her on the couch, ringing her hands and reciting the Holy Rosary in Spanish.

"I still don't think you should do it," Ida said, whispering into Olivia's ear. "It's just not right. We came here to pay our respects."

"We can't afford to wait," Olivia whispered back. "We have to talk to him now. Sometimes, you just have to follow God's will."

"This has nothing to do with God's will," Ida insisted. "We should just leave it alone."

For someone who professed to be a devout Catholic, Ida didn't have an ounce of faith.

Olivia kept an eye on Phillip as he chatted with two employees from Big Buy. She'd never known anybody who was grieving to smile as much as he did. She recalled the first time Judi had introduced them to her new man. Olivia's first thought was that Phillip Peterman had certainly found himself a sugar mama.

When the two women who were talking to Phillip finally left his side, Olivia sprang up from the couch.

"C'mon," she said, tugging Ida by the arm. "Let's get this over with."

They followed Phillip into the kitchen and waited while he retrieved a beer from the refrigerator.

Olivia couldn't believe the man was drinking at a time like this. But what did she expect? Judi did pick him up in a bar.

"Hello, Phillip," Olivia said. "We worked with Judi at Big Buy. We're so sorry about Judi. How are you holding up?"

Phillip smiled weakly, then popped open the beer. "It's hard. I really miss her. Thanks for coming."

"Well, just know that the Lord will never leave you, nor forsake you."

"Uh, yeah...okay." He walked over to the counter, poured the beer into an orange tumbler, then tossed the can in the trash.

"If there's anything we can do to help, please let us know," Ida offered.

Phillip nodded. "Thanks."

"Do you know yet when the service will be?" Olivia asked.

"We have to wait until the coroner releases the body before we can finalize the funeral arrangements."

Olivia's whole face crumpled into a frown. *The body?* He made Judi sound like a piece of furniture.

Phillip placed the tumbler to his lips and started guzzling down the beer.

"I should get back to the other guests," he said, wiping his mouth with his sleeve.

He started to leave, but Olivia stopped him. "We were wondering if we could talk to you about something."

He looked past them into the living room. "I'm listening."

Olivia took in a nervous breath. "Judi told us you weren't too thrilled about her suing Big Buy."

"I just thought it was a waste of time. You don't get promoted by suing people. You get promoted by doing a good job."

Olivia wanted to respond to what she interpreted as a slight, but knew it was best to ignore it. "Ida and I are still going ahead with the case."

"You gotta do what you gotta do."

"And we need your help."

Phillip's face clouded. "I'm not sure how I could possibly help you."

"Judi told us about those Big Buy financial documents she received in the mail," Olivia explained.

He took a long sip of beer. "Judi never mentioned any Big Buy documents to me?"

Olivia wasn't sure she believed him. But then again, Judi probably didn't trust the man enough to tell him about the documents.

"Well, Judi received some documents about the company that could help our case. I'm sure they must be somewhere around your house."

"Have you checked with her attorney?" Phillip snapped his fingers. "Come to think of it, I think Judi did mention that she'd turned over a bunch of documents to her attorney. What's her name?"

"Vernetta Henderson." Olivia smacked her lips suspiciously. "Just a second ago you said Judi never mentioned any documents to you."

Phillip bristled. "I think you misheard me. I said Judi never mentioned any Big Buy documents to me."

"Well, we already spoke with Vernetta. She doesn't have them. Maybe we could come over and—"

"That's okay, Phillip." Ida gave his forearm a motherly pat. "We're sorry to bother you at a time like this. Let's go, Olivia."

Olivia fired off a heated look at her co-worker. "As I was about to say, if you don't mind, maybe we could set up a time to come over and look for them. Judi told us she put them in a safe place. So maybe—"

"No way I'm letting you snoop around my home," Phillip said, his voice laced with annoyance. "You should forget about that lawsuit and be glad you both have jobs."

He stalked back into the living room.

"Didn't I tell you this was a bad idea?" Ida complained. "I hope he doesn't tell people we came here to bug him about our lawsuit instead of paying our respects. Those documents are gone because Big Buy paid somebody to take 'em when they murdered Judi."

Ida stomped back into the living room and Olivia reluctantly followed.

Olivia refused to buy into Ida's paranoia. Judi had always been extra cautious about the case. She'd probably hidden the documents so well no one would be able to find them.

Olivia would just have to pray and ask God to lead her to them.

CHAPTER 19

"I can't believe you waited this long to call me!"
I had just arrived home from work and was standing in my bedroom, listening in shock as Benjamin recounted being attacked two nights earlier at the Center for Justice.

"Well, I'm fine now."

Benjamin sounded as if he was trying to talk with a mouth full of cotton balls. After the beating he described, I could only imagine how he looked.

"I'm coming over," I said.

"No need. My mother's here. She's insisting on staying with me for a few days."

We were both silent, reluctant to say what we were obviously both thinking.

"Maybe Ida was right after all," I finally admitted. "Those documents, whatever they were, got you beaten up and probably got Judi killed."

"Maybe," Benjamin agreed.

"Olivia asked Judi's boyfriend about the documents. He claims Judi never told him about them."

"Maybe he's lying?"

"Maybe," I said.

"If there's some evidence out there that the company was willing to kill for, then this case is much bigger than either of us thought it was," Benjamin said. "If you want to drop the case, I'll understand."

I looked up to see Jefferson standing in the doorway. The grim expression on his face telegraphed that he'd been listening to my conversation.

"I'm not abandoning Olivia and Ida, or you," I said. "Judi may've lost her life because of this case. That makes me even more determined to win. We just need to be extremely careful until we figure out what's going on."

A second after I hung up, Jefferson stepped inside the bedroom. "What happened?"

I told him about the attack on Benjamin.

"This isn't good," Jefferson said. "First your client is murdered, now this. I really think you need to—"

"I'm not dropping the case."

Jefferson sighed. "I can't believe how short your memory is."

He was referring to my representation of Micronics Corporation in a case which also involved some missing documents. Things got a little rough and it was Jefferson who ultimately came to my rescue.

"The case just got going," he said. "It wouldn't be hard for another attorney to step in. I can't believe you aren't concerned."

What happened to Benjamin did have me pretty freaked out. The burglar's demand for those Big Buy documents was a fact that could not be ignored. But I was not frightened enough to abandon my clients.

I headed into the den with Jefferson close behind me.

"I'm not dropping the case, so let it go."

"Fine," he said. "I know how hard-headed you can be. But let's make a deal. If anything else crazy happens, promise me you'll tell them to find another attorney."

"Nothing else is going to happen."

"Okay," Jefferson said. "But if it does, you'll drop the case, right?"

The doorbell saved me from having to make a commitment I didn't want to make.

I made my way to the front door. "That's Special. I'll get it."

Special had called an hour earlier asking to borrow one of my purses for some big Community of Islam function. She might be a

Muslim woman now, but fashion was still high on her list of priorities.

When I opened the front door, I was surprised to see Clayton standing behind her.

"So what have you two lovebirds been up to?"

"We just saw the new Tyler Perry movie," she said, stepping inside. "It was hilarious."

Confusion glazed my face.

Special looked over her shoulder at Clayton. "Baby, Vernetta thinks being a Muslim means we have to stay locked up in the mosque all day."

Clayton laughed. "Not true."

I was embarrassed that Special was making me look so uninformed. But to be honest, I did think going to the movies was prohibited by their faith.

"I'm not big on the movies," Clayton said. "But Perry's films usually have a positive message. Since that's what my woman wanted to see, I didn't have a problem supporting her."

Special glowed up at Clayton. I had never seen her this enamored with any man.

I took a step toward a table in the entryway. "Here's the purse you wanted."

"That's not it," Special said. "It's the one with the silver button on the front."

"You're going to have to come look for it yourself."

I pointed Clayton toward the den. "Jefferson's in there."

In the bedroom, I tugged a large straw basket out of the closet.

"Girl, you have enough purses in here to open up your own booth at the swap meet."

"Some women have a shoe fetish," I said, laughing. "But for me, it's shoes *and* purses."

I sat down on the edge of the bed while Special sifted through the basket.

"Business must be good, counselor." She admired the new suit laid out on the bed. "'Cuz Donna Karan ain't cheap."

"I figured I owed it to myself after Lamarr's case."

"See, that's what I like about your business. Win or lose you still get paid the big bucks. How's he doing?"

"Not good. The Legends still haven't notified him if he'll be able to play again."

"He should've thought about that when he picked up that skank."

Special finally found the right purse.

I'd been so busy with work, and Special was always at the mosque, that we still hadn't found time to discuss her conversion to Islam.

"So you're really serious about this?" I asked.

"Yep." She didn't bother to look at me as she piled the purses back into the basket.

"So you don't believe in Christianity anymore?"

Special huffed. "Can you please just support me for once without giving me the third degree?"

"I just asked a question."

"This is what Clayton wants to do and I want to support him."

"But what do *you* want to do? And more importantly, what do you believe?"

"We need to talk about this another time. We're running late."

"Okay," I said. "You let me know when you have time."

We walked back into the den where Clayton and Jefferson were deep in conversation.

"People have a lot of misconceptions about the Community," Clayton went on. "They're often surprised once they check us out."

"I know at least six dudes I grew up with who turned their lives around once they became Muslims," Jefferson told him. "And I'm talking about hard-core, rob-your-own-mama kind of guys. If the Black Muslims can change brothers like that, they must be doing something right."

"We're not Black Muslims." Clayton's face hardened. "The white media gave us that title. We're Muslims."

"Hey, uh, okay, man. Uh, my bad." Jefferson turned awkwardly to me. "Clayton's been kicking me down with the four-one-one on the Community of Islam. I had no idea this brother was so deep."

"Hey, I'm just learning myself. If you really want to get some knowledge, you should come down to the mosque to hear a lecture. You too, Vernetta."

My normally talkative husband was suddenly tongue-tied. "Uh, yeah. We'll have to do that."

"How about this Sunday?" Special suggested.

Jefferson blasted me with a look that told me it was my job to come up with an appropriate excuse for turning down my friend's invitation.

"I promised to go to church with my mother this Sunday," I said.

"Me too," Jefferson chimed in.

"Puh-leeze," Special said to Jefferson. "You've never even seen the inside of her mama's church. You can go there anytime. Y'all are both coming down to the mosque with us. I'll make reservations for brunch afterward. It'll be fun."

Jefferson and I walked them to the door.

"I ain't going," Jefferson said, the second the door closed. "'Cuz if we do, they're gonna be bugging us about going to a bunch of meetings all the time. I'm down with what the Community's trying to do for black folks, but it ain't for me."

"You were the one acting like you were all interested. *If the Muslims can change brothers like that, they must be doing something right,*" I said, mimicking him.

"I was just trying to be nice."

"Well, too bad. You know how Special is. If we don't go, I'll never hear the end of it."

"I don't care," Jefferson said. "She's *your* best friend, so that's *your* problem. I ain't going."

CHAPTER 20

Benjamin stood in the far corner of my office, walking in tight circles, muttering under his breath. "This is a good sign," he said. "This is a very good sign."

He was reacting to a call I received earlier in the day from Girlie Cortez. To our surprise, she wanted to drop by to discuss early resolution of the Big Buy case.

I, however, was not nearly as excited as Benjamin. Girlie's offer of an olive branch this early on was reason for suspicion, not celebration.

"Can you please sit down?"

Benjamin flashed me a grin and stilled himself. But only for a nano-second.

He still appeared bruised and beat up. Red marks were visible on his face and neck and I could see a line of stitches on the left side of his head where hair used to be. We'd agreed not to tell Olivia and Ida about the attack until we had more information about exactly what was going on. I just hoped they weren't next on the assailant's list.

My iPhone rang. I saw that it was Lamarr, so I ignored it. He'd taken my advice and gone to visit his grandmother in Cleveland, but was still calling me every other day to find out if I had any new information about his case. Nothing I said got through to him.

A minute later the receptionist announced Girlie's arrival.

"I'm going out to the lobby," I told Benjamin. "When I come back, make sure you have your game face on."

"Got it." Benjamin puffed out his chest and balled up his fists. "This is war."

When I reached the lobby, Girlie was standing near the window talking on her cell phone. I stood a few feet away, waiting for her to finish her call. Girlie smiled at me and held up her index finger, instructing me to wait. I didn't have time for her games. I waited two more seconds, then headed back to my office.

Halfway down the hallway, Girlie caught up with me.

"I'm sooooo sorry," she gushed, stuffing her phone into her purse. "That was an important call I had to take."

She extended her hand and shook mine way too hard. I never understood what women who shook hands with the force of a man hoped to prove.

Girlie smiled big when I introduced her to Benjamin. "Is it okay if I call you Ben?"

"Sure." Benjamin smiled back. His game face nowhere to be seen.

Girlie took one of the chairs in front of my desk and maneuvered it until she was partially facing Benjamin.

"The Center does great work. You help so many people in the community." She was fixing her charms on Benjamin and he was eating it up. "What happened to your face?"

"Don't you know?" I asked. If Big Buy was responsible for Benjamin's injuries, I wouldn't be surprised to learn that Girlie was somehow in the mix.

"Why would I know?"

I couldn't gauge whether her puzzled look was sincere or not.

"I fell off my motorcycle," Benjamin said uneasily.

"Sorry to hear that. You should be more careful next time. So where should we start?"

"You tell us," I said. "You requested this meeting."

"True."

She pulled two sheets of paper from her briefcase. "Big Buy would like to avoid the unnecessary expenditure of legal fees and has authorized me to make a settlement offer."

Liar, liar, pants on fire. Her presence in my office had nothing to do with saving legal fees. Big Buy was running scared and it probably had something to do with those missing documents.

"If I had known that you wanted to discuss settlement, I would've had my clients here."

"No need for that. This isn't really a true settlement discussion since what we're offering isn't negotiable. I have authority to give both women three months' salary, one-thousand dollars in outplacement assistance, and company-paid medical coverage for three months."

"Three months' salary?" A crude laugh masked my anger. "You're joking, right?"

Girlie straightened in her seat. "Big Buy is making this offer in good faith."

Bull. "And why would my clients need outplacement assistance and medical coverage? They have jobs."

"Our offer would require them to resign."

Benjamin's face flushed with agitation. He looked so perturbed I thought his yarmulke might shoot off the top of his head. "Resign for what? Complaining about being discriminated against?"

"Obviously, after litigation, it can be very difficult to restore the trust in the employer-employee relationship," Girlie explained. "This is a great offer. We'd even be willing to convert the outplacement assistance to cash so they can use the money for tuition should they decide to go back to school. As you know, neither plaintiff has a college degree. That's one of the reasons they haven't been promoted."

"More than a few of your highly paid male managers don't have degrees either," I pointed out.

"And who's going to pay their household bills while they're going to school without a job?" Benjamin added. "A grand wouldn't even cover books."

Girlie leaned back and crossed her legs. "They could go to school at night. Many community colleges in the area have night programs. They shouldn't have trouble finding another job. Both of them have excellent retail experience."

"They certainly do," Benjamin snapped. "Which is why Big Buy should promote them using the same criteria it uses to promote men."

Girlie formed a teepee with her fingers. "I'm not sure how much actual litigation you do, but—"

"I do enough." Benjamin was now scowling at her.

"Pre-litigation settlement discussions aren't generally used to argue the merits of the case," Girlie said in a tone more appropriate for a first-grader. "This is merely an attempt to reach a speedy compromise."

"If Big Buy wants to settle this case, three months' salary isn't even in the ballpark," I said. "And since you said your offer isn't negotiable, I guess this meeting is over."

"Shouldn't you present my offer to your clients before you reject it?"

"I intend to do that. But I'm certain they won't take it."

"So exactly what *are* they looking for?"

I never opened with my bottom line.

"They want three years' salary. They want to be enrolled in the company's Management Training Program, and if they successfully complete it, they want a guarantee that they'll receive the next promotion to department manager at any store within a 20-mile radius of their homes. They also want Big Buy to implement diversity training for all employees and to commit—in writing—not to discriminate against women in the future."

Girlie chuckled. "Your demands aren't at all realistic. And Big Buy decides what programs it implements, not the employees who sue them."

"Fine. We'll put twelve in a box and let them decide what my clients deserve. Based on what I know about the company, I wouldn't be surprised if a jury came back with a seven-figure award."

"Your clients still have jobs," Girlie said. "No jury's going to give two store clerks seven figures."

"They're not store clerks," I said, knowing she was just trying to rile me. "And just so you know, those documents Judi got her hands on could really be problematic for your client."

Benjamin blinked nervously like he had something in his eyes.

Girlie's smile faltered at the mention of the documents and I enjoyed seeing the brief crack in her normally arrogant demeanor.

"So you have the documents?" she asked casually.

I wish. "You'll find out when I respond to your discovery requests."

Girlie slid two sheets of paper to my side of the desk. "Here's a copy of the offers in writing. Tell your clients they have seven days to consider them. After that, they're off the table."

Girlie stood up.

As I escorted her out to the lobby, I fantasized about pushing her down the elevator shaft.

"Is Lamarr appealing the jury's verdict?"

Her matter-of-fact tone didn't fool me. Tonisha was probably itching to get her hands on that money. I bet she was driving Girlie crazy just like Lamarr was testing my last nerve.

"Definitely."

An elevator car dinged and Girlie stepped inside.

"Don't forget my deadline. Big Buy's offer is only open for one week."

I gave her a wide fake smile as the elevator doors began to close. "If you don't hear from me, then you'll know our answer."

CHAPTER 21

Detectives Mankowski and Thomas parked at the bottom of a shallow hill at Forest Lawn Cemetery in Glendale and watched as the small cluster of people gathered around Judi Irving's gravesite meandered back to their cars.

They decided not to attend Judi's funeral services, but figured they could easily observe their two prime suspects at the burial site without being obtrusive. Phillip and Robby stood on opposite sides of the crowd of mourners as Judi's casket was lowered into the ground. Both men wore vacant expressions, no tears or other apparent signs of grief on their faces. Within minutes, most of the crowd had traipsed back to their cars and driven off.

Detective Thomas opened a folder and pulled out copies of two drivers' license photographs. He scrutinized the pictures, then aimed his binoculars at two women who lingered near the open grave.

"I think I just spotted the two women who were part of Judi Irving's lawsuit," he said. "Olivia Jackson and Ida Lopez."

The detectives waited until they began walking down the hill before exiting their sedan. They approached the women right before they reached a mid-size SUV.

"Excuse us for interrupting you at a time like this," Thomas began. "We're with the LAPD."

He held out his badge. "I'm Detective Thomas and this is my partner, Detective Mankowski. We'd like to speak with you for a moment."

Ida reached for the door handle of the SUV. Mankowski could tell from her red eyes that she'd had a good cry.

"About what?" Olivia asked.

"We're looking into Judi Irving's death," Mankowski said. "We understand that you worked with her."

"Yes, we did." Olivia extended her hand. "I'm Olivia Jackson and this is Ida Lopez."

Mankowski noticed that the Hispanic woman had stepped behind the black woman as if she was using her as a shield. "We'd like to ask a few questions about your lawsuit."

"Oh, mi Dios!" Ida pressed both hands to her cheeks. "I knew it. I told you our lawsuit had something to do with Judi's death."

"You think her death was connected to your lawsuit?" Thomas asked.

"No, we don't," Olivia said, quickly dismissing her co-worker's fears. "We don't have any evidence of that."

Mankowski pinned his gaze on Ida, wanting to hear her speak for herself.

Ida kept her eyes on the ground. "I just have this feeling."

Mankowski leaned against the rear of the SUV.

"What can you tell us about the relationship between Judi and Phillip Peterman?" Mankowski asked.

"We don't know a thing," Ida replied quickly.

Mankowski decided to direct his questions to the more forthcoming black woman. "Did Judi ever tell you they fought?"

"No," Olivia said. "Judi was crazy about him."

"So they had a good relationship?"

Olivia inhaled. "To the outside world it probably looked like they did, but no one knows what goes on behind closed doors."

Thomas folded his arms. "If you know something," he said gently, "we'd really like you to share it with us."

"I don't know anything specific. I just didn't like the man."

"Why not?"

"Because he didn't work except for a few acting jobs that barely paid minimum wage. I'm a modern woman, but he could've at least helped around the house. Judi worked all day and came home and cooked for him. She pampered him like he was a king."

"Do you think he was involved in her death?"

"That's crossed my mind."

Ida huffed in disagreement. "I never saw anything but a happy relationship."

"Don't mind her," Olivia snorted. "She wears rose-colored contact lenses."

"What about Judi's husband?" Thomas asked.

Olivia crossed her arms. "I don't put nothing past nobody. Robby was as big a jerk as Phillip. He dumped her for some youngster, but he couldn't handle it when Judi did the same thing."

"We'd like you to come down to the station for a more formal interview," Thomas said, removing two business cards from his pocket and extending them to the women.

Ida ignored the card. "I don't know anything." She opened the passenger door and climbed inside.

Olivia smiled as she took both cards. "She's really upset about Judi's death. I'll bring her down with me."

"What can you tell us about your lawsuit?"

"Big Buy doesn't give women the same opportunities it gives men, so we're suing them for sex discrimination," Olivia explained. "A few days before she died, somebody sent Judi a bunch of documents with a note that said they would help our case. I was hoping Phillip would give them to us, but he claims he doesn't know anything about them."

"What kind of documents?" Mankowski asked.

"Judi died before she could show them to us. But they were apparently financial records which were supposedly harmful to the company."

"Who sent them?" Mankowski asked.

"No one knows. The box just arrived in the mail. Judi looked up the return address, but it didn't exist."

The more Mankowski heard, the faster his mind began to churn with possibilities.

"And Phillip claims he doesn't have them?"

Olivia nodded.

After another fifteen minutes of questioning, Mankowski asked Olivia for the name of their attorney and allowed them to leave.

As they walked the short distance to their sedan, Thomas had a pensive look on his face. "Maybe we're off track here," he said. "Maybe Judi's dead because of those documents."

"I'm not ready to let Phillip Peterman or Robby Irving off the hook yet," Mankowski said. "Three-hundred-thousand dollars in insurance proceeds is a lot of reason to want someone dead. Phillip's agent still hasn't returned our calls and Robby hasn't shown up to provide his DNA."

"Maybe those documents were the reason the house was ripped up," Thomas pressed. "Somebody was looking for them."

"Or," Mankowski said, "maybe Phillip set it up to look like somebody else took the documents when he really has them. Just like he timed it so his alibi witness would be out of the country for six weeks."

"So it looks like we have three persons of interest," Thomas said, as they opened the car doors. "Phillip Peterman, who wanted Judi's insurance money. Robby Irving, who thought he was going to get that money, and somebody else who wanted those documents. Somebody connected to Big Buy."

"Time will tell who we can cross off the list," Mankowski said, clipping his seatbelt in place. "And I doubt it'll be Actor Boy."

CHAPTER 22

Olivia and Ida listened attentively as I relayed Big Buy's settlement offer.

I could feel their disappointment casting a dark cloud over my office. "So what would you like to do?"

"Why should we have to quit our jobs?" Olivia complained. "We didn't do anything wrong."

"I've settled lots of cases like this," I explained. "Most of the time, the company does expect the employee to resign. But usually there's a lot more than three months' salary on the table."

I also explained that if a jury believed that Big Buy intentionally refused to promote them because of their sex, they could win a lot more at trial. But unfortunately, I could not guarantee a win.

Ida toyed with the strap of her purse. She had barely opened her mouth since walking into my office.

Benjamin agreed not to come to the meeting since we didn't want to lie to them about his injuries. News of the break-in would definitely freak them out, particularly Ida.

"So even if we go to trial and win, we would have to quit our jobs?" Ida asked.

"No," I clarified. "But if you're still working there at the time the case goes to trial, that would significantly reduce the economic damages the jury might award."

I stared down at the notepad in front of me and took a few seconds to collect my thoughts. Trying to explain the mechanics of litigation to a non-lawyer wasn't easy. People assumed you simply filed your lawsuit, marched into court a few weeks later, told your story to twelve sympathetic jurors, and walked out with a big fat check.

In reality, even if we won at trial, Big Buy could keep the case tied up in appeals for years. Just like I had the option of doing with Lamarr's case. And remaining in the workplace while the lawsuit was pending could take its toll emotionally. Many plaintiffs went out on stress leave, or quit.

"I have to be honest with you," I said. "We're not going to win this case overnight. The longer the case goes on, the harder it could be for you at work."

Olivia cocked her head. "But you said they can't retaliate against us for suing them?"

Just because they can't, doesn't mean that they won't.

"That's true. And the minute you tell me you think they're doing something retaliatory, I'll contact Big Buy's counsel and put a stop to it. But continuing to show up for work every day could be very stressful."

"It's already stressful. I can't even sleep at night." Ida spoke just above a whisper. She was twisting the strap of her purse around her index finger. "I want to take the settlement. At least, I can pay off a few bills. My sister's company is hiring. I won't make as much, but the benefits are good."

I was disappointed to hear this, but I didn't try to change her mind. I waited for a response from Olivia.

"I ain't quitting my job for that piddling offer. If we go away, they're going to keep right on doing this stuff to other women. Right now, I feel like Daniel in the lion's den. I want to expose those heathens."

"I don't have the time or the energy to fight for anybody else," Ida said. "I have to think about my daughters."

Olivia exhaled loudly. "What if we turn down their offer now, but decide to accept it later on?"

"The offer is only good for a week," I said. "But as part of the litigation, we'll have an opportunity to participate in court-ordered mediation. I can't guarantee, however, that the offer will still be on the table."

Olivia placed a hand on Ida's forearm. "I know you need the money," she said, "but this is bigger than us. Let's keep fighting. We can probably settle for more later on."

"There are no guarantees," I cautioned. "If there's evidence uncovered later that hurts our case, then—"

"Evidence like what?" Olivia asked.

I was trying my best to walk the balance between encouraging them to stay in the fight and telling them the real deal. I'd commenced litigation with solid cases before and had them knocked out on a legal technicality.

"There's a lot of legal maneuvering that the attorney for Big Buy is going to do. For example, some of our most helpful evidence of discrimination could be barred by the statute of limitations because it happened a long time ago. They'll argue that you should have sued when it first happened."

"But that's not right," Olivia said.

"I agree. There's a legal theory called continuing violation that should make the evidence admissible. But again, there are no guarantees."

"I can do all things through Christ who strengthens me," Olivia proclaimed. "We need to do this for Judi and every other woman at Big Buy."

Ida sighed. "If you want to be a crusader for women's rights, go ahead. I have to think about my girls."

"You shouldn't feel guilty about your decision," I said to Ida. "I'll let Big Buy's counsel know that you'd like to accept the offer."

"Can you work it out so I'll have time to apply for some other jobs before I have to quit?"

"How much time do you think you'll need?"

She hunched her shoulders. "I'll get an application from my sister right away. A month maybe?"

"That's reasonable, but let me get back to you for sure."

Olivia stared out of the window.

"What about you, Olivia? Do you want to continue with the lawsuit?"

"Absolutely." Her defiant eyes met mine. "I'm not afraid of those
devils. I'm ready to fight."

CHAPTER 23

Phillip Peterman sat cornered in the tiny interrogation room, barricaded behind a metal table.

The detectives had invited him back to the station for another round of questioning. They hadn't uncovered any additional information that might lead to his arrest. Mankowski simply wanted to see him sweat.

He was glad Phillip was arrogant enough to think he didn't need a lawyer. Lawyers only got in the way.

Thomas stood near the door, resting one shoulder against the wall. Mankowski sat directly across from Phillip on the other side of the table.

"Now tell us one more time," Mankowski said, resting his hands on the table. "What time did you leave the house that night?"

Phillip gritted his teeth. "Didn't we already cover this?"

"Yep, and now we're covering it again."

"Just before ten."

"How many minutes before?"

"I don't know. Five or ten."

"Why didn't you tell us you and Judi argued that night?"

Phillip's face turned icy white. "How did you...?"

"So you admit it?"

"Yeah, but it wasn't a big deal. She was upset because I had to go meet my agent."

"I understand it was a pretty heated argument."

"Not really."

"Your neighbor was putting out the garbage along the side of her house when she heard you guys going at each other."

"She must've heard the TV."

"Nope," Mankowski said. "She was pretty sure she heard you say something about killing Judi if she ever touched your face again."

Phillip's hands started to shake so he placed them in his lap, out of sight. "That's a lie."

"Know what I think?" Mankowski enjoyed the look of terror on Phillip's face. "I think you guys got into a vicious fight and you went ballistic when she scratched that precious mug of yours."

Phillip gripped the arms of his chair, probably to keep them still. "That's not what happened."

"I don't believe you."

"And I don't care if you don't believe me."

"What did you do with the documents?"

Beads of sweat began to form at Phillip's hairline. "What documents?"

"Those Big Buy documents that you neglected to tell us about."

"I don't know anything about any documents."

"You're lying," Mankowski said, laying on the pressure. "And you're about to go down. Just as soon as we get the results of your DNA test back."

Phillip's eyes bulged. "I didn't give you my DNA."

"We got it from that Pepsi can you drank from the last time you were here. Perfectly legal."

Mankowski had been waiting all day to deliver this bombshell.

Phillip wiped his hand down his face.

"And you know what? I'd bet good money that the blood and skin we found underneath Judi's fingernails were yours."

They expected Phillip to go into meltdown mode. Instead, he displayed a calm, cocky smile.

"If, per chance, my DNA did happen to be underneath Judi's fingernails, it's not because she scratched my face. There could be another reason."

Mankowski tilted his head to the right. "Really? Enlighten us."

Phillip mockingly tilted his head to match the angle of Mankowski's.

"We both preferred it a little rough during sex. She liked to dig her nails into my back. Deep enough to draw blood sometimes. She got off on it. I did too. We had sex right before I left that night."

"There was no semen in her body."

"We always used condoms."

"Take off your shirt and show us the scars then," Mankowski challenged.

"Why should I?"

"Because innocent people don't make up bullshit stories like the ones you keep coming up with. So if what you just said is true, show us the scars."

Phillip stood up. He took his time unbuttoning his shirt, placed it neatly on the table, then lifted his white T-shirt over his head. He slowly turned around. His broad back was grazed with long scratches. Some looked fairly recent. Others had already healed.

He turned back around and smiled down at Mankowski. "Satisfied?"

"Nope," Mankowski said.

"Well, you're going to have to be." Phillip squirmed back into his T-shirt. He slipped into his shirt, but didn't bother to button it. "I'm out of here."

"The crime lab can tell us whether the DNA underneath Judi's nails is from the skin on your back or your face," Mankowski said.

Phillip looked nervously from Mankowski to Thomas, as if seeking confirmation of what he'd just heard.

"He's absolutely right," Thomas said.

"Like I said, these scratches came from a tree branch that no longer exists." Phillip winked. "That's my story and I'm sticking to it."

As he made a move toward the door, Mankowski reached out to stop him, but Thomas interceded and let him leave.

"When we get this guy, it needs to be by the book," Thomas cautioned. "And can the lab really tell what part of the body the skin came from?"

Mankowski grinned. "Hell if I know."

Detective Hopper stuck his head into the room. Their annoying co-worker spent way too much time nosing around in other people's cases. He seemed to be particularly interested in Judi Irving's murder.

"What do you want?" Mankowski snapped.

"I just saw Phillip Peterman leave," he said with a laugh. "Couldn't get a confession, huh? You should've had me in here. I could've cracked him."

"Yeah, right," Mankowski said. "Why don't you run along back to your desk and finish a crossword puzzle or something."

CHAPTER 24

Right after my meeting with Ida and Olivia, I called Girlie Cortez to convey my clients' responses to Big Buy's settlement offer. The obnoxious, game-playing human being that she is, Girlie waited three days before calling me back.

"I got your message," Girlie said, sweetly, as if she was chatting with a dear friend. "So, are your clients going to take that great offer I made."

I so wished I could tell her that both Ida and Olivia wanted Big Buy to take its offer and shove it.

"Ida would like to take your offer," I said. "Olivia has decided to proceed with the lawsuit."

Only silence came from her end of the phone.

"Are you there?"

"Yes, I'm here." Girlie's voice had lost its cheerfulness.

"So when can you get me a draft of a settlement agreement for Ida?"

"Never."

"Excuse me?"

"Perhaps I forgot to mention it, but that offer was an all-or-nothing deal," Girlie said. "Either both of them agree to settle or my client doesn't pay either one of them."

My hand tightened around the phone. "You're kidding."

"Actually, I'm not."

"And what's your rationale for this approach? Divide and conquer?"

"I don't typically divulge my litigation strategy to my opposing counsel. Just go back and ask Ms. Jackson to rethink her decision."

"There's no need to do that. Olivia's not going to change her mind."

Girlie laughed crudely. "When I was in your office, you claimed both of them would turn down the offer. Maybe you're wrong this time too."

"Either Big Buy wants to settle with Ida or it doesn't."

"It doesn't," Girlie replied. "My client follows my advice. And my advice is no deal unless they both settle."

"I guess I understand why you're working so hard to get them out of the workplace," I said. "Maybe some of their co-workers might decide to join their lawsuit. I've been seriously considering amending the complaint and filing it as a class action."

This was pure bluff. I didn't have the financial resources, the manpower or the expertise to file the case as a class action.

Girlie laughed. "You must not be up on your legal research. After the Supreme Court's decision in the *Wal-Mart* case, it'll be difficult for anybody to convince a court to certify a class action in a case like this."

"I disagree. The *Wal-Mart* case involved over a million current and former employees all over the country. Mine would be a much smaller group of plaintiffs, with similar claims based on a corporate culture that blatantly discriminates against women. But if I have to, I'll file the lawsuits store by store."

Girlie laughed again. "Don't make threats you can't back up."

"Oh, I can back them up. And I will." I slammed down the phone.

It was rare for an opposing counsel to get me so rattled. But Girlie was in a class by herself. I grabbed a few bucks from my purse and ran downstairs for some fresh air and a Frappuccino. I had almost reached the elevators when the receptionist waved me over.

"I was just about to call your office," she whispered. "Those two guys over there are here to see you. They're detectives."

She pointed at two cops in sports jackets with their backs to us. *Detectives?* My mind immediately raced to Lamarr. I prayed he hadn't done anything crazy.

"I'm Vernetta Henderson," I said, rushing up to them. "What can I do for you?"

The big white guy extended his hand. "I'm Detective Mankowski and this is my partner, Detective Thomas. We're investigating the death of Judi Irving. We understand that she was a client of yours."

Relieved that Lamarr wasn't in trouble, I escorted them to my office.

Once we were seated, their first question took me completely by surprise.

"We understand there are some missing documents related to Big Buy," Mankowski said. "What can you tell us about them?"

"Unfortunately, you're delving into an area that could possibly breach the attorney-client privilege."

"Does that mean you have the documents, but you won't talk to us about them?"

I'd made Girlie think that I had the documents, but I didn't want to lie to the police. "How'd you find out about them?"

Mankowski skipped right past my question just as I did his. "So do you have the documents?"

"No," I finally admitted. "As far as I know, the only person who ever laid eyes on them was Judi. Her boyfriend claims he knows nothing about them. But I do think they could be connected to Judi's death."

I told him about the break-in at the Center for Justice and the attack on Benjamin.

"We'll need Benjamin's contact information," Thomas said, a grave look on his face.

"Who's the attorney representing Big Buy?"

A groan slipped out before I could catch it. "Her name is Girlie Cortez."

"Didn't you just go up against her in that rape case against the Legends wide receiver?" Thomas asked.

"Unfortunately, yes."

"If you ask me, the jury got it wrong."

"Thanks."

"Do I sense a little professional rivalry between the two of you?" Mankowski asked.

"That's a nice way to put it."

"Is it possible she might have the documents?"

"If she does, neither you nor I will ever see them."

"What does that mean?"

"It means Girlie Cortez will do whatever it takes to defend her client. And if those documents have any information harmful to Big Buy, they'll never see the light of day."

"Are you insinuating that she might do something illegal to make sure that happens?"

"I'm not insinuating anything. I'm saying it."

"That's a helluva accusation to make about another lawyer," Mankowski said.

"Don't take my word for it. Ask anybody who's litigated against her. She plays by a different set of rules. She makes them up as she goes. And she never gets caught."

Mankowski nodded slowly.

"You don't seem to be too concerned that the documents are missing," Thomas said.

"I don't take cases based on mysterious documents I've never seen. I can prove Big Buy discriminates against women with or without those documents."

"I'm assuming it's not unusual for a company like Big Buy to be sued for discrimination," Detective Thomas said.

"True."

"So if there are documents out there that prove that Big Buy discriminated against your clients, I guess it wouldn't be a big deal for the company."

"I wouldn't go that far," I said. "Clear evidence of discrimination could be a very big deal. If Judi had some explosive documents that showed a pattern and practice of discrimination against women, then Big Buy would have a whole lot of reason for concern. That kind of evidence could significantly increase the company's potential liability."

I turned around and picked up a folder from my credenza.

"The verdicts in sex discrimination cases can be substantial, particularly if the case is filed as a class action. Novartis, a pharmaceutical company, got hit with a two-hundred-and-fifty-million dollar verdict. Morgan Stanley settled a sex discrimination case for fifty-four million and a year later, another one for forty-six million." I handed Detective Thomas a *Times* magazine article about the case. "Mitsubishi paid thirty-four million. Rent-A-Center, forty-seven million. A verdict like this could force Big Buy into bankruptcy."

"I thought women had equal rights," Mankowski joked. "What's the lawyer's cut of a settlement like that?"

"Enough to retire," I said with a smile. "But we don't do it for the money. We want justice."

"Thanks for your time," Mankowski said, standing up. "I think we're going to be taking a much closer look at Big Buy."

CHAPTER 25

I couldn't remember the last time Special had requested an emergency powwow at our favorite hangout, the TGI Friday's in the Ladera Center. When she ignored my text asking what was up, I sensed that her crisis had something to do with Clayton.

I entered the restaurant and spotted Special sitting at our usual booth near the back. As I got closer, I eyed the glass sitting on the table in front of her. In light of her recent conversion to Islam, it wasn't a good sign if the glass held what I thought it did.

"You okay?" I asked, settling in across from her. "Your call really had me worried."

Her fingers fluttered in the air. "Relax. It ain't that big a deal."

"That's certainly not how you sounded on the phone. And I hope that's a regular iced tea, not an alcohol-filled Long Island."

"Girl, I needed this drink because Clayton is trippin' hard."

"What's going on?"

"You'll never believe how serious he is about this Community of Islam stuff. The Negro actually wants us to stop fornicating."

I tried not to smile, but I couldn't help it.

"You better not laugh." Special aimed a skinny finger at me from across the table. "When he first told me he didn't want to have sex again until we got married, I figured he wouldn't be able to hold out. But he was dead serious. I can't even remember the last time we slept together. He just kisses me on the cheek and goes home. And frankly, I'm getting tired of going to all them damn meetings at the mosque."

I used the menu to shield my face.

Special snatched it away. "I'm not playing. Don't you dare laugh. And you better not say *I told you so*."

"I haven't said a word."

"You don't have to. I see it on your face." She started crunching on the ice from her drink.

"I think it's great that you guys have decided not to have sex. It'll give you an opportunity to really get to know each other. It's not that big a deal."

"Yes, it is. I'm so horny I'm ready to climb the walls. There's no way I can go a year without sex."

"Stop overreacting."

"I should've known you'd side with Clayton."

"I'm not siding with anybody. I just don't think premarital celibacy is a bad idea."

"Easy for you to say, Ms. Married Woman." She rolled her eyes, then checked her watch.

"You have someplace to go?"

"Yeah, I'm meeting a friend at La Louisanne at seven."

La Louisanne was a popular neighborhood nightspot a few miles away. Definitely not an appropriate hangout for a Muslim, man or woman.

"A male or female friend?"

"Don't worry. It ain't like that. I'm meeting with a guy to find out what I have to do to get my investigator's license. And don't tell Jefferson 'cuz he might mention it to Clayton."

"Are you sure being with Clayton is worth everything you're giving up?"

Special stirred her drink with a red swivel stick and didn't look up at me. "All I know is, I love him and I can't imagine not having him in my life."

"But to give up your faith," I said. "That's asking a lot."

She exhaled. "I know. To be honest, I'm still struggling with it. I pray about it every night. To me, we only have one God. Doesn't matter whether we call him God or Allah."

I certainly disagreed with that, but Special seemed too fragile for me to push the issue right now.

"Well, I'm here if you need me. I'm just glad you're still pursuing your investigations license if that's really what you want to do."

"Just keeping my options open."

I knew my friend. She always had a backup plan in her purse. It made me feel better to know that she wasn't so blinded with love that she was giving up on her own dreams.

"Is Lamarr still driving you crazy?" Special asked.

"Yep."

"He needs to forget about that case and move on."

"I wish he would."

"Hey," Special said, springing forward. "You oughta let me investigate Tonisha. I bet I can get that heffa to confess the truth."

"That won't be happening."

"Why?"

"Because it's a crazy idea."

She flopped back against the booth. "I wish that boy was into cougars. I bet I could make his rich ass forget about that case."

"You're not old enough to be a cougar, so get your mind out of the gutter and back on your man."

"Yeah, whatever," she said. "I just wish my man wasn't such a goody two-shoes."

CHAPTER 26

O livia recited a short prayer as she trudged into the Big Buy locker room. She was leaving everything in God's hands. If she took one step, she knew He would take the next.

Two other employees walked by without speaking. After news of her lawsuit hit the workplace, some of her co-workers acted as if she was suing them. No one wanted to be seen talking to her about anything other than work, including Ida.

Since the meeting at Vernetta's office, she and Ida were no longer speaking. For some crazy reason, Ida blamed Olivia for not being able to settle her case. She decided to drop out of the lawsuit with nothing. Big Buy was only trying to pit them against each other. Too bad Ida couldn't see that.

Olivia slipped into her Big Buy blazer and closed her locker.

"Richard just called a meeting," another worker announced. "He wants everyone in the break room."

A group of about fifty employees, mostly women were already waiting when Olivia entered. Every pair of eyes in the place seemed to be avoiding hers. The woman standing next to Olivia smiled nervously then moved to the other side of the room as if Olivia had some disease. She was not going to let these fools get to her. People turned their backs on Jesus too.

The store manager, Richard Williams, walked in, trailed closely by a smiling Ida Lopez. Olivia noticed that Ida wasn't wearing her blazer. The two of them marched to the front of the room.

"I just wanted to announce Ida Lopez's promotion," Richard said, looking out at the group. "She's going to be taking over as assistant manager of Risk Management. We've had a dramatic increase in customer injuries, some of them caused by sales associates failing to ensure that their areas are safe. So Ida will be patrolling your departments looking for potential hazards."

Judas, Olivia thought. She tried to stare Ida down, but Ida refused to look her way. She just stood there cheesing as if their lawsuit had nothing to do with her promotion. Olivia couldn't believe Ida was allowing herself to be used like this.

Richard rattled on about how Ida was such a dedicated employee, then dismissed the meeting.

As everyone filtered out to the floor, Olivia overheard the conversation of two Latina employees.

"They raised her salary five dollars an hour *and* gave her a two-thousand-dollar bonus," one of the women said.

"Ida practically won the lottery," said the other one.

Olivia snorted. *Lottery my behind.* Ida sold out for chump change.

She made it to Housewares just in time to find Ida trolling the aisles like a drill sergeant on inspection. After every few steps, she stopped to jot something down on a clipboard.

Olivia marched up to her, hands planted on her ample hips. "I guess you're finally sleeping at night, huh?"

"I'm sorry, but I had to do what's best for my family," she said apologetically.

"You only got that promotion because you dropped out of the lawsuit. They're sending a message to other employees that they'll get a measly raise if they *don't* sue the company. But it's just a farce to keep us from complaining about all the dirt they're doing."

"You have no idea how hard it is being a single parent. Your husband's a teacher. I don't have any support, financial or otherwise. If you were a mother, you'd understand."

Olivia wasn't letting her off the hook. "You're certainly setting the right example for your daughters. When you tell them about your promotion, don't forget to mention that you got it because you were too afraid to stand up for yourself."

Ida squared her shoulders. "Besa mi culo."

Olivia had no idea what Ida had just said, but she knew it wasn't nice. "You want to say something to me, you need to say it in English."

"Kiss my ass," Ida repeated.

Olivia pointed a finger in Ida's face. "You better be glad I'm a Christian, or I would—"

"You certainly not acting like a Christian right now."

"I'm a Christian all right. That's why I'm going to pray that the Lord shows you the error of your ways. I heard you sold out for a measly five-dollar-an-hour raise."

Ida's body visibly bristled. "Actually, I also got—" She stopped. "It's none of your business what I got. You're just jealous. Talk to me this time next year when you're still wrapped up in that stupid lawsuit. You probably won't even get a dime."

"I'm not doing this for the money," Olivia insisted. "The way this company treats women is wrong. Do you really think you're ever going to go any higher than assistant manager of Risk Management?"

"Time will tell," Ida said, puffing out her chest. "This might not be the best company in the world, but it's certainly not the worst. I watched my mother come home every day with her back aching after slaving in a sewing factory all day. I have it good compared to what she went through. And anyway, things are changing. They're transferring a female store manager here next week."

Olivia threw up both hands. "And why do you think they're doing that? Because of our lawsuit."

"I don't care why they're doing it. I'm just glad that they are. Now get out of my way."

While neither of them had raised their voices, they had drawn the attention of a handful of employees and customers. It was obvious from their facial expressions and body language that they weren't having a friendly chat.

Olivia stayed put, forcing Ida to step around her.

"By the way," Ida called back, "you need to take care of this."

Olivia turned around and saw Ida pointing down at a wire protruding from a shelf.

"I'm going over to inspect Women's Clothing. If this isn't fixed by the time I get back, I'm writing you up."

CHAPTER 27

Girlie leered across the table at the plump schoolteacher she'd been deposing for the last hour. She enjoyed grilling her opponents and couldn't wait to get Olivia Jackson in the hot seat.

"Mrs. Mitchell, in your complaint against the Beverly Hills School District, you alleged that after you were terminated, you were too emotionally distraught to have sex with your husband, is that correct?"

A burst of red eased up Melinda Mitchell's flabby neck. Her eyes darted sideways in a wordless appeal for her slouch of an attorney to object. Bob Reed had obviously neglected to explain to his client that filing a loss of consortium claim rendered her sex life an open book.

Reed gave Melinda a remorseful shrug that told her to answer the question.

She daintily pressed her right palm flat against her chest, then nodded.

"I'm sorry," Girlie said, leaning forward a bit. "But the court reporter needs an audible response."

"Oh…um…yes," she squeaked.

To heighten the woman's embarrassment, Girlie had assembled an all-male audience. Sitting across from Melinda Mitchell were her principal, the school district's human resources manager and two associates from her law firm. With the addition of the male court reporter and videographer, plus the two attorneys, Melinda had an audience of eight.

"Mrs. Mitchell, prior to your termination, how many times a week did you have sex with your husband?"

Melinda's head whipped in the direction of her attorney again. "Aren't you going to object? This is personal."

"There's nothing for him to object to," Girlie replied.

Reed leaned over and whispered into his client's ear.

Melinda's nostrils flared as she glared across the table at Girlie. "Four times a week," she said testily.

Perfect. Melinda was lying to make her claim look more severe. No married couple had sex four times a week after twenty-five years of marriage. And Girlie couldn't imagine *any* man wanting to climb on top of Melinda Mitchell.

"And what kind of sex was it?"

"Excuse me?" Melinda's entire face blushed beet burgundy. Again, she appealed to her attorney. "Do I have to talk about this?"

Girlie smiled. "I'm afraid you do."

"Well, I don't know what you mean." She folded her arms and rested them on her cushy bosom.

"What I'm asking for," Girlie explained in a soft, matter-of-fact voice, "is a description of the type of sex you claim you were having four times a week. Was it missionary style? Or were you on top? Did you give him blow jobs or did he—"

"Objection!" This time Girlie had awakened something in Reed. He pushed his chair back from the table. "You're out of line, counselor!"

Melinda clutched her throat and appeared to be choking. The human resources manager had covered his mouth with both hands. The two associates sitting to Girlie's right struggled to keep straight faces, while the principal tried to avoid the drama by staring out of the window.

"You're just trying to upset her," Reed charged. "This is completely unprofessional."

"Let's go off the record." Girlie waited as the videographer announced the time of their break.

"Your client said she didn't understand my question, so I was just trying to help her out by offering up a few examples. And just so you know, I'll be asking her the exact same questions in front of the jury. So consider this a dress rehearsal."

That was a lie. Browbeating a witness like this in front of a jury would only produce sympathy for her. The primary purpose of this line of questioning was intimidation.

"I'm not…I…I can't…I need to take a break."

Just after Reed escorted her out, Girlie's assistant entered the conference room and called her outside for a private conversation.

"There're two detectives in the lobby who want to speak with you," she whispered.

Before Girlie could respond, Reed returned to say his client was too distraught to proceed with her deposition. Girlie started to object, but she was really curious about why two cops wanted to see her.

Girlie walked her clients to the elevator, then took the stairs to her law firm's reception area.

When Mankowski saw Girlie sashaying his way, his first thought was that she looked even sexier than she had on TV.

She stopped much closer than necessary and extended her hand. "I'm Girlie Cortez. How can I help you?"

Mankowski found himself intrigued by her in-your-face demeanor.

"We're investigating the death of Judi Irving," he explained after introducing himself and his partner. "We'd like to talk to you about the Big Buy lawsuit."

"I'm willing to help you any way I can, detectives." A hint of flirtatiousness backed up her words. "As long as it doesn't involve any privileged information or damage my client's interests."

Mankowski never dated lawyers. The female prosecutors and judges he knew were way too rough around the edges. But Girlie had a softness about her that made it hard for him to keep his mind on business.

They followed Girlie to her office. Mankowski had never seen a pink couch before. Girlie directed the detectives to twin chairs on one side of a small coffee table, while she took the couch. She crossed her legs and extended her arm along the back of the couch.

Mankowski had dated women like Girlie Cortez before, so he knew exactly how to play her. He began by ignoring her magnificent legs.

"We understand you represent Big Buy in a gender discrimination case filed by Judi Irving and two of her co-workers," he began. "What can you tell us about Ms. Irving?"

"Nothing. She wasn't my client and I never had an opportunity to take her deposition. You should be talking to her attorney, not me."

"We already did."

Girlie's lips formed a slight snit.

Mankowski smiled. The two women definitely didn't care for each other.

"It's our understanding that Ms. Irving had documents that contained damaging information about your client."

"As far as I know, that's just a rumor. You can't possibly think the lawsuit had anything to do with her death."

Mankowski shrugged. "Anything's possible. So you haven't seen the documents?"

"Nope. Does Vernetta have a copy?"

"If she does, she's not telling us."

"That's no surprise."

Mankowski wasn't about to reveal what he knew about the break-in at the Center for Justice. If Big Buy was involved, that meant their lawyer might be too. After interviewing Benjamin Cohen, he was convinced that the lawsuit and those documents did indeed have a connection to Judi's murder.

"We understand that the right discrimination case could result in a company being hit with a pretty significant jury verdict."

"True. But only if the company loses."

"Ms. Henderson thinks she has a pretty strong case."

"I disagree. But that's the nature of litigation. If attorneys viewed the facts the same way, our courthouses would be empty."

"You seem pretty confident about your case."

"There's no reason not to be. I'm good at what I do, detective." She paused. "Actually, I'm good at a lot of things."

Mankowski liked Girlie's sassy little mouth. And he could think of a thing or two he'd like to do with it.

After a few more questions, it was clear that Girlie wasn't giving up any useful information.

"We won't take up any more of your time," Mankowski said, rising.

Girlie led them back to the lobby.

"How long have you been in law enforcement, detective?" Girlie asked.

"Twenty-two years."

"Wow. I bet there's a thing or two you could teach me." She placed a hand on his forearm and squeezed ever so gently. "About criminal procedure, that is."

Mankowski did not crack a smile. He turned away and punched the elevator button.

"What was up with that?" Thomas asked, once they were alone in the elevator. "I've never seen you blow off a woman like that before."

"A little too flirty for my taste," Mankowski lied.

"Yeah, right," Thomas said.

Mankowski could barely keep his excitement in check. His partner definitely wouldn't approve of the carnal thoughts he was having about the ballsy little lady lawyer.

Actually, he had every intention of hooking up with Girlie Cortez. And sooner rather than later.

CHAPTER 28

"You owe me," Jefferson grumbled as he put on his tie. "We just better be back in time for the Vikings game."

"You've told me that three times. I got it. Just stop complaining."

Special had twisted my arm and I, in turn, twisted Jefferson's. We were on our way to a Sunday morning lecture at the mosque.

I had changed clothes three times and was thinking about changing again. This was my first visit to a mosque, so I wanted to make sure I was dressed appropriately.

Special told me not to stress over what to wear, just as long as it wasn't super short, extra tight or low cut. I examined myself in the mirror, confident that my two-piece knit suit was sufficiently respectful. Even though Special told me covering my head wasn't mandatory, I stuck a silk scarf in my purse just in case.

Jefferson and I arrived about twenty minutes before the start of the service. The closest Community of Islam mosque was only a few miles from our house. The modest storefront building was sandwiched between a bakery to the left and a 99¢ store on the right. The only available parking was on the street.

Jefferson opened the passenger door and helped me out. "Can you please get rid of that sourpuss face? We're doing this for Special."

His lips curled into an exaggerated pretend smile. "As long as I'm sitting in front of the TV with a beer in one hand and a remote control in the other by kickoff, everything will be fine."

As we walked the quarter block to the mosque, most of the people heading in the same direction didn't fit the stereotypes in my head. A few of the women were wearing loose-fitting, floor-length dresses and had their heads covered. But I saw many more women in business attire, including pantsuits. Most of the men were smartly dressed in suits with ties or bow ties.

When we reached the front of the mosque, I looked around for Special. She had promised to meet us out front.

"Let's just go on in," Jefferson said. "You know your friend is always on CP time."

I took a step toward the entrance, but a man standing near the doorway gently stopped me. "This way, sister."

He extended his arm toward another door a few feet away. He turned back to Jefferson and directed him through the door that I had just attempted to use. "You can enter here, brother."

Special hadn't mentioned that there was a separate entrance for men and women. I had already made my first *faux pas* and I was barely inside. A beautiful young woman greeted me in the lobby. Her skin was the color and texture of chocolate and her smile was so warm I could feel it. She was covered in white from head to toe.

"As-Salaam Alaikum, sister," she said.

I wasn't sure what I was supposed to say in response, so I just smiled and nodded.

"Are you familiar with our check-in protocol?"

I nodded again. At least Special had explained that.

The woman in white led me to a room about the size of a large walk-in closet. We stepped behind a partition and she waved a long metal detector over my body. She asked for my purse and briefly searched it.

"This is for your protection as well as ours," she explained, almost apologetically. "Could you extend your arms?" She demonstrated by stretching her own arms out like a scarecrow.

I followed her example and she lightly patted me down using just two fingers of each hand, starting underneath my armpits and stopping at my ankles.

"Thank you, sister." She treated me to another smile and returned my purse. Another woman was waiting for me just outside the room. She escorted me down a hallway into a room full of folding chairs separated by an aisle about the width of two doorways. Men and women were milling about as a steady stream of people continued to walk in. The atmosphere was relaxed as people greeted each other with hugs and laughter.

I assumed this room was the equivalent of the sanctuary in my church, except there was no pulpit, stained-glass windows or choir section. It actually looked more like a large classroom. I spotted Jefferson already seated a few rows up. I was about to head in his direction, when Special walked up behind me.

"I'm so glad you came," she said, giving me a hug.

She was dressed in a floor-length, peach dress and her braids were covered with a matching scarf. Her face was bare of makeup, except for a touch of lip gloss.

"Jefferson's sitting over there," I said to Special. "Let's go—"

Special linked her arm through mine. "That's the men's side of the room. Women sit on the right. I would've told you before you got here, but I figured you might trip."

That was when I noticed that the entire left side of the room was filled with men. Black men. I'd never seen so many attractive, clean-shaven, immaculately dressed black men in one place before. I paused to take in the sight.

"It had the same effect on me the first time I came here too," Special said, giving me a playful nudge. "It's something to see, ain't it? These brothers don't play when it comes to their appearance. Every last one of them is sharp as a tack."

I glanced back at Jefferson as Special and I walked past him. I assumed Clayton had already told him the deal about us not being able to sit together. He gave me a bored look and shrugged as if to say, *You're the one who wanted to come here.*

Special and I found seats up front just as the service was about to begin.

"What does *As-Salaam Alaikum* mean?" I whispered.

"It's the traditional Muslim greeting. It means *Peace be unto you.*"

"Am I supposed to say the same thing back?"

She laughed. "You should respond with *Wa-alaikum as-salaam,* which means *Peace be unto you also.*"

The service finally started, but not with the musical fanfare associated with my Baptist upbringing. All was quiet as a young man who looked to be in his twenties walked to the lectern.

"In The Name of Allah, The Beneficent, the Most Merciful," the speaker began. "To whom praises are due forever. We give praise and thanks to Allah for giving us his Prophets and Messengers. We thank Him for Moses and the Torah. We thank Him for Jesus and the Gospel. We thank Him for Muhammad and the Holy Qur'an. Peace be upon these worthy servants of Allah."

Thank you for Jesus? I leaned over and whispered to Special again. "I didn't know that Muslims believed in Jesus."

Special smiled big. "Well, you're about to be enlightened. We believe he was only a Prophet like Moses and Muhammad, not the Son of God."

We? I'd been telling myself that Special hadn't really bought into Islam and was simply doing what Clayton wanted her to do. But she was certainly acting like a true convert.

After various announcements and preliminaries from the first speaker, the main speaker, Student Minister Leon Muhammad was introduced. Minister Leon was a handsome man with smooth bronze skin and closely cropped hair.

"My message this morning is Part II of my series, *Do for Self.* As you know, independence for the black man in America is the hallmark of the teachings of the Community of Islam.

"When our people in New Orleans were devastated by Hurricane Katrina, it took them years to get back on their feet. Why? Because they were waiting on somebody else to help them. They were waiting on the mayor. They were waiting on the president. They were waiting on the government. But if they had learned to be self-reliant, which is what we teach, they wouldn't have had to wait on anybody."

Minister Leon delivered his message eloquently, without reference to notes. "You must remember that you can't expect someone who mistreats you to teach you," Minister Leon told us. "If you want to eat, grow your own food. If you want to work, create your own business. If you want to learn, seek knowledge for yourself. Don't sit around waiting for some mystery God to do it for you."

He paced back and forth, pointing at the audience. But not with the theatrics of the Baptist preachers I was used to. Minister Leon was teaching, not preaching.

"We're sitting right here in a predominantly black neighborhood. But how many businesses do we own around here? Few and far between. Every racial group in this city has their own thriving community except us," he exclaimed, tapping his chest with his index finger.

"There's Koreatown, Chinatown, Little Tokyo. The Hispanics have East L.A. The Westside is predominantly Jewish. These groups have chosen to live among themselves where *they* control their communities. But you don't see black folks running the businesses in our communities.

"Step outside this door and walk into any business on this block and you'll rarely see anybody behind the counter who looks like you and me. We might run a barbecue joint or a beauty salon, but we don't own the property. Jews own the land. East Indians own the liquor stores, Koreans run the nail shops and even the stores where our women are stupid enough to buy white folks' hair to sew onto their head."

There was an occasional chant of "Teach, brother, teach."

"The Community of Islam says, 'Why don't we build up our own community?' Black supermarkets and restaurants where we teach our people to eat healthy. Black schools where we teach our kids about their history. That's all we want. We don't teach hate. We don't teach violence. We teach doing for self."

The lecture ended about thirty minutes later to raucous applause.

After the service, Special and I found Jefferson and Clayton outside waiting for us.

"So how'd you enjoy the lecture?" Clayton asked as we approached.

"That brother's message was tight," Jefferson said, giving Clayton a fist bump. "And he didn't even ask for no money."

Whenever I could cajole Jefferson into joining me at Faithful Central, he always complained when it was time for the offering.

"What about you, Vernetta?"

"It was interesting," I said, which was true. For me, church was a spiritual experience which I didn't feel in the mosque. I went to church for the prayer and gospel music as much as the preaching.

"I really dug that brother's message about doing for self," Jefferson continued. "I wish some of the guys from my crew could have heard it."

"Bring 'em down," Clayton urged. "We're all about imparting knowledge. A few brothers are meeting at one o'clock today to discuss doing some things in the neighborhood. You should come."

I snickered to myself. The Vikings kickoff was at one. I couldn't wait to hear what excuse Jefferson would use to get out of Clayton's invitation.

"I'm there," Jefferson said.

I was dizzy with disbelief, but my husband was apparently too excited to notice the stunned expression on my face.

"Sounds like I can count on you two coming back," Clayton said.

Jefferson didn't bother to consult me before answering.

"Most definitely," my husband beamed. "We're definitely coming back."

CHAPTER 29

Olivia had made up her mind. She was not going to let these devils work her nerves. She'd knelt in prayer for a full hour that morning and felt both fortified and protected. God would make a way.

The newest demon they'd shipped in to the store, Helen Sheridan, had it in for her. The new interim store manager had stopped cold when Olivia introduced herself. Olivia could tell from the way the woman's cold blue eyes had looked her up and down that she knew all about the lawsuit.

Sheridan had been an assistant manager at a much smaller Big Buy store in San Francisco. Now that she'd been promoted, Big Buy would no doubt trot her out to show that the company didn't discriminate against women.

Entering the locker room, Olivia slipped on her blazer and checked the bulletin board for next week's schedule.

At first she thought she'd read the wrong line. Olivia used her index finger to trace the space between her name and shift time. No, she'd read it correctly. She'd been assigned to work nights on Wednesday.

Olivia marched straight to the store manager's office.

"I need to speak to Helen about the schedule," she told the office receptionist. "I can't work Wednesday night."

The woman didn't bother to look up from her computer monitor. "They changed a lot of people's schedules."

"I teach Bible study on Wednesday nights." She tried to keep her voice level, though she really wanted to scream. "I can't work that night."

"You need to talk to Helen. She did the schedules."

"Where is she?"

"Not sure. But I'll tell her you're looking for her."

Olivia glanced at her watch. If she didn't get to the floor right away, she would be late. She made a quick stop in the ladies' room.

As she approached the Housewares aisles, she heard a chorus of grumbling from other employees.

"How many people's schedules did they change?" Olivia asked a co-worker in the Shoe Department.

"About ten of us. So no use complaining about it."

Olivia began taking inventory and straightening up her aisles. When she rounded the corner to the next aisle, she spotted Helen a few feet away, talking to another sales associate.

Tall and big-boned with frizzy black hair, Helen hustled over to Olivia. "You were late getting to the floor today."

"That's because I was looking for you. I need to talk to you about the new schedule."

"You need to be on the floor on time. Next time, I'm writing you up."

Three nosey sales associates peered at them from the end of the aisle.

"I was only a couple minutes late," Olivia said. "I need to talk to you about the schedule. I never work Wednesday nights. I teach Bible Study at Hope in Christ Community Church in Compton. I've been doing it for years."

"Well, I guess you'll have to find somebody else to teach your class."

"I can't do that. I haven't missed a class in five years. Olivia's chest expanded with pride."

Helen lifted a page on her clipboard. "Well, I don't know what to tell you."

"What if I find someone to switch shifts with me that night?"

"Nope," Helen said. "If I let you do that, then everyone will want to change their schedule."

Helen started walking away.

Olivia felt fury thundering in her chest and she wasn't sure she could contain it. "This sounds like retaliation," she called after her, hands on hips. "Because of my lawsuit."

Helen stopped and marched back over to her. "I changed the schedules of several associates."

Helen's words didn't mean a thing. The smug smile on her wicked lips confirmed that she *was* retaliating against her. Changing everyone's schedule made the move look legitimate. Vernetta had warned her that there would be some trying times. She would just call Vernetta on her break and have her straighten everything out.

"Never mind." Olivia raised her hand skyward, palm forward and quietly recited one of her favorite Bible verses. "*No weapon formed against me shall prosper. No weapon formed against me shall prosper.*"

"What did you say?" Helen stepped back, her lips pursed into a paper-thin line. "Did you just threaten me?"

Olivia rolled her eyes. "I didn't threaten you. I—"

"Yes, you did! You raised your hand and said something about getting a weapon. Making physical threats is a violation of our workplace violence policy. You can go home now. You're suspended pending an investigation."

Olivia chuckled. "What're you talking about? I didn't threaten you."

Helen took a step closer and pointed her ink pen in Olivia's face. "I know what I heard. I'm ordering you to leave the store. Now."

"This is crazy. That was a Bible verse. If you weren't such a heathen you would know that."

"Oh, so now you're resorting to name-calling?" Helen hugged her clipboard to her body like a shield. "Do I need to get security to escort you out of the store?"

A crowd of associates and customers seemed to appear from nowhere. They were whispering and rubbernecking as if they were about to witness a street fight.

Olivia felt short of breath. She'd been having trouble with her blood pressure lately and she didn't need a machine to tell her that it was now sky-high.

She snatched off her blazer as she took off for the locker room. Helen was probably going to fire her, but Olivia wasn't worried. God was her protector.

Grabbing her purse from her locker, Olivia slammed the door and strutted out of the store with her head held high.

CHAPTER 30

The doorbell rang just as Special gave her outfit one final, admiring look in the full-length mirror. There was no way Clayton could resist her tonight.

She headed for the living room in her braless, thigh-high sundress with spaghetti straps. She was busty enough to have cleavage without the need of a push-up bra. The faint indentation of her nipples was visible through the thin cotton fabric.

"Hey, sweetie," she said, swinging the door open.

Clayton's eyes went straight to her cleavage, then darted away. She stood on her tiptoes and gave him a hug, directing his nose between her neck and shoulder, where she'd dabbed a smidgen of Reb'l Fleur, one of Rihanna's fragrances. Clayton kissed her lightly on the cheek and stepped inside.

"How was work?"

"Crazy as ever. They moved up the project date and now they're expecting us to bust our behinds to get it done."

"I want you to forget all about that tonight." She took him by the hand and led him over to the table. "I made you a wonderful meal. Grilled red snapper, macaroni and cheese, collard greens, salad and homemade rolls from my grandmama's recipe. And before you ask, I made the greens with smoked turkey, not pork."

Clayton frowned. "I don't eat collard greens anymore."

"Since when? You love my greens."

"Since I've been enlightened. Greens are slave food and the mac 'n cheese is way too high in fat and cholesterol. And we should only be eating wheat bread."

Special turned away and cussed under her breath. She'd spent two hours making those damn rolls.

"Fine. Don't eat it then."

"Wait, hold up." He gave her shoulders a squeeze and kissed her on the forehead. "I'm sorry, babe. I had a bad day. I shouldn't be taking it out on you. I appreciate you cooking for me. I love having a woman with domestic skills."

Special wasn't sure that statement was a positive one, but she decided not to seek clarification right now. There were more important tasks to contend with tonight.

Clayton sat down at the dining room table, where Special had lit candles and set the table with her good dishes and Kente cloth napkins.

"What's the occasion?" Clayton asked, admiring the setup.

"No occasion." She placed a piece of red snapper on his plate. "I just wanted to do something special for my man."

Actually, she was hoping a good meal and a romantic setting might loosen him up.

"Well, thank you very much, my queen." He threw an arm around her waist and pulled her close.

Clayton's embrace made her woozy. It took every ounce of restraint she could muster not to jump into his lap. Once she had filled her own plate and joined him at the table, he took both of her hands in his and began to pray.

"O, Allah, I seek Thy refuge from lack of strength and laziness. I seek Thy refuge from cowardice and being overpowered by debt and the oppression of men…"

Special tried to concentrate on the prayer, but Clayton's touch brought back memories of the last time they'd made love. She closed her eyes tighter and tried to block out her sinful thoughts.

"O, Allah, teach me what is lawful and keep me away from what is prohibited. Through Thy grace, make me free from the desires of the flesh."

Damn. The desires of the flesh were all she'd been thinking about. She was relieved when he finally let go of her hands.

"I have some good news," Clayton said, taking a bite of red snapper.

"I could definitely use some good news." *I could also use a romp in the hay.*

"Minister Malik gave us the go-ahead for our naming ceremony."

Special took a forkful of the mac 'n cheese and allowed it to melt in her mouth. She'd used three different cheeses and it tasted fantastic. It was a shame that Clayton refused to even try it.

"Naming ceremony? What's that?" Special knew exactly what he was talking about and she'd been dreading this day.

"The ceremony we have to go through to get our Muslim names. If you'd been studying like you're supposed to, you'd know that."

Special braced herself for Clayton's reaction to what she was about to say. "I ain't changing my name," she said. "I love my name."

Clayton set down his fork and laced his fingers. "If you love Allah and desire to follow his teachings, you'd no longer want to carry the slave name the white man saddled you with."

"Maybe a white man gave me my last name, but my mama and daddy picked my first name. Regardless, I ain't changing either one."

A thick vein flexed in Clayton's neck. "My queen," he said, tone measured, "I'm trying to be patient with you. I know it's going to take some time before your level of commitment to the Community equals mine. But I do expect you to get there. Eventually."

"I will. But I ain't—" Special caught herself.

She wasn't changing her name. Not now, not ever. But she didn't want to start an argument. Tonight all she wanted was to get laid. They could have it out over her slave name another day.

"I'm sorry. Maybe I'm overreacting. This is all pretty new to me so it's going to take me a little time to get used to everything. I've had this name for more than three decades." *And I plan to have it another three.*

After their meal, Clayton remained at the table, reading the Community of Islam newspaper while Special cleared the table and loaded the dishes into the dishwasher.

"Let's watch TV," she said, leading him into the living room. She left a suitable distance between them on the couch. Clayton picked up the remote and flipped from one channel to another.

"This is nothing but trash," he complained. "All this reality TV junk is just a way to fill our minds with self-hatred." He finally settled on *The Tavis Smiley Show*.

Special waited a few minutes, then closed the gap between them and rested her head on Clayton's shoulder. She waited another five minutes, then reached up and pressed her lips to his. After all, kissing wasn't fornication.

For the first time in a while, Clayton returned her kiss with the energy and passion of their pre-celibacy days.

Special pressed her hand flat against his chest and began massaging his nipples through his shirt. She lowered her other hand to his upper leg. At first she just rested it there, but as their kissing intensified, she began to caress his upper thigh.

When Special felt him grow hard, she took his physical response as a green light. She eased onto his lap, pinning her knees at his sides. She slid her hands underneath his shirt and massaged his chest. Their kisses made loud, slurping sounds as their heads twisted and turned and their tongues darted in and out of each other's mouths.

Clayton was a fully active participant now, grinding up toward her as she pressed down to meet him. His hands roamed beneath her dress, gripped her narrow waist and grinded her body against his. He was breathing in heavy, intermittent gasps.

"Damn, I missed this so much," Special moaned through the kisses.

Leaning forward, Clayton stood up, still holding Special in his lap. Her legs coiled easily around his waist as he walked toward the bedroom.

They stumbled down the hallway toward the bedroom. As they stepped inside, Clayton pressed Special's back against the wall. He unbuckled his pants and let them fall to his ankles, then reached under her dress and pulled down her thong panties.

Special's right breast popped out of her sundress and Clayton bent down to take it into his mouth. At that moment, Special's left shoulder hit the light switch. A blast of light inundated the room.

Clayton froze.

Special reached a hand across her body and flicked off the light. Clayton still didn't move.

"What's the...what's the matter?" She continued to pepper his face with kisses.

Clayton abruptly dropped her to the floor, stepped back and pulled up his pants.

"This is wrong," he said. "The light coming on like that was a sign. A message from Allah. What happens in the dark will eventually come into the light."

"What the hell are you talking about?" Special grabbed his arm with both hands. "That wasn't a sign. My shoulder just hit the light switch. C'mon, baby, I'm so horny I don't know what to do."

"I gotta go," Clayton said. "Thanks for dinner." His voice was formal and distant, and he refused to look at her.

"*You gotta go?* You have to be kidding!"

He zipped up his pants. "No, I'm not kidding. This is wrong."

"Fine then! Go! I don't care!"

When she heard the front door open and close, she fell onto the bed and started pounding the mattress with her fists. This was insane. She lay there hot, horny and frustrated.

In a matter of seconds, though, her mood shifted and she started to laugh. It was just her luck to end up with the one man in L.A. who *didn't* wanna have sex. She rolled over on her side, clutching her stomach, overcome with laughter.

When her giggles had finally subsided, she walked barefoot into the kitchen and popped open a wine cooler. She'd hidden it in an empty milk carton at the back of the refrigerator in case of an emergency. This definitely fit the bill.

Special took an extra-long chug straight from the bottle. The evening hadn't ended the way she had planned, but she *had* made progress. Getting Clayton this far showed that he wasn't as committed to their celibacy as he professed. He was, after all, a man. And Special had never met a man she couldn't entice.

Tonight they'd made it past first base. Next time she would lure him all the way in to home plate.

CHAPTER 31

When I saw Olivia's cell phone light up my caller ID display, I had a bad feeling. It was after five. Her shift didn't end until six.

"Hey, Olivia," I said, bracing myself.

"I'd like to drop by to talk to you." Her voice was low and controlled.

"That's fine. When would you like to come in?"

"Right now. I'm downstairs in the lobby."

It took ten anxiety-filled minutes before Olivia made it up to my office.

She was casually dressed in black slacks and a white blouse. Her smooth face appeared calm, but her body was erect and tight, as if she was trying to hold back an eruption.

"What's going on, Olivia? Why aren't you at work?"

"Those heathens need to be glad I'm a Christian." She plunked down in a chair in front of my desk. "They had the nerve to suspend me this morning."

"What happened?" I grabbed a legal pad from the corner of my desk. "Why didn't you call me right away?"

"I went straight to Hope in Christ and got on my knees. And thank God I did, because I was seriously considering going back to that store and strangling that old she-devil. But I had a long talk with Reverend Robinson. Then I went over to the school and had lunch with my husband. I'm okay now."

"Tell me what happened?"

Olivia recounted the confrontation she'd had with the store manager over her schedule. "We can't let them get away with this," she said. "This is retaliation."

"I agree."

I started peppering her with questions. Who witnessed the incident? How long did it last? Did Helen do anything she considered threatening?

She could only remember the names of three employees in the area, though she was sure several others witnessed it.

"I promise you I'm going to take care of this."

As soon as the words were out, I wished I could take them back. That was not a promise I should've made, but my own emotions were getting the best of me. The truth was, if Big Buy wanted to make an example out of Olivia, it could take months or years to avenge her rights via the legal system.

"Go home and relax," I said. "I'm going to give Big Buy's attorney a call. I'll do everything I can to get you back to work as soon as possible."

"I'm not worried about a thing," Olivia said, getting up from her seat. "I'm a child of God."

I walked her to the elevator and returned to my office just in time to grab the phone before it clicked over to voicemail.

The voice on the other end of the line took me totally by surprise. I hadn't heard from Ida Lopez since she'd emailed me saying she wanted out of the lawsuit. A few days later, Olivia called to tell me about Ida's promotion."

"How are you doing?" I said.

"I'm fine."

"Congratulations on your promotion."

"Thank you."

"So what can I do for you?"

"I uh…I wanted to talk to you about what happened to Olivia this morning. I saw everything."

I propped my elbow on the desk and massaged my eyes. I wanted to know what Ida had to say, but ethically, I needed to cut the conversation short.

"Ida, now that you're a member of management, I can't talk to you."

"But I'm not in the lawsuit anymore. I'm calling you on my own. I know Olivia hates me for dropping out of the lawsuit, but I want to help if I can."

"It doesn't work like that. Since you're a member of management now, you represent the company. I can't speak to you without the store's permission. I could get in trouble with the state bar if I did."

And Vernetta wouldn't put it past Girlie Cortez to raise a stink about it if she found out.

"But—"

"I'm sorry. I'm assuming you're calling me because you have some information helpful to Olivia. If you really want to help her, you should go to Human Resources and make sure your information gets to the company's attorney."

I didn't need to see Ida's face to know that my suggestion mortified her.

"I…I can't do that. It'll get me in trouble. Can't we just talk confidentially? No one will know we ever had this conversation."

"I can't. Good-bye, Ida."

I placed the phone back into the base. Sometimes my job really sucked. Girlie wouldn't have done what I just did. She would've taken the information, then lied about doing so.

I took a few minutes to collect myself before dialing Girlie's number. I was surprised that she actually picked up. I usually got her secretary or her voicemail.

"I have a problem," I said, hoping to sound forceful rather than pissed. "And I need your help fixing it."

"And good afternoon to you too, Ms. Henderson," she said cheerily.

"Olivia Jackson just advised me that she was suspended based on a trumped-up charge of workplace violence. I have the names of three employees who witnessed the incident. After you have Human Resources interview them, I'd like you to instruct your client to return Olivia to work with full pay for today and no reference to this bogus incident in her personnel file."

"I think your client and mine have differing views about what happened. As I understand it, your client physically threatened the new store manager."

"That didn't happen."

"How do you know? You weren't there."

"I know my client. If she says it didn't happen, then it didn't happen. Just talk to Barbara Sykes, Linda Beed, and Robyn Gant. They saw the whole thing."

"Your client called the store manager a heathen. I'm sure your witnesses will confirm that. Name-calling is also a violation of company policy."

"Girlie," I said, trying to keep my cool, "Ms. Sheridan made completely false allegations against my client, who was merely reciting a Bible verse. In light of that, I think it's understandable why Olivia got a little upset."

"So you're admitting that your client called Ms. Sheridan a heathen?"

"I'm not admitting anything."

"Well, I'll look into this when I get some time. But I have a deposition that I need to prep for, so I won't be able to get to it for a few days."

"Is my client on a paid or unpaid suspension? No one made that clear to her when they ordered her out of the store."

"We don't pay people when we suspend them."

"Olivia didn't do anything wrong and she can't afford to sit home without a paycheck, waiting for the company to finish a drawn-out investigation."

"Well, that's what she's going to have to do."

"Girlie, what happened to my client was nothing short of retaliation. You can fix this and that's what I'm asking you to do. You don't want to go to war with me on this one. Trust me."

"Wow," Girlie said laughing. "Sounds like you're threatening me just like your client threatened Big Buy's store manager."

I closed my eyes and sucked in a breath. It wouldn't do Olivia any good for me to go off on Girlie. I needed to do whatever it took to get my client back to work.

"That wasn't my intent," I said, trying my best to sound pleasant. "I'm just a little concerned about my client."

"If Ms. Jackson had taken my settlement offer, we wouldn't have this problem."

"That settlement offer wasn't worthy of acceptance." I suddenly realized that my hand was throbbing. I'd been clutching the phone so tight, I'd cut off my circulation. "So can I count on you to look into this?"

"I'll see what I can do."

I slammed down the phone, feeling outraged and powerless because I knew Girlie Cortez wasn't going to do jack.

CHAPTER 32

Mankowski took a sip of wine and refused to allow his eyes to linger on Girlie Cortez's outstanding breasts. She was wearing a red satin blouse with the top three buttons undone.

"Your dinner invitation was a pleasant surprise," Mankowski said, struggling to keep his slight smile from expanding into a sunbeam. Giving Girlie even an inkling of how excited he really was would blow everything.

"Really?" Girlie angled her head, causing her hair to fall across her right shoulder. "I thought I sensed some sparks between us the other day. I hope I wasn't imagining things."

Damn. He'd never met a woman this direct. "Unfortunately, I don't think it's a good practice to mix business and pleasure."

"Oh, so you think being with me would be a pleasure?"

Mankowski could feel himself go rigid. If she kept talking like this, he'd probably come in his pants. To help quell his excitement, he eyed a lanky redhead, passing their table. She was a six to Girlie's ten-plus.

He tried reading the menu, but the lines kept running together. She was giving him nothing but green lights. Mankowski would continue to play it cool while they were in the restaurant, but when he walked her to her car, he was going to take charge and kiss her. He could already feel those plump breasts pressing against his chest, already taste the sweetness of her—

"Hey, big guy? Are you there?" Girlie reached across the table and placed a soft hand on top of his.

"You're a very direct young lady," Mankowski said.

"I don't like playing games. When I see something I want, I go for it."

Mankowski eased his hand away and grinned. "You and I teaming up right now isn't a good idea. We met in the course of an investigation that's still open. Even my having dinner with you tonight poses a bit of a conflict of interest." Of course, he'd violated department policy in this regard more than a few times before.

Girlie winked. "I won't tell if you don't."

He had to change the subject. "So how was your day?"

Girlie smiled. "I got a call from an irate opposing counsel right before leaving the office. I really enjoyed pissing her off."

"Sounds like you get a kick out of being a lawyer."

"I really do. It gives me a real sense of power."

That was a telling response. Mankowski should've cut the conversation short and run out of the restaurant, but his brain didn't seem to be functioning properly.

He hadn't even realized that Girlie had eased her hand across the table again. Her dainty hand appeared childlike next to his.

Mankowski felt like a geeky high school kid about to get a piece from the head cheerleader. He didn't want to make any wrong moves. If he screwed this up, he'd have to pull out his .38 and shoot himself in the head.

The waiter approached and spouted off the specials. He was talking to both of them, but giving Girlie all of his attention. Mankowski could tell that the guy wanted her too and he was probably gay.

Girlie was about to place her order when Mankowski did something he'd never done before. "Let me order for you."

He sensed that this powerful woman preferred a man who knew how to take control. He did not wait for her permission.

"The lady will have the grilled salmon. The rib eye for me. Medium-well."

The waiter stood there for a second as if waiting for Girlie's approval. But she only smiled.

"Anything else?" the waiter asked.

"A red wine. Something sweet," Mankowski said. "Like the lady."

Girlie leaned forward as the waiter disappeared. Her shift of position gave him a better view of her phenomenal tits.

"I like that," Girlie said softly.

"What?" Mankowski asked, knowing he had just scored big.

"The way you took charge and ordered exactly what I wanted. Most guys I meet are in awe of me. I like meeting a man who's..." she paused in search of the right word. "Fearless."

"It's the gun and the badge," he joked.

She leaned over the table and gave him a blazingly intense look that made him shiver inside. "I don't care what it is. I like it."

He tried to hold her gaze, but after a few seconds he had to look away. He'd had sex last week with one of the assistants in the crime lab and he wasn't even this turned on when he came.

"Tell me something about yourself." Mankowski was desperate to change the subject. "Are you the only lawyer in your family?"

Girlie's smile fell away. "Not really."

Not really? It was a yes-or-no question.

Had Girlie's response come from a suspect, Mankowski would have pressed for more. But he didn't care. He was willing to talk about whatever she chose to share.

"Where'd you grow up?"

Girlie softly inhaled and looked away.

Strike two.

"Cerritos," she finally said. She took a sip of water and averted her eyes.

Okay, so family stuff was off-limits. He got it. Maybe she'd had a tough childhood. He didn't really care how or where she'd grown up. He was just trying to make conversation.

Girlie leaned in again. "What about you? What led you to law enforcement?"

"I like protecting people." That was a line he'd just made up, but there was a great deal of truth to it.

"I'd like you to protect me," Girlie said. She reached across the table again and squeezed his hand.

"And just what do you need protecting from?"

She shrugged. "Nothing at the moment, but you never know. Having my own personal detective to call on any time of the day or night could be quite an asset. So can I call on you?"

Mankowski knew he had her and tried not to smile.

"Please do."

CHAPTER 33

By the end of the day shift, the news of Olivia's confrontation with the new store manager was swirling around the store like a swarm of pissed-off bumblebees. Associates were emailing and tweeting each other and gossiping about it on Facebook. In one version, Olivia had spat in Helen's face. In another, she'd been fired and escorted out by security.

Although most of Olivia's co-workers were afraid to be seen talking to her, many secretly envied her for having the guts to stand up for herself. After her suspension, they were ready to back her up.

"I think we should do something," Robyn Gant had told a handful of sales associates only minutes after Olivia marched out of the store. "It wasn't right what they did to Olivia. I saw the whole thing. She didn't threaten Helen."

"We can't do anything?" another worker griped. "They're probably going to fire her. And if we complain they'll fire us too."

"They can't fire all of us," Robyn insisted. She was an outgoing woman who pranced around the store in three-inch heels all day, then pretended that her feet didn't hurt after eight hours. "I don't know about y'all," she said, "but I'm going to do something."

So rather than tending to the Shoe department where she worked, Robyn had spent the rest of her shift secretly talking to other sales associates about her plan. Robyn enlisted five other workers to help get the word out to employees on the other shifts. She also contacted her cousin, who worked the assignment desk at KABC-TV.

The next morning, more than a third of the sales associates, including Robyn, had called in sick. Such a high absenteeism would've been a problem on any day, but it was definitely a near-catastrophe the day before the Fourth of July. The store was packed with shoppers making last-minute purchases in preparation for the holiday.

The store manager traipsed up and down the aisles like a confused puppy trying to catch its tail.

"I need you to cover register six," Helen barked at a worker who'd been assigned to Housewares in Olivia's absence.

"I haven't worked the register in over a year," the woman said, shrinking away. "I'm not sure I even remember how."

"Just go over there," Helen shouted at her. "It'll come back to you."

"But I don't have an access number anymore," the woman complained.

Helen threw up her hands and walked off.

Near the front of the store, only three of the ten registers were open. Each line of waiting customers was thirty-deep.

"Why don't you open up some more registers," a man called out as Helen hurried by.

"Yeah," another customer yelled after her. "This is ridiculous."

Ida Lopez walked up behind Helen. "I think you need to contact the corporate office," she whispered. "This is getting out of hand."

Helen ran a hand through her frizzy hair. "I have everything under control."

"No, you don't. Do you even realize what's going on?" Ida asked.

"What do you mean?"

"The sales associates organized a sick-in. That's why so many people called in sick." She pointed toward the registers. "And the employees who did show up are staging a work slowdown. That's why it's taking customers a half hour to get through the line."

"Why are they doing this?"

"Because of what happened to Olivia."

"That woman threatened me!" Helen pouted.

Ida held her tongue. "I really think you need to call corporate."

"I can't do that. They'll think I can't handle things. This is my chance to show I can run a big store."

"I think your problems just got worse." Ida pointed toward the sliding glass doors that led out of the store. "Look who's here."

A KABC-TV news van was illegally parked just outside the entrance. A reporter was stopping customers for an interview as they exited the store.

Helen rushed outside just as the reporter turned away to commence a live shot.

"If you still have some last-minute shopping to do for your Fourth of July celebration, you may want to avoid the Big Buy store in Carson unless you have a lot of extra time on your hands. More than a third of the store's sales associates called in sick today, and the ones who did show up are staging a work slowdown.

"The employees have banned together to protest what they believe was the unfair and retaliatory suspension of a fellow worker. I just spoke to one customer, who says she had to wait in line for thirty minutes to pay for a barbecue grill..."

Rather than react, Helen started to hyperventilate.

"Like I told you," Ida said, "you need to call the corporate office. Now."

CHAPTER 34

The employee protest at Big Buy led every local newscast in the city and resulted in tons of negative publicity about the store on Twitter and Facebook. The general counsel immediately called Girlie, who dropped everything and rushed over to the company's Anaheim headquarters.

Girlie sat across an ocean-size conference table, facing the interim store manager. Helen Sheridan kept ringing her hands and apologizing. She was flanked on either side by Evelyn Kimble, the general counsel and Rita Richards-Kimble, the CEO. There was no need for Rita to be present, but it was clear that she didn't trust her general counsel to properly manage this situation.

"I have no idea how everything got so out of control," Helen whined.

"Just tell us what happened with Ms. Jackson," Girlie urged.

"I approached Olivia Jackson because she was late getting to the floor. She got all loud and started demanding that I change her schedule. Then she raised her hand as if she was going to hit me and said something about getting a weapon and prospering."

"What?" Evelyn and Rita said in unison. "Getting a weapon and prospering? What does that mean?"

"I didn't understand it myself," Helen said. "But when I heard her say weapon, that's when I got scared. And then she called me a heathen."

Girlie frowned. "Ms. Jackson's attorney claims her client was simply quoting a Bible verse."

"Well, if she was, I'd never heard of it."

"Tell me, to the best of your memory, exactly what Ms. Jackson said to you."

Helen looked skyward. "No weapon...can...prosper over me. Yeah, I think that's what she said. I know for sure that she said *weapon* and I'm pretty sure she said *prosper.*"

Girlie didn't know much about the Bible, having only been to church for funerals and weddings. She picked up her smartphone and Googled the words *Bible verse, weapon* and *prosper."* The search instantly pulled up Isaiah 54:17.

Girlie read the verse out loud. *"No weapon formed against thee shall prosper.* Is that what she said?"

"Yeah, that's it!" Helen said, snapping her fingers. Her excitement dulled a second later, once she realized that Olivia's words were not a threat. "But, like I said, she did say it with a lot of hostility."

Girlie set her smartphone back on the table. "Weren't you advised about Ms. Jackson's lawsuit when you came to the store?"

"Yes, she was," Rita said. "Which is why I have no idea why she would do something stupid like changing that woman's schedule without clearing it with anybody."

Helen slid down a few inches in her seat. "I didn't think it would be a problem."

"Exactly why did you alter her schedule?" Evelyn asked.

"I just think it's a good idea to change employees' shifts from time to time. If you don't, they start thinking they're entitled to a particular shift. Then, when you need to move them for some reason, they start complaining. I switched about a dozen associates. Nobody else made a big deal about it."

"Do you know how much your actions have damaged this company's reputation?" Rita yelled. "You made it look as if we retaliated against Ms. Jackson because of her lawsuit."

"But I didn't," Helen protested.

"That's it for now," Girlie said, as exasperated with Rita as she was with Helen. "Please send Ida Lopez in and wait outside."

Seconds later, Ida entered the room with her eyes cast downward, her right pinkie finger wrapped around the strap of her purse.

Girlie introduced everyone and explained that she was investigating the incident involving Olivia Jackson.

"I understand that you were in the area when it happened," Girlie said. "Were you close enough to hear their conversation?"

Ida nodded, but didn't speak.

"Tell us what you saw?"

Ida began recounting a story that was completely different from what Helen had just reported. "Olivia explained to Helen that she couldn't work on Wednesday night because she teaches Bible study."

"Did Ms. Jackson raise her voice?" Girlie asked.

Ida glanced over at Rita, who was tapping her fingers on the desk. "No."

"Was her tone hostile?"

"No."

"Did it appear to you that she was going to hit Helen?"

"No."

"Did you hear Ms. Jackson say, *No weapon formed against thee shall prosper?*"

"Yes."

"Did you view that as a threat?"

Ida laughed softly. "No. Olivia is always praying and quoting the Bible."

"So you recognized what she said as a Bible verse?"

"Of course," Ida said, giving Girlie a look that said she should have too.

"What's the atmosphere like among the employees at the store?"

Ida hunched her shoulders. "I don't know."

"We really need you to be candid with us," Evelyn said.

When Girlie had urged the general counsel to promote Ida, Evelyn had initially resisted, thinking that any employee who sued the company couldn't be trusted. But Ida was a struggling single mother. Girlie figured the promotion would make her loyal to the company and, more important, create a wedge between her and Olivia. Girlie just hoped this incident didn't send Ida running back to the other side.

Girlie gave Ida as much time as she needed to answer the question. "Nobody really likes Helen," she finally admitted. "She acts like a drill sergeant, always trying to find something you're doing wrong. Our old store manager wasn't like that. He just let us do our jobs. So when she suspended Olivia, everybody took Olivia's side. They didn't think it was right."

"Did you think it was right?" Rita challenged.

Again, Ida took her time answering the question. "No," she said, her gaze on Girlie, not Rita. "It wasn't right."

They dismissed Ida after a few more questions.

"Well," Girlie said, "it looks like we have a problem. I think we need to reverse that suspension and concentrate on restoring order at the store."

"I guess we have to," the general counsel agreed. "We can't take another day of negative publicity like the one we just had. We need to get these employees calmed down. I don't want them calling up Vernetta Henderson too."

"I just hate that the sales associates are basically dictating how we discipline our employees," Rita said grudgingly.

"I'll call Ms. Henderson right after this meeting," Girlie said.

They called Helen back into the room.

"We've made the decision to bring Ms. Jackson back to work," the general counsel announced.

Helen sulked back in her chair. "But she—"

"Ms. Jackson is involved in ligation against this company," the CEO said sternly. "How you manage this situation going forward will have a direct bearing on whether we keep you on as the permanent store manager. From now on, don't make a move involving Ms. Jackson without clearing it with me personally."

Evelyn maintained her usual fake smile, but Girlie could see something bubbling beneath the surface. She was the general counsel and this was a matter within her chain of command. But Rita had stepped in and rendered her meaningless.

"I understand," Helen said with a stiff smile.

Girlie shook her head. Helen was a nightmare and had no busi-ness in charge of other workers. When they'd made the decision to bring in a female store manager, there were very few employees to pick from. Fortunately for Girlie, more workplace strife meant more billable hours for her.

"Tomorrow morning," Evelyn said, reasserting herself, "I want you to call a staff meeting and announce that there was a misunder-standing and that Olivia Jackson is returning to work."

CHAPTER 35

Jefferson pointed up at the theater marquee like an excited five-year-old. "We have plenty of time. The previews haven't even started yet."

We were standing in line at the Howard Hughes Promenade about to purchase movie tickets. When we left home twenty minutes ago, we'd agreed to see the new Julia Roberts movie. Jefferson was now welching on the deal and trying to convince me to see some action flick.

"I heard the reviews weren't that good," I said.

"I don't care about reviews. The last four movies we saw were chick flicks. You owe me."

A Thursday night movie was rare for us, but after getting Olivia back to work, I felt like celebrating. My overworked psyche needed a sappy romantic comedy, not a bunch of car chases and explosions. Still, I gave in.

We purchased tickets and I ran off to the ladies' room while Jefferson waited in line for popcorn.

Minutes later, he was walking toward me, carrying a jumbo tub of popcorn and two sodas, a frown stretched across his face.

"What's the matter?"

"I think somebody's following us." He did a slow three-sixty turn, examining every inch of the theater lobby.

My eyes trailed his. "Following us? Who?"

"I don't see the dude now. A short black guy in a beige shirt."

"What makes you think that?"

"Because I saw him at the red light right after we left the house. Then I saw him in the parking lot and I could swear I saw him just a second ago. I'm thinking this might have something to do with your Big Buy case and those documents."

"Uh…did you consider the possibility that he might want to see a movie too?"

Ever since that beating Benjamin took, Jefferson had been overly concerned about my safety. I'd been trying to forget what happened to Benjamin, but Jefferson was making me paranoid.

We headed inside theater six. When I stopped in the area where we normally sat, Jefferson continued up the stairs.

"Let's sit up here," he said, taking the aisle seat on the very last row. "I wanna be able to see if homeboy comes in."

I followed him without comment, knowing that protesting wouldn't change anything.

Jefferson shifted in his seat every few minutes and kept gazing around the theatre. Not that there was anything to see in the dark.

I tried to watch the movie, but after about twenty minutes of non-stop explosions, I nodded off.

"Wake up." Jefferson nudged my arm. "Do I fall asleep when you drag me to a chick flick?"

I opened my eyes to find him standing over me. "I was just resting my eyes. Is the movie over already?"

"Yeah, and you missed a good one."

He extended his hand and helped me to my feet. We walked the short distance to Wild Thai for dinner.

"How's the shopping-center project in Inglewood going?" I asked, after we'd placed our orders.

"Pretty messed up. The general contractor is having some problems and—"

Jefferson's attention was suddenly focused on something over my shoulder. I turned around to see what he was looking at. The spacious walkway out front was empty.

"I thought that was dude again," he said. "But maybe it wasn't."

I sighed. "If you're trying to scare me, it's working."

"So you're ready to drop the case?"

"No way. Let's get off of my job and finish talking about yours."

"The general contractor may not have enough money to finish the job, which means me and all the other subcontractors will be left holding the bag. But I'm not sweating it. It'll work out."

We finished our meal, picked up cookies from Mrs. Fields and headed to the parking garage. When we stepped into the elevator, Jefferson was about to press our floor, then stopped and pinned me with a blank look.

"Don't ask me," I said. "I don't remember what level we parked on either."

"You're the super-smart one," he quipped with a smile. "You should automatically remember stuff like this."

He punched the second floor and when the doors opened, he stuck his head out and looked to the left.

"Not this one. Must be level three."

When the elevator doors reopened, I made a move to step out ahead of Jefferson, but he took my arm and pulled me back inside.

"Hold the doors open, while I check first." He trotted a few feet up the first aisle, then waved me over. "The car's over there," he said, pointing.

I had almost caught up with him, when Jefferson suddenly took off, running past me at top speed.

I whirled around. "Jefferson, what are you—"

"Hold up, asshole!" Jefferson yelled.

My stomach flip-flopped when I realized that Jefferson was chasing after someone. A man in khakis and sunglasses was zigzagging between cars with Jefferson only a yard or two behind him. Another couple, headed for the elevators, stopped to watch.

"Jefferson, what are you doing?" I yelled, jogging toward him.

The man cut right and stumbled as he tried to make his way around an Escalade. That put him within Jefferson's reach. I watched in complete shock as my husband grabbed the man by the back of his collar.

By the time I reached them, Jefferson had the guy pressed up against a car with his arm twisted behind his back.

"Why you following us?" Jefferson demanded.

"I don't know what you're talking about," the man snarled, trying to twist himself free. "Ain't nobody following you. Let me go."

Based on his height and clothing, he appeared to be the guy Jefferson had described earlier.

"You're lyin'!" Jefferson yelled at him. "I saw you in that Honda when we first drove in here. Then you followed us into the theater and I saw you walk by the restaurant too. So what's up?"

"Get offa me! This is assault!"

We had now attracted a small crowd.

I tugged hard on the tail of Jefferson's shirt. "Are you crazy? What are you doing? Let him go!"

Jefferson ignored me. Using his body weight to keep the man pinned against the car, he dug out a wallet from the guy's back pocket. He flipped it open and studied the license.

"Antoine Davis, I don't know who told you to follow us, but I have your name and your address," Jefferson said. "And I'm not going to forget it. If I ever see you within fifty feet of me or my wife again, I'ma beat you down."

He pulled the man up toward him, then hurled him between two cars. He landed on all fours. Jefferson flung the man's wallet, hitting him in the head with it. He grabbed it and scurried off.

"Jefferson, are you crazy? Why did—"

A motorized cart carrying two security guards screeched to a stop just in front of us.

"What's going on here?" The guard on the passenger side jumped out first. A dark-skinned Hispanic, he was barely five feet.

"That punk grabbed my wife's purse," Jefferson said, breathless.

"That's not the report we got," the man challenged, puffing out his chest.

Jefferson tugged at the sleeves of his shirt. "I don't know what report you got, but that's what happened."

The other guard, taller and heftier, had a harder time climbing out of the cart. "Looks to me like your wife is holding her purse."

"That's because I got it back," Jefferson lied. "He grabbed it just as we stepped off the elevator. Maybe we need to sue this place for inadequate security."

An apprehensive look ping-ponged between the two guards. The threat of a lawsuit seemed to spark an immediate change in their attitude.

The first guard turned his attention to me. "Are you okay, ma'am? We'll need to take a report."

"Forget it," Jefferson said. "We're leaving." He grabbed my hand and started tugging me toward the car.

I waited until Jefferson had started the engine before erupting. "Are you nuts? They have cameras in here! You could be facing assault charges!"

"That dude ain't filing no police report," Jefferson said, backing his Chrysler 300 out of the stall. "*He* was following *us*, not the other way around. And I bet it has something to do with that Big Buy case. That was probably the same guy who attacked Benjamin."

"You don't know that."

"And you don't know that it wasn't him. You need to drop that case. 'Cuz the next time somebody's following you, I may not be around to save you."

CHAPTER 36

"I ran into a little problem."

The man was not prepared to hear this. Not less than a week after his other guy had screwed up.

"What kind of problem?" His voice was stretched tight enough to snap.

"Um...they made me."

"They?"

The assignment was simple. Follow Vernetta Henderson. Don't talk to her. Don't ask her about the Big Buy documents. Just follow her. Who was this *they*?

"She was with her husband. And, um...there was a little mishap."

The man pinched the bridge of his nose until it hurt. "I need specifics."

The caller, his voice shrinking in volume, recounted how the target's husband had spotted him in the garage at the Howard Hughes Promenade.

The man's fingers drummed lightly on the desk as he stared out of the window at nothing. "I said I wanted specifics," he snapped.

"He grabbed me, okay. Took my license. But it's not a big deal. I was carrying a fake."

This was indeed a big deal. A very big deal. This kind of thing was not supposed to happen on his watch. He provided the highest echelon of surveillance services. The people who hired his company had a lot at stake. Screw-ups like this were unacceptable.

"How in the hell did he make you? That place is usually packed."

"I don't know. The guy is good."

"Or maybe you're just an idiot."

He would not be mentioning this incident to his client. Just as he had not reported the botched break-in and assault at the Center for Justice. If Benjamin Cohen had been killed, his client would have been linked to a murder.

The man closed his eyes. It was good that this conversation had not taken place in person. He would have assaulted the clown himself.

"I...I don't know how it happened," the caller stuttered.

"It happened because you're incompetent," the man spit into the phone.

That's what he got for relying on amateurs, something he only did when his regular crew was unavailable. He pressed a button, ending the call. He would deal with this lackey later.

This was very disappointing. The man had hoped that the documents could have been easily retrieved. A search of Cohen's office had been a bust. They'd already crossed Phillip Peterman off the list. Three days after his girlfriend's death, they had snuck into the house late one night and searched every crevice of the place, even though it was still roped off as a crime scene.

Based on his intelligence, it was clear that Ida Lopez and Olivia Jackson didn't have them. That left their attorney, Vernetta Henderson. Searching her office without being detected was too risky. Until they had a feasible plan, he just wanted to keep an eye on her.

The man took a long, deep breath. If he could not find the mystery documents, it was not the end of the world. But it would very much please his client and the man took great pride in always delivering, even under the most challenging circumstances.

And this one was indeed turning out to be quite a challenge.

CHAPTER 37

"Rounding up plaintiffs is hard work," I said to Benjamin, who was sitting across the table from me at the Center for Justice.

"No pain, no gain," he mumbled, rubbing his eyes.

For the past four hours we'd been conducting telephone interviews with Big Buy employees from all across the state. We had a thirty-minute break before the arrival of fifteen women from three different Big Buy stores in Los Angeles County.

Benjamin's bleary eyes told me that he was just as tired as I was. Purplish scars were still visible on the side of his face, but hair now covered the stitches near his hairline.

Both of us were stunned by the flood of calls we received after Olivia's exile from the store. Suddenly, employees who'd shunned her were applauding her as a hero. Dozens of female employees had contacted us about joining the lawsuit. We were now seriously considering refiling the case as a class action.

A local law firm with class action expertise was interested in partnering with us, but wanted to see what evidence we had first. So far, our interviews told us there was a clear pattern and practice of discrimination at Big Buy.

Benjamin and I spent a few minutes comparing notes from our interviews.

"I spoke to a woman who worked at a store in Bakersfield," Benjamin said, perusing the notes on his legal pad. "She claims a regional manager told her women weren't fit for management because God made men to rule and females to serve."

"Was he trying to be funny?"

"She certainly didn't think so. That was the response she got when she asked him to submit her name for a promotion to department manager. He said his views were backed up by the Bible."

I lowered my head. "It's hard to believe this kind of stuff could even come out of someone's mouth."

I thought about Special and the Community of Islam. Was this the kind of sexist thinking she was buying into?

We traded a few more stories, then I ran down to the lobby to pick up a pizza I had ordered. On my way back, I grabbed two Cokes from the lunchroom vending machine.

"So you really think we can pull off a class action?" Benjamin asked, popping open one of the Coke cans.

"Sure, provided we find the right firm to partner with. There's no way we could handle all the work involved in a class action by ourselves."

I was on my second piece of pizza but noticed that Benjamin hadn't eaten one. I was about to ask why, when it hit me. Benjamin only ate Kosher food.

I covered my eyes in embarrassment. "I'm sorry about the pizza."

"No big deal. I'm not really hungry."

"Can I ask you something?" I said, my voice full of curiosity. "If you can only eat Kosher food, how can you drink that Coke?"

He smiled, then picked up the can and pointed to a symbol that looked like a circle with the letter *U* inside. "See that?"

I examined my own Coke more closely. "Yeah."

"That's the symbol of the Union of Orthodox Jewish Congregations," Benjamin explained. "Which means this Coke is Kosher. It's the oldest organization that certifies Kosher products. You'll find it on a lot of things."

Between Benjamin and Special, I was learning quite a bit about other faiths. I continued to eat in silence.

"So is Jefferson still upset about you staying on the case?" Benjamin asked.

"Yep. Especially after he thought that guy at the Promenade was following us."

"How do you know for sure that he wasn't?"

Actually, I wasn't sure. But I refused to buy into the fear.

"I'll be honest. What happened to you really scared me. But not enough to drop this case. We don't have the documents, and hopefully whoever wants them knows that by now."

My iPhone buzzed. I glanced at the display, rolled my eyes and hit the *decline* button.

"That's Lamarr bugging me again. I'm working with an appellate attorney to get his notice of appeal filed. But it's highly unlikely that he'll get a new trial. He's having a hard time understanding that he'll eventually have to pay Tonisha two-million dollars, plus interest. He can't seem to get it in his head that we lost."

Benjamin's face grew pensive. "And what if *we* lose?"

"Anything's possible with litigation," I said. "But I don't see how we can. The evidence we've been collecting clearly shows that Big Buy has an ingrained culture of discriminatory practices toward women."

An hour later, only three of the fifteen Big Buy employees we were expecting had shown up for our meeting. Not even Olivia had shown up. I was bummed by the turnout but didn't dare show it.

"I want to thank you for agreeing to meet with us," I began. "Suing your employer isn't an easy thing to do. I know that it was a tough decision for you to come here today."

The women focused their attention on me and had barely said a word to each other.

"What we've discovered is a good-old-boys' network in effect at Big Buy where the men promote their friends, who happen to be other men," I continued. "Our class action lawsuit will challenge that system because it's unlawful."

"There's definitely a good-old-boy thing going on at the Gardena store," said Marcia Watkins, the only white woman present. She had six years' tenure with the company.

Robyn Gant, a bubbly African-American sitting next to her, nodded. "I second that."

Robyn's gregarious, opinionated personality reminded me of Olivia. She had teetered into the room wearing expensive shoes that looked like stilts. I wasn't surprised when I learned that she was the architect of the work slowdown.

"What exactly is a class action?" asked Janice Miller, the other African-American sales associate brave enough to show up.

Benjamin decided to field that question. "It's basically a way to address similar claims involving a large number of people in one lawsuit, rather than everyone filing their own individual case."

"But how can we do that?" Janice asked. "We don't even all work at the same store." She looked over at Marcia. "The store manager who discriminated against her didn't discriminate against me."

"We'll be showing that there's a pattern and practice of discrimination that's condoned at the upper levels of the company," I explained.

Marcia inhaled and wrung her hands. "When my boss finds out that I'm suing the company, I'm going to be scared to death to go to work."

"You shouldn't be," Benjamin said. "It's unlawful for Big Buy to retaliate against you for suing them."

"That doesn't mean they still won't do it," Janice pointed out. "Look at what they did to Olivia."

"And we were also able to quickly get her back to work with no repercussions."

Janice was the only one taking copious notes, which gave me a bad vibe.

"According to my husband," she continued, "the only people who really make any money off of a class action are the attorneys."

Benjamin caught my eye. I could tell he was thinking the same thing I was. Janice sounded like trouble.

"If you're a lead plaintiff, you'll receive more than the other plaintiffs," I said, intentionally side-stepping her comment because she was right. The legal fees we recovered would likely be far more than what the plaintiffs received individually.

But Benjamin and I weren't doing this for a big payday. This lawsuit was personal for us. We wanted to put an end to the way Big Buy treated its female employees.

"I could certainly use a big settlement check," Robyn said. "I saw a new pair of Christian Louboutins I'd love to have. And I'm definitely up for a promotion."

"Me too," Marcia chimed in.

"Do all of us need to have our names on the lawsuit?" Janice asked.

"No. We just need two or three women to be class representatives. Only their names will appear on the front page of the complaint."

"You can definitely use my name," Robyn said. "I ain't scared of them."

"Doesn't a lawsuit take a long time?" Janice asked.

"It can," I said.

"My cousin had a disability case against his company. He won at trial, but it's been a year and he still hasn't seen a dime."

I paused, trying to figure out the best way to combat Janice's negativity, when Olivia walked in.

"Sorry, I'm so late everybody," she said, out of breath. "I had a last-minute meeting at the church. I would've called but my cell ran out of juice."

"I'm glad you're here," I said, pulling out a chair for her. "We were just talking about the challenges of filing a lawsuit like this. I know it hasn't been easy for you. Why don't you talk a little bit about your experiences?"

Olivia sucked in a long breath. "No, it certainly hasn't been easy. But I refuse to sit back and let them get away with this. If you all join this lawsuit with me, it's going to mean better working conditions for us and every woman who comes through the door after us."

The women nodded. Olivia's frankness had resonated with them in a way my assurances had not.

"I don't know about your relationship with God," Olivia said, "but mine is solid. And I have nothing but faith that He'll help us through this, every step of the way."

CHAPTER 38

Phillip refused to put his life on hold a minute longer. Screw those asshole cops. He was in desperate need of cash, plus he was dying to get laid.

He drove slowly down his street, then circled the block twice before finally beginning to relax a bit. On his third lap, he bypassed the house and headed for the grocery store three blocks away. Once inside the store, he meandered in the bread aisle, pretended to read the label on a loaf of bread, then pulled out his throwaway cell phone.

"I think we're good," he whispered into the telephone. "The back door is unlocked. I'll be there in twenty minutes."

Phillip took his time shopping for items he didn't really need, then headed home. He found her sitting on the living room couch, legs crossed, dressed in a brightly colored kimono that barely covered her crotch. Damn she was sexy.

"Nice to see you again," he said, giving her a seductive grin.

He pulled her to her feet, gripping her ass as he kissed her.

"Shouldn't you still be grieving?" she purred, tossing a thick mane of hair to the side.

"I am grieving," Phillip mumbled between kisses. "And this is exactly what I need to cure it." He buried his nose between her breasts, then sucked on her left nipple, which prompted a low moan.

They didn't bother to disengage as they walked lockstep into the bedroom. While Phillip stripped down to his boxers, she sat cross-legged on the bed, propping her back against the headboard, watching him.

He walked over to a large chest in the corner of the room and started rummaging through a stack of DVDs. Judi had never liked watching porn.

"I'll let you choose," he said with a wink. "*Mr. Rockhard is Cumming* or *Riding Bareback?*"

"*Mr. Rockhard,*" she laughed. "I like the sound of that."

He removed the disk and tossed the DVD cover on the bed.

"Big Buy's Board of Directors would die if they knew their TV pitchman was addicted to porn."

Phillip winked at her over his shoulder. "I won't tell 'em if you don't."

He placed the disk into the DVD player, then crawled into bed next to her. She took a joint from her purse, lit it and passed it to him.

He took a long hit, then held it up to her lips. Marijuana was his drug of choice, but he did not indulge frequently. Other than beer, he wasn't much of a drinker either. He'd seen how booze and drugs had aged some of Hollywood's finest. That wasn't going to happen to him.

Phillip stared thoughtfully at the TV screen. "Maybe I should do porn."

His lover smiled and patted his groin. "You certainly have the equipment for it."

He liked the feel of her hand, but wasn't ready to get down to business just yet. Where women were concerned, Phillip preferred to call the shots. In the beginning, Judi had played along, eager to follow his lead. He wondered how long it would be before his current lay would turn on him and get mouthy.

The performance on screen had obviously gotten his guest all revved up. She started gently massaging his crotch through the hole in his boxers.

He placed his hand on top of hers, stilling her movements. He was stone stiff and ready to roll, but he had a big surprise for her and it wasn't between his legs.

"I have a present for you," he said at the same time his lips took another taste of her nipple.

"I can see that," his companion whispered, raking her manicured nails along his erection.

He winked at her. "I think you'll want this even more."

Her hand stopped moving and her playful expression turned serious.

"You found them!?"

Phillip nodded and grinned.

"I thought you'd given up looking for them. Where were they?"

"Judi definitely did a good job of hiding them. I was cleaning out her car and found them in the trunk, underneath the carpeting where the spare tire was supposed to be."

"Oh, my God! I can't believe you found them. So show me!"

Phillip leaned across the bed, opened the bottom drawer of the nightstand and pulled out a thick packet of documents.

He dropped it into her lap. "As promised."

Delight crept across the woman's face. "Oh, my God," she repeated, pulling the documents from the package. "I've been dying to see these."

She took her time studying the first page, then flipped through the remaining pages with increasing speed. Deep worry lines lodged across her forehead.

"So how bad is it?" Phillip asked after a few minutes.

She looked up at him. "You didn't read them?"

"I took a look, but none of it made any sense to me."

"They look like earnings reports."

Phillip leaned over and nuzzled her neck. "So where's that reward you promised me?"

She smiled, then placed the documents inside her overnight bag on the floor.

"You most definitely deserve a reward." She playfully pushed him down on the bed, straddling his body.

"Uh, this isn't exactly the kind of reward we talked about."

The woman giggled. "Is this the only copy?"

"Of course."

"So how much do you want?"

"Just a little something to tide me over until I can get the cops off my back and collect on Judi's insurance."

She stared intently into his eyes. "Will you actually be able to get the cops off your back?"

Phillip's entire body tightened. He knew what she was really asking.

"I already told you, I had nothing to do with Judi's death. You don't believe me?"

"I wouldn't be here if I didn't believe you." The doubt dancing in her eyes contradicted her words. "So how much is a little something?"

"Fifty grand should do it."

She grimaced. "I'll need some time to—"

Phillip reached across her body and grabbed her bag from the floor. He retrieved the documents and shoved them back into the nightstand. "Maybe I should just give them to Judi's co-workers. Or perhaps to their attorney."

"No need to do that." She raked his chest hairs with her nails. "C'mon, give them back."

"I will. *After* I get my money."

A child-like pout clouded her face.

Phillip noticed that her nipples had grown hard, which aroused him more than the thought of the fifty grand he knew she could and would pay.

"We'll work out the precise terms later," he said, "After we're done."

He pulled her back on top of him.

"Can I really trust you?" she asked, bending to give him a kiss that was all tongue. "My career is over if anyone connects me to these documents."

"Sure, you can trust me." Phillip gripped her firm butt with both hands and rammed himself deep inside her.

About as much as I can trust you.

CHAPTER 39

The second I stepped into the house, something didn't feel right. For one, I didn't hear the television blasting play-by-play from a sports announcer.

I stuck my head into the den anyway. Jefferson wasn't there. I walked down the hallway toward the bedroom and stumbled to a stop in the doorway. Jefferson was sitting up in bed reading. Not a blueprint or a sports magazine, but a book.

"What are you reading?" I asked, kicking off my pumps.

Jefferson held up the cover for me to see. "*The Black Man and the Community of Islam.*"

It took a minute for this to compute. "And where'd you get that?"

"You know where I got it. Clayton."

"I didn't realize you two had become so buddy-buddy."

"There's a lotta stuff I do that you don't know about."

"Oh, yeah. Like what?"

Jefferson laughed. "Not like that. Anyway, we ain't buddy-buddy. But the guy is so passionate about this Community of Islam stuff, I just wanted to check it out for myself."

"And?"

"It's pretty interesting."

I sat down on the edge of the bed. "What's so interesting about it?"

"The chapter I'm reading now is basically a comparison of the Bible and the Holy Qur'an."

"So you're questioning the Bible now?"

"No. I'm just investigating. This book was written in the nineteen-sixties and it's still relevant today. Nothing much has changed as far as black folks are concerned. In fact, we're probably worse off."

"You're kidding me, right?"

"Nope."

"Did you forget that there's a black man in the White House?"

"Yeah, that's cool, but black unemployment is at fifteen percent, brothers are still going to prison at a rate six times higher than whites, and in some states, fifty percent of black males don't graduate from high school. Something's wrong with that picture."

"So when did you become so well-versed in black sociology?"

"Clayton's been kicking me down with the facts. I never knew how heavy that brother was."

"Sounds like you're thinking about trading Christianity for Islam too."

I waited for Jefferson to flatly reject that possibility. Instead, he continued reading.

"Did you hear what I just said?"

"Yeah, I heard you. I'm not even focusing on the Christian versus Islam thing right now. I just like the fact that these brothers are all about uplifting black people. You're always complaining about me never reading. Well, now I am."

I didn't have a comeback for that.

"There's a lot of knowledge in here," Jefferson said, tapping the book with his index finger. "You should check it out."

I was too exhausted to engage in the pros and cons of Islam versus Christianity. I stood up and headed for the bathroom.

"By the way, Clayton was telling me about a lecture at the mosque Friday night. I told him we'd come."

I stuck my head back into the room. "You made that commitment without checking with me first?"

"Don't even trip. After all the boring law firm crap you've dragged me to, don't even try to get out of doing something I wanna do." He turned a page in the book. "I would think you'd want to support your friend. We can all go out to dinner afterward."

I was not thrilled about my husband's sudden infatuation with Islam. I viewed his interest as a rejection of my faith, our faith. But he was right about always supporting me.

"They may not want to go out to dinner," I said, walking back into the room. "Things are a little strained between them right now."

Jefferson placed the book face-down on the bed. "I spoke to Clayton earlier today. He never indicated that anything was up."

"From Clayton's perspective, it probably isn't. He told Special he wanted them to be celibate until they got married. Special's having a little trouble with that."

Jefferson whistled long and low. "Damn. I knew the brother was serious about the Community, but that's a sacrifice for your ass."

I couldn't help laughing. "I guess you couldn't be an unmarried Muslim man then, huh?"

"Not if it means giving up pus—"

I raised my hand, cutting him off. "I get it."

Jefferson shook his head. "I most definitely have a newfound respect for that brother."

CHAPTER 40

For the second time in a matter of days, Girlie received an emergency call summoning her to Big Buy's headquarters.

Janice Miller, a sales associate, and Helen Sheridan, the store manager, were waiting in the general counsel's office. Girlie didn't know why the CEO wasn't present, but she didn't ask since she preferred it this way.

Janice, a short, pear-shaped woman, looked to be in her late thirties, but you could never tell with black women.

"As I told you on the phone," Evelyn Kimble, the general counsel explained, "it appears that Vernetta Henderson is moving forward with her class action. Go ahead and tell Ms. Cortez everything you told me," she said to Janice.

The woman's eyes flickered around the room.

"Don't worry," Girlie assured her. "Everything you tell us will be kept in the strictest confidence." *Unless I need to use it.*

"Well, I got this call from Ms. Henderson a few days ago," Janice said.

"Were you contacted at home or at work?"

"She called me on my cell and left a message. I called her back during my break."

"How did she get your number?"

"Another employee, Robyn Gant, gave it to her. She was the one who got everyone all riled up about Olivia being suspended."

"Did Ms. Gant have your permission to give out your number?"

"Uh, well, kind of. After what happened to Olivia, a lot of the women were talking about joining her lawsuit." Janice turned to the general counsel. "Of course, I never planned to sue, mind you. I was just playing along so I could find out what they were up to so I could let you know."

The woman was the biggest brownnoser Girlie had come across in a while.

"Okay," Girlie said. "Go on."

Janice retrieved Vernetta's business card from her purse and slid it across the table to Girlie. "She started asking me all kinds of questions about the store."

"Like what?"

"Whether I was happy working at Big Buy. Whether I felt I had ever been passed over for a promotion. Whether I thought the company discriminated against women."

"And what did you tell her?"

Janice responded with a big cheesy smile. "I told her everything was fine as far as I was concerned."

"How long was the conversation?"

"That first conversation? Not even five minutes. I lied and said I had to get back to work."

"So how did you get her business card?" Girlie asked.

"She invited me to a meeting at the Center for Justice on Crenshaw. She said she was filing a class action lawsuit against Big Buy and wanted to discuss the case with a few female employees."

Helen, the store manager, appeared ready to bounce out of her chair. "Why didn't you come to me when you got that first call?"

Girlie held up her hand. She didn't want to scare this woman off before they got all the information they needed.

"Don't worry about that, Janice," Girlie said. "I'm glad you went to the meeting. Tell me what happened there."

"Only two other employees showed up besides me. Robyn Gant and Marcia Watkins. Olivia Jackson came later. A bunch of employees were supposed to come, but they didn't."

Ethically speaking, Girlie should have asked Janice if she signed a retainer agreement with Vernetta. If she had, this conversation was barred by the attorney-client privilege. But Girlie wasn't known for letting legal obligations get in the way of her personal ethics.

"I'd like to know everything said in that meeting," Girlie continued.

Janice gave them a play-by-play, then pulled several pieces of lined yellow paper from her purse.

"I didn't feel right about being there," Janice said. "So I took good notes so I could report everything back to you. I also wrote down the names of the sales associates who said they were coming but didn't show up."

She handed the pages to Girlie.

"Thank you," Girlie said. "This is going to be very helpful."

This would give her a good idea of which Big Buy stores Vernetta had poisoned.

"Do you have any idea whether Ida Lopez might be involved?" Girlie asked.

"Nope. Since she got that promotion, Ida's been a total company girl. She barely even speaks to Olivia anymore. I didn't think it was right what they were doing," Janice continued. "Ms. Henderson was trying to entice us with money. She said the plaintiffs who have their name on the complaint would get more money. But I told her not as much money as the attorneys get."

"That's exactly right," Girlie said. "You make sure your co-workers understand that. Ms. Henderson might be talking to you about discrimination, but she's only filing this lawsuit for what she can get out of it."

Evelyn dismissed Janice, but the woman seemed reluctant to leave.

"Is there something else you have to tell us?" Girlie asked.

"Uh…well," Janice said, "I was wondering if there're going to be any more promotions soon. I think I'm ready to be promoted to manager of the Cosmetics Department."

The store manager grunted. "Why don't you just—"

Girlie raised her hand again. She could definitely use a snitch like Janice to her advantage. Girlie believed in rewarding people for their loyalty. She was going to urge Evelyn to find some way to promote the woman.

"We're definitely going to consider that," Girlie said with a smile. "In the meantime, you keep your ears open and let us know if you hear anything you think we might need to know."

CHAPTER 41

Special was trying her darnedest to be a model Muslim woman. Dating a man as fine as Clayton and having to forego sex was hard enough. But this was a bit much.

She glanced at the gathering of women in the small room at the mosque and wished she was someplace, anyplace else.

"Welcome, sister."

A young, soft-spoken woman greeted Special, then introduced her to everyone in the room. Most of the women were friendly enough, but she already had enough friends. Attending the women's meeting, however, was a mandatory part of her training for becoming a model Muslim wife.

Of the twenty or so women present, there was a mix of modern and traditional Muslim dress. Several women wore business suits. Special was dressed in a knee-length skirt and white blouse. She didn't feel like covering her head, but had a scarf in her purse just in case it was required.

The women arranged their chairs in a semi-circle with an older woman at the top of the circle. She had creamy, maple-colored skin and a gentleness about her that immediately put Special at ease.

"I'd like to welcome Sister Special," Mother Jackie, the elder woman began. "She's the intended of one of our most dynamic young men, Brother Clayton. She's new to the Community, so we need to make her feel welcome."

Akila, a woman sitting directly across from Special, had attitude all over her face. Special heard from another sister that Akila had expressed an interest in meeting Clayton before finding out he was engaged.

"One of the reasons for our meeting is to help Sister Special understand a wife's obligations as dictated by the Almighty Allah," Mother Jackie explained.

Akila addressed Special directly. "Sister, under Muslim law the female is her husband's helpmate. He is head of his family. We are gladly subservient to him because—"

"Hold up," Special interrupted. "I don't mean any disrespect, but why do we have to be subservient? Why can't we be equals and help lift each other up?"

The temperature in the room fell ten degrees as the other women eyed each other in dismay.

"I see y'all looking at each other out of the corner of your eyes," Special boldly continued. "I just don't understand why we have to consider ourselves less than a man."

"We don't question Allah's teachings," Akila sniffed.

Mother Jackie raised both hands palms out as if to hold down the tension in the room. "We understand your concerns and we're here to answer any questions you may have. In Islam, obedience is our first rule. Obedience to Allah and obedience to our husbands. And while you may have concerns at this point, as you continue to grow in your faith, Allah will reveal the truth to you. There is a place for women in the Community. But foremost, you should understand that honoring and serving your husband does not make you less than him."

Special pursed her lips and folded her arms. "I'm sorry. That just don't make sense to me. Women fought for equal rights. This is like taking ten steps backward."

This time, there were audible sighs along with shakes of the head.

"We don't think less of ourselves." Mother Jackie's tone was firm, but gentle. "Supporting our husbands does not take anything away from us as women. I have some readings for you that will help enlighten you."

"Sister Special," said a voice to her right, "I understand your frustrations. I was raised in the Church of God and Christ and I work in the corporate world."

Special turned to face the speaker, a woman named Carol. Special was relieved to be hearing from someone who could see things from her vantage point.

"When I met my husband and found out he was a minister in the Community, I never thought we would make it. He just asked me to be open to the teachings and once I did that, I was enlightened."

"But how can you come from corporate America and deal with someone telling you to be subservient?"

"Just as the media has painted all Muslims as violent extremists," Carol said, "you're relying on the Western interpretation of Islam as sexist. You'll see many women in leadership roles in the Community of Islam."

Another woman, Malia, spoke up. She was covered from head to toe in powder blue. Special could still tell from the small swatch of her face that she was a beautiful woman.

"If more of our people embraced the teachings of Islam, we wouldn't see our young girls walking around looking like hookers. I don't view Islam as making me less than a man. My husband honors me and in turn, I honor him."

The other women murmured their agreement.

"You're also forgetting that the Christian faith can be just as sexist as Islam is perceived to be," Carol pointed out. "My aunt graduated from divinity school and set out to become a minister in a Southern Baptist church. You want to talk about sexist? Just listen to a few of her stories."

Special nodded. She was well aware of the imperfections of Christianity.

"Knowledge is held extremely high in the Muslim faith," Carol continued. "The Holy Qur'an teaches us to seek knowledge from the cradle to the grave. And that is what I urge you to do."

Mother Jackie reached over and squeezed Special's hand. "What we're saying to you, my sister, is please come to us with your eyes open and your heart receptive. Judge us for what we are, not what non-Muslims perceive us to be."

CHAPTER 42

Girlie didn't like the lack of enthusiasm in Eli's voice when he'd called that morning asking to meet with her. She assumed his investigation probably hadn't uncovered any earth-shattering information.

She welcomed Eli into her office and directed him to a chair in front of her desk, rather than her pink couch. Today her focus was all about business.

"Got anything good for me?"

She placed her clasped hands on the desk and waited as he pulled three red folders from a beat-up leather briefcase.

Eli shrugged. "A few interesting tidbits. Unfortunately, nothing earth-shattering enough to make or break your case."

He handed her a folder labeled *Background Checks*.

"Olivia Jackson didn't have anything unusual in her background. She spends all of her free time at Hope in Christ Community Church in Compton. No kids, an equally religious husband who teaches history at Centennial High School in Compton. Nothing much in Ida Lopez's past either. She has a lot of debt. Lives paycheck to paycheck."

"Ida's out of the case now," Girlie said. "Anything on Benjamin Cohen or Vernetta Henderson?"

"Not really, both of 'em are pretty clean. The Jewish dude basically lives for his job. The worst thing I saw Vernetta Henderson do was purchase a couple of bootleg movies on the way into the beauty shop. But I have to say, I was a bit surprised to see her at a Community of Islam meeting."

Girlie's spine straightened at that news. "That black separatist group?"

"I don't think they would describe themselves that way, but yeah."

"So she's a member?"

"I'm not a hundred percent sure. Her best friend definitely is. Here's a snapshot of Vernetta and her husband standing outside the mosque."

Girlie stared at the photograph as Eli handed her another folder labeled *Big Buy*.

"You didn't ask for this," Eli said, "but I stumbled across some interesting information about your client. The company's about to be bought out by the Welson Corporation."

Girlie looked up from the picture. "That merger is supposed to be top secret. I can't believe you found out about it."

"Damn!" Eli slapped his thigh. "So you already knew about it? Did you also know that the day the deal closes the CEO will walk away with one-hundred-and-twenty-five mil?"

Girlie whistled. "*That* I didn't know."

She had figured Rita Richards-Kimble would get a windfall from the deal, but nothing that massive. Now she understood why the CEO was so concerned about making sure the case didn't turn into a class action. She was worried that it might kill the deal.

"There's more," Eli said. "I didn't run across any information about those missing documents, but why don't you open that folder and skip ahead to page three of my report."

Girlie did as instructed. She read the first paragraph, blinked, then read it again.

"Is this true?" she asked, looking across her desk at Eli.

He held up his right hand. "Nothing but the truth, so help me God."

"And you confirmed it."

"Absolutely."

"Wow," Girlie said, placing a finger to her smiling lips. "This is excellent information. It'll be very, very useful to me."

The investigator glowed with pride.

"And now I have a follow-up assignment for you," Girlie said, pulling an envelope with Eli's cash payment from inside her purse.

"I want you to find out everything you can about Vernetta Henderson's involvement with the Community of Islam."

CHAPTER 43

When Special heard the heavy pounding on her front door, she already knew who was standing on the other side.

As soon as she swung open the door, she could tell from Clayton's hooded eyes and dour expression that he had been filled in on the women's meeting at the mosque. That conniving-ass Akila had probably called him the second it ended.

Special stuck her head out of the door and looked in both directions before letting him in. "Are you sure you wanna come in? Don't we need a chaperone?"

"That's not funny," Clayton said, brushing past her.

"So what's up?" She wasn't in the mood to be subservient. If he started fussing at her, she planned to fire right back at him.

Clayton looked disapprovingly at her body. "We need to talk. But first you need to go put on something more appropriate."

Special glanced down at her body. She was wearing shorts and a tight-fitting tank top. She was about to remind Clayton that this was *her* body and *her* house and she could dress any way *she* wanted, when an idea popped into her head.

"Okay," she said with a sinister grin. "Give me a second."

Five minutes later, Special stalked back into the living room.

"Is this *appropriate* enough for you?"

She was now dressed in a pair of baggy sweatpants and had pulled her shorts on over them. Her burgundy-and-gold USC sweatshirt was underneath a black sweater that was buttoned up to her chin. The scarf wrapped around her head made her look like Little Red Riding hood pretending to be a mummy.

Clayton's eyes blazed. "Don't make fun of my faith."

"I don't know what you're talking about. You told me to cover up and that's what I did."

If Clayton's faith was everything he claimed it to be, she should have been able to walk into the room butt naked without it fazing him.

"You know women aren't required to cover their heads at home."

Special snatched off the scarf and tossed it on the coffee table.

Clayton sat down on the couch. "Have a seat," he said tightly.

She took the far end of the couch, facing him, her arms locked across her chest.

"I love you," Clayton began. "You know that, right?"

Damn! She hated the way he could aim straight at her heart. The anger built up inside of her started to seep away. She nodded her response for fear that if she moved her lips, a cry might escape.

"Maybe before we got back together I should've told you how serious I was about the Community. I don't think I gave much thought about how hard this might be for you. You're pretty outspoken. Frankly, that's one of the things I like most about you."

She was on the verge of blubbering any minute.

"I know that this is *my* chosen faith, not yours. I understand that and I'm trying to be patient with you. But what I don't understand and what I will not accept is you disrespecting me and disrespecting Allah. Akila told me how you acted down at the mosque today."

The swell of emotions she had felt just seconds ago melted into mush. An explosion of words—cuss words—danced on the tip of her tongue.

"I love you just as much as you love me," Special said. "The only difference is, I don't expect you to change overnight and—"

"I don't expect you to change overnight. I—"

"Hold up." Special raised her hand high above her head. "I let you talk without interruption and I would appreciate it if you showed me the same courtesy."

Clayton looked away and rubbed his chin. If one of his Muslim brothers were around, they'd probably tell him he didn't know how to handle his woman. But this was *her* house and she was going to speak *her* piece.

"I don't know what you heard about that meeting, but it wasn't my intent to disrespect anybody. I just had some questions and I asked them. I'm not comfortable being told that I need to be subservient to a man. I will love you and support you and lift you up, but not at the expense of my own self-worth."

Clayton stared straight past her.

"I'm done," she said. "You can talk now."

He rubbed his chin again and looked into her eyes for a long time before speaking. "I'm not sure this is going to work out."

Tell me something I don't know. Special had been wanting to say those very words herself.

"Okay, fine." She stood up. "So you want your ring back?"

"This ain't about the ring. This is about us. This is about whether we can really do this. I feel like we're at opposite ends of a rope, pulling in different directions. We need to be pulling in the same direction."

"Maybe you need to put a little slack in your rope and I'd be willing to meet you halfway."

"There's no halfway with Allah. I'm committed to my faith and I need my woman to be equally committed."

"Well, I have my own faith."

"That's funny. I barely remember you going to church. And you certainly agreed to convert to Islam without even a second thought. So you couldn't have been too much of a Christian."

"That's because I love you."

"But the question is, do you love Allah more?"

"Why can't you just love your God and let me love mine?"

"The Holy Qur'an says a man is supposed to lead his family. I can't do that if I'm going to the mosque and you're off at some church."

They locked eyes in a wordless standoff.

"So, I guess this means we're breaking up," Special said, anxious to get it over with.

"I didn't say that."

"So what *are* you saying?" Both hands were on her hips now. She had no idea why she was pushing the issue. She didn't want to break up.

"I don't know what I'm saying."

"Then I guess that says it all." She started to pull the ring from her finger.

"Don't do that." He reached up and grabbed her hand. "Keep the ring. I want you to have it."

Clayton rose from the couch and headed for the door. When he reached it, he turned back to face her. "Maybe we should have a hug for the road."

"You sure we don't have to run down to the mosque and get somebody's permission first?"

He ignored her crack and wrapped his arms around her, holding her close. Special folded into him, reveling in the security of his embrace, the comfort of his scent. They remained glued together for a long, long time. So long, that Special felt his erection press against her.

When she tried to pull away, Clayton held on tighter. He finally leaned down and pressed his lips to hers and she eagerly kissed him back. Seconds later, his hands groped their way through her layers of clothing until he found flesh. Clayton quickly stripped off her bulky sweater, helped her shimmy out of her sweatshirt and unhooked her bra.

Special stood before him, bare-chested, as he gently cupped her breasts, licking them with the slow, careful precision of a cat cleaning its fur. She moaned and leaned her head back, relishing the sound and feel of Clayton's lips and tongue pleasuring her neck and chest. She let out a low, guttural moan when his tongue began to slowly encircle her right nipple.

Clayton abruptly stepped away from her, but only long enough to hoist her off the ground and cart her down the hallway in the direction of the bedroom.

CHAPTER 44

I pulled my Land Cruiser to a stop in front of the Center for Justice and scanned the cars and vans parked along the street. We'd flooded the media with press releases about our class action and I had hoped a couple of reporters would show. I happily counted five local TV news vans.

I hopped out and hurried past the receptionist into Benjamin's office. He had a big smile on his face. "Can you believe it? The conference room is packed with reporters!"

"This is wonderful," I said.

"They're all talking about the sick-in and the work slowdown. That's what got them here."

"How many of the women showed up?"

"Just Olivia, Robyn and Marcia," he said with a shrug.

We had hoped more employees would show, but I'd rather have three solid fighters than fifteen shaky ones.

I followed Benjamin into a small office next door where the women were waiting.

"I'm really proud of you," I said, giving each of them a hug. "What you're doing isn't just for yourselves, but for other women too. Let's go fight this fight."

The five of us walked single file into the conference room. Camera shutters clicked and lights flashed on, brightening up the room. We sat down at the conference table with the three women in the middle, Benjamin and I on either side of them. I introduced everyone, then gave Benjamin a nod.

"Thank you for coming today," he said, a nervous quiver in his voice. "I'm Benjamin Cohen, Executive Director of the Center for Justice. As you know, the Center has been in this community for more than fifty years, fighting for the rights of those who don't have the resources to fight for themselves. The lawsuit we're filing today against Big Buy department stores is a cause the Center for Justice is proud to take on and so is attorney Vernetta Henderson, who will be litigating the case, along with the Usher, Davidson law firm. I'll let Vernetta tell you more about the case."

He slid the group of microphones to my end of the table.

"I've litigated dozens of discrimination cases in my career," I began. "But none as egregious as this one. Big Buy's treatment of women is not only discriminatory, it's archaic. During the course of this litigation, we're going to produce evidence which shows that the company blatantly refuses to pay women equal wages for the same job that men perform.

A female reporter from KNX news radio grimaced and shook her head.

"Big Buy refuses to consider women for promotion to department manager, store manager and higher positions in the company solely because they are women. Female employees at Big Buy are also subjected to crude and sexist jokes. The three women sitting at this table were all given the message that management jobs were for men, not women. Their lawsuit is going to change things at Big Buy for the benefit of all women."

With that, I handed out copies of our complaint and opened it up for questions.

The reporters were anxious to hear directly from the plaintiffs. The first question was directed at Olivia.

"After working at Big Buy for several years, what made you decide to finally file suit?" asked a reporter from KNBC-TV.

"Right is right and wrong is wrong," Olivia said. "I couldn't stand by and continue to allow this company to treat us like second-class citizens."

I made eye contact with Benjamin. His smile told me he was thinking the same thing I was. Olivia's sound bite was going to sound great on the six o'clock news.

And, I hoped Girlie Cortez was watching.

CHAPTER 45

Clayton and Special lay on opposite sides of her queen-size bed, sweating and panting and staring up at the ceiling.

Special wasn't sure what to say, so she didn't say anything. They had just broken up and here they were having sex.

And it wasn't just sex. It was skillet-hot, off-the-chart sex. Maybe committing to celibacy wouldn't be so hard after all. After what they'd just done, she could survive off the wet dreams for months. They should break up more often.

There was no need for her to look over at Clayton. She didn't need to see his face to know that he was upset about what had just happened. She could feel his disappointment sucking the air out of the room.

The bed shifted as Clayton sat up and flung his legs to the floor. He stood, picked up his shirt from the floor and slipped into it.

"I better go," he mumbled.

Special admired his strong legs as he stepped into his boxers and slacks. When his eyes finally met hers, he stared at her nakedness as if it repulsed him.

It wasn't her fault that he was just as horny as she was. She sat up and looked around for her top, then remembered that Clayton had stripped off her clothes in the living room.

Why in the hell was she feeling guilty? This was crazy. She was glad they were breaking up. Good riddance. She didn't need his phony ass.

If he was too damn religious to have sex, he should keep it in his pants.

Clayton disappeared into the bathroom and Special grabbed a robe from the back of the door. After about ten minutes, Special figured Clayton must've been in there on his knees praying to Allah for forgiveness.

When he finally walked out of the bathroom, she saw shame in his eyes. She followed him down the hallway into the living room, where he began looking around for his keys.

"Over there," she said, pointing to the coffee table.

Clayton picked up his keys and moved toward the door.

"Hold up," Special said. "I know you're not about to just walk up out of here without another word. So exactly where do we go from here?"

"I have no idea where we go. I need to clear my head. I'll call you."

"Oh, hell naw. You need to tell me something. One way or the other."

"I've asked you on more than one occasion not to cuss. It's unladylike and it's disrespectful."

Special's head whipped from left to right in rhythm with her words. "*Hell* is not a cuss word. *Damn* is a cuss word. And I'm tired of you telling me what to do like you're my daddy or something. I'm a grown-ass woman. If I wanna cuss, I can cuss. Damn it!"

"You know where we are?" The curves of Clayton's jawline transformed into sharp angles. "We're nowhere. You've just shown me once and for all that we can't be together."

"Fine. I don't wanna be with your hypocritical ass anyway. I'm tired of you judging me."

"I'm not judging you. Only Allah can judge you. All I've asked is that you make the same commitment that I've made. I need a woman who can stand behind me."

"That's the problem. I shouldn't have to stand behind you."

"That was just a figure of speech. You know what I mean. You obviously aren't the woman I thought you were."

Special could not hold back her tears. "And you're not the man I thought you were. At least I tried to support you. You won't even try to compromise."

"Compromise? Is that what Christianity teaches you? Compromise? I've made a decision to live by the Holy Qur'an, which I don't find all that hard to do. I know a lot of women who would love to be with a brother who wasn't constantly trying to get into their pants. But all you've done lately is try to trick me into bed."

"Trick you into bed? Oh, hell naw! I know you're not blaming this on me. You started it. You came on to me."

"And you didn't have the strength to stop me. A true Muslim woman would've never let that happen."

"Screw you!" Special shrieked. "A true Muslim man wouldn't have let it happen either. Don't blame me because your ass is weak."

"Like I said, thanks for showing me your true colors."

Special jumped in front of him and snatched open the door. "Get out!"

"Gladly."

Clayton stepped onto the porch a split second before the door slammed shut behind him.

CHAPTER 46

"I don't believe this prick," Mankowski said, both amazed and annoyed at what he was seeing. "Is he stupid or what?"

Mankowski and Thomas sat in an unmarked sedan, peering across Beverly Boulevard as Phillip strolled around the lot at Mercedes Benz of Beverly Hills.

"We've been on his ass like white on rice." Mankowski gripped the steering wheel. "He has to be stupid to go out and buy a hundred thousand dollar Benz. He's messing with us. He's saying, *I killed Judi, but you can't touch me.*"

"That insurance money is still tied up. Where's he getting the dough?" Thomas asked.

"Maybe he's got a sugar mama. Let's get out and mess with him."

"We have plenty of time to razz him," Thomas objected. "Maybe he's dealing with his grief by window-shopping."

"Grief, my ass."

They remained parked for close to forty minutes, watching as Phillip examined nearly every car in the showroom. He ultimately test drove the SL-class coupe.

"That car costs a hundred grand easy," Mankowski said.

"I'd say more like a buck fifty," Thomas corrected.

Thirty minutes later, Phillip drove an apple red Mercedes-Benz convertible off the lot.

The detectives exited the car and jogged across the street. They pretended to be checking out a black SUV and waited for a salesman to approach them. Ten minutes later, no one had.

Mankowski began to tap his foot in frustration. "They're ignoring us. Don't I look more like a rich guy than that prick Phillip Peterman?"

Thomas grinned. "Maybe it's your cheap suit."

Mankowski tugged at his collar. "This is the most expensive suit in my wardrobe. Got it on sale at the Men's Warehouse for half off."

A salesman finally walked over to them, but not the one who'd been working with Phillip.

"How can I help you gentlemen?"

"What's your best offer on this SUV?" Mankowski asked, patting the hood.

"Fully loaded, eighty-five grand. But I could probably get you in a stripped-down version for a lot less."

"Do I look like I need a stripped-down version?" Mankowski said, indignantly. "What makes you think I can't afford the fully-loaded model?"

The salesman raised his hands in surrender. "No offense intended. Why don't I go get the keys so you can take it for a test drive?"

Mankowski saw the salesman who'd helped Phillip approaching. "Forget it. I'd rather deal with that guy."

"We're interested in this SUV," Mankowski said, walking up to the other salesman. "Your colleague here was rather rude to us, so we're giving you our business. Why don't we talk in your office?"

The guy gave his co-worker an apologetic shrug and happily escorted the two detectives to his office. Once the door was closed, Mankowski flashed his badge. The man's vision of a commission on the sale of a second Benz disappeared with his smile.

"You just sold a red convertible to a man by the name of Phillip Peterman. We'd like to know how he paid for it?"

"Our customer's financial information is confidential. I can't—"

"So you telling me you want us to come back with a search warrant?"

"You definitely don't want that," Thomas chimed in. "There'll be so many cops converging on this place, you'll have to shut down for at least a day."

"What you're asking me to do is illegal." The salesman's voice was now several octaves higher.

Mankowski had been standing to the right of the salesman's desk and noticed Phillip's sales' contract on top of a stack of papers. He gave Thomas a signal, which he quickly picked up on.

Thomas kept the guy engaged by recounting a long list of bad things that could happen to the dealership if he didn't cooperate, while Mankowski scanned Phillip's contract.

Finally, the salesman had enough of being threatened. "I don't care. I can't give you that information. You need to see the general manager. I'm not losing my job over this."

"Alright, alright," Mankowski said. "Thanks for nothing."

As they passed the first salesman, Mankowski scowled at him. "We're taking our business to another dealership."

"What did you find out?" Thomas asked as they waited for the traffic to clear so they could jaywalk across the street.

"For one, Phillip didn't buy the car," Mankowski said. "He's leasing it. Almost two grand a month."

"That's more than my mortgage."

"And he prepaid the first three months."

Thomas arched a brow. "Maybe he did have those Big Buy documents and did some bartering with them."

"If he did," Mankowski said, "I wish I knew who in the hell he was bartering with."

CHAPTER 47

My phone rang and I made the mistake of answering it without checking the number on the caller ID display.

"Glad I finally got you," Lamarr said. "Why haven't you called me back?"

"I've been wrapped up with another case."

"I just got off the phone with my agent. The team just dropped me because of this bullshit with Tonisha."

"I'm sorry to hear that."

"Sorry ain't good enough. I ain't letting this go. We need to meet so we can talk about my appeal. That bitch was on another talk show yesterday. She's still tryin' to—"

"I've asked you repeatedly not to use that kind of language in my presence."

"Yeah, okay. Sorry."

"The notice of appeal is ready to be filed."

"And how long is it gonna take after that to get my new trial?"

"A long time, Lamarr. It'll be months before we even get a briefing schedule. The courts are seriously backed up due to budget cuts."

"Well, I can't wait months. I got some new information for you to put in my appeal. Word on the street is that Tonisha admitted to one of her girlfriends that she lied on me. I got somebody lookin' into that."

"I don't think that's a good idea."

"I have to do something. I wanna make her take a lie detector test."

"There's no way we can do that."

"Well, you need to set up a press conference. I saw that press conference you did for those women at Big Buy. I wanna have a press conference too. If Tonisha's gonna keep slandering me, I need to say something in my defense."

"We have to have some news to announce in order to have a press conference."

"You said you're filing the appeal. That's news, ain't it?"

Actually, it was. But it wouldn't help Lamarr's case to put him in front of a bunch of TV cameras and let him lash out at Tonisha. I wouldn't mind doing a press conference if I knew Lamarr would behave. It might not further his case, but it would definitely piss off Girlie Cortez.

"So you gonna get me a press conference?"

"No."

"Why not?"

"Because I don't think it's a wise move. You can't just go around attacking Tonisha."

"Why not? That's what she's doing to me."

"People see her as a victim."

"She ain't no victim. I'm the victim!"

"Who told you she admitted lying?" I asked, simply to steer him away from the idea of a press conference.

Lamarr proceeded to tell me about a guy whose sister heard it from her hairdresser, who heard it from her cousin's best friend. I gave absolutely no credence to the tale.

"I'll look into it."

"You don't have to do that. I already got my peeps lookin' into it. I can't live my life with everybody thinkin' I'm a rapist."

"Lamarr, please don't make your situation worse by doing something stupid."

"I'm not," he said. "But I am gonna prove that I didn't rape that 'ho. So when are you setting up my press conference?"

"Were you listening to me? I said I can't do that."

"Why not?"

"I don't have time for this. I have a meeting."

"I'm not done yet. I wanna know why I can't have a press conference."

I pulled a bottle of Advil from my desk and swallowed two tablets dry. "I'm sorry, Lamarr, I have to go." I placed the phone back into the base.

Lamarr called right back. I let it go to voicemail, then erased the message without listening to it.

Lamarr "The Hero" Harris was turning out to be a nightmare of a client. After I filed his notice of appeal, I planned to put him in the hands of an able appellate attorney and let somebody else deal with his craziness.

CHAPTER 48

Girlie studied the bored faces scattered around the table in the Big Buy board room. She found it odd that none of the six board members were talking to each other. Three were pecking away on their smartphones. Two were on their cell phones. Another was reading the newspaper.

"Rita should be here any minute," Evelyn Kimble announced. Making excuses for the CEO must have been written into her job description.

This was Girlie's first appearance at a Big Buy board meeting, her presence necessitated by Vernetta Henderson's recently filed class action. Girlie always had the impression that Evelyn intentionally kept her out of reach of the Big Buy board. Some general counsels feared that allowing their outside counsel access to their board might result in their replacement. But now that her ass was on the line, Evelyn was glad to put Girlie on the chopping block.

To Girlie's surprise, Vernetta's press conference had generated a groundswell of national media coverage, from *The Wall Street Journal* to the *Nightly News* to the Huffington Post. A *60 Minutes* producer had even contacted the company, requesting an interview. All of the news outlets reported the allegations as if they were fact. *The New York Post* ran the outrageous headline: California Store Tells Women, 'Stay in Your Place.'

"So what are we going to do about this?" board member Keith Rogers asked, finally putting away his phone. "My colleagues know

I'm a member of this board. All this bad publicity could impact me personally."

Interesting comment, Girlie thought. The board members had a fiduciary duty to the company, but this guy was worrying about his own skin.

"I don't understand how they can accuse this company of sex discrimination," Rogers continued. "The CEO *and* the general counsel are both women."

He'd neglected to acknowledge that the board of directors was entirely male. Rogers probably had no idea of the company's equally disgraceful stats outside of this room. Diversity wasn't a word the Big Buy board even knew how to pronounce.

"Getting a handle on this negative publicity is precisely what we're here to discuss," the general counsel replied. "But let's wait until Rita arrives before we begin."

At that instant, Rita bolted into the room, followed by the company's Chief Financial Officer. Fred Hiller had been a partner with Big Buy's longtime accounting firm, Wynn, Miller & Gold. Rita hired him on as CFO three months after her husband's death. Girlie had learned from one of her partners that Rita and the very married Fred were an item, but the two foolishly believed that no one knew about their affair.

Rita took a seat at the head of the table and immediately turned her wrath on Girlie.

"I don't like hearing that my company is the target of a class action on the local news. If you had settled with that woman, we wouldn't be in this mess."

"We knew this was coming after receiving information from one of your employees that Ms. Henderson was talking to them about filing a class action," Girlie said. *And by the way you were the one who told me to play hardball.*

"Do you know how embarrassing this is for me?" Rita continued to rant.

Girlie hadn't come here to be publicly berated. She had hoped for some support from Evelyn, but the general counsel wouldn't meet her eyes.

"You said you had the case under control." Rita pounded the table with her fist. "And now the news of the Welson merger has leaked out. But there won't *be* a merger unless you fix this."

It always baffled Girlie that clients thought it was her job to fix their screw ups. *There wouldn't be a problem to fix if your company didn't blatantly discriminate against women.* The CEO was only worried about her $125 million.

"Well, say something," Rita challenged. "How are you going to resolve this?"

Girlie could feel heat sting her cheeks. She fought off the urge to put Rita in her place. No matter how much she resented the woman's disrespect, losing Big Buy as a client would not be a good career move.

Before she could respond, Rita's executive assistant rushed in carrying a monogrammed cup and saucer. Her hands were trembling so badly the tinkling of the cup hitting the saucer blared across the room.

Rita narrowed her eyes and shot the woman a hateful, intimidating glare. Jane Campbell's premature gray hair and frail demeanor made her appear much older than her late fifties. She shakily placed the tea on the table, lowered her head and backed out of the room.

"Please get back here," Rita huffed, snapping her fingers in the air. "This isn't hot enough." Rita hadn't even tasted it.

"I'm sorry," Jane mumbled. "I'll bring another cup."

Rita waved her away. "Just forget it. I guess I'll have to make it myself."

Girlie wanted to jump to the poor woman's defense and set Rita straight. It was just like Rita to pick on the weak. Girlie learned from her former partner that Jane had been the longtime executive assistant to Big Buy founder, Harlan Kimble. They'd shared a close relationship, which Rita had always resented. In an effort to protect her, Harlan's will mandated that Jane receive four-hundred-thousand dollars if she was terminated before reaching the company's retirement age of sixty-two.

Harlan had assumed the provision would protect his beloved assistant, but it had just the opposite effect. Rita didn't want to keep

Jane on and she also didn't want to pay her four-hundred grand to leave. So instead, Rita treated her like a dog, hoping she would quit.

Everyone waited for the uncomfortable silence to fade.

Evelyn finally found her voice. "Girlie and I have been discussing a number of strategies for dealing with this situation," she explained. "We've also retained a PR firm from New York which specializes in crisis management. They're putting together a PR plan to get our side of the story out there."

Rita pounded the table again. "I just want to know how fast you can make this nonsense go away."

"If you really want to resolve this quickly, we should approach the other side about settlement," Girlie said. "In another case, we agreed to put the court proceedings on hold, then conducted some limited discovery and proceeded to mediation. We got rid of the case in about three months. I suspect we can do the same here."

"Three months!" Rita screamed. "That's not fast enough. The Welson deal is supposed to close in eight weeks. I've already gotten a call from the company's general counsel asking about this mess. I told him we have it under control."

Girlie's hands tightened around the arms of her chair, but she wished she could wrap them around Rita's neck.

"There is another approach we can take that could put an end to the case almost immediately. It'll be costly, but not nearly as costly as a class action."

She briefly summarized her plan. The board members listened, but said nothing. Girlie realized that everyone was waiting to hear what Rita thought before expressing their own opinion.

Rita bit down on her ink pen and rocked back in her leather chair. "I like it. I like it a lot."

Now that Rita thought it was a great idea, so did the board. Evelyn remained mute.

Girlie smiled at her own brilliance. She was certain that her clever little plan would quickly short-circuit the class action. And by the time Vernetta saw it coming, there would be absolutely nothing she could do about it.

CHAPTER 49

It was unusual for Jefferson to be privy to information about my best friend that I didn't know. So his call telling me that Special and Clayton had broken up was a bit of a shock.

I immediately hung up and called Special's office. One of her co-workers told me she'd been out sick for the second day in a row. I drove straight to her house, even though she hadn't answered her home phone or cell. The fact that Special had not bothered to tell me about the breakup meant that she was really in bad shape.

I knocked on the door, but got no response. I was about to leave when I heard the approach of footsteps. When she finally opened the door, all I could do was stare. She did not look like a wreck. Her skin had a bronzy glow and her makeup had been expertly applied, complete with eyelash extensions. Her micro braids had been re-placed with a shoulder-length weave streaked with reddish-brown highlights. The tight, short-sleeved shirt and black jeans made her look like a Banana Republic model.

"Hey, girl, what's up?" She stepped aside to welcome me in.

"I ran over here to check up on you."

"And why would I need checking up on?"

"Because you broke up with Clayton and didn't bother to tell me."

She crossed her arms and fixed her lips with indignation. "He called to tell you we broke up?"

"No. He told Jefferson, who told me."

I followed her into the living room where we sat down on the couch.

Special let out a heavy sigh. "I wasn't ready to tell anybody yet. Not even you. I guess I didn't want to hear *I told you so.*"

"I wouldn't have said that."

"Probably not. But you definitely would have been thinking it. I just had to get myself together first."

"So you're okay about it?"

"Nope." She tried to smile, but halfway there it faltered.

"Well, you certainly look good."

This time her attempt at a smile was more successful. "Girl, you know me. Whenever I feel like crap on the inside, at least I can fake it by looking good on the outside. After lying in bed crying all day yesterday, today I decided to stop feeling sorry for myself. I went to the gym this morning and worked out really hard. Then I had a facial and got my hair and nails done."

She spread out her bony fingers for me to see. Then her eyes started to water.

I reached over and gave her a big hug. As I did, I glanced over her shoulder and was surprised at what I saw sitting on the coffee table next to the couch. A large leather-bound Qur'an sat next to a Bible. Both were open.

"I see you've been doing some reading."

She followed my eyes to the coffee table, then picked up the Qur'an.

"You know what the weird thing is? Since Clayton and I broke up, I've been reading the Holy Qur'an. I mean *really* reading it. Before I was only doing it because Clayton wanted me to. But now, I'm doing it for me."

She set it in her lap and ran her hands over the cover.

"Thank God, I got into the habit of praying five times a day. That's the only thing that's gotten me through the last couple of days. Ain't that a trip? I've been fighting Islam all along, but it's brought me peace when I really needed it."

My eyebrows fused in surprise. "Are you saying you couldn't have found that same sense of peace with Christianity?"

"I've been reading the Bible too. I've always loved Psalms. I guess I'm trying to figure out what I really believe spiritually. I was brought up as a Christian and I've never questioned that. But for the first time in my life, I'm taking a deeper look at my faith. I guess I have my experience with Islam to thank for that."

I didn't know what else to say, so I decided to lighten the mood. "I know how we can get you and Clayton back together. We can kidnap him and get him deprogrammed."

Special flinched. "Clayton doesn't need deprogramming." There was a defensiveness in her tone and the narrowing of her eyes echoed it.

"I'm sorry. I didn't mean it like that."

"Yes, you did. Everybody thinks anybody who joins the Community of Islam is a black racist, but that's not true. I understand Clayton's attraction to the Community. They're about helping black people help themselves. But the reality is, I'm just not committed enough to make the kind of sacrifices he's willing to make."

She hung her head, then laughed softly. "Especially if it means I have to spend all my time at the mosque and give up Long Island Iced Teas and pork. I'm kinda shallow, huh?"

I laughed. "Not at all. I'm actually impressed at how you're handling this. I ran over here expecting to find a basket case."

She slapped her thigh. "You shoulda been here yesterday. But I got tired of waking up in the fetal position, with puffy eyes and Don King hair. So this morning I decided to stop feeling sorry for myself." She stood up. "I wanna show you something."

I followed her over to the dining room table. Papers and brochures covered the table.

"I've been researching my new career." She held up a brochure entitled *Do You Have What it Takes to be a Private Investigator?*

"So you're really serious about this?"

"Yep. I'm just trying to decide whether I want to take night classes or do it online."

"You'll make a great private investigator," I said.

Her eyes twinkled with hope. "Does that mean you're going to hire me for one of your cases once I get my license?"

"Uh…I'm not sure we should work together. It might ruin our friendship."

"That's cold. You should hire me to look into Lamarr's case. I still say Tonisha set him up. Maybe I can find some information you can use in his appeal."

"Appealing that case is an exercise in futility. No court's going to overturn the jury's verdict. So don't waste your time."

"Okay," she said with a syrupy smile. "Whatever you say."

"I'm not playing, Special. Leave it alone. Don't go nosing around in that case."

She placed a hand on her hip. "Okay, okay. Want something to drink? All I have is cranberry juice. I drained my secret stash of wine last night."

I followed her into the kitchen where she filled two glasses and handed one to me.

I glanced down at her ringless finger. "So did Clayton take the ring back?"

"Nope."

"Are you going to give it back?"

"Nope." She smiled sheepishly. "I also visited a couple of jewelry stores today. Got it appraised."

"Why doesn't that surprise me?"

"'Cuz you know me. Clayton was a lot of things, but the brother definitely wasn't cheap." She picked up her purse from the kitchen counter, took out a red velvet box and popped it open.

"This bad boy right here," she said, pulling out the ring, "is gonna finance my new career *and* allow me to spend a couple weeks in Jamaica getting my groove back."

CHAPTER 50

Mankowski sat on the side of the bed, dressed in nothing but his blue silk boxers, sending silent messages of thanks straight up to God.

At this very moment, the smart, gorgeous, incredibly sexy Girlie Cortez was in the bathroom—his bathroom—showering. The anticipation of what was about to occur might just cause his heart to give out.

As he was imagining the touch of her creamy skin rubbing against his, she walked out of the bathroom. Completely naked. No robe, no negligee, not even a towel.

She gave him a smile that was so tantalizing he thought he might come right that second.

"Hope I wasn't too long."

"Not at all."

She walked over to the foot of the bed and stopped in front of the mirror. With her backside facing him, she bent to rub oil on her upper thighs. He hoped it was some Asian herb that would hypnotize him and keep his dick hard for four hours.

Stepping out of his boxers, he slid underneath the thin sheet, never once taking his eyes off of her. She was rubbing the oil on her ass now. Her beautiful, tight, flawless ass.

He lay back with his hands laced behind his head, enjoying the preview. Girlie had cantaloupe-shaped breasts that were disproportionately large for her small frame. She'd probably paid for them, but he didn't give a shit. He most definitely preferred manufactured tits over those mushy-looking cow udders on the cougars he'd been dating lately.

Girlie turned around to face him as she replaced the cap on the bottle. The perfectly shaved triangle at the gathering of her thighs looked like it had been sculpted by an artist. He couldn't wait to brush his lips across that.

"So, are you any closer to finding out who killed Judi Irving?" Girlie asked.

Mankowski grimaced. This wasn't a good sign. Girlie should have been concentrating on all of the nasty little things she had in store for him, rather than asking about his case. Phillip Peterman was still his number one person of interest, but Mankowski was beginning to seriously consider the possibility that Big Buy was also involved somehow. And if that was true, he was about to bed someone who could end up being a witness in the case, or even worse, a suspect. Unfortunately, things had gone way too far to put the brakes on now.

"Why are we talking about Big Buy?"

Girlie tilted her head, causing her hair to sweep across her right shoulder. "My mom taught me that men like to talk about their work. It makes them feel good."

"I can think of a few other things that might make me feel good."

Girlie grinned and perched herself at the edge of the bed facing him. She sat upright with her legs crossed like a model preschooler. He hated no longer having a clear view of her sweet spot. But at least he could still ogle her impressive rack.

Mankowski took in a deep breath of anticipation. He was more than ready to get this show on the road.

"Okay," she said, her voice as soft as he imagined her skin to be. "Tell me what you like."

"Everything," he said, grinning. "I like everything."

"C'mon," she teased, sucking the tip of her baby finger, "there has to be something special that you like."

He smiled. "I like seeing you in the buff. Most women aren't comfortable with their bodies."

Girlie shrugged. "Most women don't have a body as fabulous as mine."

"True."

He wallowed in the pleasure of staring at her for a few more seconds.

"Unfold your legs," he ordered, in the same commanding voice he used with criminals. *Put your hands up. Now!*

Girlie did as instructed, forming a long V with her legs.

Wow! The view was fantastic. "Now touch yourself."

Without hesitation, Girlie followed orders. As Mankowski watched her masturbate, he had to struggle to refrain from grabbing himself and joining her. He was going to do everything in his power not to screw up this good thing for at least three months. Maybe five or six.

Once Girlie had brought herself to climax, she recovered quickly and crawled toward him on all fours, like a sleek, bare-assed cat.

She stopped when her head was hovering over his crotch. "We're going to play a game." She leaned down and took him deep into her warm, wet mouth.

Mankowski palmed the back of her head. "Oh, mother of—"

Girlie abruptly pulled away and winked at him.

"That was just a preview. The game we're going to play is called *Hands Off.* So if you touch me in any way, the game stops. I get to do all the work."

He grinned. *God really, really loved him.*

Mankowski watched as Girlie maneuvered her body like a gymnast on top of a balance beam. In seconds, her legs were extended, parallel with his body, her feet inches above his head, balancing herself only with her hands. It took incredible strength and control for her to lift her own body weight. He was in pretty good shape, but there was no way he could do that.

Mankowski wanted to grab her ass and plunge into her, but he had to play by the rules. He gripped the side of the headboard and bit his lip.

Finally, Girlie pinned her knees at his sides, straddling him. As her body welcomed him inside, he reflexively reached out and clutched her right butt cheek.

"You're being a bad boy," Girlie said, easing herself off of him. "Hands off, remember?"

"Uh...oh, yeah. Sorry. I forgot."

Girlie waited almost a full minute, then eased back down onto him, slowly, way too slowly. He closed his eyes and reluctantly submitted. In seconds that seemed like minutes, he was finally inside her.

"You like this?" She swayed from left to right like she was riding a slow-moving bucking bronco. At the same time, she was doing some reflexive move that tightened then loosened around him. Girlie was in full control and he didn't mind being her humble subject.

Mankowski wanted to moan or curse or something, but his voice failed him. He opened his eyes, salivated at her gorgeous body, and wished he could pinch one of her nipples.

As he was seconds away from coming, he could hear his partner's voice spewing disapproval. But right now, Mankowski felt too damn good to care about ethical considerations or department policies. He would enjoy the hell out of Girlie Cortez and deal with the consequences later.

CHAPTER 51

Olivia's voice sounded so garbled that I could only make out every other word between her sobs.

"Olivia, please," I said into the phone, "I need you to calm down. I can't understand a word you're saying."

"Big Buy just killed the lawsuit!"

"Killed the lawsuit? What are you talking about?"

"They gave all the female employees a letter."

"A letter? Olivia, you're not making any sense. I need you to take a deep breath and speak slowly."

I couldn't believe she was actually having a meltdown. Not Olivia, my Rock of Gibraltar. Her faith never faltered. It took a few more minutes, but when I finally understood what she was telling me, I was the one diving into panic mode.

"I need to see a copy of that letter," I said. "Did they give you one?"

"No," she sniffed. "Robyn either. I don't know about Marcia because she works at the Torrance store. But every other female employee got one."

I instructed her to get a copy from a co-worker and go to Staples on her lunch break to fax it to me.

It took another forty minutes before the fax arrived. Once I read the letter, I wanted to strangle Girlie Cortez.

Dear Valued Big Buy Associate,

I'd like to thank you for your contribution and dedication to our company. A recent lawsuit has alleged that Big Buy's promotional practices have not been fairly applied to women. We believe these allegations have no merit and our own investigation has found no evidence supporting these claims.

Nevertheless, we have decided to use this opportunity to demonstrate Big Buy's commitment to ensuring a workplace that is free from all forms of discrimination. As a sign of our good faith, we are offering every female sales associate three-thousand dollars ($3,000.00) in exchange for signing the attached release agreement. Signing this agreement will mean that you waive your right to participate in the pending class action lawsuit.

To further demonstrate our commitment, we are implementing a new Diversity Task force to examine our promotional and pay practices. Going forward, promotions in all of our stores must be approved by a corporate human resources panel.

I balled up the letter and hurled it across the room.

The company was undermining my class action by waving a fake apology and a measly three grand in front of these women's faces. This was probably the largest lump sum most would ever receive in their lives. There was no way they would turn it down for the possibility of a larger payment months or years from now.

I charged out of my office and headed next door to talk to Nichelle Ayers, a close friend and one of the partners at the law firm where I rented space. I barged in without knocking.

"Sorry to disturb you," I said, "but I have an emergency."

"Hey, girl. Have a seat. What's going on?"

I was too peeved to sit down so I remained standing, gripping the back of the chair. "Big Buy just pulled the rug out from under me."

I told her about the letter. "Can they do that?"

"That's crazy," Nichelle said, her eyes expanding in surprise. She punched three numbers on her phone. "Can you come over to my office?" she said, when her law partner picked up. "We need your help with something."

"I've never heard of a company doing that," Nichelle said, as we waited for Russell Barnes to join us. "But when you think about it, paying off the women now means they'll probably save millions in attorneys' fees and engender some good will from their employees. It's actually quite brilliant."

"Yeah, it's brilliant," I grumbled, "but is it legal? I've met with some of the women in person and had telephone conversations with others. So as far as I'm concerned, there was an attorney-client relationship between us. And Big Buy violated it by sending them that letter."

Tall and studious-looking, Russell Barnes towered into the office. "What's up?"

"Wait until you hear this," Nichelle said, then shared my predicament. "Can they get away with that?"

Russell scratched his head. "I think I have heard of companies doing that before."

"But those women are my clients," I insisted. "They can't contact them directly. They have to communicate with them through me."

"Did they sign representation agreements?" Russell asked.

"Only the three lead plaintiffs did and I know for sure that two of them didn't get the letter. The other women we spoke to were really nervous about the lawsuit and weren't willing to be listed as plaintiffs, so I didn't ask them to sign agreements."

"Then you may be out of luck. Technically, you don't represent anybody else because the class hasn't been certified by the court yet. So Big Buy may be perfectly within its rights to pay off the women."

As I stood there, all I could see was Girlie Cortez's gloating face.

I had no idea what I was going to do, but there was no way I was going to let her defeat me a fourth time.

CHAPTER 52

For the last twenty minutes, Mankowski and Thomas had been hot on Phillip's tail as he drove north up La Cienega Boulevard. They were reasonably sure they hadn't been spotted because Mankowski had borrowed his cousin's new Porsche.

Thomas gripped the steering wheel like he was holding the woman he loved.

"Man, if I could afford one of these, I'd trade in my firstborn."

Mankowski smiled. "I'll be sure not to mention that to your wife."

Phillip transitioned to San Vicente Boulevard. "Get in your left lane," Mankowski barked. "Don't lose him."

"We're in a Porsche. He's in a Benz," Thomas said. "That's not going to happen. He's got luxury, but we've got luxury *and* speed. He's probably headed to another acting class. This dude needs to get a job."

Mankowski chuckled. "I'm betting Actor Boy's found himself a replacement cougar."

"What a lucky guy," Thomas said wistfully. "A woman willing to pay all the bills and screw your brains out too."

Mankowski started whistling as he thought about his mind-blowing tryst with Girlie Cortez. He was dying to brag to Thomas about it, but he knew better.

"Speaking of screwing around," Thomas said, "meet anybody new?"

A chill swept through Mankowski. "Nope."

He had been extra careful. There was no way Thomas could know that he had hooked up with Girlie. "Why'd you ask?"

"I dunno. Maybe it's your rosy cheeks and the fact you're whistling all the time."

Mankowski stared out of the window. "Hey, man, I'm just a happy-go-lucky kinda guy."

Even though he'd screwed her, Mankowski was still playing Girlie the way she needed to be played. When she suggested dinner the night after their hookup, he'd put her off. It wasn't that difficult pretending to be aloof. He was still jacking off from the memory of his evening with her.

They continued northwest on San Vicente Boulevard until Phillip made a left onto Burton Way.

"Where the hell is he going?" Thomas asked.

"I'm telling you, he's got a new woman," Mankowski insisted. "This is a pretty nice neighborhood, so she probably has some bucks. I think he's just been laying low for the past few weeks. But now he can't hold out any longer."

After a moment, Mankowski snapped his fingers. "I bet I know exactly where he's going."

Thomas turned to face him. "Well, hurry up and let me in on it."

"The Four Seasons Hotel on Doheny."

"He can't afford that place. The cheapest room there has to be at least five-hundred bucks a night."

"He can if the chick he's screwing has dough."

They followed as Phillip did indeed turn onto Doheny and then made another quick right into the small half-circle driveway in front of the Four Seasons Hotel.

"Crap," Mankowski said. "We can't follow him in there. He'll spot us."

The front of the hotel was hidden from street view by a large brick wall and tall shrubbery. The wealthy relished their privacy.

Thomas drove past the hotel, then did a U-turn and pulled over to the curb across the street.

"So now what?" Thomas asked.

Mankowski glanced at his watch. "Let's give him a chance to get inside, then we're going in. I'm figuring that after he gets through pumping his girlfriend, we may get lucky and catch them walking out together."

After another ten minutes, they pulled up in front of the hotel and climbed out of the car. Thomas was slow to hand over the keys to the Porsche. "How about if I park it myself?" he said to the valet.

"I'm sorry, sir. We don't have self-parking."

"Give him the damn keys," Mankowski barked.

"Don't scratch it," Thomas said, staring wistfully as the valet drove off.

"I see now that I'm going to have to pry the keys from your hands when it's time to give it back."

Thomas whipped his head around. "We gotta give it back?"

Mankowski chuckled. He was about to reach for the door when a doorman opened it for him.

Thomas whistled as they stepped inside the lobby. "This place even feels like money. It's a shame how the other half lives."

They found a deserted area of the bar, after first making sure Phillip wasn't in there.

Thomas pulled out his iPhone to check on his most recent stock trades. "So how long are we waiting?"

"I figure a stud like Phillip would need about an hour to do his thing. It's the middle of the day so his princess probably has a job or a husband to get back to. In another thirty minutes, let's find a spot where we can see them leave."

Exactly forty-two minutes later, they spotted Phillip walking out of the hotel. Alone.

"There he is," Thomas said. "There's a pep in his step. I'd say he definitely got laid."

Mankowski groaned. "No matter how many women walk out of here after him, there's no way for us to figure out who he was with."

So far, except for a few men who looked like businessmen, only couples had gone in and out of the hotel.

"Let's stay put a little while longer. Keep an eye on any woman walking out alone," Mankowski said. "We can jot down the license plate numbers of each one and check her out."

Just as the words left Mankowski's lips, a strikingly hot brunette floated through the lobby carrying a dainty leather briefcase. Every man in the vicinity stopped to gawk at her.

Thomas looked from the woman to Mankowski. "You okay?"

Mankowski didn't answer right away. "Why wouldn't I be?" he snapped.

"I don't know. Just checking."

"Checking for what?"

Thomas frowned. "Man, don't think you can keep any secrets from me. I know what you've been up to. I *am* a detective."

Mankowski tried to keep his face as neutral as possible. He could not let Thomas see the mix of emotions churning in his chest. Regret, embarrassment, and most of all, anger. The fact that his partner knew his little secret made it even worse.

They both sat speechless, watching from the ritzy lobby of the Four Seasons Hotel as the parking attendant helped Girlie Cortez into her silver blue Jaguar.

CHAPTER 53

I was sitting in the gallery of Department 36 of the Los Angeles Superior Court waiting for the judge to take the bench. I was surprised that Girlie hadn't arrived yet. Maybe she'd been hit by a bus.

The day after getting word of Big Buy's underhanded attempt to derail my class action, I moved for a temporary injunction to prevent the company from paying off the Big Buy employees.

While the law wasn't clearly in my favor on this issue, it wasn't a slam dunk for Big Buy either. No matter what the precedent directed, the judge always had the option to go off on a tangent if he so chose. That was my hope for today.

Olivia had informed me that Janice Miller had reported to Big Buy everything that went on at our meeting at the Center for Justice. I should have listened to my gut. I should have known she was taking copious notes for a reason.

I waited patiently as two attorneys battled over a discovery motion. They finished and the judge called my case number. As I rose to head into the well of the courtroom, Girlie strolled in as if on cue.

She handed a business card to the judge's clerk, who didn't seem to mind that she should've been there to do that long before the judge took the bench.

"Your motion poses a rather unique legal question," Judge Ezra Goldberg began, peering down at me from the bench. "My law clerk didn't find much California law on point."

I was about to respond when Girlie cut me off.

"That's because there isn't much, Your Honor," Girlie said. "But what's out there is enough to support Big Buy's position that its action was completely legal."

"I disagree," I said, trying to regain control. "Your Honor, Big Buy was well aware that the meeting I held with its employees at the Center for Justice was for the purpose of discussing legal action against the company. It was a confidential, privileged discussion. Yet Big Buy's lawyer questioned one of the attendees, intentionally violating the attorney-client privilege that I had established with these potential class members. Then the company used the information that it had improperly gathered as the basis for its decision to entice its female employees not to join the class action."

Girlie puffed out a breath. "I'll concede that Ms. Henderson represented three of the employees, and none of them received our letter. Maybe I missed it in her moving papers, but I wasn't aware of any agreement she had with Big Buy's other one-thousand-plus female employees across the state."

Judge Goldberg grimaced. Girlie's sarcasm wasn't winning her any points with him. Nor was the low-cut blouse she was wearing. Prior to joining the bench, Goldberg had been a semi-radical activist for Jewish causes. He was the father of eight and as straight-laced as they came. I had appeared in his courtroom many times and always felt he fairly and accurately interpreted the law.

"Your Honor," I began, "this is not just an issue of whether a formal representation agreement exists. The issue here is the sanctity of the attorney-client relationship. The policy underlying the privilege is to encourage open and honest communication between attorneys and their clients. Big Buy intentionally infringed upon that relationship. If Ms. Cortez wanted to discuss an early settlement, she should've contacted me."

The judge focused his gaze on Girlie. "Counselor, I have to say that I am quite concerned about your actions. In that you were aware that Ms. Henderson was meeting with those employees in preparation for legal action, your discussion with Janice Miller appears highly inappropriate."

"Your Honor, I'd like to point out that we did not approach Ms. Miller. She came to us, which means she willingly waived the privilege, if one even existed. In addition, before allowing her to share any information with us, I confirmed that she had not signed a representation agreement with Ms. Henderson."

"Is it your position, Ms. Cortez, that the privilege doesn't exist in the absence of a written representation agreement?"

"Uh, well…no, Your Honor." Girlie looked down at her notes and shifted her weight from one of her red patent leather pumps to the other. "But it is my contention that no privilege existed between Ms. Henderson and any Big Buy employee who had not signed a retainer agreement because the class hasn't been certified yet."

Judge Goldberg hesitated, then proceeded. "I'm going to grant Ms. Henderson's request for a temporary injunction. Big Buy is prohibited from issuing checks to any employee until this matter has been fully decided by this court. I will make a ruling as to Ms. Henderson's request for a permanent injunction by the end of the week."

My smile was so bright it could have lit up the whole courthouse.

I exited the courtroom ahead of Girlie and politely held the door open for her. This time I was the one gloating and it felt fantastic.

"Tell your client to start saving up," I said, as Girlie pushed past me. "Because I'm going to make sure Big Buy pays those women a hell of a lot more than the peanuts they're offering them now."

Girlie's eyes hardened and her nose lifted into a sneer. "Don't bet on it."

CHAPTER 54

Girlie stood in the lobby of Big Buy's corporate headquarters, wishing she could be someplace, anyplace, else.

The CEO and general counsel wanted to be informed of the results of the judge's ruling as soon as the hearing ended. Girlie could've taken the coward's way out and delivered the news by phone, but it was her style to face a difficult situation head on.

Evelyn Kimble, the general counsel, greeted her in the lobby.

"So how did it go?" she asked.

"Why don't we wait until we get to Rita's office?"

Evelyn exhaled. "Doesn't sound like you have good news for us."

Girlie followed her into an elevator. Right before they entered the CEO's office, Evelyn slowed.

"If the news is bad, Rita's going to go off," she said sympathetically. "Don't take it personally. I never do."

Rita Richards-Kimble rose from her seat as soon as they stepped inside. "Is it time to pop open the champagne bottles?"

Girlie simply smiled and took a seat in one of the chairs in front of the CEO's desk. Evelyn sat down next to her. Girlie inhaled and braced herself for the coming onslaught.

"The judge granted the temporary injunction," she said quickly. "We can't pay out the checks until Goldberg rules on whether he's going to issue a permanent injunction."

"I don't believe this shit!" Rita yelled and pounded the desk with both fists like a spoiled five-year-old. "I just got off the phone with

Welson's CEO. I assured him that this case was history. They're not going to buy this company if they'll have to defend a costly class action. When you came up with this harebrained idea to pay off those women, you told me it was perfectly legal."

"It is," Girlie tried to explain. "One of my partners did it successfully in a similar case. I'm confident that the court's final ruling will go our way. The judge just wanted some time to study the issue."

"If the court grants that permanent injunction, *then* what are you going to do?" the CEO demanded.

Rita was the reason women had a hard time gaining respect in the business world, Girlie thought to herself. They were way too emotional.

"That's not going to happen."

"Is that a guarantee?"

"No," Girlie said. "But the odds are on our side."

"I don't want odds. I want guarantees! You also told us you'd be able to find those documents Judi Irving supposedly had. You didn't come through on that either."

"No," Girlie corrected her, "I said *if* they existed, I would find them. And so far the only thing I've been able to track down about those documents are rumors."

Rita ranted for a few more minutes, then stormed out of her own office, leaving Girlie alone with the general counsel.

"Please excuse her," Evelyn apologized. "She can't help herself."

"You deserve an award for being able to work with her."

Evelyn smiled. "I don't let her get to me. I stay with this company because my brother built it. If I left, she'd destroy it."

"Why is she so worried about those documents?"

"Your guess is as good as mine."

Evelyn was being just as closed mouth as Mankowski had been. Girlie had hoped that having sex with the detective would ultimately produce some useful information. Now, she realized, that wasn't going to happen. Still, the handsome cop had turned out to be a nice lay. She was a little perturbed that he'd turned down her invitation for dinner. He was probably just freaked out about the whole conflict-of-interest thing. Maybe she would invite him out again.

Girlie said her good-byes and headed for her car, mulling over her next steps.

When she had advised Big Buy to pay off its female employees, she had carefully researched the law and believed her legal analysis was solid. She was actually surprised at the course that the hearing had taken. Based on his comments from the bench, Judge Goldberg might actually rule that Big Buy had violated the attorney-client privilege and issue a permanent injunction, preventing the company from paying off the women. Girlie couldn't let that happen.

Too bad Goldberg was such a straight arrow. Trying to screw him would be a waste of time. So Girlie had no choice but to resort to Plan B. There was no guarantee that her backup plan would produce the desired result, but it was worth a shot.

Girlie felt a warm tingle course through her body. Her Plan B was so creatively scandalous that every time she thought about it, she almost wet her pink lace panties.

CHAPTER 55

"So tell me again?" Mankowski said, talking and chewing at the same time. "What's this called?"

Girlie reached across the table and wiped the corner of Mankowski's mouth with her napkin.

"Lumpia. It's basically a Filipino egg roll. I guess you like it, huh?"

Mankowski wasn't big on Asian cuisine, but the food she'd been stuffing him with wasn't bad.

"Pretty tasty," he said, reaching for another one.

Girlie had called him up and insisted on taking him to her favorite Filipino restaurant not far from her home in Cerritos.

It hadn't been easy for Mankowski to pretend as if everything between them was hunky-dory. After seeing Girlie walk out of the Four Seasons seconds behind Phillip Peterman, he realized just how dangerous the woman was. Mankowski was also pissed that she was playing him. He was now more determined than ever to bring down Phillip Peterman and Girlie Cortez right along with him.

He pointed to a chicken dish in the middle of the table. "How do you pronounce that again?"

"Adobo," she said, puckering her lips. "Ah-doo-bo. It's the Spanish word for seasoning or marinade. The chicken is slow cooked in soy sauce, vinegar, and garlic, then pan-fried."

"Uh, why do you guys use a Spanish word to describe a Filipino dish?"

"I guess you don't know your history. The Philippines was colonized by Spain. Most Filipinos have Spanish surnames. Ferdinand and Emelda *Marcos*. Manny *Pacquiao*. Girlie *Cortez*."

Mankowski nodded thoughtfully. "Actually, I'd never thought about it."

They enjoyed their food in silence for the next few minutes.

"So why is this place called Goldilocks?" he asked.

Girlie laughed. "The two women who opened the restaurant thought naming it after Goldilocks would bring them luck. And I guess it did. It's now a chain of restaurants in the Philippines, the U.S. and Canada."

"This is quite a history lesson I'm getting."

They munched in silence for a minute or so.

"So how's the Irving murder investigation going?" Girlie asked, trying to appear casual.

Mankowski had been waiting for her to get around to asking about the case.

"I think we may be close to cracking it," he lied. "Her boyfriend's about to go down."

"You really think he killed her?"

Mankowski took a sip of Coke. "Actually, I do."

He waited for another question, but Girlie didn't ask one.

"Have you ever met the guy?" he asked, carefully studying her face, looking for a tell.

"Nope."

Mankowski felt his gut clench.

"I heard he was a pretty handsome guy who made the rounds."

Girlie's narrow shoulders rose and fell. "Not my type."

"How would you know he's not your type if you never met him before?"

"Sounds like I might be a suspect," Girlie said, playfully. "After Judi's death, I read about her murder on the Internet. One of the articles had a photograph of Peterman. He's a starving actor, right?"

Nice. A slipup and a fast recovery. The girl was good.

"So exactly what is your type?"

Girlie smiled. "I like big, strong manly men like you."

He grinned. "You're really good for my ego."

"I didn't think a guy like you needed your ego stroked. And speaking of stroking…"

She seductively sucked on her lumpia. The same way she had sucked on him.

Although he was trying hard to play it by the book, the lower half of his body refused to cooperate. He shifted in his seat and tried to erase the image of a naked Girlie sitting at the foot of his bed playing with herself.

Mankowski decided to ask about her background again, no longer caring if it made her uncomfortable.

"Tell me about yourself," he said. "You told me you grew up not far from here, but that's all I know about you."

She cocked her head. "Not much else to tell."

Just like the last time he asked about her personal life, Girlie's demeanor instantly grew dark.

"I was raised by my mother. She died several years ago."

That explained a lot. No father in the picture. That had to be why she thrived on manipulating men. Daddy issues.

"My mother put me through school working as a nursing assistant at Long Beach Memorial."

"And your father?"

"Wasn't around."

"A serviceman?"

Girlie laughed. "That's pretty stereotypical of you. What? You think my mother was snatched from the Philippine rice fields by a U.S. soldier who got her pregnant and dumped her once he got back to the states?"

Boy, she was touchy. "No, I just—"

"Well, that's not my story," she said, her tone now snippy. "It was just me, my mom and her unending series of boyfriends who never hung around long enough to marry her or become a father figure to me."

"So you never had any contact with your father at all?"

"He never claimed me, okay? Can we just leave it at that?"

"Well, your father was an asshole," Mankowski said. "Because you're an amazing woman. It's definitely his loss."

Girlie shrugged.

A heavy silence hovered over the table. "Maybe we should change the subject," Mankowski said.

"Good idea." Her smile returned as she took another bite of her lumpia. "Now, tell me again why you can't come home with me tonight," she said coyly. "And this time, make me believe it."

CHAPTER 56

I'd been an irritable ball of nerves since the court hearing. I couldn't wait for the end of the week to arrive to hear Judge Goldberg's ruling. Meantime, I was still acting as if I had a class action to litigate.

My telephone rang and I recognized the number as Olivia's cell phone. It had been a tough week for both of us. Olivia's co-workers all blamed her for delaying payment of their three grand. I prayed nothing else had gone wrong.

"Hey, Olivia," I said, trying to sound cheerful. "How's it going?"

"Not too good."

"What's wrong? Did something happen at work?"

I heard her take a deep breath, then slowly exhale.

"I wanna thank you for everything you've been doing for me, but I had a talk with my husband last night. He thinks I should drop the lawsuit. I'd like to see if you can go back to the company and get them to give me the three months' pay they originally offered. I'll just resign."

I didn't respond.

"Are you there?" Olivia asked.

"Yes, I'm here. I know this is tough on you, but what Big Buy's doing is wrong."

"*I* know that and *you* know that, but we can't fight big business."

"Yes, we can."

"But *we* aren't fighting," Olivia reminded me. "You're not the one who has to work with these heathens every day. Last week somebody let the air out of my tires, and a few days after that, somebody keyed my car. I don't know how much longer I can deal with this."

I wished I could give her some kind of guarantee of our future success, but the law was simply too unpredictable. Based on the judge's questions at the hearing, I was reasonably confident that we were going to get a permanent injunction preventing Big Buy from paying off the other women. But then things would be even tougher for her at work.

Jefferson was still bugging me about dropping the case, convinced that I was in danger. He called me several times a day just to check on me. If I was five minutes late getting home, he assumed the worst.

"Just do me a favor," I said to Olivia. "Don't make a final decision until after the judge rules on our motion later this week. Then we can sit down and talk about it. Even if the class action is thrown out, we can still pursue your case on an individual basis."

Olivia's silence conveyed that she didn't even want to do that.

"I don't know. It just doesn't seem worth it anymore. Maybe this is God's will."

I knew my next statement was a cheap shot, but it was the only way I knew to reach her.

"You've always had a strong faith," I said. "God never puts more on us than we can bear. Why don't you pray on it?"

"I already have," she said weakly. "And to tell you the truth, I still want to fight. But my husband thinks I should—"

"Ask him just to wait until we get the judge's ruling," I pleaded. "That's only a couple of days from now."

"Okay," she said uneasily, bowing to my pressure. "But I doubt that I'm going to change my mind."

CHAPTER 57

The best police work, Mankowski knew from experience, often resulted from a slow, careful analysis of the evidence. Cold cases were solved all the time by different officers reviewing the same case file years later and finding something significant that was missed the first time around.

So Mankowski figured that if he thought about it long and hard enough, he could solve the puzzle of Judi Irving's death *and* the mysterious Big Buy documents.

Mankowski and Thomas drove out of their way to pick up hotdogs at Pink's on LaBrea and Melrose. They spent the lunch hour chowing down in their sedan.

"We just gotta think everything through." Mankowski took a big bite of his Bacon Chili Cheese Dog and chased it down with a swig of Strawberry Crush. "We're probably missing something. Something simple."

Thomas grunted. "You really think so? That's actually quite insightful."

Mankowski ignored the sarcasm.

"Let's look at what we've got," he continued. "Judi Irving is attacked in her home. There are these documents that Judi told everybody she had but nobody's seen. And we have Actor Boy driving off in a Benz when he doesn't even have a job or two dimes to rub together."

"And let's not forget about Robby Irving," Thomas reminded him. "He hasn't shown up to provide his DNA. I think we need to light a fire under his rear end."

"I agree," Mankowski replied, but his money was still on Phillip Peterman.

"I'd love to get Girlie Cortez in an interrogation room," Thomas said, talking with his mouth full. He'd ordered a Brooklyn Pastrami Swiss Cheese Dog and was almost done. "I'd bet anything that when she walked out of that hotel behind Peterman, she was carrying those Big Buy documents in her briefcase."

"Maybe she isn't screwing him," Mankowski said. "Maybe she's the front man Big Buy used to negotiate the deal with Peterman for the documents."

His partner shot him a skeptical look.

"I guess that's a possibility," Thomas said. "She's a classy lady. It's hard to see her lowering herself for a weasel like Peterman."

"Except she claims she never met the guy."

Thomas paused mid-bite. "Exactly when did she tell you that?"

Mankowski winced. He hadn't meant to let that slip. "Couple days ago," he admitted.

"Man, please tell me you're not still sleeping with that chick. She's a person of interest or at least a potential witness."

"Who said I was sleeping with her?"

"I did," Thomas said. "I didn't buy it for a minute the way you were ignoring her blatant flirting when we were in her office. You didn't want me to know you planned to screw her because you know I would've told you that you'd be stupid to risk your career for a lay."

Mankowski squeezed his Strawberry Crush bottle. He hated having a bright partner.

"Okay, so I screwed her. But now I'm playing her, just like she thinks she's playing me."

Thomas brushed his palm down his face. "I know you don't want to believe it, but that woman is trouble. I felt it from the day we first met her."

"Yeah, whatever."

The ringing of Thomas' iPhone filled the car. He retrieved it from the pocket of his jacket.

"If that's another call from your stockbroker, I'm turning you in," Mankowski said.

Thomas placed the phone to his ear. His brows fused into one as he listened. After a minute or so, he lowered the phone and turned to face his partner. "You won't believe this. Phillip Peterman just crashed his brand new Benz."

Mankowski almost spit up his Strawberry Crush. "What?"

"Wrecked it off Sunset. Sounds like he's pretty banged up."

Mankowski stuffed his hotdog in the cup holder, turned on the engine and screeched off from the curb.

CHAPTER 58

I'd been telling myself all week to think positive thoughts. Judge Goldberg was going to side with me and prevent Big Buy from gutting my class action. And in less than an hour, I'd have a permanent injunction order in my hand.

I exited the Harbor Freeway at 4th Street and made my way to Grand. I was just pulling into the underground parking garage when my iPhone rang. I let it go to voicemail as I searched for a parking space. Once I parked, I pulled the phone from my purse and saw that the call was from my mother.

I listened to her message.

"This is your mama." Her tone was uncharacteristically curt. "You need to call me as soon as you get this message."

What was that about? I racked my brain, trying to figure out if I'd missed a birthday or family event, but I couldn't think of anything my mother might be upset about. I didn't need to be rattled before going into court. I would return her call after the hearing.

I joined a long line of courthouse visitors waiting to go through the metal detectors. I had just made it to the elevators, when one of my law school classmates rushed past me.

"Hey, girl," Angela Evans called out to me. "That was an interesting article in the *L.A. Times* today. I'm running late, but we'll *definitely* have to talk."

Before I could ask what article she was talking about, Angela disappeared down the corridor. When I reached Judge Goldberg's courtroom, the clerk was busy checking in the attorneys who had matters on the judge's docket.

"Hey, Candy, how's it going?" I handed the clerk my business card.

I always made a habit of getting to know the judges' clerks. Some attorneys failed to realize that the clerks ran the courtroom. Candy had been with Judge Goldberg for more than ten years.

Candy did not return my greeting. Instead, she snatched the business card from my hand.

Dang. She was obviously having a bad day.

"Did the judge issue a tentative?" I asked.

She looked me up and down. "Not in your case."

Who pissed you off this morning?

The fact the judge had not issued a tentative ruling concerned me. I took a seat in the gallery just as Girlie walked in. As usual, she drew more than her share of admiring stares, probably because her skirt was halfway up her ass.

Girlie sat in the first row, directly in front of me. After a minute or so, she turned around and smiled. "That was a nice article in the *L.A. Times* today."

"You're the second person to mention the *Times* to me," I said. "What article are you talking about?"

"The article about you." The deviousness in her smile radiated pure evil. "On the front page. You haven't seen it?"

"No, I haven't."

"You should definitely check it out." She waved at an older man in a tailored suit standing near the clerk's desk, then went over to talk to him.

I glanced at my watch. We still had thirteen minutes before the judge took the bench. I walked out into the corridor and tried to pull up the *Times* website on my iPhone, but couldn't get a signal inside the courthouse. I glanced down the corridor looking for someone reading the newspaper.

I spotted a discarded copy of the newspaper left on a bench two courtrooms down. I picked it up and stared at the front page in disbelief. Right there in living color was a photograph of Jefferson and me standing in front of the mosque chatting with Special and

Clayton. All four of us were wearing broad smiles. When I read the headline, I was glad I had skipped breakfast.

THE COMMUNITY OF ISLAM ATTRACTS
NEW BREED OF BLACK PROFESSIONALS.

The story discussed the growing number of young, African-American professionals joining the Community of Islam. The article included quotes from an Inglewood dentist, a McDonald's franchise owner and a UCLA sociology professor. My name wasn't mentioned in the story, but the caption beneath the photo identified me as *Attorney Vernetta Henderson.*

I was at a complete loss. *Was this Girlie's doing?*

I slumped down on the bench and tried to gather myself. Now I understood the gruff tone of my mother's voicemail message.

"Miss, are you okay?" an elderly Latina wearing a juror's badge touched me on the shoulder.

I could only imagine how distraught I must have looked.

"Oh…uh, yeah. I'm fine."

I stood up and marched back into the courtroom and charged straight up to Girlie. I stepped in front of the man she was talking to and got right up in her face.

"Did you have anything to do with that *Times* article?" I spoke in a tone that was appropriately low for the setting, but sufficiently venomous for the target.

"Did you like it?" Girlie smiled as if she was proud of herself. "A close friend of mine freelances for the *Times.* He's always looking for interesting feature stories. When I found out that you were a member of the Community of Islam, I told him about it."

"I'm not a member of the Community of Islam. And if I was, it wouldn't be any of your business."

The man who'd been talking to Girlie backed away from us, his eyes wide.

Girlie shrugged. "The way you were happily chatting outside that mosque, it sure looked like you were a member to me."

I pointed my index finger inches from her nose. "You are the most unethical—"

"Please come to order," the clerk called out. "The courtroom of the Honorable Ezra Goldberg is now in session."

Unfortunately, we were the first case on the docket. The clerk called our case number and we both headed into the well of the courtroom.

My head was still reeling and I couldn't think straight. I had no idea what Girlie had hoped to gain from this little stunt.

"After a careful review of the moving papers and case law," Judge Goldberg began, "I'm lifting the temporary injunction against Big Buy and denying plaintiff's motion for a permanent injunction. I find that Big Buy's settlement offer to its employees did not violate the attorney-client privilege as the employees were not represented by counsel at the time of the relevant communications since the class had not been certified."

"Your Honor," I said, "I'd like to direct your attention to *Mallory v. Sommers*, which we cited in our moving papers. The facts of that case are similar to this one in that—"

"I'm not taking any additional argument on your motion, Ms. Henderson." There was an impatience in his voice that I'd never seen him exhibit before.

"Your Honor, I would just like to—"

The judge banged his gavel. "Next case."

It wasn't until this precise moment that I understood the motivation for Girlie's vicious little stunt. She feared Judge Goldberg would grant my request for a permanent injunction. So she maneuvered to get that article published, banking on the likelihood that our Jewish judge would allow his personal feelings about the Community of Islam to color how he decided my motion.

Girlie had gathered her papers and was on her way out of the courtroom. I just stood there like a frozen stick figure.

"We're done here, Ms. Henderson," Judge Goldberg said brusquely. He turned to his clerk. "Please call the next case."

I all but stumbled out of the courtroom. I looked around for Girlie, but she was long gone. I tried to wait for an elevator, but I was so filled with rage that I finally jogged down the escalators.

Girlie Cortez had done it again. She'd defeated me not with legal talent, but with a blatantly underhanded tactic. I had spent my entire career playing by the rules, something that was foreign to Girlie. Maybe it was time for me to start doing things her way.

The second I stepped outside the courthouse, I pulled out my iPhone and speed-dialed Special. "I have a job for you."

"A job? What kind of job?"

"You said you want to be an investigator, well, I'm hiring you. And this is a paying job."

"Oh, snap! I'm definitely down with that. What do you need me to do?"

"I need you to find me some dirt on Girlie Cortez. And I don't care what you have to do to get it."

"Whooaaa. This doesn't sound like the uber-ethical Vernetta Henderson I know. What did that cow do to piss you off now?"

"Read the front page of today's *L.A. Times*," I said. "That little story she planted just sank my class action. And whatever information you dig up on her ass, make sure it's enough for me to bury that bitch."

CHAPTER 59

Mankowski and Thomas reached the crash scene just as an ambulance whizzed by, rushing Phillip to UCLA Medical Center.

"Was he conscious?" Mankowski asked a uniformed officer as he reached into his breast pocket for his badge. "We're homicide. The guy's a person of interest in one of our cases."

"He was pretty banged up, but conscious."

Phillip's new Benz was now a mangled piece of steel. The entire front end looked like an accordion, but the back half was mostly intact.

Mankowski scanned the area. "The pavement's dry, the weather's clear. What in the hell caused him to crash in broad daylight?"

Another officer standing nearby answered the question. "A witness said he was texting and drifted into another lane. He swerved to keep from hitting another car and ran off the road into that tree."

Mankowski and Thomas approached the wreckage and looked inside the car.

"What a waste," Thomas said, admiring the car.

Mankowski turned back to the first officer. "Did you find anything of interest inside the car?"

Even if Phillip had sold the documents to Girlie, the scumbag probably would have double-crossed her and kept an extra copy.

The cop gave him a blank look. "Interesting like what?"

"Like documents or a file folder."

"We haven't searched it yet. They usually do inventory at impound."

Mankowski couldn't wait that long. "Can't you do it here?"

The officer shrugged. "I guess we could."

Mankowski felt a sense of anticipation as the officer searched the car's interior. They found a throwaway cell phone, but the Big Buy papers weren't there.

The tow truck driver grabbed a crowbar and wedged it into the back of the trunk near the key slot. This was it. Mankowski was sure of it. Those Big Buy documents were in there.

He felt like he was in the closing scene of some TV crime show, seconds before the discovery of the smoking gun.

The trunk finally sprang open and the two detectives stepped forward. When Mankowski saw a thick stack of loose papers, his pulse sped up three notches. He reached for them, but Thomas snatched his hand away.

"We're doing this by the book," Thomas declared. "We don't have probable cause to touch those documents, but these guys do."

They waited as the officer picked them up and began to peruse them.

"Is that it?" Thomas asked, peering over Mankowski's shoulder.

They scanned the pages as the officer flipped through them.

"Damn!" Mankowski said, turning away. "It's only his friggin' lease papers."

The officer searched the rest of the trunk, but found nothing.

"Let's head over to the hospital," Mankowski said, already walking in the direction of the car. "Maybe seeing his life flash before his eyes will make Actor Boy more willing to talk."

The drive to UCLA Medical Center took less than twenty minutes, but it took close to an hour to track down someone who could provide information on Phillip's condition. A nurse finally explained that Phillip was critical, but stable, but wasn't well enough to undergo an interview.

"Can you get a doctor down here who can tell me when we can talk to him. It's very important."

Thirty minutes later, a young doctor in green scrubs approached the two detectives. Mankowski hopped to his feet.

"I understand that you're here about Phillip Peterman," the doctor said. "Are you family?"

"No, we're with LAPD." He showed his badge. "When can we talk to him?"

The doctor cleared his throat. "I'm sorry, but you won't be able to do that. We weren't able to stop the internal bleeding. Mr. Peterman didn't make it."

CHAPTER 60

I spent the next three hours after leaving the courthouse huddled in my office alternately sulking and cursing Girlie Cortez.

I had no idea how I was going to break the news to Olivia about the dismissal of the class action. I didn't even want to call Benjamin. I could file a writ asking the California Court of Appeal to reverse Judge Goldberg's ruling, but that was a longshot.

Before facing my client, I needed to return my mother's call and let her know that I had not abandoned my Christian upbringing. I'd planned to make sure Olivia knew that too.

"Hey, mama," I said, when she picked up.

"I was beginning to think you were never going to call me back."

"I had a court appearance this morning."

"Did you read the newspaper today?"

I rubbed my forehead. "Yes, and that article isn't true."

"Pictures don't lie. Since when did you start going to the mosque?"

"I only went that once with Special and her boyfriend, Clayton. He's a Muslim."

"Does Special's mama know about this?"

"There's nothing to know. Anyway, they recently broke up."

"Everybody I know saw that article. I've been getting calls all day. Reverend Hamilton even left me a message, but I couldn't bring myself to call him back."

"Well, please tell Reverend Hamilton and everybody else at Community Baptist that I'm still a God-fearing Christian, okay?"

"I should hope so. We raised you right."

"Yeah, I know, mama. I have to go, okay?"

"I'm not done yet. What about Jefferson? Is he mixed up with them Muslims?"

"Jefferson and Clayton are friends, mama."

"That's not what I asked you."

"Mama, I really can't talk about this right now. I'm late for a meeting. I'll call you later."

That witch Girlie even had me lying to my mama.

Rather than face Olivia, I headed home to sulk some more. I heated up some leftover Thai food and spent the afternoon plotting my revenge against Girlie Cortez. I wanted to call Jefferson to tell him about the article, but he had an important meeting about the problems with that shopping center project. I didn't want to interrupt his day with my troubles.

He arrived home just after six, looking as perturbed as I felt.

"How did your meeting go?" I asked.

"Not good." He untied his work boots and joined me on the couch in the den.

"I hate to add more gray clouds to your day, but I suspect you haven't seen this yet."

I tossed the *L.A. Times* onto the coffee table in front of him. He sat forward, glanced at the headline, then picked up the paper. I waited while he read the entire article. He set the newspaper back on the table, then picked up the remote and changed the channel to ESPN.

"So?" I said.

Jefferson looked over at me. His face had no inkling of the concern that I had expected. "What?"

"You don't have anything to say about the article?"

"Oh," he shrugged. "I thought it was a good story. I think I know that dentist they quoted. I didn't know he was a Muslim. That's some nice pub for the Community."

My mouth fell open. *"Nice pub for the Community?* Are you crazy? Did you see that big-ass picture of us? What about the bad pub for you and me? People think we're members of the Community of Islam."

"So?"

"I just lost a very important motion because the judge assumed I was a member."

"And if you were, what would that have to do with your motion?"

"Absolutely nothing but—"

"Okay, then tell the judge to kiss your ass."

"Unfortunately, it doesn't work like that."

"This is exactly what the Muslims are talking about. We're always too busy bowin' and scrapin' and worrying about what white folks think. The Muslims are about teaching black people to think for themselves and take care of themselves. If that judge—or anybody else—has a problem with that, that's on them. You don't work for O'Reilly & Finney anymore. You have your own law practice. You're off the plantation now. So stop acting like a slave."

I was certain I felt the room sway. "I'm not a slave. I'm a realist. Because of that article, people are going to think I hate white people."

"When we went to the mosque, did you hear anybody say one word about hatin' white people?"

"No, but—"

"Whenever black folks try to come together, white folks get threatened and try to sabotage us. And as long as we're walking around with our tails between our legs, they can. If people wanna think that building up black folks means hatin' on white folks, then so be it."

I was too stunned by my husband's harsh words to form an appropriate retort. "I don't know why I even tried to talk to you about this." I stood up and marched out of the room.

"I don't know either," he called after me as I headed down the hallway. "I think that article is good for us."

I screeched to a stop, then charged back into the den. "*Us?* So you're a Muslim now?"

"Maybe. I like what they're about."

"If that's the choice you've made, it impacts me as much as it does you. So it's something *we* need to discuss."

"*We* can't discuss it because *you* go ape shit every time you hear me mention the Community. Like right now. I've never seen you be so closed-minded about anything."

"I'm not closed-minded."

"Yes, you are. You don't see the Community for what it is. You see it for what the white media's been telling you it is."

"What's going on with you, Jefferson? You were raised as a Christian. Are you saying those aren't your beliefs anymore?"

"Right now, I'm not sure what my beliefs are. But the Community of Islam is a much better fit for me than trying to turn the other cheek and wait for my rewards in heaven. The Muslims are about improving the lives of black folks here on earth, now. And that just makes sense to me."

"Well, that's not what *I'm* about. So it sounds like you might have some choices to make."

Jefferson snatched the remote from the end table and settled deeper into the couch.

"I like going to the mosque and I like hanging out with the brothers down there," he said, staring at the TV screen and not me. "If anybody has a choice to make, it ain't me. It's you."

CHAPTER 61

I'd made four calls to Benjamin over the last few days. It was
unusual for him not to call me back. I immediately feared that he
might be in danger again.

Rather than call his direct line or cell phone, I called the main
office this time.

"Hey, Reesa," I said when his Intake Administrator picked up.
"I've been trying to reach Benjamin for a few days, but he hasn't
called me back. Is he there?"

"Yeah, he's here," Reesa said with a chuckle. "But I don't think
he wanna talk to you."

Reesa was a bus driver who volunteered at the Center three days
a week. She ran the place like she owned it.

"And why wouldn't he want to talk to me?"

"Girl, how many degrees do you have? Benjamin is Jewish.
You're a black Muslim. I think it might have something to do with
your religion."

Then it hit me. That damn *L.A. Times* article.

"I'm not a Muslim," I said curtly. "Can you please put Benjamin
on the phone?"

"If you ask me, and I know you haven't, you need to come down
here and talk to your friend in person. You guys go way back. Come
talk to him."

Thirty minutes later, I walked into the lobby of the Center for Justice and approached Lisa Goldman, the law school intern who ran the front desk. "Could you tell Benjamin I'm here?"

She looked me up and down. "Do you have an appointment?"

"I don't need one," I said, and walked right past her.

I stopped a second before entering the open door of Ben's office. I didn't need to barrel in there angry at him for being angry with me. I took a big breath, then stepped inside.

Benjamin was reading something on his computer screen, his back facing me.

"We need to talk." I plunked down on one of the rickety chairs in front of his desk.

Benjamin didn't turn around. "Uh, I'm a little busy right now."

"I'm not a member of the Community of Islam."

"Okay."

"This is nuts. Benjamin, you know me. We need to talk."

Benjamin turned around, finally giving me his full attention. He propped his elbows on the arms of his chair and laced his fingers.

"Okay, you're not a member," he said. There was no anger on his face, just resignation. "But you just drop by for the weekly lectures?"

"C'mon, Benjamin, you know my friend Special. Her boyfriend or ex-boyfriend is a member. That's why she joined. They asked me and Jefferson to attend a lecture. We just went to be nice."

Benjamin knew Special pretty well. The three of us had even gone out for dinner together a few times.

"Special being a member doesn't surprise me. But you…" His words trailed off.

"I'm not a member," I repeated.

"I wonder how you'd feel if you'd seen a snapshot of me with some extremist group chatting it up with my racist buddies."

"I'm not sure how I'd feel, but I would ask you some questions rather than make assumptions. Because I know you so well, I'd give you the benefit of the doubt. I wouldn't presume you were a racist. I'd go on what I know about you. Not what I read in the newspaper. And the Community of Islam isn't racist."

He leaned back in his chair. "Really? Based on everything I've read it certainly appears to be."

"Everything you've read was probably written by a non-Muslim with a bias against them."

"Excuse me, but didn't you just say you *weren't* a member? You certainly sound like one by the way you're defending them."

"I'm not defending them. I'm defending their right to exist and their right to believe what they believe. Just like you have the right to believe what you believe. They're not anti-white. Their focus is uplifting the lives of black people."

"I recall one of their leaders making some pretty nasty statements about the Jewish faith. I think he called it a filthy religion. That doesn't sound very uplifting of black people to me."

I wasn't sure why I felt the need to defend the Community, but I did. "And what else do you know about them?"

He dropped his hands and rested them on the desk. "I don't need to know anything else."

"Like I said, I'm not a member and I don't support statements like that. But they have a right to their beliefs."

Splotches of red stung Benjamin's cheeks. "You're not talking to someone who doesn't know about discrimination," he said. "I just don't think slavery and discrimination are a justification for promoting hate."

"I agree. And from what I've learned about the Community, they don't promote hate."

"Whatever you say." Benjamin abruptly turned back to his computer.

"Benjamin, this is nuts! Your friendship means a lot to me. Plus, we have work to do. I still want to do everything I can to help Olivia."

He started typing on the keyboard and acted as if he hadn't heard me.

"You're the one who brought this case to me," I said. "So basically, it's yours. Are you telling me you want me off of it?"

He waited a long beat, then shook his head.

"Then we need to talk about our next steps," I said. "Girlie has derailed our class action, but I'm determined to find a way to get some justice for Olivia if it kills me."

CHAPTER 62

Detective Thomas slapped a sheet of paper on the corner of Mankowski's desk.

"Peterman's DNA results are in," he said. "And you're not going to believe it."

Mankowski leaned back in his chair and continued his intense examination of the *Sports Illustrated* Swimsuit Edition. He turned the magazine sideways to admire the luscious brunette centerfold.

"What's not to believe? It was Actor Boy's DNA underneath Judi Irving's fingernails, right?"

Following Phillip's death, his agent had finally called back and admitted that Phillip hadn't been at his house that night. For Mankowski, Phillip's lack of an alibi only confirmed that he had killed Judi. His gut was right again.

Mankowski had wanted Phillip to pay for Judi Irving's death, but that was impossible now. Without Phillip, he knew it would be difficult, if not impossible, to tie Girlie in. He could not and would not let Girlie walk away scot-free. Vernetta Henderson might believe that Girlie Cortez never got caught, but Mankowski was determined to prove her wrong. He'd cracked difficult cases before and he'd do it with this one too.

"Yep," Thomas said. "It was Phillip's DNA."

This news didn't excite Mankowski since he knew his gut had been right all along. He flipped a page in the magazine.

"At least we kept that scum from getting the insurance money before he kicked the bucket. I just wish we knew where he'd gotten the cash to lease that Benz."

"We already know where he got it," Thomas said. "From your girlfriend."

"She isn't my girlfriend," Mankowski snapped, finally looking up. "Go ahead and admit that my gut racked up another one."

"Hold on a minute, partner." Thomas took the magazine from Mankowski's hands and shoved a piece of paper in its place. "Your gut's not getting credit for solving Judi Irving's murder just yet. Take a look at this."

Mankowski scanned the DNA report.

"What's the deal?" he said, glancing up at his partner again. "You just said Phillip's DNA was a match."

Thomas smiled. "The test confirmed that the blood and skin underneath the fingernails of Judi's right hand belonged to Phillip. But believe it or not, she apparently sunk her nails into two people. Phillip *wasn't* a match for the DNA underneath the nails of Judi's *left* hand."

Mankowski sprang forward in his chair. "You're shittin' me."

Thomas pointed at the report. "Nope, it's right there in black and white. You know what I think? I think Judi did scratch Phillip's face that night. But also she scratched somebody else."

"Maybe Actor Boy had help," Mankowski said, thinking out loud.

Thomas shook his head. "I think your gut's been way off on this one from the start. You and your tunnel vision have been too focused on Phillip."

Sometimes Mankowski hated it when his partner made sense.

"Robby Irving hasn't shown up to provide his DNA," Thomas continued. "Maybe the neighbor heard Judi fighting with Robby, not Phillip. Robby Irving has the same motive as Phillip—that insurance money. We've been letting your gut, as well as your dick, lead us down the wrong path."

Mankowski started to get huffy about his partner's snide remark, but suddenly snapped his fingers and turned away. He dug through a stack of pink message slips on his desk.

"Robby Irving's ditzy girlfriend called me a couple of days ago."

"Uncooperative Camille? What did she want?"

"I don't know." Mankowski pulled Camille's message from the stack. "Haven't had a chance to call her back yet. It looks like Robby Irving needs to go to the top of our persons-of-interest list."

"He never came off mine," Thomas reminded him.

"And we still gotta figure out how those documents fit in," Mankowski said, reenergized. "Maybe Judi's death isn't connected to Big Buy at all."

"I hope it doesn't turn out that we wasted all this time looking at Peterman, when Robby Irving's our guy," Thomas said, getting in another dig.

The police had officially ruled Phillip Peterman's death a case of distracted driving. Three witnesses reported seeing him looking down at his phone seconds before the crash. Unfortunately, they found no useful information in his phone.

Mankowski was unwilling to admit that he was wrong on this one yet.

"Don't get all happy. We can't rule out Actor Boy as the killer yet. The guy definitely had something to hide. Otherwise, why was he using a throwaway cell phone? We just gotta figure out how Girlie Cortez is connected."

"Good to hear that you're finally willing to admit that Girlie punked you."

Mankowski grimaced. "Nobody punked me."

"Really? She screwed you, she screwed Phillip and who knows who else."

Mankowski had nothing to say to that.

"Let's go." He grabbed his jacket from the back of the chair. "We can call Camille from the car and tell her we're on our way over. And after we finish with her, we're going to pay Robby Irving a visit."

CHAPTER 63

I'd just returned to my office after a trip downstairs for coffee when I heard my iPhone ring. I picked it up and saw that I had missed two calls from Jefferson.

He was probably calling to ball me out for breaking my promise to leave the office by six. Since the incident at the Howard Hughes Promenade, Jefferson had started calling me several times a day just to check on me. While I was glad he was concerned about my safety, he was starting to make me feel a little nervous.

We still hadn't resolved our differences over his interest in the Community of Islam. Jefferson was continuing to attend lectures at the mosque every Tuesday night and most Sundays. For now, we both avoided the conflict by never bringing it up.

Now that my class action was history, I was pouring all of my energy into Olivia's individual case. I'd convinced her not to dismiss the lawsuit just yet, but I didn't know how long she could hold out.

Turning off my computer, I began packing up to leave. Once I got to my car, I would let Jefferson know I was on my way. I bent down to retrieve my purse from the bottom drawer of my desk. When I stood up, Lamarr was standing in the doorway of my office.

"Hey, counselor," he slurred. His right hand was tucked behind his back. "You workin' pretty late tonight. Hope that's my case you slavin' over."

A jolt of panic hit me at the sight of my wealthy client. His sluggish speech pattern told me he was either intoxicated or high, or both. He was usually immaculately dressed. Today, his jeans were dirty and his white T-shirt was stained with brown splotches that looked like dried gravy. The stench of body odor tainted with alcohol wafted all the way across the room.

"How'd you get up here?" I said. "The guard is supposed to call me before letting anyone up after hours."

Lamarr shrugged, stepped further into my office and closed the door behind him.

"Everybody know me," he bragged with a smile. "And everybody know you're my lawyer. I told the guard I wanted to surprise you, so he let me up. After I gave him my autograph, of course."

"Well, I'm surprised alright."

This wasn't the first time our poor excuse for security had ignored after-hour procedures. I planned to complain to the building manager first thing in the morning.

Lamarr was sporting thick cornrows now and facial hair that was too unkempt to be called a beard. He was squinting so much I couldn't tell if his eyes were even open. His dirty T-shirt draped over his low-hanging jeans gave him a hard-core gang-banger look.

His slovenly physical appearance wasn't what concerned me most.

"What are you holding behind your back?" I asked.

My mind had already raced to the worst-case scenario. Dissatisfied clients have been known to take out their frustrations on their lawyers. Was I staring at a client who was upset enough to pull out a gun and blow me away?

Lamarr snickered and took several long strides toward me. He was now inches away from my desk, his right hand still tucked behind his back.

"You know, I really don't like it when people hang up on me. I paid you over two-hundred grand. You'd think I'd get a little more respect for that much dough."

"I hung up because you weren't listening to me. What are you holding behind your back?" I asked again.

"I bought you a present."

I held my breath and wondered when the security guard would be making his rounds. Not that it mattered since none of the guards carried weapons.

"What kind of present?"

Instead of answering, Lamarr slapped a bouquet of red roses on my desk. Petals scattered everywhere.

I must've jumped a good foot off the floor.

"Why you so jumpy, counselor?" A cloud of alcohol rolled past my face as he spoke. "You ain't afraid of me, are you?"

I stared at him a long time before answering. The fact that he was carrying flowers and not a .38 did little to reduce my anxiety level. Actually, I was afraid, very afraid. But I couldn't let him know that.

Show no fear.

I folded my arms across my chest. "Do I have a reason to be afraid?"

"I don't know. Do you? By the way, you never told me you was a black Muslim. I was glad to hear that. That means you can relate to how the white man tries to keep a brother down. That's what this is all about. The same way they tried to bring down Tiger Woods and Mike Tyson. That's what they're trying to do to me."

He was obviously delirious.

I grabbed the strap of my purse and hoisted it on my shoulder. "Thanks for the flowers. I was just about to leave. So—"

"Have a seat," he said. His tone was serious now.

"We'll have to talk another time. I have to get home."

He slapped the desk with his open hand. "I said, sit your ass down!"

Lamarr was no longer squinting and I could see the whites of his eyes, except they weren't white. They were bloodshot red.

I eased back into my chair.

"I wanna know why you won't hold a press conference for me like you did for those women at that store?"

Lamarr was a large man, but he seemed twice as large as he glowered down at me.

"I don't think it's a good idea to call a press conference right now. We don't have anything new about the case to announce."

"So? Make some shit up."

"That's not how it works."

My eyes slid sideways toward the closed door. Since Lamarr was intoxicated, maybe I could make it to the door before he caught me. But then what? It would take forever for the elevators to arrive. The stairs were not an option. I'd seen too many bad B movies where stairwell chases end badly to even consider that as an option.

"I have a question for you," Lamarr said. "All that nice stuff you said about me in court during your closing argument, did you really believe it?"

I swallowed. "Yes, of course."

His chin jutted forward and his lips tightened. "I think you lyin'. You think I raped that bitch, don't you?"

My heart thudded against my chest. "You told me you didn't do it and I believe you."

Lamarr angled his head as his expression switched from one of anger to seduction. He stepped around the desk, licking his lips.

"You ever thought about gettin' with me?"

My hands squeezed the arms of my chair. "No. I'm married."

"That don't mean shit. I screw married women all the time."

I tried to slow the pace of my breathing. *Show no fear.*

"I never told you this, but one of the reasons I picked you for my lawyer was 'cuz I thought there was a vibe between us. You smart and shit, but you also got a hella phatt ass."

He laughed and fell into one of the chairs in front of my desk.

I immediately bounced to my feet. It felt much better to be staring down at him rather than the other way around.

"I'm not comfortable with this conversation, Lamarr."

"*I'm not comfortable with this conversation, Lamarr,*" he mimicked in a high-pitched voice. "And I'm not comfortable with paying that bitch no two-million dollars."

I flinched when my iPhone rang. Before I could get to it, Lamarr grabbed it from my desk and tossed it across the room. It fell to the carpeted floor with a thud just to the right of the door.

"We don't need no interruptions."

Internally, I was in full panic mode now. I was ready to tell Lamarr whatever he wanted to hear to get him out of my office.

"Fine, Lamarr. If you want me to hold a press conference for you, I will."

"Oh, so now, you wanna cooperate." He slid so low into the chair that his huge head hooked over the back.

"What else you wanna cooperate about, counselor?"

"You're really making me uncomfortable, Lamarr. You need to leave."

"Maybe I should show you why that bitch Tonisha did all that scheming to get with me. It wasn't just because I play pro ball." He winked. "I really know how to please the ladies."

He hopped up and started walking around the desk toward me. I jumped behind my chair, using it as a shield.

"C'mon, counselor, you ain't scared of me, are you?"

I took a step back, at the same time that I pushed the chair forward. I was trying to get within reach of the paperweight on my desk just in case I needed to use it.

"I'm not playing, Lamarr. You need to leave."

"Stop actin' like you don't wanna get with me." He lifted his T-shirt to show off his solid, ripped abs, then slapped his stomach with his palm. "You like this? Bet your husband ain't got a body like this."

"Is this how it went down with Tonisha?" I asked.

My question stopped him cold. His body stiffened and he seemed to awaken from his high.

"I told you I didn't rape that bitch!" His tone was angry and this time he didn't slur a single word.

"Considering the way you're acting right now, that's kind of hard for me to believe."

Rather than upset him, my comments seemed to wound him. I could see that expressing disbelief in his innocence was the only weapon at my disposal.

"Frankly," I continued, "I'm wondering if the way I'm feeling right now is how Tonisha felt right before you raped her."

"I'm not no damn rapist!" he yelled, his voice quivering. "I wasn't gonna do nothing to you. I was just playin' with you, girl."

He threw up his hands and fell back into the chair. "I just want you to get me a press conference. That's all. Can't you just—"

The door of my office suddenly flew open and Jefferson stepped inside. "What's going on in here?" His narrowed eyes scrutinized me, then Lamarr, then me again.

The rage and frustration on Lamarr's face had been replaced with a smile. "I was just talking a little late-night business with my counselor here. You're Jefferson, right? Good to see you again, bruh." He extended his hand.

Though I hadn't said a word, Jefferson apparently sensed that I was in distress. He ignored Lamarr's hand and walked up to me.

"You okay, babe? I heard yelling in here a second ago."

He took in the rose petals scattered everywhere, then walked across the room to retrieve my iPhone from the floor. "What's this doing on the floor and what's that all over your desk?"

"Everything's cool," Lamarr said, easing toward the door. "I'll holla back at you tomorrow about that press conference, counselor."

When the door finally closed, I collapsed into my chair and dumped my face into my palms.

"Babe, what's going on in here?" Jefferson demanded, standing over me. "Did he get out of line?"

If I told my husband what had just happened, he'd be on his way downstairs after Lamarr.

"What made you come down here?" I asked, trying to keep my voice from trembling.

"You didn't answer my calls. I even called just before I came up here. Why didn't you pick up?"

I stood and buried my face in his chest. "I'm so glad you're here."

"Tell me what happened?"

"I can't talk about it," I lied. "It's privileged."

"You're lyin'. Did Lamarr get out of line? Do you need me to kick his ass?"

I laughed. "I don't think you could."

"I know that. I'd bring some of my boys with me."

I sat back down and turned on my computer. "I have a short letter I need to prepare."

"Now?" Jefferson asked with a frown. "Can't that wait until tomorrow?"

"Nope. I have to do it now so it can be hand-delivered first thing in the morning. We'll be out of here in ten minutes."

Jefferson took a seat. "A letter to who?"

"Lamarr," I said, anxious for the computer to boot up. "Telling him to find himself a new attorney."

CHAPTER 64

The detectives found Camille standing in the doorway of the salon when they pulled up out front. Before they could park, Camille pranced over in leopard-print leggings and a matching lace blouse.

Detective Mankowski rolled down the window as Camille squatted down to talk to them.

"Meet me at the coffee shop," she whispered, pointing across the street. "Too many nosey Nellie's in the salon. Go on over while I run back inside and grab my purse."

They were seated at a table near the door when Camille sashayed in.

"This won't work," she complained, looking around the tiny cafe. "I don't want anybody to overhear us."

She selected a table for four in the back near the emergency exit.

Camille dropped her rabbit hair purse in the empty chair. "First of all, I need to know if you guys are willing to slice me a deal?"

This time both men laughed.

"*Cut* you a deal for what?" Mankowski asked.

Camille rolled her eyes. "For information."

"We don't cut or slice deals. Prosecutors do that. But once we hear what you have to say, we'll see what we can do."

"The cops on *Law & Order* do it all the time," she whined. "I want a deal!"

"Did you commit a crime?" Mankowski asked.

Camille leaned back in her chair and folded her bony arms. "You're not tricking me into a confession. I'm taking the Fourth."

"It's the Fifth," Mankowski corrected her. "Did you have anything to do with Judi Irving's murder?"

She pressed a hand to her cheek. "Oh, heavens no!"

"Then you don't need a deal."

Camille took a few seconds to ponder that.

"You're the one who called us, remember?" Thomas said. "So whatever it is you called us about, you need to start talking."

Camille nervously glanced around the restaurant, then leaned her head close to theirs. "Okay, here it is," she said in a hushed tone. "I wasn't exactly truthful with you before."

"About what?"

"About being home with Robby. I wasn't at his house the night his wife was murdered."

Mankowski cocked his head. "So why did you lie?"

"To help Robby."

"So you think he killed Judi?"

"I dunno. Maybe."

Camille's new version of events didn't smell right.

"The last time we spoke to you, you were pretty certain that Robby couldn't hurt a fly," Thomas said.

Camille huffed. "Let's just say he's not the man I thought he was."

"So when did you reach that conclusion?" Thomas asked.

"A few days ago."

"Did you guys break up or something?"

Camille's eyes began to well up. "How'd you know?"

"Just a lucky guess," Thomas said. "What happened?"

"He had the nerve to tell me that we weren't a good fit," she whimpered. "After all I've done for him."

Mankowski scratched his chin. "And now you want to get back at him."

She dabbed her eyes with a table napkin. "All's fair in love and battle."

"I'm not sure we know which story to believe," Mankowski said. "The first story you told us or this one. Maybe you were telling the truth before and now you're lying to get back at Robby for dumping you."

"I'm telling the truth now," she pouted. "I wasn't with him that night. I swear."

CHAPTER 65

Girlie hadn't felt this great since the day she'd made partner.

She was seated in the boardroom at Big Buy headquarters, trying to look humble as the board of directors sang her praises.

"That was an incredible result," said the CEO. "An absolutely brilliant strategy. Any other attorney would've had the company tied up in litigation for years, billing us up the whazoo. But you were thinking outside the box."

Rita's tirade in her office just a few days ago was totally forgotten now.

Girlie glanced to her right at Evelyn. The general counsel's stoic expression conveyed that this love fest didn't exactly please her.

"I was just doing the job I was paid to do," Girlie said, her best imitation of humility.

Fred Hiller, the CFO, picked up an envelope and walked around to the side of the table where Girlie was sitting.

"This is just a small token of our appreciation," he said, handing it to her. "There's a check inside for fifty-thousand dollars. That's a bonus for you, not your firm," he stressed. "I've already made that clear to your managing partner. Having us pay out those measly bonuses will save us far more than fighting a class action."

The general counsel had staunchly opposed Girlie's idea to pay off all the potential class members, but Rita had overruled her. Girlie decided to throw Evelyn a bone.

"Thank you all very much. But this has really been a team effort. I've worked hand-in-hand with your general counsel. So let's not leave her out."

The board members took about ten seconds to applaud Evelyn, then turned back to heaping praise on Girlie.

Evelyn apparently decided to interject some gloom into the celebration.

"We still have one plaintiff left," she said. "We shouldn't really celebrate until we're able to get rid of Olivia Jackson's case too."

The CEO swatted away her sister-in-law's concerns. "That'll be easy. Even *you* would be able to settle that case."

Girlie looked from the CEO to the general counsel and wondered how they'd been able to work together for as long as they had.

"I don't think it will be that easy," Evelyn said. "I suspect Ms. Jackson's attorney will dig in her heels even more."

"Don't worry." Girlie's tone was full of assurance. "It's my plan to have that case resolved very shortly as well."

"So are we going to try to settle with her too?" the CFO asked.

Girlie smiled. "Not right away. The plaintiff already turned down an offer of three months' pay. I'd like to drag this process out a bit. Teach her and her attorney a lesson."

The CEO smiled, but only for a second. "What if her attorney really has those documents?"

"I don't think she does," Girlie said confidently. "Trust me. If Vernetta Henderson had something on the company, you can bet she would've played her hand by now."

"I like your style, young lady," said Bob Zimmerman, one of the board members. "I can tell that you enjoy going for the jugular."

"Yes, I do," Girlie said proudly. "And when I'm finally done with Ms. Vernetta Henderson and her one remaining client, it'll be a bloodbath."

CHAPTER 66

Special was more than proud of herself. She had waited four whole days before returning Clayton's call. But the second she heard his voice, all the resolve she'd built up sapped right out of her.

"How you doin'?" Clayton asked.

She took in a deep breath. "I'm good."

Actually, she was pretty messed up. She had no appetite, still couldn't sleep through the night and her heart felt like someone had trampled on it with a pair of football cleats. Love sucked.

"I miss you," he said.

I miss you too, she felt, but didn't say.

"Did you hear me?"

"Yeah, I heard you."

Brothers were forever trippin'. First they can't get enough of you, then they dump your ass, then they want you back.

"Have you eaten yet? I wanna take you out to dinner."

"Why? Sister Akila's not available to cook for you tonight?"

"It's not like that. I'm not with her."

Men were so friggin' stupid. That tattle-tale had her eye on Clayton. Six months from now, he'd be walking Akila down the aisle instead of her.

"So can I take you to dinner?"

"Nope. Gotta do my nails."

Clayton chuckled. "So it's like that?"

"Yep, it's like that."

"Don't you miss me?"

Of course, I do. "A little."

"Alright," he said. "I won't push it."

That was an hour ago. Now his fine ass was standing on her porch, smiling like he was about to get some. *Damn him.*

"Aren't you going to let me in?" He held up a bag. "Since you wouldn't let me take you out to dinner, I brought dinner to you."

Special searched for the strength to tell him to leave, but had none left. She stepped back and let him in.

Damn. He smelled good too.

"So what's in the bag?"

"I stopped by Simply Wholesome. Got us some tofu burgers."

A stiff smile concealed her disappointment. *If you really wanted to impress me, you shoulda stopped by Woody's and picked up some pork ribs.*

Clayton marched in like he owned the place. Like everything between them was great. He placed the bag on the kitchen table.

"I wanted to let you know that I changed my name." His face swelled with pride. "I'm Khalil Ali now."

"Wow, you really did it. The name fits you. I like it." And she really did.

Special opened the cabinet and pulled out two plates. When she turned around, Clayton was standing directly in front of her, his body almost touching hers.

She tried to breathe, but couldn't.

"I miss you," he whispered. His sweet breath warmed her face.

She tried to take a step back, but she was trapped between Clayton and the counter. He wrapped his arms around her.

"What are you doing?" Her protest had little force behind it.

"I don't know what I'm doing. I just know I miss you." He pressed his lips to hers.

They connected in a soft, slow kiss, then Special turned her head away.

"So what's this? A booty call?"

"You and I were never about that. You know that."

He kissed her again and this time, she let go, kissing him back.

Their lips still pressed together, Clayton lifted her up and sat her on the counter. Special's legs easily wrapped around his waist. Clayton quickly scooped her up by the butt and started carting her toward the bedroom.

They were almost there when Special had a change of heart. "No," she said, trying to pull away. "I can't do this."

Clayton acted as if he hadn't heard her. He kept walking, his face buried in the crook of her neck, peppering her with kisses.

"I'm serious. Clay—I mean, Khalil. I can't do this."

Just before they entered the bedroom, Special reached out and grabbed the doorframe, then pressed her hand flat against the hallway wall, stopping him. She unwrapped her legs and jumped from his embrace.

She backed away from him until the wall stopped her.

"Why are you here, Clayton? Sorry, Khalil. You made your choice very clear to me."

Breathing heavily, he slumped back against the opposite wall, facing her. There was barely enough light in the hallway to make out each other's face.

"I'm here because I miss you and because I want you in my life."

"We've been through this already. I can't be what you want me to be."

"How do you know that for sure? You didn't really give it much of a try. I've been praying for Allah to show you the way."

The first tear hit her cheek before she even felt the moisture in her eyes.

"That's not going to happen," she said. "I can't be your Muslim wife. I have my own faith and I don't want to change it."

He twisted his lips to the side. They just stood there for a long, sad moment. Special wanted to tell him to leave. She also wanted to beg him to stay.

"I don't want you to ever have any doubt that I love you," he said quietly. "Because I do. A lot."

"I know that. I need you to go because I don't know how much willpower I have left. If you stay too much longer, we're going to end up in bed."

He smiled. "For real?"

Special grabbed his forearm and led him back into the living room and opened the front door. When he bent down to kiss her, she leaned her head back, out of his reach.

"Please, don't. We can't—"

He ignored her lukewarm protests, pulled her to his chest. "How about this?" he said with a devious smile. "What about one last booty call for the road?"

She laughed and squirmed free. "How about you take your horny behind home?"

After he stepped outside, Special closed the door, then hurried over to the front picture window. She lifted the curtain just an inch and watched Clayton walk to his car. She continued to sit in the window long after he was gone. She imagined that she must have looked like a jilted heroine from some sappy chick flick.

Only one more night, Special promised herself. She would cry herself to sleep one more night. Then she was moving on.

CHAPTER 67

Detectives Thomas and Mankowski agreed wholeheartedly on how they should approach Robby Irving. No more Mister Nice Guy.

They stormed onto his porch and banged on the door with the urgency of a fire.

"You have a problem," Mankowski announced, when Robby opened the door.

He was chewing and they could smell something spicy wafting through the open doorway.

"No," Thomas corrected his partner, "he has two problems. You and me."

"What's going on?" Robby swallowed the last of whatever he'd been eating.

"You lied to us," Mankowski bellowed. "And we don't like that."

Robby looked right, then left, as if he was concerned that his neighbors might be watching. He didn't say a word, but opened the door wider and allowed them inside. He did not offer them a seat.

"I didn't lie about a thing," he finally replied.

"You said you were coming down to give us your DNA. You never did that."

Robby inhaled. "I've been busy. I didn't want to take time off work to come down to the station. And since you guys didn't call me about it, I figured it wasn't a big deal."

Mankowski looked him in the eye. "Well, you not showing up to provide your DNA like you said you would *is* a big deal."

"So, we're here to collect it now." Mankowski pulled an envelope from his pocket. He opened a plastic packet. "No needles, remember? Just a cotton swab."

"I didn't kill Judi. You can't force me to do that."

"You're right," Thomas said. "We can't force you. But if you didn't have anything to do with Judi's murder as you claim, it shouldn't be a problem."

Robby's chest heaved in frustration. His expression conveyed more annoyance than worry.

"So what's it gonna be?" Mankowski asked. "I'll be honest, if you have something to hide, you probably shouldn't do this."

Robby's eyes met Mankowski's. He seemed to be weighing the pros and cons in his head. "Okay, I'll do it. I need to go rinse out my mouth." He turned toward the kitchen.

Both officers were close on his heels. They watched as he filled a cup with water, swished it around in his mouth and spit it in the sink.

Robby walked up to Mankowski. "Let's get this over with."

Mankowski swabbed the inside of Robby's cheek and placed the swab in a sterile plastic envelope.

Robby led the detectives back into the living room. "So is that it?"

"Nope. Where's your girlfriend?" Mankowski asked. He scanned the small living room. It had the stark feel of a bachelor's pad.

"We broke up."

"She told us."

His left brow arched in surprise.

"She also told us you asked her to lie for you."

"What are you talking about?"

"Camille says she wasn't with you the night Judi was murdered. She says she lied to us to help you out. So where were you?"

"That bitch is lying!"

The bug-eyed rage that distorted his face gave the detectives pause. Robby Irving didn't look like a harmless pharmaceutical sales rep anymore. He looked like a killer.

"She only did that to get back at me because I dumped her."

"Well, you no longer have an alibi so you need to come up with somebody else who can confirm your whereabouts that night."

"There isn't anybody else. I was here with Camille all night."

"We don't believe you." Mankowski glanced over his shoulder. "Mind if we look around?"

"Yeah, I do mind. I didn't kill Judi. So there's no reason for you to be nosing around my house. You need to go arrest Phillip Peterman."

"We can't," Mankowski said. "He's dead."

Robby rocked back. "Really? How?"

"Car accident."

"Then why are you hassling me? You should be closing the case since your primary suspect is dead. Hey, wait a minute?" A look of delight crossed his face. "Does this mean I get the insurance money now?"

"Nope," Thomas said gleefully. "It doesn't work that way. It goes to Phillip's next of kin. His mother in San Francisco."

Robby's fists curled up tight. He looked as if he wanted to punch a hole in the wall, but somehow managed to restrain himself.

"The case is still open," Mankowski said. "And now we have time to focus on other suspects. Like you. You actually remind me a lot of Peterman. You're almost as evasive as he was."

Robby's nostrils flared. "Don't compare me to that gigolo," he spat. "I'm glad he's dead!"

"Seems you have quite the temper, Mr. Irving," Thomas said, goading him. "The kind of temper that might make a man pound his wife's head in for her insurance money."

"You don't know what you're talking about. I—"

It seemed to dawn on Robby that by showing his rage, he was only confirming the detectives' belief that he had killed Judi. A forced smile replaced the brief glimpse of his fury.

"I understand your divorce got kind of ugly," Mankowski said, hoping to push him to the point of an explosion. "You leave your wife and she shacks up with a hunk of a kid who's way better looking than you. That could put a lot of men over the edge."

"We're done here," Robby said.

Mankowski kept at it. "I think you killed her for that insurance money. Next time, you should make sure you're the beneficiary *before* you commit murder."

"You guys must be hard of hearing. Get out! Now!"

Robby marched over to the door and pulled it so hard the whole room rattled.

"I didn't kill my wife and you can't prove that I did. Hurry up and get the results of that DNA test so you can leave me the hell alone!"

CHAPTER 68

Special relaxed in a booth at TGI Friday's, thumbing through the latest issue of *PI* magazine.

The best thing about her breakup with Clayton was having plenty of time to focus on getting her investigator's license. The second best thing was her guilt-free reunion with Long Island Iced Teas.

As she took a sip of her drink, she spotted her friend's bald head hovering above a small crowd gathered near the door. Special waved to get his attention.

Eli squeezed into the booth and planted his muscular forearms on the table. "You couldn't wait for me before you started imbibing?"

"I've been on alcohol lockdown," she said with a laugh. "I have a lot of catching up to do."

Eli asked the waiter to bring him a vodka on the rocks, then some nachos for them to share. "So how can I help?"

Special opened one of the folders. "Is the written test hard?"

"Naw, you can buy a study guide. The BSIS only requires—"

"Hold up. I don't speak the language yet. What's BSIS?"

"The Bureau of Security and Investigative Services. They license investigators in California."

He went through the list of things she would need to do to get her license.

"I get to carry a concealed weapon, right?"

"Yeah, but that's way down the road. And you may end up re-thinking that. If you want to carry, you'll need at least a million dollars in liability insurance."

"Okay, then," she said. "I guess I won't be needing a gun after all."

"You know about the hours' requirement, right?"

Special nodded. "Three years of paid experience, totaling at least two-thousand hours."

"Okay, sounds like you've been doing your homework. I'm impressed."

The waitress set Eli's drink and a plate of nachos on the table.

"Once I get my license, I wanna try to get on staff at *Cheaters*. I'd be good at tracking down cheating husbands and wives."

Eli grinned. "I could definitely see that."

"I already have my first unofficial case," Special bragged. "I'm doing some research for my best friend Vernetta. Wink, wink."

He took a sip of his drink. "What kind of research?"

"There's this lawyer who screwed her over big time. I'm just nosing around in her background trying to see if I can find some dirt on her. Her name is Girlie Cortez. You know her?"

Eli smoothed a palm across his baldhead and looked away.

"Uh oh! Looks like I might have an inside track!" Special reached for her notepad on the seat next to her. "Tell me everything you know about that wench."

Eli solemnly shook his head. "Girlie Cortez is off-limits."

"Why?"

"You don't need to know why."

Special peered at him over the rim of her glass. "You screwing her, aren't you?"

"I wish," Eli said wistfully.

"Then what's the deal?"

"The deal is I don't know anything about her and even if I did, I wouldn't tell you."

"Aw, c'mon Eli, we go way back. This is just between us. That heffa screwed over my girl big time. She had the *Times* run this story saying she was a member of the Community of Islam. It really caused some problems for her."

Eli stared down at his drink.

"You *definitely* know something," Special challenged. "Is she a client?"

"I'd never tell anybody who my clients were and if you're serious about being an investigator, you better understand that client confidentiality is crucial to staying in business."

"So she is a client!"

"I never said that."

"C'mon, Eli. You don't need her. I can get you work from my friend's law firm."

Eli's expression grew stern. "We need to change the subject. Now."

Special slumped back in her chair and pouted.

"I'll tell you this much," Eli said, lowering his voice. "Girlie Cortez isn't sloppy about anything she does. If you find any dirt on her, then you have a long, successful career ahead of you."

CHAPTER 69

Whenever Mankowski and Thomas had a serious disagreement over approach, as the senior detective, Mankowski usually held his ground until Thomas relented. This time, Mankowski sensed that he would be the one saying uncle.

"Not yet," Mankowski said. "We need to hold off until we have some solid evidence to work with."

Thomas was pushing for another meeting with Girlie Cortez, but Mankowski was against it.

"You don't want to interrogate her because you screwed her," Thomas charged. "That's exactly why you—"

"That has nothing to do with it. I just think we need to gather all our facts first. We're playing our hand too soon. Girlie Cortez is no dummy."

Thomas' iPhone buzzed. "Hot dang! My new penny stock just reached a fifty-two-week high. I'm telling you man, this is going to lead to my early retirement." He slipped the device back into his shirt pocket.

Mankowski hung his head.

"Okay, how about this?" Thomas said. "What if we just drop by her office and let her know Phillip Peterman is dead? We can at least see how she reacts."

Mankowski grunted. "Fine."

As they drove to Girlie's Beverly Hills office, Mankowski was uncharacteristically mute. He was hoping his poor judgment in getting involved with Girlie didn't blow up in his face.

"I think she was the front man for Big Buy," Thomas surmised.

Mankowski shook his head. "It doesn't make sense that a talented attorney like Girlie Cortez would risk her career doing something underhanded like that for a client."

"It's all about the money," Thomas explained. "You need to watch *American Greed* on CNBC sometimes, dude. Super wealthy guys with a whole lot to lose do incredibly unethical stuff all the time. It's a way of life in corporate America. The more you have, the more you want. Maybe Big Buy offered her some big money if she found those documents."

Mankowski didn't want to believe that Girlie was really wrapped up in all of this. But it sure looked that way.

Seconds after they told the receptionist they were there to see Girlie, she walked out to greet them in a short black skirt and white tailored blouse.

"Do you have a few minutes?" Mankowski asked, trying to ignore her cleavage.

"For you," she said with a wink, "absolutely."

Thomas pursed his lips and looked away.

As she led them back to her office, Mankowski stared at her tight ass and remembered how she'd slathered it with oil.

Girlie sat down across from them on her pink couch. She leaned back and made a show of crossing her legs.

"So how can I help you, detectives?"

"We're still trying to track down those Big Buy documents," Thomas said. "But we're not having much luck."

"You really think they exist?"

"Judi Irving certainly told enough people that they did."

Girlie shrugged. "Doesn't really matter now. She's dead and that lawsuit is almost dead. Only one plaintiff left and if I have anything to do with it, she won't see a dime."

"I heard you like playing hardball," Thomas said.

Girlie smiled. "Then you obviously have some reliable sources."

Thomas laughed. "I do. We figured the documents might turn up now that Irving's boyfriend is dead."

Girlie swallowed hard then put on a poker face. "Phillip Peterman is dead?"

Thomas didn't take his eyes off of her. "Yep."

"How?"

"Car accident."

"When?"

"A few days ago."

"You seem concerned," Mankowski interjected. "I thought you didn't know him?"

"I don't." Girlie crossed, then uncrossed her legs. "So did your investigation conclude that Phillip killed Judi Irving?"

"Why do you ask?"

"I don't know. Just curious."

"Yeah," he lied. "We're pretty sure he's the killer."

"So exactly what is it that you need from me?"

"We just wanted to make sure you hadn't learned anything more about the documents."

"No, I haven't."

Mankowski stood up. "Then we won't waste any more of your time."

Thomas didn't speak until they were back in their sedan. "Your girlfriend's a liar," he said, starting up the car. "Since she's lying about knowing Phillip Peterman, it's a good bet she's also lying about where those documents are. I'd bet every share of stock in my portfolio that she knows exactly where they are."

Mankowski stared out of the passenger window. He hated it when he was wrong and his partner was one-hundred percent right.

CHAPTER 70

The Conga Room was not one of my favorite haunts. It was too crowded, too trendy, and the music was way too loud. Despite those complaints, I had agreed to meet Special for drinks after work. As usual, she was late.

I tapped my feet to a spicy Latin number as couples twirled around the dance floor. This was the spot where serious salsa dancers showed off their stuff. The main room of the club was a kaleidoscope of bright yellows and oranges, accented with striped couches and velvet curtains. A humongous screen showed music videos in one corner. There was a concert stage a few feet away and three strategically placed bars.

I was about to text Special when I spotted her snaking her way through the crowd. The old Special was definitely back. She was dressed in all black: satin skinny jeans, a tight mesh top, and four-inch sandals. Her eyelashes were long enough to be butterflies and her glittery eye shadow sparkled like new diamonds.

"You look fabulous," I shouted over the music as she sat down. "You still doing okay?"

"As well as can be expected under the circumstances."

She glanced around the club. "You spot any prospects for me?"

"Don't you think you should fly solo for a while?"

"Absolutely not. The best way to get over one man is to hunt down another one."

She leaned sideways and pointed over my shoulder. "Now *that* brother right there might be a suitable prospect."

I glanced back to see the profile of a guy with chiseled features sitting at the bar. "You can't even tell what he really looks like."

"I'm not looking for perfection right now. Just something to do."

"I thought you were busy preparing for your private investigator's exam."

"Ooooh! Speaking of investigations, guess who gets her hair done at the Emerald Chateau?"

I took a sip of my Diet Coke. "I have no idea."

"Tonisha Cosby! You know Darlene is the weave queen, right? Well, I was getting my weave hooked up last week when Tonisha called Darlene to make an appointment. Now tell me that ain't fate?"

"Exactly why would that be fate?"

"'Cuz I'm gonna be her new best friend and make her confess that she lied on Lamarr. And once I take credit for solving that case, my investigative career is gonna skyrocket. I plan to drop by the shop the next time Tonisha shows up to get her hair done."

"Well, don't waste your time. I don't represent Lamarr anymore."

"What? Why not?"

"Nothing I can to talk about. I just wish the fool would stop sending me flowers and blowing up my phone."

"What happened?"

"Let's just say I used to think that *maybe* he forced himself on Tonisha. Now I *know* he did."

Special frowned. "I have no idea what that boy did to make you dump his behind, but I still think that girl is lying. I plan to get a confession out of her and it won't be forced. You know how strangers love to tell me all their business."

Telling Special to back off wasn't going to do any good. So I didn't even try.

"And just so you know, Darlene and everybody else in the shop thinks Tonisha is lying too. Darlene told me Tonisha used to brag about all the professional athletes she slept with."

"Unfortunately, that won't help Lamarr get a new trial."

Special surveyed the room. "I need a drink. Where's the waitress?" She glanced over her shoulder, then turned back to me.

"I have to tell you," she said with a pout, "that heffa Girlie Cortez is like Teflon. Don't nothing stick to her devious behind. I haven't been able to find even a speck of dirt on her."

"Forget about it," I said. "I can't believe I even asked you to do that. But I was fit to be tied when I walked out of that courtroom."

"Well, I ain't giving up yet. There's gotta be something out there."

Special was talking to me, but her gaze was fixed on the guy at the bar. "Uh-oh, I swear baby just smiled at me. This might be a good night."

"Are you going to spend all your time gawking at him or talking to me?"

"I'm multitasking." She finally turned back to me. "So is Jefferson making out okay?"

"What do you mean? Why wouldn't he be?"

"He didn't tell you?"

"Tell me what?"

"Oh…uh, nothing. Never mind." She picked up her phone and acted like she was checking her messages.

I grabbed it from her. "What's going on?"

"Damn. I hate being the bearer of news your husband obviously doesn't want you to know."

"Cough it up."

"Jefferson was having problems with one of his subcontractors. He was talking to the Community of Islam about getting a loan."

I felt my face tighten. "Who told you that?"

"Clay—I mean, Khalil."

"You're still seeing him?"

"Nope. But he still calls me every now and then. Now, don't go off on your husband," Special advised me. "You know how brothers are when they're having problems. They don't always tell their woman. It's a pride thing."

"This is something he should've talked to me about."

Special was staring over my shoulder again. "O-M-G! He's coming over here." She sat more erect in her chair and puffed out her chest.

The guy reached our table, but kept walking. That was when I noticed where and who he was headed toward. "Don't turn around," I warned Special.

But of course, she did.

The man Special was all excited about was now smiling and laughing it up with Girlie Cortez.

Special pounded the table with her fist. "That heffa just stole my man!"

"You don't even know him."

"I was about to know him if she hadn't messed it up."

Girlie and the guy breezed past us to the dance floor. We watched as they did a sexy salsa, grinding their bodies in rhythm with the music.

"Look at her," Special said in disgust. "She dances like the skank that she is."

When they finished dancing, Girlie slowed at our table.

"I thought that was you." Girlie batted her eyes up at her dance partner. "Carter, this is my colleague, Vernetta Henderson." She turned to Special. "And you are?"

Special ignored Girlie and extended her hand to Carter. "Hi, I'm Special."

"*Special?*" Girlie said, cracking up. "Is that really your name?"

Special looked Girlie up and down. "Yes, it is and yes, I am. Special, that is. And you have some nerve talking about somebody's name. *Girlie.*"

I needed to put some distance between my best friend and my archenemy.

I smiled up at Girlie. "I don't mean to be rude, but we were in the middle of an important conversation."

She rolled her eyes. "Well, forgive me for interrupting." She grabbed Carter's hand and fluttered away.

I could see that I would need a fire extinguisher to cool Special down.

"Bring me a Long Island Iced Tea," Special growled at a passing waitress. "And make it a strong one."

She glared over her shoulder at Girlie, who was hanging all over Carter.

"To hell with finding some dirt on that skank. We need to wait for her in the parking lot and beat her ass down."

That was my cue. I flagged the waitress and cancelled Special's drink order.

"We're leaving," I said, grabbing my friend's arm and pulling her to her feet.

"I haven't even had a drink yet," Special complained.

"Okay, I owe you one."

Special stared back at Girlie and Carter as I tugged her toward the exit. "We need to find her car so I can key it."

"You're not keying anybody's car."

"That heffa messed up real bad tonight," Special muttered. "The only thing I had against her was what she did to you. Now it's personal."

CHAPTER 71

I had managed to get Special calmed down by the time we made it to the parking garage. Then she spotted Girlie's Jag with the *HotGirl* license plates and revved up all over again.

"That's just trashy." Special walked up to Girlie's car like she wanted to punch it. "And did you see the way that heffa was grinding all up against that man on the dance floor? I think she—"

"Good night, Special." I gave her a hug and tugged her toward her car a few feet away. I waited as she climbed inside, still fussing about Girlie.

I knew my buddy better than I knew myself. I wouldn't put it past her to actually come back to key Girlie's car. So I waited for her to pull out and I drove behind her to make sure she actually left the parking garage.

As I entered the on-ramp for the southbound Harbor Freeway, I started to grapple with my own emotions. Having to hear about my husband's money problems from Special and not from him, left me both hurt and angry. I had no idea that it had gotten serious enough for him to consider getting a loan from the Community of Islam.

I was about to transition from the Harbor to the Santa Monica Freeway when I changed destinations. I continued south on the Harbor Freeway, toward Jefferson's worksite in Inglewood. He'd been putting in some long days, so I knew he'd still be there.

When I stepped inside the trailer, I found Jefferson and his business partner, Stan, sitting around a scarred, metal table that was too large for the small space. The dingy, makeshift office smelled of leftover Mexican food.

"Hey," Jefferson said, his face bunched up in surprise. "What're you doing here?"

"We need to talk." Both of my hands zoomed to my hips.

"Hey, bruh," Stan teased, "looks like you're in some serious trouble."

"I'm in the middle of something right now, babe. Can this wait?"

"Nope."

Stan picked up a blueprint from the desk and started rolling it up. "I think I better give you some time to talk to your woman."

"If I hear you in here gettin' an ass whippin'," Stan said, "I'll be sure to call nine-one-one." He backed out of the trailer on his tiptoes as if he was afraid of me.

Jefferson's jaw tightened. He waited until Stan was gone before speaking. "What was that about?"

"I need to know why you didn't tell me you were having financial problems?"

It took him a long time to respond. Jefferson had a habit of measuring his words when he was upset. It was probably a trait I needed to learn.

"What you just did was way out of line. I didn't tell you what was going on because I know how to handle my business."

"We're married. This is something you should've talked to me about. Particularly if you're getting a loan from the Community of Islam."

"Oh, now I get it. That's exactly why I didn't tell you. Like I said before, whenever you hear the words *Community of Islam*, you go ape shit."

"I need to know what's going on."

"Nothin's going on. I'm handling my business. And right now I gotta get back to work. Stan and I need to finish going over those blueprints."

He tried to move past me, but I took a step sideways, blocking his path. "We need to talk, Jefferson."

"Babe, this is not a good time. If you wanna talk, we'll do it when I get home."

He blew out a long breath and I could tell he was exhausted. But I didn't want to talk at home. I wanted to talk now.

Jefferson finally stepped around me and grabbed his baseball cap from the top of the file cabinet.

"This is some bullshit. A Muslim woman would never pull no crap like this. She would respect her man."

My body's thermostat lurched ten degrees higher. "What did you just say to me?"

"You heard me. That's the problem with black women. Y'all don't know when to back the hell up."

"Maybe you need to take your ass down to the mosque and find yourself a nice, obedient Muslim woman."

Jefferson slapped on his cap, then snatched the doorknob so hard the entire trailer shook. "Right now I wish I could."

It was well past midnight when I finally returned home. After leaving Jefferson's worksite, I stopped by my parents' place in Compton for a long visit, then went to Special's house in Leimert Park. I wanted to spend the night, but Special insisted that I go home and make up with my husband. To his credit, Jefferson had called my iPhone three times, but I didn't pick up.

When I walked in, Jefferson was in the den watching television and nursing a beer. I walked right past him toward the bedroom.

I had just unzipped my skirt when I noticed him standing in the doorway.

"We need to talk."

"Oh, so now you want to talk?"

"Yeah, I do. I'll be in the den."

I had no intention of talking to him tonight. I finished undressing, slipped into my nightgown and climbed into bed. But after only a few minutes of sulking, I changed my mind. I entered the den and took a seat in the armchair adjacent to the couch where Jefferson was sitting.

"So, you ready to tell me what's going on?" I began.

"One of my subcontractors on the project in Inglewood took some shortcuts. I need about seventy-five grand to make everything right."

"If you needed money, why didn't you come to me?"

"Because it's my problem, not yours."

"We're married. Your problem *is* my problem."

He raised the beer can to his lips and took a sip.

"You know what I like most about going to the mosque?"

I didn't like the fact that he was changing the subject, but decided not to point that out.

"Hanging out with those brothers makes me feel like a man." His voice was almost wistful. "I ain't saying I didn't feel like a man before I walked in there, but it's just cool to connect with some brothers who are all about lifting each other up."

"You trying to tell me that I don't make you feel like a man?"

He ignored my question. "You were wrong for coming at me like that tonight."

"And you were wrong for telling me I need to act like a Muslim woman."

The sound of nothingness filled the room.

Jefferson reached for the remote control. "I want you to watch something."

"I don't want to see a Community of Islam video. It's late and I have to—"

"Just hold on a minute and do this for me, okay? Come sit over here."

I took my time joining him on the couch. I waited while he browsed the list of shows he'd TiVo'd. When he finally found what he was looking for, it surprised me. It was a segment of *Oprah*.

"This is what you wanted me to watch?"

"Yep. I recorded it the other night. And can you do me a favor and watch it without offering any legal analysis?"

I huffed and clasped my hands.

The show was about a young black man convicted of robbing a check-cashing store. Surveillance cameras caught the entire robbery on tape. What made the show *Oprah* worthy was that in the midst of the robbery the female clerk asked the robber to pray with her. The man actually dropped to his knees and they tearfully prayed together.

Now I was really confused. Was my husband trying to tell me he was ready to go out and rob somebody to get the money he needed?

"Why are you showing me this?"

"Just hold on." Jefferson fast-forwarded through the first commercial break. "You need to see the rest of it."

In the next segment, the robber was Skyped in live from jail, while his mother, his wife and the store clerk were on set with Oprah. The young man talked about losing his job and being at wit's end. His tearful mother and wife expressed regret about constantly riding him for not being able to support his family. When the show ended, Jefferson muted the television.

"When I was watching that show the other night," he said, "I could imagine that brother coming home day after day listening to his wife and his mama constantly telling him he wasn't shit because he didn't have a job and couldn't support his family." He turned and smiled at me. "And you know you sistahs have tongues sharp enough to slice steel."

I was not pleased that he was putting me in that category. "That's not me. I've always supported you."

"I know that. But sometimes a man doesn't want to lean on anybody else. That dude had never even been arrested before. If he'd gotten just an ounce of support at home, he might've made some different choices."

Jefferson paused to take a sip of his beer.

"So my point in saying all this is that I need your support right now. I don't need you demanding answers or offering me your help or even your money. This is my problem and it's a problem I have to fix."

"But why can't I help you? I'm a lawyer. There might be legal grounds to—"

"I understand all that. And it if gets that serious, I'll come to you. But right now, I need you to back up off me and let me handle my business my way."

He embraced me with both arms and rested his chin on top of my head. "Okay?"

No, it was not okay.

I wanted to know whether he'd borrowed money from the Community of Islam, but I was bright enough to realize that now was not the time to demand an answer to that question. So I backed off and said exactly what my husband needed me to say.

"Okay."

CHAPTER 72

Mankowski wasn't happy about his immediate predicament, but it was a little late for regrets now.

He was sitting on Girlie's living room couch, waiting for her to return from the kitchen with their drinks. Mankowski had accepted Girlie's invitation in hopes of getting information. He just had to remember that. He was here for official business. Nothing else.

Mankowski stared down at his groin. "This is business," he mumbled. "Don't forget that."

The place, like Girlie, was pretty snazzy. Shiny, high-tech furniture, oddly shaped couches and chairs, lots of greenery.

"Two rum and Cokes," she said cheerily, gliding back into the room and setting the glasses on the bamboo coffee table in front of them. To his dismay she had slipped out of her business suit and into a long, red silk robe. Knowing Girlie, she had nothing on underneath it.

It was going to be damn hard to keep it inside his pants tonight. But he would. Screwing her now would be far more trouble than it was worth.

She eased closer to him on the couch. "So tell me why I shouldn't take it personally that you've been avoiding me?"

"Work," Mankowski replied.

Girlie brought the glass to her lips. "Not buying it. Even now, you're acting like you're afraid I'm going to bite you." She winked. "But if you're into that kind of thing, I can definitely accommodate."

Mankowski smiled and pretended to take a sip from the glass. Drinking on the job was also a definite no-no.

"I really don't like your quiet side, detective. And I have to tell you, I usually don't get this kind of frigid reaction from men who've experienced me in bed."

I'll bet.

Mankowski smiled as Girlie extended her arm along the back of the couch, allowing her robe to fall open, giving him a peek at her shapely headlights. He had to summon all of his mental powers to fight off an approaching boner. Thinking back to seeing Girlie walking out of the Four Seasons right behind Phillip helped quite a bit. The thought of Girlie doing what she'd done to him to that sleazebag disgusted him.

They were still waiting to get the results of Robby Irving's DNA test. Despite his declarations of innocence, Mankowski figured there was a 50/50 possibility that his DNA would match. If it did, they'd still need more evidence to conclusively determine whether Phillip or Robby was the killer. Neither had an alibi and both had a motive.

Regardless, it didn't mean that Phillip and Girlie hadn't cooked up some scheme involving those Big Buy documents. Maybe he should just follow Thomas' advice and tell Girlie that he knew she was screwing Phillip and see how she reacted.

"I have something I need to ask you," Mankowski struggled to keep his eyes off her breasts. Then he noticed that her nipples had hardened and were protruding against the silk fabric. He could still remember how they tasted.

"Okay. Ask me anything you want." She stirred her drink with her index finger, then stuck it into her mouth and sucked on it.

Mankowski looked away. What he really wanted was to have those lips suck him off again. But he had to keep his mind on business.

"Why didn't you tell me you were screwing Phillip Peterman?"

"What?" Girlie flinched, spilling her drink on the couch. "What are you talking about? Wait. Let me go get a towel first."

Damn, she's good. He figured she was in the kitchen getting her story together.

Girlie returned, dabbed at the wet spot on the couch, then sat back down.

Mankowski noticed that she had loosened the belt of her robe, exposing a wider view of her breasts. She was trying to knock him off track with those gorgeous tits.

"Why would you ask me that? I already told you I didn't know the guy."

"Then what were you doing with him at a hotel last week?"

This time a subtle twitch of her right eye gave her away. "I don't know where you're getting your information, detective, but it's wrong. I wasn't with him at a hotel last week."

"Are you saying you weren't at the Four Seasons on Doheny a week ago Monday?"

This was the real test. Mankowski knew what he'd seen with his own eyes.

Girlie stomped over to a sofa table, picked up her purse and pulled out her smartphone. He assumed she was checking her calendar.

"Yeah, I was there last week." She turned to face him, her face as red as her robe now. "I had a meeting with a client, an in-house attorney for Paramount. He suggested that we meet for lunch at the hotel."

Everybody said she was smart. Of course, she would have a legitimate reason to be there in case she got caught.

"So you weren't there to meet Phillip Peterman?"

"No."

"And you didn't see him at all while you were there?"

"Absolutely not." She held up her palm.

"And you've never seen those Big Buy documents Judi Irving supposedly had?"

"Nope."

He was pretty good with lying criminals. But he was at a loss with Girlie. He had no clue from her demeanor whether she was lying or telling the truth.

"Next question."

"My partner thinks either you screwed Phillip for those Big Buy documents or paid him for them. Maybe both."

"I don't care what your partner thinks. But I do care what you think."

He shrugged. "I think either scenario is possible."

Anger tightened her lips. "Why in the world would I do that?"

"I understand that those documents could've damaged your client's case. I hear you like to win."

"I do like to win. But I didn't need any help doing that, as demonstrated by the way the case was resolved. I got Vernetta Henderson's class action dismissed. You need to check your facts before you go falsely accusing people. Especially people you're sleeping with."

Was that a threat?

Maybe getting him in bed was all part of her plan from the beginning? He remembered seeing cameras outside the front of her house, which meant she now had videotape of him coming to her place. She could get a lot of mileage out of that. If charges were ever filed against her, she would of course argue that their relationship tainted his investigation.

"What do you want me to do? Take a lie detector test?"

"That might be a good start," he said, knowing she never would.

"Those tests aren't reliable."

"I disagree."

"And they're also inadmissible in court. Anyway, I'd never advise a client to take a polygraph and I'd be a pretty stupid lawyer if I did it myself."

Mankowski stood up. "That wouldn't matter if you didn't have anything to hide."

Girlie laughed. It was the kind of nervous laughter he'd heard from criminals who thought they were too smart to get caught. "I can't believe this. You really don't believe me."

"No, I don't."

He headed for the door and had pulled it open when Girlie placed her hands on top of his.

"I'm telling the truth."

Mankowski wanted to shake her hand away, but he also wanted to ram it down his pants. Her eyes pleaded with him and he almost gave in.

"I gotta go," he said. "And for the record, I really do think you're lying."

Girlie's hand squeezed his forearm.

"I can't believe I'm doing this." She spoke hesitantly, as if she was uncertain of her next words. "I'll take the damn polygraph," she said. "Set it up."

CHAPTER 73

The most important lesson that Special had learned from her buddy Eli was that a good investigator always started at the beginning, meticulously turning over every stone from the past to the present. No matter how insignificant a piece of evidence might seem, there was always the chance that it might lead to something that could break a case wide open.

With that approach in mind, Special had spent hours scouring the Internet, reading anything she could find about Girlie Cortez. But so far, nothing. Special refused to become discouraged. If she gave up this easily, she might as well forget about being a private investigator. Patience, Eli had said, was just as important as perseverance.

Her job in collections at Verizon gave Special the freedom to sneak in time on the Internet when she should have been working. She hit a few keys on her desktop computer and called up Girlie's Facebook page. Everything there was related to her law practice. Girlie wasn't stupid enough to put all her business on the web, so she didn't find out anything helpful. She did learn that Girlie graduated from Cerritos High School.

She moved on to Girlie's LinkedIn page.

"Interesting," Special said out loud. All of the LinkedIn connections from Girlie's high school, college and law school were men. Not a single female was listed. That was certainly weird. "She must've been a man stealer from birth."

What Special needed was someone who was connected to Girlie's past. Special wanted to know what she was like growing up. But she didn't know anyone who'd gone to Cerritos High. She did have a few Filipino friends. Calling one of them up was a longshot, but you never knew.

She pulled out her Droid and started flipping through her phone book. When she came across Manny Manalo, one of her high school classmates, her spirits lifted. She immediately called him.

"Wazzup, homegirl?"

Unfortunately, for Manny, his Filipino parents forgot to tell him that he wasn't black. "You don't never call a brother."

Special had to get past a few minutes of his flirting before bringing up the real purpose of her call.

"I need your help," she finally said. "Do you happen to know anybody who graduated from Cerritos High School around the same time we graduated? Preferably a woman."

A woman was more likely to have some dirt on Girlie and be willing to spill it.

"Manny know everybody," he bragged. "And if I don't know her, I can find somebody who does."

He'd been referring to himself in the third person since tenth grade. It was part of the wise-guy demeanor he tried to portray. When you were five-foot-four, you had to sound large and in charge since you couldn't look it.

"Well, can Manny hook me up?"

"Manny gotta know the real deal before Manny gets involved."

Manny wasn't stupid. That was why she liked him despite his self-absorbed persona. She had already come up with a cover story to tell him.

"Okay, I'll tell you the truth. I'm trying my hand at being an investigator. A friend of mine thinks a woman who graduated from Cerritos High is screwing her husband. I want to find out if there's anything interesting in her background I might be able to use."

"Now that's more like it. You gotta be up front with Manny."

"So can Manny help me? Is there some Filipino nightspot in Cerritos you can take me to? We might get lucky and run into somebody who might know the woman from way back."

"What's her name? Maybe Manny knows her."

Special couldn't tell him too much because he had a mouth the size of a manhole cover. But it was possible that he might know Girlie.

"Her name is Girlie Cortez. She's a lawyer."

"Naw. Manny don't know her. Manny don't do lady lawyers. They talk back too much."

Special laughed. "Can you take me to some Filipino joint in Cerritos? Maybe somebody there might know her or her family."

"That's going to be tough. You're an outsider. Nobody's gonna give you the four-one-one. But let me call some of my ladies. I'll holla back at you."

Manny called back two hours later and told Special to meet him at Joe's for Happy Hour. As it turned out, he had two female friends who actually knew Girlie Cortez. He arranged for them to meet us for drinks. According to Manny, if they had any dirt on Girlie, by their second Mango Margarita, they'd tell it all.

Special ignored all the stares as she walked into the club. She was the only black person in the whole joint. She spotted Manny sitting on one side of a small booth, sandwiched between two petite, dark-eyed women with hair down to their butts. Manny was wearing a leather coat, dark shades and a baseball cap that read *The Man.*

Manny introduced Special to Suzie and Janie as his co-worker. She had asked him not to tell them the reason she wanted to talk to them. Special sat down across from the three of them.

Manny gave her a wink and a nod, which told Special he'd already gotten the women nice and loosened up.

"Manny told me you guys went to Cerritos High and that you know Girlie Cortez," Special began, after ordering a Coke.

Both women simultaneously turned up their pert little noses. One of them looked as if she wanted to spit in Special's drink.

"Yeah, I know her," Suzie said. "I went to elementary, middle school and high school with that slut. She's got issues."

Great. So Girlie *had* been a bitch from the cradle.

"Sounds like you hated going to school with her as much as I hated working with her."

"You got that right," Janie chimed in. "I'll never forgive her for what she did to me in the tenth grade. I made the mistake of telling her I liked a guy. The next day, guess who was all over him? I thought we were friends."

"Wow. Sounds like she was a hot mess," Special said laughing.

"A hot, slutty mess," Suzie clarified. "We'd been best friends since fourth grade. A week after I broke up with my boyfriend, she invited him to the junior prom. Don't ever bring your man around her. You'll leave to go to the ladies' room and she'll be under the table giving him a blow job."

This was juicy gossip, but Special already knew from firsthand experience that Girlie was a man-stealing 'ho. She needed something she could actually use.

"To act that way, I suspect she must've had a rough family life," Special said.

Janie shrugged. "Kinda." She reached into her purse, pulled out her phone and started texting.

Special was dying to snatch the phone from the girl's hands so she could have her full attention. "Tell me more."

"She's half-white, you know," Suzie said. "She thought she was better than everybody because of that."

Special feigned surprise. "I didn't know that. Was her mother or her father white?"

"Her father. I know the whole story about him," Suzie continued. "Like I said, we were pretty close before she stole my boyfriend."

"Do tell." Special leaned in over the table.

Just then, the MC called Suzie's name and she sloshed her way to the stage. Special endured the most painful version of Beyoncé's *Single Ladies* that she'd ever heard. She had no idea how these people could sit there and listen to such bad singing.

When Suzie returned to the table, she was ready to move on to another topic, but Special was dying to know Girlie's *whole story*.

Suzie downed the remainder of her drink and got up to go to the ladies' room. Special waited a couple of minutes, then followed.

She stood in the mirror, pretending to be freshening up her lipstick when Suzie came out of the bathroom stall.

"You know," Special said, "I really feel sorry for Girlie. She didn't have any female friends at work and from everything you told me, she didn't have any at school either."

"That's because she's a conniving bitch," Suzie huffed.

"You said she had a rough childhood. What exactly happened?"

Suzie opened her purse, pulled out a lipstick and took her time painting her thin lips with a grape-colored lipstick that gave her a hideous Goth look.

She turned to face Special. "Girlie's mother went after nothing but married men. She even tried to hit on my father."

"Really?" Special opened her purse and hit the *record* button on her Droid.

Suzie matted her lips with a tissue. "You think Girlie's a slut? She ain't got nothing on her mother."

CHAPTER 74

"I know you don't take walk-ins," the receptionist said when I picked up the phone. "But there's a woman out here who says she needs to speak to you right away. She's pretty upset."

I glanced up at the clock. It was a quarter to five and I was bushed. A new client, especially one in distress, could mean a couple more hours in the office.

"Tell her I'm sorry, but she'll have to make an appointment."

I hung up and started straightening up my desk. A minute later, the receptionist called back.

"The woman asked me to tell you that she works for Big Buy. Says she's the executive assistant to the CEO of the company."

That tidbit of information changed everything.

I walked down to the reception area to find a woman who looked thin and matronly. She was totally gray, with deep age lines in her face. Her eyes were sad and vacant.

The woman struggled to get to her feet when I approached. "Thank you for seeing me," she said in a shaky voice. "I really need your help." She wiped at the corner of one eye with a handkerchief.

I needed to get her out of the lobby. I led her to my office and closed the door.

"I think she's going to fire me," the woman blurted out before I could even ask her name. "She's going to try to send me to jail!"

"Who?"

"The CEO of Big Buy, Rita Richards-Kimble. She's my boss."

"I need you to slow down," I said, ushering her to a seat, then returning to the chair behind my desk. "First tell me your name. Then I want to know why you think you're going to be fired and why you think you're going to jail."

The woman, who identified herself as Jane Campbell, recounted an incident with her boss earlier that day. Rita Richards-Kimble had accused her of looking at confidential records on her desk and threatened to fire her if she did it again. She'd come to me because she knew about the sex discrimination case I had filed against Big Buy.

"You just told me you worked for the company for close to thirty years," I said. "It doesn't sound like you did anything wrong. She's not going to fire you."

"She knows I know," Jane whimpered.

"You know what?"

"Everything she's been doing."

"And what has she been doing?"

Jane opened her small purse and unfolded a piece of paper. "Take a look at this."

I reached across my desk and took the paper she held out to me. There was no heading on the page, but the document appeared to be some type of financial statement. There were several columns of numbers on the right, and several categories on the left.

"What is this?"

"Information from our last earnings statement. I had to copy and paste it from another document."

"Okay," I said.

"We get an earnings report from each of our divisions and the information is used to compile our quarterly earnings statements. The information you have is what the divisions reported last quarter. Those numbers don't match the numbers in the final report prepared for the board of directors. Those earnings are significantly lower than what was reported to the board."

My heart began to patter with excitement. "Sounds like you're telling me the CEO of Big Buy might be cooking the books."

"That's precisely what I'm saying."

"I'll need more evidence than this," I said, looking down at the paper again.

"And I have it. Lots of it. She started doing this about two years ago. I've been keeping a copy of the original documents for about a year."

"I want to see them," I said. "In the meantime, you'll need to go back to work and act as if everything is fine, but continue to keep your eyes open."

"I don't know how long I can continue to put up with Rita. She's always been a spiteful person, but lately she's been absolutely vicious. She's determined to make sure that—"

She paused. "Is everything I tell you confidential?"

"If you're here for the purpose of retaining me as an attorney, then yes, our communications are confidential."

"The CEO is obsessed about making sure the Welson deal goes through because she's going to make millions."

"What's the Welson deal?"

She told me about the pending sale of Big Buy, which would net the CEO $125 million.

Then it hit me. This could be the reason Judi was murdered. Maybe those missing documents had a connection to the fraudulent earnings reports and the CEO's attempt to push through the sale of the company at a price much higher than it was really worth.

"How'd you find out about Judi Irving's lawsuit?"

"Everybody knows about it. I was in Rita's office when the company was served with the complaint. She had quite a temper tantrum. Rita's even asked me if I knew anything about a rumor that Judi Irving had confidential company records."

Jane averted her eyes in a way that signaled that she wasn't telling me everything.

"Do you?" I asked.

Still not making eye contact with me, Jane slowly nodded, then broke into a full-fledged wail. "That's why I think they're going to put me in jail!" she sobbed.

"What are you talking about?"

"I need to be completely truthful with you," Jane cried. "I did do something that I know could get me fired."

I stared across my desk, unconsciously holding my breath. "I'm listening."

"I was the one who mailed those Big Buy documents to Judi."

My mouth sprang open. "You?"

"Rita is an evil, hateful woman," Jane said, her emotions having grown from anxious to angry. "When I heard those women were suing the company for sex discrimination, I wanted to help them. I figured that if they had information that the CEO was engaging in fraud, it would help them with their lawsuit."

My mind was racing too fast to take this all in.

"The documents you mailed Judi," I said, "what were they?"

"I sent her copies of the company's true earnings reports. If you compared them to the fake reports actually submitted by the company, you would see that they don't match."

I was too dumbfounded to form another question.

"She thinks I'm stupid," Jane said angrily. "She gave me documents to shred, figuring I wouldn't look at them. But I did. And when I figured out what she was doing, I started taking the documents home instead of shredding them."

"Do you have a copy of the documents you gave to Judi?"

She nodded.

I sat there, lost in my own thoughts, trying to put this all together.

"That's not everything I have to tell you." Jane's eyes started to water again. "It's my fault that Judi's dead."

"What? Why would you say that?"

She cupped her forehead. "Judi was murdered because of those documents I sent her."

I could tell she was about to rev up for another good cry. I got up from my desk, sat down next to her and gave her a hug. "You don't know that."

"Yes, I do," she shrieked.

It took several minutes for Jane to regain her composure.

"I've been listening in on Rita's calls," she admitted, her voice hoarse from crying. "Rita was determined to make sure Judi Irving's case didn't jeopardize the Welson deal. When I told you that woman is evil, I meant it."

Her moist eyes met mine head-on.

"I think Rita hired somebody to kill Judi Irving because of those documents I sent her."

CHAPTER 75

Special spent the next thirty minutes in the ladies' room, getting the 4-1-1 on Girlie Cortez from her former best friend.

"I used to overhear my mom and her friends talking about Girlie's mom a lot when I was growing up," Suzie said. "They didn't like her. If Ms. Cortez saw a man she wanted, she went after him. She didn't care if he was married. I heard that a couple of families moved out of Cerritos because of her."

"She must've been an attractive woman."

"Absolutely gorgeous," Suzie said. "Even more beautiful than Girlie. She was one of those women men just gravitated toward. Even as a kid I remember thinking how beautiful she was. And she had a really nice body. Even back then, she was always working out."

"Did she ever marry?"

"Nope. But she had lots of married boyfriends who lavished her with all kinds of gifts. She always drove the newest model Lexus or Mercedes. Once she got tired of a guy, she'd dump him and move on to somebody else's husband. It was like a game to her."

"This must've had a bad effect on Girlie."

"I think she was really embarrassed by the way her mother behaved," Suzie said. "Every few months there would be a different boyfriend. Most of us had large, close families, but Girlie only had her mom."

"What do you know about Girlie's father?"

"Rumor is, he was loaded. I heard he made a lot of money in the stock market. He was supposedly the only man her mother really loved. She thought having his child would convince him to leave his wife, but he refused. And after his wife found out that Girlie's mother was pregnant, she demanded that he never see her or his daughter again."

"So Girlie's father never played a role in her life?"

Suzie shook her head. "Nope. I guess he loved his wife more than Girlie's mom. Or Girlie," Suzie said, almost as if she felt sorry for her former friend.

"Did he support them financially?"

"He supposedly paid off their house and gave her mother a six-figure check, but she blew it in a couple of years. Her mother didn't make much money as a nursing assistant. When she was between boyfriends, things were really tight. There were times when Girlie couldn't afford to go on ski trips and things like that. One time, my dad paid for her to go on a ski trip."

"Did she ever tell you who her father was?"

"When we were growing up, I don't think she even knew. In exchange for that check her mother got, she agreed to never disclose his identity to Girlie. But I heard that Girlie found out who he was a few years ago. After her mother died in a car accident, her aunt told her everything."

"I'm surprised Girlie never tried to find him."

"She really resented him when she was growing up. So I don't think she had any interest in finding him. By the time she learned who he was, he had supposedly died."

What a messed up story.

"Was Girlie close to her aunt?"

"Nope. Girlie didn't have much of a relationship with any of her relatives. Her family didn't approve of the things her mother did. Her aunt runs a drycleaners over on South Street near the Cerritos mall."

Suzie's suddenly suspicious eyes met Special's through the bathroom mirror. The girl's buzz was apparently wearing off.

"You sure are asking a lot of questions about Girlie. Why do you wanna know all this?"

"I didn't mean to be so nosey." Special gave a big phony smile. "But everything you just told me explains a lot about why Girlie is the way she is. Thanks for talking to me."

Special walked back into the club and said good-bye to Manny and Janie.

As she walked to her car, Special wondered if discovering the identity of the white man who had abandoned Girlie Cortez could lead to some useful information for Vernetta. A strong gut instinct was signaling that it might be worth her while to keep digging.

Suzie claimed Girlie's father had *supposedly* died. What if he was still alive? The fact that he had paid off Girlie's mother and never looked back, meant he must've had something to hide. Maybe he was a prominent politician or a celebrity who couldn't risk the bad publicity of an affair and a bastard child.

Special's investigative juices began to bubble with excitement. Her next task was to track down Girlie's aunt.

CHAPTER 76

Benjamin sat in the passenger seat of my Land Cruiser, his face a muddle of contemplation. We were on Wilshire Boulevard, headed for the West Coast office of *The Daily Business Journal.*

I was completely hyped about the information that my new client, Jane Carson, had disclosed to me, certain that it would provide the leverage we needed to get Olivia the justice she deserved. Benjamin wasn't as enthused.

Jane had given me her copy of the documents she'd anonymously sent to Judi. A high school friend of mine, who was a financial reporter for the *Journal,* had agreed to take a look at them and help us decipher the financial jargon.

"I just think we should just turn everything over to the police," Benjamin said. "The people Big Buy hired to find those documents are dangerous. I still have the scars to prove it."

Though he rarely brought it up, the trauma of the beating Benjamin took went much deeper than the slowly fading bruises on his face. The fact that we now had a plausible basis for believing that Big Buy was behind Judi's death, meant that we had to be extra careful.

"I'm going to turn it over," I replied. "But first I want to know exactly what we're dealing with."

Our tiff over my supposed membership in the Community of Islam had been put aside. It wasn't quite like old times between us yet, but almost.

"Figuring out the scam Big Buy is involved in is going to give us some ammunition for Olivia's case," I said. "For Olivia's sake, I just hope she can hang on long enough for that to happen."

Benjamin looked over at me as if he had something to say, then turned away.

"Are you sure you want Olivia to stay in this case for her sake or yours?" he asked a minute later.

I took my eyes off of the road for much longer than I should have. "What does that mean?"

"You know exactly what I mean," he said without facing me.

I took a second to think about his question before responding. I wanted a victory for Olivia because I truly believed she was the victim of discrimination. And I also wanted to avenge Judi's death, which appeared to be at the hands of Big Buy. But I couldn't deny that there was also another more personal motive driving my desire for a win on her behalf. I could not let Girlie Cortez trounce me again.

My quest for vengeance against Girlie aside, dropping the case was not in Olivia's best interests.

"I would never jeopardize my client's interests for personal reasons," I finally said. "I want to get a decent settlement for Olivia because she deserves it. And I want it to be a lot more than three months' pay or a measly three-thousand dollars."

We pulled into a parking lot across the street from the high-rise where *The Daily Business Journal's* offices were located.

My friend, Dennis Dickerson, greeted us after a short wait in the lobby.

"Thanks for making time to see us," I said.

Dennis was a lanky, non-athletic type with black-rimmed glasses that gave him a studious look. Back in high school, he'd been a math whiz.

He led us to a small conference room with a front wall made of glass that looked out onto the newsroom.

I took out the documents Jane had given me. All references to Big Buy had been blacked out. I only wanted Dennis to explain what the documents were, not sniff out a story he could run under his byline.

He opened the package and began to slowly peruse the pages. "This appears to be information from a company's financial statement," he said. "Who's the company?"

"I can't disclose that right now," I said. "Can you go through one of the statements and explain what each line means?"

Dennis went into a long technical explanation about profit and loss, rate of return and a lot of other financial terms. Most of it was way over my head.

"What if the company didn't actually earn the sums listed there and falsified those reports?" I asked.

"That would be fraud."

"What if it's a privately owned company, not a public one?"

"Different laws cover private and public companies, but same difference. Private companies still have legal obligations. Just because you're private doesn't mean you can do whatever you want."

Dennis scratched his head, then bit his lip. "Mind if I show these to another reporter?"

"Why?" Benjamin asked. He'd been unusually quiet.

"Billie Wilson covers privately held companies headquartered in Southern California. She might have some additional information."

I looked at Benjamin, then shrugged. "I guess that's okay."

We watched as Dennis walked across the newsroom and handed the documents to a woman sitting at a desk on the far side of the newsroom. We couldn't hear what they were saying, but we could see the woman's face glisten with astonishment as she leafed through the pages. She looked up, her eyes laser beaming in our direction. The two of them hurried across the newsroom.

"This is Billie Wilson," Dennis said, introducing a tall blonde in khakis with a long, pointed nose. Her weathered skin and sun-bleached hair gave her the appearance of an aging hippie.

"Where'd you get these documents?" she asked, her voice bathed with urgency.

Her anxious demeanor concerned me. "I'm not at liberty to say."

She frowned and placed both hands on her narrow waist. "They're records from Big Buy department store, right?"

Benjamin and I exchanged a mystified look. "How could you possibly know that?" I asked.

"It wasn't exactly hard to put two and two together," Billie responded. "I saw your press conference announcing the class action against them. I cover companies like this so I'm usually tuned in to what's going on. We ran a few paragraphs about your lawsuit."

I started to accept her explanation, but it seemed too convenient. She would've needed more to make the connection between the documents and Big Buy.

"You're not being straight with me," I challenged. "Are you guys already on to this story?"

Dennis took in a healthy gulp of air, then gave Billie a go-ahead nod.

"Okay," she said, taking a seat. "I can't give you any specifics, but yes, I've been working on a story about Big Buy. When Dennis showed me your documents, I realized that they were duplicates of records that I have."

"Wait a minute." Benjamin gripped the edge of the table. "Someone sent you a copy of these same records?"

Billie should never play poker. Her lips didn't move, but her brown eyes blinked nervously up at Dennis. "I'm not at liberty to say how I got them."

"Our client may have been murdered because someone wanted to get these documents back," Benjamin said.

"Murdered?" Billie's eyes expanded as wide as saucers. "Let's back up a minute. That's way outside the scope of my story. You need to tell us exactly what's going on."

A splash of anticipation ricocheted through me. We were definitely on to something. I just prayed it was something that could help Olivia's case.

"We're willing to put our cards on the table," I told Billie. "But only if you agree to do the same."

CHAPTER 77

Special strolled into the Emerald Chateau Hair Salon and made a beeline for Darlene's booth in the far left corner of the shop. Tonisha was sitting in Darlene's chair, getting her hair French braided in preparation for her weave.

"Hey, everybody," Special called out to the other customers and hair stylists.

Darlene glanced over at her appointment book. "What're you doing here? Your appointment isn't until next Tuesday."

"Is it?" Special pulled out her Droid and pretended to check it. "Dang. I must've read it wrong. The calendar on this thing is so hard to read."

Special narrowed her eyes and peered down at Tonisha. "Hey, girl, I recognize you. You're a celebrity."

Tonisha half-smiled.

"It was really brave of you to go through all of that. They tried to drag your name through the mud, but you stood your ground. You deserve every dime of that two mil."

Tonisha distorted her lips into a sour pucker. "I ain't seen a dime of it yet 'cuz Lamarr is supposedly filing an appeal. I just wish he'd stop playing games and pay me my money."

"You just need to be patient," Darlene said. "You'll get paid."

Special quietly snorted. *Not if I have anything to do with it, you won't.*

"You just stay prayerful, girl." Special gave her a quick pat on the shoulder. "Everything's going to work out just fine."

She turned to Darlene. "Since I'm here, can you squeeze me in? I just need you to tighten up the back."

"Yeah," Darlene said, "but it may be a while."

Special smiled. That was exactly what she wanted to hear. "You want something to eat? I'm going to run over to Popeyes."

Darlene shook her head. "No, thanks. I just ate."

"What about you, Tonisha?"

She hesitated. "Yeah, get me a two-piece with some red beans 'n rice."

Tonisha grabbed a large Coach bag from the floor and started rummaging around in it. "Oh, never mind. I changed purses last night and forgot to put my wallet in here."

Darlene's hands froze in mid-air. She dropped the braid she was holding and whirled the chair around until Tonisha was facing her. "If you can't buy a two-piece, how you gonna pay me?"

"I'm sorry. I didn't realize I'd left my wallet at home."

Darlene lowered her chin. "Maybe you should go get it."

"Uh...I have to be in Santa Monica at eight. I won't have time to go all the way back to Hawthorne. Is there an ATM around here?"

"You don't have your wallet, but you have your ATM card?" Darlene asked skeptically.

"Uh, I don't keep my ATM card in my wallet."

"Yeah, right," Darlene said. "Well, there's an ATM across the street at Vons and another one around the corner at Bank of America. Take your pick. You go get some money while I wash Keekee."

Darlene complained all the way to the shampoo bowl. "If she can't pay for a damn two-piece, I don't know how she thinks she can afford a weave. Hell, I don't work for free."

"Don't worry about it, girl," Special whispered. "I got you on the grub. You're about to become a millionaire. I don't have a problem hookin' you up."

When Special returned with the food, Keekee was sitting in Darlene's chair. As it turned out, Tonisha only had enough money in her checking account to pay for a press 'n curl. So she was busy unbraiding her own hair while Darlene worked on another client.

That gave Special and Tonisha time for a nice long chat over their chicken. By the time Tonisha left the shop with her short, thin hair pressed into a sad-looking flip, they had exchanged telephone numbers and email addresses. They also agreed to meet for drinks at the Cheesecake Factory later that night.

"You know you wrong," Darlene said, wagging her finger at Special after Tonisha walked out. "You trying to be friends with that girl 'cuz she got two-million dollars coming."

"That's not true. You know I ain't like that."

Special was actually feeling quite a sense of accomplishment. She really had a knack for this investigation stuff. Thanks to Suzie, she had located the drycleaners owned by Girlie's aunt and now she was about to get up close and personal with Tonisha.

"I just feel sorry for the girl," Special said, thrilled at how easily she'd gotten Tonisha to open up to her. "She's been having a rough time. Tonisha Cosby needs a B-F-F and I'm it."

CHAPTER 78

"You wanna kiss my ring finger now or later?"

Their annoying colleague, Detective Hopper, planted his flat ass on the corner of Mankowski's desk.

Thomas grinned and readied himself for the impending confrontation. He could tolerate Hopper, but Mankowski had no patience for the guy.

Mankowski didn't bother to look up from his computer. "Why don't you run along and find somebody else to play cops and robbers with, okay?"

The lieutenant never assigned Hopper to a decent case, so he was always running around, trying to solve everyone else's.

"You guys should be nice to me," Hopper replied. "I just solved your murder case."

"Sure you did," Mankowski said. "And I just found Jon Benet Ramsey's killer."

"So what case did you solve?" Thomas asked, amused.

Hopper smiled. "The one in Mar Vista."

"The Irving murder?"

"That would be the one," Hopper said with a self-assured chuckle. "I even got a confession."

Detective Mankowski continued to work on the report he was typing and wished Hopper would just hop away. Thomas, however, wanted to hear more.

"A confession from who?"

"The wannabe thug in interrogation room four. Armando Ortiz."

Mankowski finally stopped typing. "What the hell are you talking about?"

"You're a detective. You're supposed to have better listening skills. I *said* I solved your case."

"How?" Detective Thomas asked.

"Solid police work."

Mankowski rocked back in his chair. "Stop jerking us around and tell us what you're talking about?"

Detective Hopper stood up. "Why don't you come with me and see for yourself?"

They followed him into an interrogation room near the end of the hallway. A dark-skinned Hispanic kid who could have passed for fifteen was handcuffed to a metal table, sniveling into his forearm.

"Armando, this is Detective Thomas and this is Detective Mankowski. I want you to tell them everything you told me."

"I...I...I didn't kill that white lady. I swear!"

Mankowski glared back over his shoulder at Hopper. "I thought you said you got a confession."

"Just hold on and listen to the kid's story," Hopper said, holding up both palms in an appeal for patience. "He's been locked up for two weeks. Picked up on his second DUI and couldn't bail out. One of the deputies heard him mouthing off to another inmate about a murder."

It took a few seconds for Armando to compose himself. "I...I was hanging out with my buddy Hector and he asked me for a ride to Mar Vista to get some weed. I swear I didn't know he was gonna kill that lady."

Armando cried and hiccupped in tandem. "We was gonna score some weed. That's it. That's all I thought we was gonna do."

"Where do you live?" Mankowski asked.

"Pico Rivera," Armando sniffed.

Mankowski laughed. "You live in East L.A. and you want me to believe you drove all the way to Mar Vista to buy some weed. Were the drug dealers in your neighborhood on strike or something?"

"Just hold on," Hopper said, coming to Armando's defense. "Let him finish."

"Tell them where you and your friend Hector went," Detective Hopper prodded.

"We went over on Rose Street in Mar Vista. Another dude told Hector about this white guy, some college dude, who sold weed out of his house. Hector found out the dude had just bought a big stash of weed, but was out of town. We went to steal his weed. That's all."

Mankowski interrupted. "So how did Judi Irving end up dead?"

"I let Hector out in front of this house. About twenty minutes later he came running out carrying a jewelry box and a flat screen, screaming at me to take off."

Thomas and Mankowski locked gazes. Only someone involved in Judi's murder would know that the only items taken were a jewelry box and a small flat screen. They'd intentionally withheld that information from the media.

"I swear I didn't know that he was gonna kill that white lady." Armando started crying again. "I swear I didn't!"

Mankowski sat down in the chair facing Armando. "What white lady?"

"The one in the newspaper. I don't know her name. Hector said he hit her in the head with his big metal flashlight he had. He just wanted to knock her out until he had time to search the place to find out where the guy hid his weed."

"What guy?" Mankowski asked.

"I already told you," Armando cried. "Some white dude Hector knew."

"So where's Hector?"

"He ran, man. He went back to Mexico. He's never coming back."

"Let's talk outside, gentlemen," Detective Hopper said. "I'll fill you in on the rest."

"His story checks out," Hopper said, when they stepped into the hallway. "Judi Irving had just rented that house a month earlier. Before that, it was the residence of Kenneth Murphy, a sophomore at

UCLA. He was doing so well in the weed trade that he was able to upgrade to a condo in Westwood. Unfortunately for Ms. Irving, Mr. Murphy forgot to send a change-of-address notice to his customers."

"I'll be damned," Thomas said. "So it wasn't Phillip Peterman *or* Robby Irving?"

Mankowski wasn't buying this tale just yet. "What else you got? We can't just take the word of this whimpering thug."

"How about this?" Hopper said. "Armando told me Hector turned off the breakers, cutting the electricity to Judi's unit before he broke in. If I'm correct, that information was withheld from the media. Hector Ortiz has a long record of petty crimes. I ran his prints and they match the ones found at the crime scene. The kid's telling the truth."

"Wait a minute," Mankowski said, growing angry. "We submitted those prints weeks ago. How'd you get word of a match before we did?"

"When you're nice to people they don't mind putting your request ahead of others."

It was incredibly annoying, not to mention embarrassing for a sap like Detective Hopper to have cracked their case simply by lucking up on this cry baby.

Thomas and Mankowski were too stunned to react with anything other than stone silence.

Detective Hopper treated them to a goofy gap-toothed smile. "Like I said, gentlemen. I just cracked your murder case."

CHAPTER 79

"Hey, girlfriend!" Special greeted Tonisha with a big sisterly embrace in the crowded lobby of the Cheesecake Factory.

As usual, the trendy restaurant in Marina Del Rey was packed. Special could see that all eyes were on Tonisha. Probably because of her leather hot pants, gold halter top and the blonde page-boy wig that looked more like a football helmet. Her foundation was thick enough to scrape off with a knife. Special wished she had time to teach the girl a little class. But that wasn't her job.

What Special was about to do was straight-up backstabbing, but if she was going to be a top-notch investigator, she had to do whatever it took to solve the case without any trace of guilt.

"Thanks for inviting me out," Tonisha said. "I've just been hanging out at home with nothing to do. When you go through the kind of craziness I've been through, you learn pretty fast who your real friends are."

Tonisha probably didn't have any real friends before she'd accused Lamarr of sexual assault, so it was understandable that she didn't have any now. When Special had Googled her name, the venomous posts shocked her. There was one whole website dedicated to attacking her. The girl definitely needed a BFF.

Special had chosen this restaurant because it was always crowded. She wanted Tonisha to feel as uncomfortable as possible. That way, she would rely on Special even more. Special did not expect to work a confession out of Tonisha tonight. That would take time. This was simply a build-a-friendship dinner. Real investigative work took time and patience.

"Girl, you're a celebrity." Special gazed around the restaurant. "Everybody's checking you out."

Tonisha turned up her nose. "I don't feel like no celebrity the way everybody's hatin' on me."

Special gave her forearm a squeeze. "Don't let it get to you, girl. You got two-million dollars coming."

"I hope so. My attorney is trippin' hard. I told her I'm tired of waiting. I need my money now. She won't even return my calls."

The hostess led them to a choice table.

Their waitress, a thick black woman with a wide smile, came over to take their drink orders.

"What will you be drinking, ladies?" she said, pleasantly to Special.

She wanted a Long Island Iced Tea, but had to stick to her rule about not drinking on the job. "I'll have a Coke. I'm taking some medication, so I can't drink," she explained to Tonisha.

When the waitress' eyes bounced over to Tonisha, her nose crinkled as if she had smelled something foul.

"And what do *you* want?" the waitress said with a hand on her hip.

"Hold up," Special said, her hand in the air. "What's up with the attitude? I hope I don't have to ask the manager to have someone else serve us."

Special leaned across the table. "What you drinking, girl?"

"I'll have an apple martini," she said. "And some avocado eggrolls."

The waitress waddled away without writing down their order.

"Girl, you can't let people treat you like that. You gotta put them in their place."

"Thanks for standing up for me." She let out an exasperated breath. "It's been rough."

"Don't worry about it, girl. I got your back."

Special spent the next hour telling Tonisha details about her own life—her made-up life—that she hoped would engender trust.

Tonisha was gulping down her drink and munching on the avocado eggrolls as if this would be her only meal for the day.

Tonisha was clearly a lightweight when it came to alcohol. Her tongue was running a mile a minute by the time Special asked the waitress to bring her a second apple martini. The more Tonisha talked, the more Special realized things about the girl that she had not picked up while watching the trial on TV.

First, Tonisha suffered from serious self-esteem issues, having been bounced around eight different foster homes, starting at the age of ten. Though she had attractive facial features—wide brown eyes, full lips and nice cheekbones—she distorted her appearance with too much of everything. Too much eye shadow, too much blush, and way too much hair. Although she'd worked as a stripper for years, she didn't have the street sense Special assumed came with that territory. She was beginning to think that Tonisha might be on the slow side.

They finished their meal—a meal Special insisted on paying for—shared a piece of Tiramisu Cheesecake and headed out of the restaurant. The valet brought Tonisha's car up first, a beat-up Ford Escort.

"Where you going now?" Tonisha asked, ignoring her car.

"Home," Special said, rubbing her stomach. "I'm stuffed."

Tonisha pouted. "I ain't ready to go home yet. Can I come over?"

That was a no-no. She didn't want Tonisha to know where she lived. Special could sense that she didn't want to be alone. The girl was actually pretty pitiful. Special felt a pang of guilt again, but brushed it aside.

"Girl, my house is a wreck. Let's go to Starbucks. We can sit outside and have some coffee. Just follow me."

Tonisha smiled and scampered toward her car.

Special deliberately chose the Starbucks that was most likely to put Tonisha in the most uncomfortable position. When she pulled up in front of the Ladera Center Starbucks, the place, as usual, was crammed with people just hanging out. Special parked and walked over to Tonisha's car, wondering why she hadn't gotten out yet.

Tonisha rolled down the window. "Can we go to a Starbucks in a white neighborhood? I'm tired of black folks hatin' on me."

"You ain't gotta worry about that. You're with me."

Tonisha inhaled and reluctantly climbed out. Special looped arms with her new BFF as they walked up to the Starbucks.

"Save us that table over there," Special said, pointing. "I'll go inside and order our drinks."

When she returned with two Caffè Mochas, Special pulled a flask from her purse, opened it and poured a healthy dose of brandy into Tonisha's drink.

Tonisha took a sip and smiled. "Whoooo, this is good!"

Special only pretended to spike her own drink.

"*Lyin', money-hungry skank,*" someone yelled out.

Tonisha tried to scrunch down in her chair. "See why I didn't wanna come here."

Special looked around with a daring grimace on her face. "Who said that?" she yelled out.

The heckler didn't respond.

Special gave Tonisha's hand a squeeze. "Girl, don't you let these fools get to you. This is a free country."

Tonisha picked up her napkin and dabbed at her eyes. "I wish I never would've gone through with this," she said, caressing her coffee cup.

Special had made up a story she planned to tell Tonisha after they knew each other better, but they seemed to be developing a bond much faster than she had expected. So Special decided to share her tale now.

"You shouldn't feel that way, girl. I had something similar happen to me in college during my sophomore year. I was dating this football player, but he kicked me to the curb for some freshman who wasn't even cute. But I got his ass back good. I told the campus police he tried to force himself on me. When they expelled him from school everybody was hatin' on me. So I know exactly how it feels to be ostracized."

Tonisha's blank expression conveyed that she wasn't quite sure what *ostracized* meant.

"So, did the guy really force himself on you?"

Special lowered her voice and checked their surroundings. "No. But that asshole got what he deserved. If he'd had some money, I would've sued his ass."

Tonisha nodded absently.

"I'm just proud of you for standing up for yourself. What these people are sending you through is ridiculous. You're the victim. They're treating you like a criminal."

Tonisha took a sip of her drink. "They're treating me worse than a criminal."

They were both quiet, enjoying the warm early evening air.

"Can I tell you something?" Her face held the sad innocence of a little girl.

Special's heart skipped three beats. Was Tonisha ready to spill her guts already? She looked casually across the table at her new friend. "You can tell me anything."

"I'm thinking about leaving L.A. and changing my name. I'm tired of all these L.A. haters. I made good money as a stripper. I gotta find a new club where nobody knows me."

Dang. "That sounds like a good idea. Maybe you should."

"That damn Lamarr's been talking to people and it's been getting back to me. He's going around telling people that I got drunk and told somebody I made up the charges against him."

Did you?

"I ain't stupid," Tonisha said. "I'm getting my money. My attorney told me to keep my mouth shut. So that's what I'm doing."

Keep your mouth shut? OMG! Special was getting close. She just had to calm down and take it slow. She slipped her Droid out of her pocket, and pretended to check her email. Instead, she turned on the recorder and set it on the table.

"Your attorney was really good," Special said. "I would definitely use her if I had a case."

Tonisha sucked her teeth. "They say attorneys are vultures and they are. Including her."

"What?" Special lowered her chin, feigning shock. "She got you two-million dollars. How can you talk about her like that?"

"'Cuz it's true. And she ain't got me nothin' yet. She's just as un-ethical as the rest of 'em."

"What makes you say that?"

Tonisha smiled, then swung her head slowly from side to side. Her stiff wig didn't move an inch. "No way," she said sheepishly. "I can't tell nobody this."

"No problem, girl. I ain't trying to get in nobody's business."

Tonisha seemed disappointed that Special didn't press her for more.

Special looked at her watch. "I guess I better be going."

"No, don't go yet," Tonisha begged. "I ain't ready to leave."

Tonisha looked around, leaned her head close to Special's and lowered her voice. "Can I really trust you?"

Special frowned. "The way I've been standing up for you and you have the nerve to ask me that? I'm offended."

"Okay, okay," Tonisha said. "I'm sorry. It's just hard for me to trust people."

"Well, you can definitely trust me."

Tonisha looked over her shoulder. "Okay, but you gotta swear not to tell *nobody* what I'm about to tell you."

"Okay," Special said, trying to play it cool.

"I can definitely relate to what you went through in college," Tonisha said with a wink. "Sometimes you just gotta do what you gotta do."

Special gave her a fake laugh. "It's all about looking out for number one. You were lucky to have an attorney like Girlie Cortez looking out for you."

"Forget her! I can't stand her!" Tonisha said. "She better get me my money. If she don't, I got something on her ass. She'll be just as unemployed as I am if I start telling what I know."

OMG! She was about to get two for the price of one. *Maybe Tonisha and Girlie were working together to frame Lamarr.*

Special folded her arms and pretended to be checking out a cutie who could've passed for Denzel's buffed-up brother. In reality, she was trying to contain her excitement. She refused to ask another question for fear of interrupting Tonisha's flow. The girl wanted to talk and Special was going to let her spill her guts.

Tonisha surveyed the area again. "Let's go sit in your car," she whispered. "'Cuz I can't let nobody hear when I tell you what really went down."

CHAPTER 80

"**M**an, you're nuts if you don't pick up a few shares of this stock. It's the next Apple."

Detective Thomas sat on the corner of his desk, browsing the CNBC website on his iPhone. It was almost four and he'd been on the thing all day.

"Front me a few grand and maybe I'll give it a go," Mankowski said, leaning back in his chair.

"*Me* front *you*? No wife, no kids. You should have a boatload of discretionary cash."

Thomas looked up from the device, but just for a second. "So you really think Girlie is going to show up for the polygraph?"

"We'll find out in two days."

"She ain't coming," Thomas said. "No way a lawyer would agree to take a lie detector test. Especially a lawyer as shrewd as Girlie Cortez."

Mankowski was hoping like hell that she did show. The fact that Judi Irving died as a result of a botched burglary, still left a lot of unanswered questions. There was a definite connection between Girlie and Phillip Peterman. Even though Girlie swore she'd never met Phillip, Mankowski refused to believe the two of them being at the Four Seasons Hotel at the same time was a mere coincidence. He couldn't rest until he knew for sure how Girlie was tied to Actor Boy.

At least there were no lingering questions about the cause of Phillip's death. Based on the reports of four eyewitnesses who saw Phillip fiddling with his phone right before the crash, his death was officially attributed to distracted driving. Too bad. Even though he hadn't killed his girlfriend, Mankowski wanted him around to badger some more.

"Holy shit!" Detective Thomas jumped off the desk. "This is it!"

"What? Another one of your stocks hit an all-time high? Just don't retire before we tie up all the loose ends in this case."

Detective Thomas shoved his iPhone inches from Mankowski's nose. "Read this. This is it! "

Mankowski took the device from his partner, squinting as he tried to read the CNBC website on the small screen. "How do you scroll down on this thing?"

Detective Thomas swiped his index finger down the screen and Mankowski continued to read.

"This is what Big Buy was trying to keep under wraps," Thomas insisted. "I bet you anything, this is what those missing documents were all about. The reason nobody could find Judi Irving's documents was because somebody turned them over to *The Daily Business Journal.*"

The CNBC website, quoting an article in the *Journal,* reported that a bid by the Welson Corporation to purchase Big Buy department stores had been called off amid allegations of fraud by Big Buy executives. According to the report, Big Buy CEO Rita Richards-Kimble and the company's CFO Fred Hiller had been part of a scheme to falsify the company's financial statements for the past two years. The company's Big 10 accounting firm, Wynn, Miller & Gold had also allegedly participated in the fraud.

The article stated that Hiller, a former managing partner at the accounting firm before joining Big Buy, was the architect of the scheme. The newspaper also noted that Big Buy's CEO would have netted $125 million dollars had the Welson deal gone through.

Mankowski handed the device back to his partner as he grabbed his sports jacket from the back of his chair.

"I think we need to take a trip over to Big Buy and shake some trees to see what might fall out. But first, I want to talk to that reporter at the *Daily Business Journal* who broke the story."

It was no real surprise to Mankowski that *Journal* reporter Billie Wilson would hide behind the First Amendment and refuse to divulge the source of her article about Big Buy.

Wilson sat next to the newspaper's in-house attorney as the detectives leered across the table at her. Unfortunately, she had the upper hand and there was really nothing they could do about it.

Mankowski thought about getting forceful with the woman. But treating her like a suspect wasn't a good idea since being in the glass conference room was like sitting in a fish bowl.

"Would you at least be willing to tell us when you received the Big Buy documents?" Mankowski asked.

Journalists were second only to criminal defense attorneys on his list of the earth's lowest creatures.

Wilson arrogantly protruded her pancake-flat chest. "I never admitted to receiving any Big Buy documents."

Mankowski grunted. "I know that, and I also know that you did. You wouldn't have printed that article without having some direct proof of the fraud."

"We're prohibited from divulging any information about our sources," she repeated for the umpteenth time. Her sharp nose already made her look like a parrot, now she sounded like one too.

The newspaper's attorney, a balding Latino in a three-piece suit, was uncharacteristically mute for his species.

"We really need your help," Mankowski said. "Someone may have died because of those documents."

Not even that revelation moved her.

"Sorry." Wilson cocked her head ever so slightly. "Can't help you. Freedom of the press is at stake here."

Thomas stood up, never one to push too hard unless he was fairly certain of a payoff.

His more stubborn partner took his time getting to his feet. Mankowski was keenly aware that several sets of eyes from the newsroom were peering at them through the glass. They could probably sense it when one of their own was being pressed for information.

He thought about saying something crass, but decided he'd save his insults for the folks on his next stop.

CHAPTER 81

I left the office early, planning to have a hot, soapy bubble bath, then plant myself in front of the TV with a big bowl of kettle corn. I'd have the house to myself tonight since Jefferson would be attending a lecture at the mosque.

I definitely needed a break after my stressful day. That morning *The Daily Business Journal* broke the story about Big Buy's financial fraud. I spent almost an hour on the phone with Jane, trying to calm her down. She claimed the CEO was treating her even worse than before, so she wanted to quit. But after Jane told me about the four-hundred-thousand dollars Big Buy's founder left for her in his will, I wasn't about to let her leave that money on the table.

Right after hanging up with Jane, Olivia called me. She was also ready to throw in the towel. I listened sympathetically as she told me how she was being shunned at work. I didn't share the information Jane had revealed to me, but I did tell her that I'd uncovered some information that might allow me to negotiate a decent settlement for her. By the time we hung up, she was holding on, but the thread was pretty thin.

Since my blowup with Jefferson over his talking to the Community of Islam about a loan, we hadn't discussed the issue again. On Sunday mornings, I continued to head off to Faithful Central Bible Church, while Jefferson went alone to the mosque. Prior to his interest in the Community, Jefferson occasionally attended church with me, but most mornings he slept in.

I eased my Land Cruiser into the driveway, surprised to see Jefferson's car parked on his side of the driveway.

When I entered the house, the familiar sound of the TV welcomed me. Jefferson was in his usual spot on the couch in the den, drink in one hand, the remote no farther than arm's reach.

There was still a dubious tension between us that we'd been ignoring, something we were both pretty good at. A disagreement could hover below the surface for months before finally exploding in our faces.

"I'm surprised to find you home," I said, kicking off my shoes. "Isn't there a lecture at the mosque tonight?"

"What? You're not happy to see me?" His tone was neither serious nor playful.

"I just didn't expect you to be here. You always go to lectures on Tuesday nights."

He lazily hunched his left shoulder. "I decided to skip a night."

When my husband was in one of his moods, it was usually best to give him some distance. Most of the time, I wisely did so. Tonight, though, curiosity wouldn't let me.

I eyed the brown liquor in his cocktail glass and assumed that it wasn't tea.

I plopped down next to him on the couch. "I thought Muslims weren't supposed to drink alcohol."

His gaze remained on the television screen. "I thought Christians weren't supposed to judge people."

"Okay, I get it. You're in a bad mood."

I motioned to get up, but before I could, he placed a hand on my forearm.

"Don't go."

I settled back in, my mood about to become as funky as his.

"I've decided not to join the Community," Jefferson announced. "So you happy now?"

Hell, yeah, I'm happy. "Is that why you're in such a funky mood tonight?"

"I'm not in a funky mood." He swirled his drink, which made a clinking sound when the ice hit the side of the glass.

"Then what would you call it?"

He twisted his lips sideways as he thought about my question. "I'm in a reflective mood."

I laughed. "Okay, then."

Several minutes passed with the only sound in the room coming from the Jaheim music video on the television screen.

I tried hard to keep my lips sealed, but the questions bouncing around in my head needed answers. "Did you decide not to join the Community because of me?" I finally asked.

Jefferson didn't rush to respond.

"Don't get me wrong," he said. "I definitely didn't wanna deal with the drama of seeing your lips poked out every time I went to a lecture. But that wasn't what led to my decision."

It was easy to see that my husband was in the midst of a serious internal struggle. I snuggled closer and decided to let him talk when he was ready.

"Those brothers are on a mission," he said after a few more minutes had passed. "And I really respect that. But I didn't wanna half-step. I don't have time for all the meetings or the patience for all the rules and regulations. If I couldn't do it with the kind of passion and commitment that Clayton—I mean, Khalil—has, I wouldn't feel right."

He held his glass high in the air, then took a sip. "And I can give up bacon. I might be able to cut back on cussin'. But I ain't giving up Cognac."

I chuckled. "So that's what it came down to?"

Jefferson smiled. "I am who I am."

"What about the loan?"

"The general contractor got his act together. I didn't need it after all. Now go ahead and just say it so we can get past this."

"Say what?"

"How glad you are that I'm not joining the Community. You probably wanna do some cartwheels across the room."

"You did have me worried," I confessed with a laugh. "I really thought you might get as deep into the Community as Clayton is."

"And if I had?"

"My faith is important to me, so that would've been a big problem."

"I still don't understand why you were trippin' so hard. Especially since I rarely even went to church anyway."

"Yeah, but you were raised as a Christian. Despite your willingness to dabble in Islam, I know your religious beliefs are the same as mine. Our faith and our upbringing in the church shape who we are."

"You act like we agree on everything. We don't."

"I know that. But some aspects of a marriage are more important than others. For me, my faith is one of them. And on that, we need to be on the same page. I've been praying about it. If that didn't work, I was gonna call your mama and tell on you."

"Oh, that would've been messed up," Jefferson said, laughing. "I'm just lucky she hasn't seen that *Times* article.

The room fell silent again.

"Thanks for backing off and letting me work this out on my own."

"No problem," I said, briefly looking skyward. *Thank God.*

CHAPTER 82

It took Mankowski and Thomas close to ninety minutes in rush-hour traffic to make the drive from *The Daily Business Journal* to Big Buy's headquarters in Anaheim. In light of the media firestorm the company found itself in the midst of, the detectives had correctly predicted that the CEO would still be in the office despite the fact that it was almost eight.

It hadn't been easy to get an audience with Rita Richards-Kimble. Only after Mankowski threatened to drag her down to the station for questioning, did she suddenly become available.

"As you can imagine, we've had a pretty rough day with all of these scandalous news reports about our company," Rita said, when they entered her office. "So obviously I'm not happy to have two detectives in my office right now."

She rounded her desk, gave both detectives a firm handshake and showed them to an adjoining conference room. The impressive space had windows on two sides and a long, black lacquered table sur-rounded by sixteen black leather chairs.

Mankowski sank down into one of them and felt like he was rest-ing on a mound of cotton.

The CEO sat at the head of the table and faced the detectives who sat on either side of her. She was a weird-looking woman, Mankowski thought. Something about her face seemed a little off, but he wasn't quite sure what. Probably too much nipping and tucking.

"My general counsel will be here in just a second," Rita said, the tips of her fingers pressed together. "In the meantime, can you give me a little more information about why you're here?"

"We believe the news reports about your company's financial ir-regularities are tied to a case we've been investigating."

Her perfectly arched brows furrowed. "And what case would that be?"

"The murder of Judi Irving. We understand that Ms. Irving was suing Big Buy for gender discrimination. We believe she had copies of documents with information about the company's fraudulent financial statements that somehow got into the hands of *The Daily Business Journal.*"

"That's as ridiculous as the media's lies about our finances."

Another woman entered without knocking and curtly introduced herself as the general counsel. She was better looking than the CEO, but was way too buttoned-up.

"I hope you haven't answered any questions without me," Evelyn Kimble gently chided the CEO.

The general counsel pulled out a chair and sat down next to Thomas. She looked from Mankowski to his partner. "It's very unusual for us to get a visit from law enforcement."

Mankowski repeated what he had just told the CEO. Almost im-mediately, he picked up on a restrained friction between the two women. They had yet to make eye contact. Maybe now was a good time to turn up the heat.

"We also have evidence that Phillip Peterman, Judi Irving's boy-friend, was intimately involved with someone who had close ties to your company."

"Who?" both women blurted out in the same shrill voice.

"Your attorney, Girlie Cortez," he said.

It was Thomas' idea to ambush them with the information so they could observe their reactions.

The general counsel's rosy cheeks whitened. "Are you saying Girlie was sleeping with Mr. Peterman?"

"That's what we believe," Mankowski confirmed, then waited a beat. "Is it possible that Ms. Cortez may've turned over your company's records to *The Daily Business Journal?*"

"That's absurd," the CEO bristled. "Girlie didn't perform the kind of legal work that would have given her access to our financial records."

"She could've gotten access to them if somebody sent them to Judi Irving and Ms. Cortez was screwing Judi Irving's boyfriend," Thomas pointed out.

Neither woman could muster a response to that scenario.

"We're also looking into the possibility that Ms. Cortez obtained the documents from Peterman at the company's request," Thomas continued. "That might explain Mr. Peterman's untimely death. Maybe someone had him killed to keep him quiet about what he knew."

Mankowski gave his partner an attaboy grin. That was complete bull, but he liked it.

"That's ridiculous!" Rita pushed away from the table. "Our earnings reports aren't fraudulent and Girlie Cortez is way too smart to ruin her legal career by doing something that stupid. And if we *had* hired her to recover those documents, you can bet they would've never ended up in the hands of *The Daily Business Journal.*"

He could see why this woman was the CEO. She had some grapefruit-size balls. She'd immediately zeroed in on the one big flaw in their little theory. If Girlie was doing the dirty work of her clients, she wouldn't have given the documents to the *Journal.*

"Girlie told us Mr. Peterman died in a car accident," Evelyn said quietly. "I didn't think his death was the result of foul play."

Mankowski hunched his shoulders and spread his arms. "I'm not at liberty to disclose the evidence we've gathered."

No one spoke until the general counsel rose from her chair. "We have no knowledge about any of this. So I think we're done here, gentlemen."

Mankowski didn't want to leave. His chair was softer than his bed.

"We'd appreciate it if you didn't tell Ms. Cortez that we know about her relationship with Mr. Peterman," Thomas said, as he neared the door. "Our investigation is still ongoing and we don't want to tip her off."

"I can assure you that nobody connected with Big Buy had anything to do with those documents or the death of Judi Irving, her boyfriend or anybody else," the CEO insisted. "Especially not one of our attorneys."

"Shouldn't you talk to Ms. Cortez before making that representation?" Thomas asked.

"We don't need to talk to her," Rita insisted. "The attorneys we hire don't engage in unscrupulous or illegal conduct. And neither do we."

CHAPTER 83

Special pounded on Vernetta's front door with both fists, then pressed the doorbell in rapid succession.

"It's me!" she yelled. "Open up. This is important!"

It took a couple of minutes before she heard the click of the deadbolt lock. "Do you know what time it is?" Jefferson groaned, as he eased the door open.

He had one hand on the door, the other on the door jam, blocking her entrance. He was dressed in a rumpled T-shirt and flannel pajama bottoms.

"It's not even nine o'clock yet. That ain't late." Special ducked under his arm and into the house.

"Vernetta's not answering her cell. Is she home? I need to talk to her. A-S-A-P."

Jefferson yawned and closed the door. "She had to take her parents to LAX. She should be home any minute."

"Well, I gotta wait up for her. You see this right here?" She waved a yellow folder back and forth in front of his face. "What I got in here is gonna clear Lamarr *and* nail that heffa, Girlie Cortez."

"I doubt Vernetta cares about clearing Lamarr. She doesn't represent him anymore."

"She'll care once I tell her what I found out."

Jefferson yawned and stretched his arms. "So what did you find out?"

Special tucked the folder behind her back. "Sorry, it's top secret. I'm a private investigator now. I'd be breaching my ethical obligation to my client if I divulged confidential information."

"Okay, whatever. You can wait for Vernetta in the den. I have to be up at five, so I'm going back to sleep."

He turned to leave, but Special grabbed the tail end of his T-shirt.

"I don't wanna wait by myself. Anyway, I need to talk to you too."

She tugged him toward the den, where he fell onto the couch. Special placed her file on the coffee table and sat in an adjacent chair.

"What's the four-one-one on Clayton—excuse me—Khalil. Did he hook up with that blabbermouth Akila yet?"

Jefferson hooked his head over the back of the couch and closed his eyes. "I ain't getting into that."

"That's a very evasive response," Special replied. "Now that I'm a private investigator, I'm a lot more perceptive. If you didn't know anything, you would've said so. Now spill it."

Jefferson pinched the bridge of his nose. "I haven't talked to Clay—Khalil—in a few days. I have no idea what's going on with him. And even if I knew something, I wouldn't tell you. He's not the guy for you, okay?"

Jefferson's words quieted her. "And why would you say that?"

"Clay—hell, it's gonna take me some time to get used to his new name. He ain't here, so I'm calling him Clayton. That brother really wants to change things for black folks. He needs a woman who's down with him on that."

"And that's not me?"

"You tell me. The woman Clayton hooks up with is gonna have to make a lot of sacrifices. She's gonna have to share him with the Community. You willing to do that?"

"Maybe."

"Stop lyin'," Jefferson said. "Move on. You're crazy as hell, but you're a good woman. There's a guy out there for you."

Special sucked her teeth. "I wish you would tell me where the hell he is."

"Just stop lookin' so hard. Sistahs like you scare men. The next dude you meet, just kick back and enjoy his company."

"Easy for you to say. Your clock ain't tickin'."

"I thought you didn't want kids."

"That's beside the point."

Jefferson chuckled and massaged the back of his neck. "I have no idea why women are so anxious to get married. Marriage ain't the be-all and end-all."

"I won't tell your wife you said that."

"I don't mean it in a bad way. I like being married. But it's hard work sometimes. Me and Vernetta have been through some stuff. And, by the way, thanks for telling her I was talking to the Community of Islam about a loan."

"Oh," Special said sheepishly. "That kinda slipped out. Sorry."

"Yeah, I bet it did."

"So you think Clayton's going to marry Akila?"

"Did you hear anything I just said?"

"Yep. Now answer my question."

"I don't know. But if he doesn't marry her, he'll probably marry some other woman he meets at the mosque."

Hearing Jefferson's confirmation of what she already knew made her heart shudder.

"And if that does happen, it's no reflection on you." After a long stretch of silence, he looked over at her. "Are you gonna be okay if he does?"

Special didn't respond. Her head could definitely handle the loss, but her heart was another story.

Neither one of them heard Vernetta walk into the room. "Hey, what's up?"

"Girrrlllll," Special said, jumping up from the chair, "you won't believe what I dug up. First, we gotta go talk to Lamarr right away. And after that, we're going to stick it to Girlie Cortez. The information I found out about her will blow your mind!"

"I don't have a thing to talk to Lamarr about," Vernetta said, kicking off her shoes. "But I'm very interested in what you found out about Girlie."

"Lamarr didn't do it," Special said. "We need to go over to his house right now so I can tell him about my investigation. He'll probably be so happy he'll hook me up with some rich football player."

Vernetta sat down on the couch next to Jefferson. "Just tell me what you found out about Girlie."

"Nope," Special said, stubbornly. "Not until you agree to go with me to Lamarr's place. And I *do* know where the brother lives. So either you go with me right now or I'm going by myself."

CHAPTER 84

Evelyn escorted the two detectives to the lobby and returned to the CEO's office. She found her sister-in-law staring out of the window.

A somber silence draped the room.

"Those detectives are wrong," Rita said, in a soft, but menacing voice. "Girlie Cortez didn't turn over those documents to the *Journal,* but I know who did."

"You do?" Evelyn said. "Who?"

When Rita finally turned around, rage had disfigured her face. "That bitch sitting just outside my office. And after all I've done for her!"

She leaned across the desk and slapped the intercom button on her telephone.

"Jane! Get in here!"

"Hold on a minute." Evelyn ran over to her. "You don't know that for sure. We should let Human Resources conduct an investigation first."

Jane scrambled into the room, her hands trembling so badly she could barely hold on to her pad and pen.

"Have a seat," Rita ordered, pointing to a chair in front of her desk.

Jane sat down and Evelyn protectively stood next to her. "Rita, I really think we should—"

"Did you really think you could get away with this, you stupid bitch!"

Jane drew back in her chair. "I…I…get away with what? I don't know what you're—"

"You were the one who turned over those documents to *The Daily Business Journal*. Did you send them to Judi Irving too?"

"I don't know what you're talking about. I wouldn't do anything like that."

"You're a liar!"

The CEO walked around the desk and charged toward Jane. Evelyn jumped in front of her, arms extended, blocking her path.

"Please, Rita," Evelyn pleaded, "don't say another word. I'm advising you to cut this conversation short and let Human Resources handle this."

"You're the general counsel," Rita said. "So this is an attorney-client privileged conversation. We don't need Human Resources."

"The privilege doesn't extend to—"

"I don't care what it extends to. We don't need to waste time on an investigation. I'm taking care of this here and now."

Rita stepped around Evelyn and peered down at Jane, pointing a finger inches from her nose.

"I know you gave those documents to *The Daily Business Journal*. I can't believe you would jeopardize the sale of this company by stabbing us all in the back."

A tear rolled down Jane's cheek. "I…I didn't—"

"You're a goddamn liar! After all Harlan did for you, this is how you pay him back? And if you think you're going to testify against me or anyone else connected with this company, you better think again. You stole confidential records and you're going to jail for it. Now get out of here. You're fired!"

Jane rose and staggered out of the office.

Evelyn covered her mouth. "What you did was—"

"Call up Girlie Cortez and fire her too."

"I thought you just accused Jane of turning over those documents, not Girlie."

"Weren't you and I in the same damn meeting? That whore was sleeping with Judi Irving's boyfriend. That's a major conflict of interest. I should call up her firm's managing partner right now."

"You can't do that," Evelyn said. "Those detectives don't want her to know she's under investigation. And if we fire Girlie now, that'll definitely tip her off."

Rita stopped to consider that, then turned her wrath on Evelyn.

"So how are you going to fix this?"

"I've been on the phone doing damage control with the PR firm that helped us with that store protest. They've already issued a statement denying the story. They're working with Johnson in Media Relations to develop some talking points."

"Little good that's going to do. That report claimed to have documents with my signature on it. But I had no idea any of this stuff was going on."

Evelyn stared at her sister-in-law with disbelieving eyes. "These charges are serious," she said. "Investigators are going to go through our books with a fine-tooth comb."

"I know that," Rita snapped.

"These are the kind of charges that land CEOs in prison."

Rita's back straightened indignantly. "I only signed what I was asked to sign. I had no knowledge of anything inappropriate or illegal."

"It doesn't matter how much you knew or didn't know," Evelyn advised her. "You're the CEO and chairman of the board of directors. All fingers are going to be pointing at you."

"I'm not going down alone on this. You're my legal counsel. You had a duty to protect me."

"How could I protect you when you and Hiller kept everything from me?"

"You're the general counsel of this company. It's your job to know."

Evelyn folded her arms defiantly across her chest. "My job is to defend the best interests of this company. And that's exactly what I've been doing."

"No, you haven't," Rita yelled. "If you had, none of this would be happening."

"You're unbelievable!" Evelyn said, throwing up her hands. "I'm sorry, but this is one mess that I can't clean up for you. If you want my advice, you need to find yourself a good criminal attorney because you're going to need one."

CHAPTER 85

It took a lot of prodding, but Special finally told me what she had uncovered about Tonisha and Girlie. It actually did blow my mind.

Still, I didn't feel it was necessary to drop everything and run over to Lamarr's house tonight. I only relented because I feared Special would go without me and because Jefferson agreed to drive us there.

Lamarr lived in Brentwood, a ritzy neighborhood not far from the UCLA campus. His house was near the top of a winding hill, hidden behind high stone walls. During all the time I'd represented him, I'd never visited his home. I was surprised that there was no private gate or intercom system. We drove straight up a wide, cobblestone driveway and parked a few feet from the front door.

"This is going to be fantastic," Special exclaimed, hopping out of the car. "He's going to be so happy when he hears what I have to say."

I opened the car door, but didn't get out. Despite all the flowers he'd sent and apologies he'd made via voicemail and email, I was still reluctant to face him again. Being here brought back the terror I'd felt that night in my office.

"You okay?" Jefferson asked.

"Yeah," I lied.

"Are you ever going to tell me what really went down that night in your office?"

Nope. "Nothing went down."

"Then why are you afraid to face him?"

"Who said I'm afraid?"

"I did."

My husband knew me far too well. "I'm fine," I said, and finally climbed out of the car.

Special was already on the front step, ringing the doorbell like she was the UPS man with a special delivery.

Spotlights powerful enough to light up a football stadium almost made the New England Style two-story glow in the darkness.

"I could definitely see myself living large like this," Special said, looking around.

Jefferson threw an arm around my shoulders and we fell in behind Special.

"Wait until you see the inside," Special continued, excitedly. "I saw it on *MTV Cribs* last year. It's over eight-thousand square feet."

"Don't worry," Jefferson whispered in my ear as we waited for Lamarr to answer the door, "if he gets out of line, I'll beat him down. Just make sure you're waiting outside for me with the car running."

My husband could always make me laugh.

A few seconds later, Lamarr opened the front door. Jefferson and I gaped at him. Special emitted a sharp gasp.

He'd looked a mess that night he showed up at my office, but now Lamarr resembled a homeless bum. He had a few weeks' growth of beard and his cornrows were loose and ratty like cotton. His puffy eyes were barely open. He was wearing black sweatpants and a filthy T-shirt that used to be white.

Lamarr squinted and shielded his eyes from the light. "What y'all doing here?" There was no anger in his voice, only bewilderment.

"I'm a close friend of Vernetta's and I have some information about your case," Special said, taking a step back, bumping into me and Jefferson. "It's really important and we wanted to tell you about it right away."

That news sparked no visible reaction from Lamarr. "C'mon in," he mumbled.

Lamarr's physical appearance was nothing compared to the interior of his home. The place appeared to be in pre-hoarder stage and smelled like it too. The entryway opened up into a massive sunken living room littered with beer cans, liquor bottles, uneaten food and piles of clothes.

"Uh, excuse the place," he said, bending down to pick up an empty Cristal champagne bottle. "I had a party a few days ago and my peeps got a little wild."

All the curtains were closed, which gave the room a cave-like feel. A small table lamp provided the only light.

Special pressed the back of her hand to her nose as we stepped over trash on our journey to the living room.

"This is a damn shame," Special whispered to me. "It smells like feet up in here. This place was immaculate on *MTV Cribs*."

We all stood awkwardly in a ragged circle in the middle of the living room.

"Have a seat," Lamarr finally said.

He didn't appear to be under the influence of any substance. He just looked beaten down, as if he'd given up on life.

Special sat down first, then shot right back up. "Yuk! That chair is wet!"

"Oh, yeah," Lamarr said. "Why don't you sit over there?"

He pointed to a garish mink-covered chair that looked like it might bite. Special decided to join Jefferson and me on the couch.

"So why y'all here?" Lamarr asked.

"I'm a private investigator—well, not yet, but I'm going to be—and I've uncovered some information about Tonisha Cosby and her attorney, Girlie Cortez," Special happily announced. "I have information that proves that you didn't rape Tonisha."

Again, no reaction at all from Lamarr.

"Yeah, that's cool," he said, frowning. "But it won't do me any good now. The Legends cut me. Sent me some bullshit letter claiming my conduct was detrimental to the integrity of the league. The police didn't even charge me with nothin'."

"You don't understand," I said. "We have proof of your innocence."

"Don't matter. People still ain't gonna believe I didn't rape that girl. You wouldn't believe how everybody's been dissin' me. My agent dropped me before I even got that damn letter. Can you believe that shit? After all the money he made offfa me."

"Don't you even want to hear what Special found out?" I asked.

Lamarr shrugged. "Not really. But I would like to uh…" He looked down at his hands. "Can we, uh, have a private conversation? There's some stuff I need to say."

I was about to respond, but Jefferson beat me to it. "Whatever you need to say to her, you can say in front of us."

"It needs to be an attorney-customer discussion."

Lamarr's botched reference to the attorney-client privilege made me smile. Despite the way he'd treated me, I was actually feeling sorry for him. I was no longer afraid to be alone with him. At least not with my husband within rescuing distance.

I got up from the couch. "Let's talk in the kitchen."

Jefferson gave me a confounded look. "You don't have to—"

I squeezed his shoulder. "It'll be fine."

Lamarr led the way into the kitchen. The place was twice the size of my bedroom and was just as nasty as the rest of the house. Plates with moldy food sat out in the open. A liquid that had spilled on the countertop had hardened into a glaze and a sticky substance on the floor made a squishy sound with every step I took.

"Don't you have a housekeeper?" I asked.

"I used to." Lamarr rested his body against the cabinet. "But she quit 'cuz her family told her I might rape her."

Now that I knew he was an innocent man, my heart went out to him. I almost wanted to give him a hug, but his body odor made me keep my distance. "So what did you want to talk to me about?"

"I just wanted you to know that I…uh…I wasn't gonna hurt you that night in your office. I was pretty messed up, but I wasn't gonna do nothin'. I was just messin' around. I'm not like that. I appreciate everything you did for me."

"I know."

"So you believe me?"

"Yeah, I do."

My response seemed to please him and he smiled for the first time since we'd arrived.

"The information Special uncovered could do a lot to change your situation."

He hunched his shoulders. "Is it gonna get that verdict reversed?"

"Yeah, I think it might."

Lamarr's eyes brightened and he gave me an even bigger smile. This one much more hopeful.

"Okay, then," he said, scratching his chin through his scraggily beard, "let's go hear what your homegirl's got to say."

CHAPTER 86

The news that Jane Carson had been fired left me outraged and even more determined to go after Big Buy.

I'd spent most of the morning drafting Jane's wrongful termination complaint. Instead of going to lunch, I had an hour-long telephone conference with two experienced appellate attorneys. I needed their advice on the best way to get the new information about Lamarr's innocence before the court. Unfortunately, we had some daunting legal hurdles.

First, Tonisha wasn't aware that Special was recording their conversation. That made the recording illegal since California law requires both parties to consent to a taping. We could argue that Tonisha didn't have a reasonable expectation of privacy when she spilled her guts to Special, but her own words on the recording contradicted that. We could have Special prepare an affidavit detailing everything Tonisha told her, but that wouldn't be nearly as convincing as hearing Tonisha confess in her own words.

Another problem was the likelihood that Girlie would argue that Special, as my close friend, was acting at my instruction when she spoke to Tonisha. It would be inappropriate for me or anyone acting as my agent to speak to a plaintiff whom I knew was represented by counsel. Both Special and I could swear under oath that I had no knowledge of her actions, but the judge might not believe us.

We also discussed rolling the dice and going public with the recording. Since it revealed that a miscarriage of justice had taken place, it was possible that the D.A. wouldn't pursue criminal prosecution against Special for secretly taping Tonisha. Because of the likely public outrage over the contents of the tape, it might not be worth it for the D.A. to spend time trying to convene a jury to convict Special.

With regard to my other client, Olivia, I was still gently pressuring her to hang on just a little while longer. I felt bad that her case had taken so many wrong turns. I even swallowed my pride and called Girlie to discuss trying to settle Olivia's case. The witch rudely told me that all deals were off the table and hung up in my face.

But now, *I* was about to be calling the shots again. I couldn't wait until Girlie learned about the information Special and I planned to turn over to those two detectives tomorrow morning.

The telephone rang and I intended to ignore it, until I saw the 714 area code and *Big Buy* flash across the display screen. I snatched up the phone.

"This is Evelyn Kimble," said the curt voice on the other end of the line. "I'm the general counsel of Big Buy. I'm calling about the lawsuit you filed on behalf of Olivia Jackson."

I leaned forward in my chair. *Why was the general counsel calling me?* It was unusual for a company's in-house lawyers to get directly involved in a case when they had outside counsel. All communications were handled through their counsel.

"Isn't Girlie Cortez handling this case?"

"We'd like to resolve this matter quickly and quietly," Kimble said, ignoring my question. "What exactly is your client looking for?"

"A promotion and compensation for past wrongs," I answered without missing a beat.

"How much compensation?"

I was not about to bid against myself. "You initiated this call. Make me an offer and I'll let you know if you're in the ballpark."

The general counsel's arrogant sigh told me she considered this task beneath her.

"I'm prepared to offer your client a transfer to a new store where she'll be placed in the management training program. If she successfully completes the program and continues to perform her job satisfactorily, she'll be promoted to department manager within six months. I'll also include a settlement payment of one year's salary."

This offer was nothing short of a blessing. Still, I knew there was room for more. The general counsel wouldn't be calling me if she didn't want to settle. Olivia had gone through hell over the past few months. I wanted to get her as much as I could.

"Make it two years and a fifty-thousand-dollar donation to the Center for Justice, plus thirty-thousand dollars to cover my fees. But if Olivia wants to leave the company, you'll need to increase the settlement payment to three years, plus a letter of recommendation."

The phone line went dead for several seconds.

"Fine." Kimble sounded as if she had more important things to do. "I'll need a strict confidentiality clause. If she discloses our settlement payment to anyone other than her spouse or tax advisor, we're going after her for liquidated damages."

"Confidentiality won't be a problem. Is Girlie Cortez aware of this call?"

There was a long pause. "You'll be dealing directly with me going forward. When can I expect your client's response?"

What in the world was going on between Girlie and her client?

"I'll try to reach Olivia right now. I'll get back to you within the hour."

"That's fine. I'll make sure my assistant puts your call through. Thanks for—"

"Hold on." I felt so good that I decided to shoot for the stars. "I have another client who's entitled to payment from your company. I understand that Harlan Kimble's will provides that Jane Campbell should receive four-hundred-thousand dollars if she gets fired before reaching the age of sixty-two. It would be nice to take care of both of these matters at the same time."

"Is she willing to sign a release waiving any other claims against the company?"

"Nope. She's entitled to that money. But if you want to discuss an additional sum to resolve the wrongful termination, retaliation, whistleblowing and age discrimination claims I'm planning to file on her behalf later this week, I'm sure she'd be open to hearing your offer."

A global settlement was definitely my preference. Jane did not have the emotional stamina to make it through a deposition, much less a trial.

"I'll see what I can do," Evelyn said in her lifeless voice. "Goodbye."

I started to dial Olivia's number, then quietly placed the phone back into the base. It was almost as if I could feel Judi Irving's presence in my office, applauding the end of this crazy battle. I closed my eyes and said a short prayer of thanks. "This is for you, Judi."

When I finally got Olivia on the line, I could hardly contain myself. "The Lord works in mysterious ways," I gushed.

She paused, having rarely heard this kind of talk from me.

"Indeed, He does," she agreed.

"I just got a settlement offer from Big Buy." I repeated the offer.

"Oh, my goodness! Praise the Lord! Praise the Lord. Praise the Lord!"

"I think David just slaughtered Goliath."

"And praise the Lord for that!"

"So what do you want to do?" I asked. "Stay with the company or leave?"

"Get me out of that den of inequity. I'll take the three years' salary."

"Wise choice," I said. "Why don't you call your husband with the good news? You're going to be subject to a confidentiality provision, so you shouldn't mention it to anyone else. I'll call you back to let you know when I'll have the settlement agreement for you to sign."

Olivia spent another five minutes alternately praising God and thanking me. I hung up feeling like I'd just won a million-dollar jury verdict. My devious side prompted me to make one more call.

Girlie answered, probably so she could hang up on me again. I didn't waste time getting to the point.

"I just got an offer to settle Olivia's case directly from the general counsel of Big Buy. I'm curious about why I didn't hear it from you."

The silence on the other end of the line told me that something was definitely amiss between Girlie and her client.

"Are you still handling the case?"

"What was the offer?" Girlie asked tightly.

"Perhaps you should call your client and find out," I said, then happily hung up.

CHAPTER 87

Special and I sat in the lobby at LAPD headquarters anxiously awaiting our scheduled meeting with Detectives Mankowski and Thomas.

"Girl, I can't wait to see their faces when they find out we've solved their murder case." Special beamed with pride. "And by the way, when are you going to give me my props?"

I smiled at my friend. "You are an incredible investigator, Ms. Special Sharlene Moore. But you still haven't told me exactly how you got the information about Girlie."

She waved away my inquiry. "Sorry, but my investigative techniques are a trade secret."

Knowing my friend and her antics, it was probably best that I didn't know.

I was still on a high from my call with Olivia. It felt great to have delivered for her. Now, I only hoped that I could do the same for Jane Campbell. The general counsel hadn't called back yet, but Jane was thrilled about the possibility that Big Buy would give her the money Harlan Kimble had left for her without a long legal battle. With everything going on with the company, I didn't think they'd want to take on Jane's wrongful discharge case either. So I fully expected that Big Buy would make an offer to resolve that case as well.

Too bad Girlie Cortez wouldn't be representing the company. After the police heard the information we were about to disclose, Girlie wouldn't be representing anybody.

The day before, I had called Detective Mankowski and explained that I had information regarding Big Buy and Judi Irving's murder that I thought he would find quite interesting. He asked for specifics, but I refused to divulge any information over the phone. I wanted to deliver these bombshells face-to-face.

Finally, Mankowski came out to the lobby to greet us. "Sorry to keep you waiting. Follow me."

He escorted us to a small interrogation room. Detective Thomas entered the room behind us.

"You were very mysterious about the nature of your visit when you called," Mankowski said, once we were all seated. "So let's hear it."

"Sorry," Special responded. "We couldn't talk about this over the phone. This is serious business."

Mankowski's fingers drummed the table. "Tell me who you are again?"

"Special Moore," I said. "Just a good friend who helps me with research from time to time.

Deep lines wrinkled Special's forehead. She didn't like being referred to as a lowly researcher. But I was not about to tell two cops that I was turning over information obtained by an unlicensed investigator.

"So exactly what information do you have?"

"We have evidence of criminal conduct on the part of Big Buy," I said proudly. "And we also know what was in those documents Judi Irving received, which we believe led to her murder."

"We already know all about the documents," Detective Mankowski announced. "Big Buy was cooking its books. It's been all over the news. And that information didn't lead to Judi Irving's death. She was murdered during a botched burglary. Those documents had nothing to do with her murder."

That information stunned Special as much as it did me. Big Buy's financial fraud was all over the news. So it made sense that the detectives would've put two and two together just as we had. But we were convinced that Judi was killed over the documents.

"A botched burglary?" Special said. "Are you sure?"

"We're absolutely sure. And the guys involved had absolutely no connection to Big Buy. One of them fled to Mexico. But we'll get him. Eventually."

Special and I exchanged disappointed glances. Based on the conversations that Jane had overheard, we'd assumed that Judi had been murdered over the documents. But then again, Jane didn't have any corroborating evidence. This was a real blow, but we weren't done yet.

"Do you know who sent those Big Buy documents to Judi?" I asked.

Mankowski leaned back in his chair. "Nope. Do you?"

"Jane Campbell," I said. "She was the assistant to Big Buy's CEO. She's my client now. She was wrongfully terminated and I'm pursuing a lawsuit against the company on her behalf."

"Isn't that going to be a little difficult? Sounds like she misappropriated confidential company records."

"It won't be difficult at all." I folded my arms and cocked my head. "The CEO had instructed her to shred the documents but she kept them because they revealed evidence of a crime. She was fired because of that evidence. By the time I'm done, Jane Campbell will be a corporate folk hero."

"You lawyers are something else," Thomas said with a grin. "So was Campbell also the one who turned over the documents to *The Daily Business Journal?*"

"Nope. The CEO accused her of that, but she swears she didn't."

Thomas raised an eyebrow. "And you believe her?"

"Absolutely. She has no reason to lie about it. But I do have a theory about someone else who had a motive for turning over those documents to the *Journal.*"

"We're listening."

"We believe Girlie Cortez did."

Mankowski shot up in his seat and rested both forearms on the table. His level of interest in what we had to say had suddenly spiked.

"How did she get them?" he asked.

"From Judi's boyfriend, Phillip Peterman."

Some kind of signal I couldn't decipher passed between Mankowski and his partner. "You believe that or you know it?" Mankowski asked.

I hesitated. Billie Wilson from the *Journal* never revealed how she got the Big Buy documents, but she did confirm that they had arrived in the mail from an anonymous source.

"It's a theory. But it's a theory based on Girlie's background."

I slid a folder across the table to him. "Take a look at this. I think it explains why Girlie went against her client's best interests and gave those documents to the *Journal*."

Mankowski opened the folder and picked up Special's neatly typed report. He placed it on the table so both he and Thomas could read it at the same time. We waited as the two detectives read all five pages. It took them several minutes.

Thomas was the faster reader. When he gazed across the table at me, there was a noticeable gleam in his eye.

"Where'd you get this information?" he asked.

"I dug it up," Special boasted.

Mankowski turned the report face-down. "How?"

"Research."

"What kind of research?"

"Some of it on the Internet. But most of it from talking to people."

A skeptical Mankowski pressed harder. "What people?"

Special turned to look at me. It had not occurred to her that she might be on the firing line. "Friends and friends of friends."

Her voice had a cagey edge to it and she started rubbing her palms together. I hoped Special hadn't done anything illegal to gather the information, but I knew that was a definite possibility.

Mankowski hurled a scowl across the table. It was probably the same intimidating look he used to get criminals to confess.

Special squared her shoulders. "Look, I have some Filipino friends who happen to know people, who know people who knew Girlie's family."

"So you got this information from a relative of Girlie?"

"Yes. And it's all true. I got this information from Girlie's aunt, okay?"

A long patch of silence followed. Both detectives seemed to be locked in their own thoughts.

Mankowski scratched his jaw. "If the information in this folder is true, it would definitely serve as a motive for Girlie to hand over those documents to the *Journal*."

"It's true," Special assured him. "My sources are solid."

"We'll need the names of everybody you talked to?"

"I can't. My sources are confidential."

Mankowski rolled his eyes. "Girlie Cortez denies ever having seen those documents. She even agreed to take a lie detector test to prove it."

That revelation shot a double dose of disbelief straight down my spine. "There's no way she'd take a lie detector test. She's a lawyer. No lawyer would. They're not reliable."

Mankowski spread his palms. "We've already got it scheduled. Tomorrow at three o'clock."

My head swung from side to side, then back again. "She's bluffing. No way she's going to show up. Girlie Cortez enjoys playing head games."

"And if she does show up," Special threw in, "it's only because she's figured out some way to beat the test. I read an article about how you can throw it off by controlling your pulse and breathing. That heffa is treacherous."

Thomas snickered. "Now that last statement I believe."

Mankowski muttered, mostly to himself. I didn't know if his reaction was in response to Special's comment about Girlie or his partner's confirmation of it.

"You said you also had some information about criminal activity on the part of Big Buy," Mankowski said. "Were you referring to the company's fraudulent earnings reports?"

"Nope." I opened a second folder and handed him another piece of paper. "I'm talking about a totally separate crime."

Both detectives started reading the report. Seconds later, they looked up at precisely the same moment.

"Are you saying the CEO of Big Buy authorized this activity?" Mankowski asked.

Now we definitely had their attention. "That's exactly what I'm saying."

"You also claimed Big Buy was involved in Judi's murder and you were wrong about that. Why should I believe this?"

"That information came directly from my client, Jane Campbell. As I said, she was the CEO's executive assistant. So she was definitely in a position to know. She has copies of phone records and bank transfers. And she will testify under oath to everything in that report."

I rose from my chair, reached across the table and attempted to retrieve both documents.

"Hold on," Mankowski said, placing a hand on top of the papers before I could take them back. "We'd like to make a copy."

I eased back into my seat, more than pleased with his level of interest in our information.

"That's fine. I'll allow you to copy them, but only if you agree to make a deal with us."

Mankowski frowned. "What kind of deal?"

Special's eyes darted my way. We had already agreed to leave the reports. She had no idea what I was about to propose.

"If Girlie does show up for that lie detector test tomorrow, we want to be here."

The thrill of finally bringing down my nemesis churned in my chest. "We want to be in close proximity when you catch her lying through her teeth."

CHAPTER 88

"I can't believe she actually showed up," Detective Thomas whispered to Mankowski, his words dripping with glee.

They stood in the hallway outside the room where a technician was hooking Girlie Cortez up to a polygraph machine.

Mankowski couldn't believe it either when Girlie marched into the station fifteen minutes early for their appointment. She was wearing a shorter-than-short red cotton dress with red leather boots that snaked up over her knees. Every officer in the squad room gave her a lustful double-take as she sashayed by.

Girlie was certainly no dummy. While she continued to profess that she was telling the truth and that the test would prove it, she insisted on an agreement in writing that the polygraph results could not be used against her for any purpose. She also wanted an agreement that the results would be destroyed immediately after the test. She was taking the test she said, solely to prove her innocence to Mankowski.

Mankowski was flattered that his opinion meant so much to her. He readily signed the agreement since the tests weren't admissible in court anyway. He hoped like hell that she did pass so he could screw her again. But after the information he'd gotten from Vernetta Henderson, he seriously doubted that she would.

"You think she knows how to beat it?" Detective Thomas asked.

Mankowski shrugged. "Hell if I know."

If the results turned out to be inconclusive, that would be everyone's assumption. They entered an adjacent room where Vernetta and Special were seated at a table.

"This is gonna be good," Special said, rubbing her palms together. "You guys going to arrest her as soon as she fails the test?"

This chick was way too excited about bringing down Girlie. Women bent on revenge made him nervous.

"Ladies, like I told you—"

"We know," Vernetta said, interrupting him. "Having us here is a violation of department procedure. We won't get in the way and we won't come out of this room until you tell us to. Promise."

"You sure we can't watch?" Special said, pleadingly. "Can you put us in one of those rooms with the two-way mirrors?"

"No," Mankowski said, and followed his partner out of the room.

"You think they'll really stay in there?" Thomas asked.

"I hope so. But I'm a little concerned about the mouthy one."

Thomas grinned. "I got a feeling we're in for some real fireworks."

"You have no idea," Mankowski said. "We have some additional guests to greet. Follow me."

Detective Thomas looked confused as he watched Mankowski enter a room a few feet down the hallway.

Thomas almost lost his lunch when he saw Rita Richards-Kimble and Evelyn Kimble sitting around a small table that was usually reserved for suspected criminals. They were accompanied by two men who bore all the appearances of big-firm lawyers.

"How much longer is this going to take?" said a gray-headed, Brooks Brothers' type. Mankowski presumed he was Rita's attorney because the two of them were sitting off to the side.

"I didn't catch your name," Mankowski said.

"Nelson. Barry Nelson. I'm a partner with Sheppard, Mullen & Reed and I represent Ms. Richards-Kimble." He plucked a card from a diamond-studded card case. "My client doesn't have to be here. She came voluntarily. Against my advice, by the way."

"We really appreciate your cooperation," Mankowski said. "It'll only be a few more minutes."

"Do you have a card?" the other suit asked Mankowski. "I'm Marcus Winbush and I represent Evelyn Kimble."

The fact that the CEO and general counsel had each hired their own attorney was a good sign. They were already drawing battle lines.

"Are you a partner too?" Mankowski asked, though he didn't really care.

"Uh, no." The guy had the boyish face of a twelve-year-old. "I'm a senior associate with Haskins & Summers. My client is only here to listen."

They traded business cards and Mankowski backed out of the room.

"Man, you're not just playing with fire, you're playing with dynamite," Thomas said.

"I'm just trying to get to the bottom of this and bringing all this estrogen together just might give us some answers. Let's do this."

Girlie smiled when Mankowski entered the polygraph room. Her legs were opened just enough to be enticing. Mankowski wondered if she was wearing any underwear. Maybe her goal was to get the examiner so hot and bothered that he couldn't read the machine correctly.

"You have the questions?" Mankowski asked the examiner.

Martin Grundy was a computer geek who'd been conducting polygraph tests for decades. "Yep. I already explained the process."

Girlie repositioned herself in the chair as if she was trying to get comfortable, then winked at Mankowski. Her right arm rested on a table. Wires led from her fingers and arm to what looked like a laptop that sat on the table in front of Grundy.

The two detectives left and walked into an adjacent room where they could observe the testing through a large window. They had a clear view of Grundy's computer screen. On the other side of the window was a mirror which prevented Grundy and Girlie from seeing them.

For several years, Mankowski had taught a class for rookies covering the basics of polygraph examinations. The test measured four physiological responses: breathing, oxygen usage, heart rate, and blood pressure. A subject who was about to lie had a tendency to tense up, which produced a physiological response that the polygraph could measure.

Grundy began the examination by asking Girlie a series of innocuous questions, such as her name, address and place of employment. Mankowski held his breath as the examiner asked the first substantive question.

"Have you ever met Phillip Peterman?" Grundy asked.

Girlie waited a beat. *"No."*

Mankowski stepped closer to the window, his eyes zeroing in on the graphs on the computer screen in front of the examiner. "Holy shit!"

"What?" Detective Thomas exclaimed. "Is she lying or telling the truth?"

Mankowski held up a hand to quiet his partner. "Hold on, hold on. I need to hear this."

"Did you meet with Phillip Peterman at the Four Seasons Hotel on July sixteenth?"

"No."

Mankowski pounded his right fist into his left palm. "Son of a bitch!"

"Have you ever slept with Phillip Peterman?"

"No."

"Did Phillip Peterman give you a copy of Judi Irving's Big Buy documents?"

"No."

"Have you ever seen a copy of Judi Irving's Big Buy documents."

"No."

"Man, tell me what's going on," Thomas yelled, knowing the test was being conducted in a soundproof room. "Is she passing or failing?"

Mankowski continued to ignore him, his eyes transfixed on the computer screen.

"Did you turn over Big Buy financial records to The Daily Business Journal?"

"No."

"Tell me, god damn it!" Detective Thomas yelled. "Is she passing or failing?"

Mankowski slapped his partner on the back.

"She passed with flying colors! No evidence of deception. Not a single inconclusive response."

Thomas spun away, then turned back. "No way. I'm not buying it. She must've figured out a way to beat the test. We both saw her walk out of that hotel seconds behind Phillip Peterman. I refuse to believe that was just a coincidence."

"Well, apparently it was," Mankowski said, unable to stop grinning. "Because according to that polygraph machine, she's telling the whole truth and nothing but."

CHAPTER 89

"Ladies, I feel the need to say this one more time," said Barry Nelson, patting his tie. "You have no obligation to speak to the police."

"We know that and we have no plans to submit to an interview," Rita snapped. "The only reason we agreed to come down here was to hear the information the police have about Girlie Cortez stabbing us in the back."

The attorney tugged at one of his monogrammed shirt sleeves. "The police don't give information. They gather it. Your being here is in their best interests, not yours. They aren't going to tell you a thing."

Marcus Winbush turned to Evelyn. He was tall, with sand-colored hair and a mustache that was little more than fuzz.

"I would have to agree," Winbush said. "As a matter of fact, I bet they're out there right now laying a trap for the two of you. You need to start thinking like the excellent lawyer that I know you are," he said to Evelyn.

"Excellent lawyer, my ass," Rita mumbled loud enough for everyone in the room to hear.

"You have some nerve," Evelyn spat back. "Your greed is about to destroy our company."

"Our company? You don't have a company. You're an employee, remember? Your brother left Big Buy to me. So get over it."

"Ladies, ladies!" Nelson stood up. "What's going on here? If anybody sees this display of animosity between the two of you, it's going to do both of you a lot of harm. Whatever's going on, you need to work it out for the good of the company."

Both women lifted their chins and looked in opposite directions.

Barry's smartphone chirped. He pulled it from his pocket and stared at the screen. "This isn't good, but I guess it's to be expected."

"What is it?" Rita asked.

"The state Attorney General's Office just served a search warrant at Big Buy headquarters."

He started pressing the keys of his smartphone. "I'll make sure someone from my office gets there right away."

"This is your fault!" Rita charged. "You hired Girlie Cortez and now look at what she's done to us."

"Will you ever take responsibility for *anything* you do?" Evelyn asked. "It's not Girlie's fault that you and your boyfriend decided to create fraudulent earnings reports."

"That's a lie," Rita said, not quite convincingly. "And no one can ever prove that I did."

Evelyn's eyes filled with a smug delight. "Jane Campbell can."

Rita nervously clasped her hands. "I should've fired her years ago."

"Unfortunately, you were too selfish to do that. With all the millions you have, you refused to give that woman a measly four-hundred grand that you know Harlan wanted her to have. Well, now, she's about to pay you back for all the hell you put her through."

"That woman is senile and she's a liar."

"Really? Did I tell you that Vernetta Henderson now represents Jane? I had a conversation with Henderson yesterday. Jane wants the money that Harlan left her in his will."

Rita was about to speak, then paused, suddenly looking hopeful. "Let's pay her and make her sign a confidentiality provision agreeing not to testify against the company."

"That won't work," Nelson said. "If she's subpoenaed by the authorities, she'll have to testify to what she knows."

"Anyway, Henderson would never agree to that. She wants the money her client is entitled to and this morning, I authorized Accounts Payable to send her a check for four-hundred thousand and I plan to offer her another three-hundred thousand to settle her wrongful termination claim."

Rita gripped the edge of the table. "You did what? You can't do any of that without my approval."

"Yes, I can. Those sums are well within my settlement authority. Oh, and something else I forgot to mention, as of—" she paused to check her watch—"exactly thirty-five minutes ago, you and your boyfriend Fred are relieved of your duties as CEO and CFO until the completion of an investigation into your alleged misconduct."

Rita shot to her feet. "You can't do that! You've been trying to wrestle this company away from me since the day your brother died."

"This isn't my doing. The board of directors authorized your removal. They held an emergency meeting via teleconference earlier today."

"You...I...I don't know why you're sitting there looking so self-righteous," she seethed. "You're in just as much hot water as I am."

"I beg to differ. I knew nothing about your little scheme. If I had, I would have turned you in myself."

Nelson pressed three fingers to his right temple. "Ladies, ladies—"

"Shut up!" Rita and Evelyn shouted at the same time.

Nelson's body grew rigid and his teeth were clenched tight enough to crack.

Evelyn's young attorney, boldly ventured to speak. He stood and hid his shaking hands inside his pockets.

"That's enough!" Winbush shouted. "Whatever's going on between the two of you needs to stop. Immediately. You're facing some very serious charges here."

He turned to Evelyn. "And not just the CEO. You too. Just because you weren't directly involved, doesn't mean you won't be held liable. You're an officer of this company too. The legal standard is whether you knew or reasonably should have known the alleged fraud was occurring."

Rita smiled across the room at Evelyn, who seemed shaken by her attorney's blunt words.

Winbush wiped sweat from his forehead. "So I would suggest that the two of you cut out all of this childish bickering and find a way to get on the same team."

CHAPTER 90

We heard the approach of footsteps, so Special and I were already on our feet when Detectives Mankowski and Thomas stepped back into the room.

"Did she pass?" My anxiety level was so high I might as well have been strapped to a polygraph myself.

"Yep," Mankowski said. "She never saw the documents, never met Phillip Peterman and didn't give them to the *Journal.*"

Mankowski's delivery of this news was way too cheerful.

I felt like someone had just doused me with a quart of ice water. "What? How?"

"No way!" Special exclaimed. "That test was rigged. She's probably screwing the guy who gave it to her."

"But what about that information we gave you?" I said. "We know it's true. She clearly had a motive to turn over the documents to the *Journal.*"

"Not everybody who has a motive to commit a crime actually does," Mankowski explained.

I slumped back into my chair. "I can't believe it. I don't know how she does it. She's the most unethical attorney I've ever met, and time after time she never gets caught."

"This is bullshit!" Special said, banging her fist on the desk. "That girl is dirty. I know it."

"I'm sorry," Mankowski said. "I think you're wrong."

"Why in the hell do you look so damn happy?" Special said to Detective Mankowski. "You sleeping with her too?"

Mankowski's curved lips immediately flattened and his expression changed to one of embarrassment.

"Calm down," I said to Special.

"No. He's acting like he's all happy that she passed."

"Contrary to all the TV cop shows you watch," Mankowski said defensively, "we aren't out to nail innocent people. It sounds to me like you have a score to settle with Girlie. I'm sorry we can't manufacture any evidence to help you do that."

"We're not asking you to manufacture any evidence," Special insisted. "I'm asking you to do your job."

"Let it go, Special." I picked up my purse from the table. "Thanks for allowing us to be here."

"Hold on," Special said. "We ain't done yet. Can you go back in there and ask her one more question?"

Mankowski huffed and shook his head.

"Just leave it alone," I said. "Let's go."

"It doesn't work like that," Mankowski replied. "The test is finished."

Ignoring them, Special opened her purse, grabbed a pen and started scribbling on a notepad she picked up from the table.

"Here," she said, ripping off the top sheet. "Please go back in there and ask her this last question."

Mankowski glanced at the piece of paper while Detective Thomas peered at it over his shoulder.

"Pretty please," Special begged. "If she denies *that* and the test says she's telling the truth, I'll admit I've been wrong about her. Hell, I'll even tell Girlie that to her face."

CHAPTER 91

"You going to do it?" Detective Thomas asked when they stepped back into the hallway.

Mankowski thought for a second. "What the hell? Might as well tie up all the loose ends."

He placed his hand on the doorknob that led into the polygraph room.

"Crap!" He looked back over his shoulder at the room where the Big Buy execs and their attorneys were waiting. "We told them Girlie was sleeping with Phillip Peterman. We have to tell them we were wrong."

"Are we?" Detective Thomas asked quietly.

"What do you mean?"

"What if she beat the test?"

"She didn't beat the test," Mankowski barked. "Not a single question came back inconclusive. She's innocent."

"You sure you're not a little biased?"

"She passed the friggin' test, okay? Get over it."

Just then, Rita opened the door and peered out into the hallway. "We're not waiting in here another minute. We're leaving. Now."

Evelyn was standing right behind her, purse in hand.

"Just give us ten more minutes," Mankowski pleaded. "I didn't want to tell you this earlier, but we also have Ms. Cortez here. We're waiting for the results of her polygraph test. We're asking her questions that pertain to your company. I think you'll want to know what we find out."

The possibility of hanging Girlie seemed to be enough to keep both of them corralled just a little longer.

"Fine." Rita glanced at her watch. "You have ten minutes."

The door slammed shut.

Mankowski called Grundy out of the room and handed him the piece of paper with Special's question on it. "I need you to ask Ms. Cortez one more question."

Grundy took the paper and walked back into the room. Mankowski and Thomas hurried into the adjacent room to watch.

"We have one last question," Grundy said to Girlie.

She crossed her legs and shrugged. "Just ask until your little heart's content."

"Did Tonisha Cosby confess to you that she was lying about being raped by Lamarr Harris before you put her on the witness stand at trial?"

At the same time that her physiological responses began to register on the computer screen, Girlie's face turned icicle white.

Mankowski's eyes zeroed in on the computer in front of Grundy. The colorful lines on the screen zigzagged wildly across the computer screen.

"That case wasn't supposed to be part of this examination." Girlie spoke in a tight, controlled voice. She was smart enough to try to keep her emotions in check while she was still hooked up to the machine. She stood up and started snatching off the wires pasted to her arm. She slammed down the blood pressure cuff on the table and stomped out of the room.

Mankowski and Thomas met her in the hallway.

"What in the hell was that question about?" Girlie seethed.

Before Mankowski could answer, Special scurried down the hallway with Vernetta right behind her.

"That question was for us," Special happily announced.

"What are *they* doing here?" Girlie looked at Mankowski with disgust. "I trusted you. You set me up!"

Before he could respond, the Big Buy CEO and general counsel crowded into the hallway, followed by their attorneys.

"I don't believe this!" Girlie's hands shot up in the air, then flopped back down to her sides. "I trusted you!"

"Hold on a minute, everybody." Mankowski feared he was about to lose control of this hormone-infested free-for-all. He turned to Evelyn and Rita. "I was wrong. Girlie was not involved with Phillip Peterman and she didn't give those documents to the *Journal.*"

"And just how do you know that?" Rita asked.

"Because I just passed a friggin' lie detector test," Girlie yelled at her.

"Well, I don't believe it," the CEO continued. "Your behavior is atrocious. How could you—"

Nelson grabbed Rita's upper arm. "This is highly inappropriate. I instruct you not to say another word!"

"I don't believe it either," Special said. "You probably found a way to rig the test."

"Why are you even here?" Girlie spat at Special as if she was an insect.

"I'm here because I want to make sure your ass goes to jail where you belong," Special spat back.

"I think there's somebody else here who's more likely to end up in jail," Mankowski said. "And not just for financial fraud." He looked directly at Rita. "We have information that cooking your company's books wasn't the only criminal activity you were involved in."

"I have no idea what you're talking about," Rita said, pressing a hand to her chest. "That's nonsense."

"Not according to the information Ms. Henderson provided us. According to your former executive assistant, you instructed Big Buy's chief of security to hire someone to break into the Center for Justice to search for Judi Irving's documents. In the process, your hired-goon assaulted Benjamin Cohen. You also had someone follow Ms. Henderson. Your secretary listened in on your calls and she's willing to testify to what she heard. We already picked up your security guy. It didn't take long for him to crack. He says you gave him a pretty nice bonus for his dirty work."

The very polished Nelson started to stutter and could barely get his words out. "I'm…I'm ordering you not to say another word." He gripped Rita's arm even tighter. "This is highly inappropriate. My...my...my client and I are leaving."

Special sneered as she pointed a finger in Girlie's direction. "I think we should get back to this scandalous criminal over here. I don't care what that lie detector test said, I still think you gave those documents to the *Journal*."

Special turned to face Evelyn and Rita.

"I'm not exactly sure who y'all are, but did you know that her daddy was the founder of Big Buy? He never claimed her ass, though. She turned over Judi Irving's documents to the *Journal* in order to foil the company's sale to the Welson Corporation."

Rita pulled away from Nelson and took a step forward. She stared at Girlie's face as if she was searching for something she'd lost.

"You're Harlan's daughter?"

"Yes, I am." Girlie's lips drew back in a lizard-like smile. "Hello, step-mommy dearest."

CHAPTER 92

"What the hell?" Special and I shouted in unison.

"It's really getting wild up in here now!" Special exclaimed, turning to Rita. "So *you're* the one who refused to let her father see her?"

"Sure is," Girlie said, eying Rita with a lifetime of hatred. "I'm glad to hear you'll be spending some time in jail. Just consider it payback."

I stepped forward. "Payback? So you admit turning over those documents to the *Journal*?"

"Nope," Girlie said smugly. "I didn't have to."

She maneuvered around me until she was face-to-face with the general counsel. "Don't you have something *you'd* like to confess, Auntie Evelyn?"

The general counsel hugged her purse to her chest. "Confess? I...I...don't know what you're talking about."

"My Aunt Evelyn here was the one who handed over those documents to the *Journal*," Girlie explained, turning back to Mankowski. "That's why I was at the Four Seasons that day. To confirm a report about a meeting between Evelyn and Phillip Peterman. It was their regular hangout."

"You told me you were there to meet a client," Mankowski said, his jawline now taut with anger.

"I did meet with a client that day," Girlie admitted. "But I was also there to confirm for myself that my investigator's information was indeed true. Evelyn had been screwing Judi Irving's boyfriend for weeks before Judi was killed. Phillip hit on Evelyn at a photo shoot for his Big Buy commercial. The Four Seasons was their regular hangout."

Now all eyes were on the general counsel.

"*You* did this?" Rita positioned herself nose-to-nose with her sister-in-law. "Your brother built this company from nothing. He gave you a job you weren't even smart enough to have."

Evelyn's eyes narrowed. "Get the hell away from me!" Using both hands, she shoved Rita so hard, she stumbled into her attorney.

"Hey, hey, hey! Hold on a minute!" Mankowski rushed over and grabbed Rita, before she could strike back. "This is a police station for Christ's sake!"

Thomas extended his arm across Evelyn's upper body, holding her back.

"My brother was a weak, selfish tightwad who somehow managed to marry someone who was even more selfish than he was," Evelyn shouted at Rita, as she tried in vain to push past Thomas.

"Before you two tear each other apart, let me finish *my* story," Girlie said calmly.

"All along, the general counsel here was pretending that she wanted to get the sex discrimination case resolved. But she was really hoping it exploded into a class action, jeopardizing the sale to Welson."

Girlie smiled demurely at Evelyn.

"You hated the fact that your brother's wife was going to walk away with a hundred-and-twenty-five-million dollars while you'd be lucky to keep your lousy pension. It took me a while, but I figured out your little plan. Every time I proposed something reasonable to resolve the case, you objected. I suggested an early settlement. You dismissed the idea, claiming you didn't want other employees to ask for money. You even balked at my proposal to pay off all the women employees, but Rita overruled you. So when the class action didn't stop the buyout, you sent *The Daily Business Journal* those documents you got from your lover, Phillip Peterman."

"I don't have to listen to this nonsense. I'm leaving," Evelyn said.

Thomas refused to let her pass.

"See," Girlie said with a satisfied smile, "I didn't give those documents to the *Journal.* I didn't have to. Once I found out that my Auntie Evelyn was screwing Phillip Peterman, I knew she'd get her hands on the documents. I had no idea what they were, but if they were harmful to Big Buy, I knew that she hated Rita enough to use them against the company. All I had to do was sit back and wait. And as it turns out I was absolutely right."

"This is nothing but ridiculous speculation. I haven't..." Evelyn fumbled for words. "I...I—"

All of a sudden Mankowski's face brightened and he snapped his fingers.

"Phillip Peterman was with you the night Judi was murdered," he shouted, pointing at Evelyn. "That's why he lied about being with his agent. He didn't want anybody to know that he was sleeping with you."

Evelyn just stood there, her face awash in guilt.

Her young attorney finally found his voice. "Don't say another word," Winbush ordered. "We're getting out of here."

"Nice doing business with you, ladies." Girlie slapped her palms back and forth. "As I said, I didn't do anything illegal *or* unethical. In fact, I served my client well. I helped Big Buy quickly dispose of a class action that could have cost the company millions. They even gave me a big bonus for a job well done."

Girlie whirled around until she was facing Mankowski.

"As for you, I'm quite disappointed that you betrayed me like this. And since you screwed me, I'm now going to screw you, so to speak."

Mankowski's face contorted as if he'd just swallowed his tongue.

Girlie made eye contact with the whole group as we all waited for her next bombshell.

"While my Auntie Evelyn was bedding Phillip, I was having a ball with the handsome detective here."

Everybody in the hallway gasped at once. Nobody louder than me.

"Correct me if I'm wrong, detective, but isn't it a violation of department policy to sleep with a potential witness? Don't answer that," she said with a playful wink. "It could be used against you in a court of law. I'll be contacting both your lieutenant and your captain to let them know about your highly inappropriate conflict of interest."

Mankowski reached out as if he was going to snatch her, but Thomas grabbed him from behind and pulled him away.

Girlie didn't even flinch. She seemed to be enjoying the fact that she was the star of this show.

"As we agreed in writing, fellas, those polygraph results should be destroyed. And for the record, I never responded to that last question about Tonisha, and I have no plans to do so. So I guess it's just her word against mine. Have a nice day, everybody."

I stepped in front of her.

"Take this with you." I tried to hand her an envelope, but she wouldn't take it.

"What's that?"

"It's an affidavit recounting a conversation between my friend Special and Tonisha Cosby. Your client admitted that she made up the story about being raped by Lamarr. They had consensual sex that night. Tonisha also said she told you that the night before she was scheduled to testify. You put her on the stand anyway and told her to keep her mouth shut. Lamarr will be using Special's affidavit in support of his appeal."

I tried to force the envelope into Girlie's hand, but she let it fall to the floor.

"And we're giving a copy to the State Bar too," Special threw in. "So you can forget about practicing law in this state again, Ms. Thang."

True to her nature, Girlie did not lose her cool.

She smiled and cocked her head. "I'm assuming you put your little friend here up to prying information out of Tonisha. Since she's still my client, that's a violation of the attorney-client privilege, which I'm sure you're quite familiar with. Your affidavit will never be admitted into evidence."

"Special and Tonisha are friends," I said, my bravado surpassing hers. "I wasn't even aware that Special was meeting with her."

"I don't buy that and neither will the court. And if you happen to have a recording of my client, that'll be inadmissible too."

I wasn't about to admit to Special's illegal activity while standing in front of two cops.

"Since you won't take my transcript, go home and turn on the TV so you can hear all the nice things your client said about you. I sent a copy of Special's affidavit to the media. It's the lead story on CNN, TMZ and ESPN."

This time, Girlie's entire face seemed to crack, but just for a second. She hoisted her purse higher on her shoulder, turned and strolled down the hallway.

"See you in court," I yelled after her.

Girlie pivoted and spun around in her fancy red boots, hands on hips. "Don't bet on it."

EPILOGUE

Eight Weeks Later

"These seats are tight," Jefferson said, leaning over to kiss me on the cheek. "I've never sat in the first row on the fifty-yard line at a pro game before. Not to mention a playoff game between the Legends and the 49ers."

This spur-of-the-moment trip to San Francisco had turned out to be a much-needed break from all the drama I'd been through with the Big Buy case.

"Vernetta's got it like that now," Special said, nudging Benjamin, who was sitting next to her. "After *we*—emphasis on *we*—got Lamarr's name cleared, that boy promised us season tickets for life."

"Y'all need more clients like Lamarr," Jefferson said, reaching over me to bump fists with Benjamin.

Special had suggested that we invite Benjamin along to round out our foursome. She was now on a self-imposed, six-month dating hiatus. I thought taking some solo time to heal from her breakup with Clayton was an excellent idea.

A lot had transpired over the past few weeks. Special's affidavit recapping her conversation with Tonisha made national news. We even posted it on the Internet and, at last count, it had gotten over a million hits. Every place Tonisha went, reporters hounded her for a reaction to Special's affidavit. She finally broke down and admitted everything. Special and I never disclosed the existence of the recording.

After that, Lamarr and I hit the talk show circuit with a vengeance. It took some doing, but I convinced Lamarr to refrain from attacking Tonisha. Instead, he painted her as a victim. In reality, she was a naïve, misguided young woman who used the wrong tactics to achieve the riches she so desperately desired. Lamarr even agreed to donate ten thousand dollars toward her attorneys' fees for the perjury charges she was now facing. That, too, had been my idea.

The media, impressed with the empathy Lamarr showed toward his accuser, piled on the praise. The Legends quickly rescinded its decision to cut him from the team. All of his prior endorsement deals were renewed and he picked up four more on top of those. He was now the national spokesperson for California Kids on the Mend, a group that worked to improve the lives of foster kids.

Lamarr's handsome face graced the cover of countless newspapers and magazines. Needless to say, the publicity has kept my phone ringing off the hook with new clients.

During her conversation with Special, Tonisha admitted that she had intentionally set up Lamarr, figuring she'd get lots of public sympathy and some big cash. The night before she was scheduled to testify, the guilt got to her and she told Girlie about the scam. The attorney-client privilege prevented Girlie from divulging Tonisha's misconduct to the court, but it mandated that she withdraw from the case rather than allow her client to give false testimony.

But Girlie had too much invested in the case and wanted to win. The decision to allow Tonisha to perjure herself, however, ultimately cost Girlie her career. She quietly resigned from her law firm and was being brought before the State Bar. Because of all of her connections, the District Attorney's Office declined to charge her with suborning perjury. She was still facing a lengthy suspension of her bar license. Just before she resigned from her law firm, Girlie filed papers with the court in support of my request for dismissal of the verdict against Lamarr.

Mankowski had been restricted to administrative duty while internal affairs completed its investigation into his affair with Girlie. It looked like he might keep his job, but a demotion was likely.

The Big Buy situation was still unfolding. The company's CEO, CFO, general counsel and a host of other company executives were all facing criminal charges. Rita Richards-Kimble had become the newest poster child for corporate greed. One story I saw even compared her to the likes of Bernie Madoff.

Special nudged me with her elbow. "What are you thinking about? You look like you're in a totally different place."

I slowly exhaled. "I was just thinking about Girlie Cortez."

"Please don't tell me you're feeling sorry for that heffa. She's about to get everything she deserves."

"I know. But can you imagine having a father—a wealthy father, at that—who never claimed you? That had to be rough."

"No, I can't imagine it," Special said, taking a sip of her soda. "That's why I don't have a problem with some of the things she did. I completely understand why she hated her stepmother and wanted to bring down Big Buy. But what she did to Lamarr was inexcusable."

I wholeheartedly agreed. Still, I did feel a little sorry for her. "What she went through as a kid," I said, "says a lot about who she is today."

"True." Special spread her hands, palms up. "But like my grand-mama always said, you reap what you sow."

A resounding roar filled the Legends' side of the arena. Special and I shot to our feet. Benjamin and Jefferson were already up.

I placed a hand on Jefferson's shoulder and looked toward the Legends' end zone. "What happened?"

"Your boy just scored another touchdown."

Lamarr jumped to his feet, pumped a fist high in the air, then did an Incredible Hulk muscle move. The Legends were now up by 14 points with eight minutes left on the clock.

We watched the replay on the Jumbo Tron as the words *Lamarr "The Hero" Harris Scores Again!* flashed across the screen. As we returned to our seats, I picked up the game booklet and stared at the cover. It showed Lamarr surrounded by a bunch of beaming kids from a local Boys & Girls Club. The headline brought a gigantic smile to my face.

Lamarr Harris: A Real-Life Hero After All.

ACKNOWLEDGMENTS

I am truly a lucky woman! I doubt that there's a writer alive who has friends and family more supportive than mine. It's now time for me to say thanks to the many, many people who helped me craft another page-turner.

First, to the multitude of friends and relatives who critiqued the early drafts of this novel, as always, your feedback was invaluable. A big thanks to Randy Bauer, Dawn Pittman, Malcolm Ali, Faye Gipson, Diane Mackin, Kathy Fairbrother, Carline Louis-Jacques, M.D., Donny Wilson, E. Jewelle Johnson, Debbie Diffendal, James White, Ellen Farrell, Geneva O'Keith, Paul Ullom, my prayer warrior Olivia Smith and my USC homegirl Cynthia Hebron. I couldn't buy better supporters.

To my two super fans turned friends and editors, Pamela Goree Dancy, thanks for critiquing my manuscript and pumping me up when I needed it most; and Valerie Lamar, thanks for your enthusiastic critique. One day we'll have to stop chatting by email and actually meet.

To the three Los Angeles area book clubs who read an early draft of *Attorney-Client Privilege* and joined me at my home for an evening of food, drinks and lively discussion, I am lucky to have you in my corner: Bookalicious Book Club members Arlene L. Walker, Judi Johnson, Saba McKinley, Kamillah Clayton, Helen Jingles, Raunda Frank, and Lesleigh Kelly; Sisters with Books Book Club members Cheryl Finley, Bunny Withers, Gloria Falls, Helen Merrick, Elaine Moore, Freida Smith, Janice Criddle and Beverly Newton; and Something to Talk About Book Club members Tonya Cobb, Vera

Walker-Alfred, Aleshia Johnson, Marina Young, Yasmine Johnson, Patricia Jenkins and Tanisha Johnson. Can't wait to visit your book clubs again. To the 160-plus book clubs who've invited me into their homes via speakerphone, Skype and in-person since the release of my first book, thanks for making me a part of your sister circle. To other book clubs out there, call me!

I'd also like to thank those experts who freely shared their knowledge and expertise with me: Los Angeles employment attorney Mika M. Hilaire, Oakland criminal defense attorney Colin Bowen and retired Washington, D.C. homicide detective George Blackwell. Thanks for answering my many questions and helping me fix my flaws.

To Sister Daaimah Abdulmujeeb, Sister Charlene Muhammad and my homeboy and photographer extraordinaire Brother Malcolm Ali, thank you for discussing your faith, Islam, with me. To my co-worker Jae Requiro, I really enjoyed our discussions about your Filipino heritage.

To my talented team: developmental editors Kristen Weber and Jerome Norris, copy editors Lynel Washington and Karey Keenan, publicists Dee Stewart of Dee Gospel PR and Ella Curry of EDC Creations Media Group, LLC, my lifeline to the blogging world, Tracee Gleichner of Pump Up Your Books, book cover designer Keith Saunders of Marion Designs, interior book designer Kimberly Martin of Jera Publishing, website designer Ikenna Igwe of Tranquil Black, and my wonderful virtual assistant Stacey Nikodym. I couldn't do what I do without all of you.

To my mother Pearl and my husband Rickey, thanks for picking up the slack when I'm writing or on the road promoting my books. The two of you make my job so much easier.

To my devoted readers, I hope you enjoyed this one. I'm already hard at work on the next one!

DISCUSSION QUESTIONS FOR
ATTORNEY-CLIENT PRIVILEGE

1. Do you think most attorneys will do "whatever it takes" to win a case?

2. If you were in Olivia and Ida's shoes, would you have settled out of the lawsuit like Ida did, or continued to fight the way Olivia did?

3. Do you think women, for the most part, have achieved equality in the workplace?

4. Is it important for a husband and wife to share the same religious beliefs?

5. Do you think it's a good idea to study other religions, not for the purpose of converting, but to understand the beliefs of others?

6. Were you more sympathetic toward Girlie Cortez after learning about her upbringing?

7. Have you ever worked with someone who used sex for career advancement?

8. Do you think Detective Mankowski's partner should have reported his unethical behavior?

9. Who was your favorite character in *Attorney-Client Privilege*?

10. What did you like/dislike most about *Attorney-Client Privilege*?

ABOUT THE AUTHOR

Pamela Samuels Young is a practicing attorney and bestselling author of the legal thrillers, *Every Reasonable Doubt, In Firm Pursuit, Murder on the Down Low, Buying Time* and *Attorney-Client Privilege.*

In addition to writing legal thrillers and working as an in-house employment attorney for a major corporation in Southern California, Pamela is on the board of directors of the Los Angeles chapter of Sisters in Crime, an organization dedicated to the advancement of women mystery writers. The former journalist and Compton native is a graduate of USC, Northwestern University and UC Berkeley's School of Law. She is married and lives in the Los Angeles area.

To schedule Pamela for a speaking engagement or book club meeting via speakerphone, Skype or in person, visit her website at www.pamelasamuelsyoung.com.

9 780986 436130